MW01243643

Chronicles of Virgàm: Book 2

The Warlock

of

Dunivear

Brooke J. Losee

ISBN: 978-1-954136-03-8

Her royal Excellency would like to offer thanks to all those who aided in the quest to find and apprehend an infamous murderer, and for thy dutiful services to the throne. May your efforts continue to impede the darkness and bring light to the land of Virgamor.

The Royal Steward/Master Craftsman, Ammon Losee

For thy persistent oversight and commission of the royal artistry

The Royal Advisors, Jake & Mindy Porter

For thy generous advice, late night critics, and profound guidance

The Royal Scribe, Sara Kelly

For thy clean edit of the Royal proclamation and dedicated work to its perfection

The Royal Lensman, Steven Howes

For thy boundless expertise in preparing the proclamation cover with skill and precision

And to my loyal subjects: without thy support I am nothing

Titles in Series:

The Prisoner of Magic (Novella)

The Witch of Selvenor (Book 1)

The Warlock of Dunivear (Book 2)

Chronicles of Virgàm: Book 2

The Warlock

of

Dunivear

CHAPTER
~ *One* ~

The air was cool as another spring night settled over the city. Everything was quiet except for the sound of an owl hooting from a pine just beyond the courtyard. I turned over in my bed, trying to ignore its persistent calls. Sleep had been difficult the last few nights. I seemed unable to stop the thoughts that haunted my mind. I longed for a good night's rest but feared tonight would only be a repeat of yesterday. Memories of the dark cave lying on the other side of the mountains filled my thoughts. I hated that my mind felt the need to revisit it so frequently, and I could feel my heart already racing as I watched my body enter the black space between its walls for what seemed the hundredth time.

As soon as I walked into the darkness of the cave, I could sense the same evil presence I had that day. It was still there, still lingering within the granite walls. I could see myself moving towards the back wall, the symbols illuminating in the light of the torch I held in my hand. My heart pounded harder as I tried to wake myself from the nightmare before it got worse. *This isn't real. I'm not really here. Wake up, Zynnera! Wake up!* But I couldn't seem to pull my mind back to reality. I couldn't force myself to open my eyes.

I watched as I reached out to touch the symbols on the stone wall. *Don't do it! Don't touch them!* I screamed at my mind to stop. I didn't want to relive these memories, but it seemed I had no control over them. As soon as my fingers touched the markings, I was encompassed once again by the darkness. The same voice resounded all around me, making my ears hurt. The man in the black cloak appeared in front of me, repeating the familiar words, *Pukurae mayart Virgàm.* His black hair seemed to flow backwards with a breeze coming from the cave opening. I could feel my own hair moving forward as I faced him. It felt so real. *Sounded* real.

The darkness surrounded me, and I was alone with his shadowed figure. The red streaks in his hair seemed to be the only bit of color I could see, one on each side of his head, laying just over his ears. Once again I felt trapped, unable to move or speak. The nightmare brought back every sensation I had felt in the cave. It was as though I had been transported through time to relive those moments. I could feel tears streaming down my face as he reached his hand towards me, still repeating his message. *This isn't real! Wake up! Please wake up!*

I sat up in my bed, gasping as I looked around the room. My frantic heart calmed as I realized I was still safe beneath the warm blankets of my bed. I played with their soft folds while I waited for my breathing to calm, twisting them until they wrapped tightly around my finger. At this time of night, the palace was quiet. I was likely the only one awake. This wasn't the first time my nightmares had awakened me in the dead of night, and my instincts told me it would not be the last. In fact, my nightmares only seemed to be getting worse.

I collapsed back onto my pillow, staring at the ceiling with a mix of irritation and fear. *How long am I going to have these nightmares? Why won't they go away?* I knew the answer. Until I figured out what they meant, I doubted I would ever get a peaceful night's rest. I had hoped defeating Eradoma would bring some sort of normalcy to my life, but instead it seemed things were only more confusing.

I closed my eyes, begging my mind to let me rest. It was nights like these that I missed my father most. I longed to hear his voice, his gentle tone carrying me off to sleep as he told me stories. *What I wouldn't give for one of them now. I wish he were still here.* I felt myself fading into the quiet corners of my mind. My desires were answered as one of my father's stories filled my thoughts. His soft, familiar voice swept over me in a warm wave and it almost felt as though he were sitting at my beside, just as he had so long ago.

"Dunivear. A kingdom not far from here. A city resting on the beautiful Sea of Maleze, surrounded by a dense forest of pine and birch. It existed long before Selvenor and continues to be a kingdom of wealth and resources. Dunivear became one of the most prosperous kingdoms in the land, idolized by its neighbors as the most desirable place to live. Its people lived in peace and harmony, sharing their resources throughout the land of Virgamor and welcoming all those who sought to build a life within its city walls.

"One day the King of Izarden, King Meneres, visited Dunivear. Izarden was a kingdom situated deep in the forest on the southwestern side of the Sea of Maleze. Rumors of Dunivear had spread to Izarden, and King Meneres desired to see the city for himself. The king was so impressed by the natural beauty of the city and by the vast wealth of the people that he signed a peace treaty with the King of Dunivear, opening his own kingdom to trade with the people. But King Meneres had no intention of honoring such a treaty. He desired the wealth of Dunivear for himself and secretly vowed to lay siege on the kingdom.

"Late in the darkness of night, King Meneres sent a fleet of ships carrying his entire army of skilled soldiers across the Sea of Maleze. Dunivear rested peacefully in the moonlight, unaware of the enormous army approaching its shores. By the time the King of Dunivear, King Wilhelm, was alerted to the impending threat, there was no time for him to prepare his city. The small army of Dunivear stood no chance against the tremendous power of Izarden. After nearly one hundred years of peace, Dunivear was under attack by foreign invaders.

"The King of Izarden was merciless. He overpowered the people, killing many innocents on his path to victory. King Wilhelm begged for his people to be unharmed, bowing to the subjugation of Izarden. Under new rule, Dunivear became a bleak and gloomy place to live. All of the kingdom's wealth was pillaged and taken to Izarden, leaving the people of Dunivear with almost nothing. Many lost their lives to hunger as they struggled to fight against the tyranny. There was nothing the people could do, and the fate of their kingdom seemed dark.

"After a year of living in oppression, King Wilhelm had lost all hope of saving his kingdom. But one day, two men from Dunivear requested an audience with their king, promising to help free the people from Izarden's tight grasp. The king met with the two men and they revealed their secret powers to him. They both possessed magical abilities, abilities the king knew could defeat the army of Izarden and free his kingdom from its control. These warlocks were noble men, offering their help to the king in order to return the kingdom to the peace and prosperity it once knew.

"The warlocks journeyed to Izarden, hoping to convince King Meneres to relinquish his control of Dunivear without the shedding of innocent blood. But the King of Izarden was a harsh and stubborn man. He refused to give up his power over their kingdom and threatened to send more soldiers to occupy the city. The warlocks knew the only way Dunivear would ever be free was to defeat Izarden's army, so they attacked them with their magic. The city lit up with green and blue light as the warlocks unleashed their power on the inhabitants of Izarden. They eliminated each soldier with little effort and devastated city buildings with a fiery blaze. The army of Izarden was completely destroyed, and much of the great city lay in ruin.

"With nothing left to defend him, King Meneres surrendered to the power of the warlocks, begging them to spare his life and the lives of those who remained. The warlocks agreed to leave Izarden in peace if the king promised to never again set foot in Dunivear. The king obliged, fearing the wrath of the warlocks and their power should he break his covenant.

"The warlocks returned to Dunivear, optimistic their land would now be safe from the invaders who had destroyed everything their people had built. They told the king of their battle, rejoicing in the success of their mission as a huge celebration was held in their honor. The people praised their bravery and power, and King Wilhelm made them captains in his army. The warlocks were held in the highest of respect.

"The kingdom of Dunivear once again began to thrive. The people regained their zest for life and the city returned to the prosperity it once knew. But with such wealth, the King of Dunivear became greedy. He knew his army, led by the magic of the warlocks, could not be defeated. King Wilhelm desired to extend his own power beyond the borders of Dunivear and seize the kingdoms that surrounded him.

"King Wilhelm asked the warlocks to lead his army to Izarden to take revenge for crimes they had committed against them. He knew Izarden would recognize the warlocks and surrender to their power. Exacting his vengeance upon this kingdom would be the first step in demonstrating his strength and serve as a warning for those who might resist future advances. King Wilhelm gave the warlocks his orders, but they refused to fulfill his commands. The warlocks were men of honor and stood by the covenant they had made with the King of Izarden. They refused to attack the kingdom nor any others in the name of the king's desire for power.

"King Wilhelm became angry with the warlocks' refusal to engage his commands. He knew there was nothing he could do to match their powers. Instead, he marked them as traitors. He created fear among the people, whispering rumors that they sought to destroy everything the people had built. Eventually the people turned against them, demanding the warlocks who once saved their kingdom be exiled into the forest of Arnfell.

"The warlocks did not fear the threats from the people. They knew their magic could protect them from anything the king's army should send against them. But they each had families of their own and feared King Wilhelm would seek retribution by taking his anger out on the ones they loved. So, they took their families deep into the forest, hiding amongst the trees of Arnfell away from the king's wrath. King Wilhelm sent many spies into the forest to follow the warlocks, but he dared not disturb them for fear they would unleash the same destruction upon him as they had on Izarden.

"Eventually, the king decreed all magic illegal within the city walls and vowed to destroy anyone who expressed magical abilities. The people feared the magic of the warlocks and witches who lived in the forest and, to this very day, no one from Dunivear dares go near their village. They remain hidden, deep in the forest, living in peace where they can use their powers without fear. Some say they are now as numerous as the army of Dunivear itself."

I recalled my wide-eyed expression as though it were only yesterday. "Can we go there, Papa! Can we go meet them!" As a child I had been so excited to learn there were others like me besides my mother. I couldn't help but wonder what they were like. The idea that there were witches and warlocks out there who were still good had made me happy.

I remembered how easy it was to relate to the people in his story. Even as a small child I understood what it felt like to be hated and feared. Although the people of Selvenor had not yet discovered I was a witch, I knew they would react the same way the people of Dunivear had. They hated Eradoma, not that I had blamed them. But I feared they would have the same hatred for me even though I desired to be nothing like her.

My father's soft smile flashed across my memory. "Someday perhaps, Zynnera. Someday, I do think you will meet them."

I smiled back at him. "And you'll go with me! We can meet them together!"

As a young child I hadn't understood his glazed eyes and shallow nod. I hadn't recognized the sadness and pain in his expression. My father knew then he would never take such a journey with me. He knew his life would end before I ever had the opportunity to visit the village hidden in the forest beyond the walls of Dunivear. My naive bliss was something he hadn't wanted to destroy. He wanted me to hope for such a happy event, to look forward to something beyond the walls of the palace.

I turned to my side, sobbing into my pillow. Thinking of him was painful. *I miss him so much.* I desperately wanted his comforting smile and his warm embrace. I wanted to feel his arms wrapped around me, protecting me as he had when I was a child. But I knew I would never feel his arms holding me again. He was gone, and all I had left of him were my memories.

I released another light sob. *I need to rest. I have to rest.* But how could I sleep when I was haunted by such memories, both good and bad? I allowed my eyes to drift closed. I knew I had to do something to stop the nightmares; I needed to find answers. I only wished I knew where to begin.

CHAPTER
~*Two*~

The light from the sun attempted to seep through my frosted window. I scrunched my forehead as it settled on my face, uncertain I was ready for a new day to begin. Rolling over, I pulled my blankets over my head. I wished I could escape my thoughts as easily as I escaped the bright light penetrating through the window. *Another sleepless night. Another day of exhaustion.* Part of me wanted to attempt sleeping, but I knew it would make little difference. As soon as my eyes closed, the memories would flood back in and I would once again be standing between the walls of the granite cave.

I threw off the blanket, staring up at the ceiling. *I have to do something. But what? I can't keep going like this.* I didn't know where to begin. There was so much uncertainty lingering in my thoughts that I feared my mind would soon be overwhelmed. I wanted to believe defeating Eradoma had brought peace to Selvenor. At the moment, my victory seemed to have earned it. But I could still sense *it*. There was a darkness I just couldn't deny. It lingered inside the palace walls and even on the city streets. I wondered if I was the only one who could feel it? I wondered if it was all just in my head?

Images of the man in the black cloak crept into my thoughts. My heart pounded as the flashes raced across my mind. I shook my head. *No. I don't want to think about him right now.* If only it were that easy to chase the thoughts away. Whoever the man was, he seemed to be linked to the darkness I felt. *I need to figure out who he is. I need to understand what he wants.*

I sighed, sitting up in order to convince myself to leave the bed. The frost was nearly gone now that the sun had fully emerged from behind the mountains. I slowly moved from my bed towards the window, allowing the light to warm my skin. I rubbed my arms with my hands, hoping to chase away the chills that had appeared when I left the warmth of the blankets. Peering out the window, I could see the frosted meadow glistening in the morning light. Everything seemed so peaceful.

But something still seemed *off.* I couldn't explain it. I couldn't wrap my mind around the idea that there was still an evil presence out there. My thoughts wandered back to my father. *Is this how he felt? Is this what it had been like for him, knowing the events of the future?* I felt shivers run across every inch of my skin as my bores became large bumps in response to my thoughts. *The future. Is that what my nightmares are?* It certainly wasn't out of the realm of possibilities, although my visions of the black-haired man hadn't really seemed like a glimpse into the future. I wished there was someone I could ask, someone who could tell me what it was like to be a Seer. I wished Larena was still alive.

I could have learned so much from her. I still didn't know what gift I had been born with, or if I had one at all. My victory over Eradoma made me believe that I was likely a Protesta, but ever since my nightmares had become more frequent and clear, I found myself doubting. If these nightmares were glimpses into the future, then that meant I was a Seer, but I wasn't sure that's what they really were, and there was no one to guide me to the answer.

I moved closer to the window, peering at the stone paved area below. The courtyard was empty now, but soon it would be full of workers. After Eradoma's downfall, the people had been eager to rebuild their lives. Anaros had insisted on reconstructing the courtyard, eliminating the ruins that reminded everyone of Eradoma's destruction. The new wall was nearly finished, yet I couldn't help but worry it would not keep out the threat I sensed beyond the grassy meadow. If it was as dark as my instincts led me to believe, no amount of stone and brick would keep it at bay.

The urgency to find answers seemed to grow. I knew they were the only chance my soul had of obtaining peace. There *was* one person in Selvenor who might have answers. There was one person who could shed light on my nightmares and the questions about my powers. But did I dare ask her? After our battle, Eradoma had been imprisoned in the dungeon, left to live out her mortal days in cold darkness. I knew it was where she belonged after everything she had done, but I still felt a bit of sympathy for her. That sympathy was something I also knew she would never return. Even if I were brave enough to go speak with her, I doubted she would give me any answers. I, the daughter who betrayed her and the one who stole the thing she valued most, would probably be the last person she would talk to.

Several people had now entered the courtyard and began working on the new wall. I watched as they lay bricks, piece by piece, to create a strong structure that would defend against physical assaults. Figuratively, I knew what it was like to build walls. I'd spent my entire life keeping my identity a secret, keeping my magic hidden. I had built a strong wall to keep everyone out, never permitting anyone to get close to me. But those same walls that kept those close to me out also kept me inside, trapped in a prison of my own creation. Anaros had torn down part of that wall. Rhemues, Hachseeva...Reynard and Delamere, they had all played a role in removing pieces of my prison. But the structure around my soul remained. I still felt the need to hide myself, protect myself. *Or protect everyone else.*

My father's story once again permeated my thoughts. I thought about the warlocks of Dunivear. The people had honored them for saving them from Izarden's tyranny, but their praise had not lasted. It had not taken long for their admiration to turn into fear and for the people to desire their exile. I wondered if my fate would be the same. I had saved the people of Selvenor from Eradoma's wrath, but was it enough? Would they also begin to see me as a threat and desire that I leave? I wanted desperately to believe the people trusted me, but my heart wasn't convinced.

I moved away from the window and sat down at the small

wooden desk near my bed. From my chair I could feel warmth emanating from the smoldering flame in the fireplace a few feet away. My thoughts reflected back to my mother, sitting in the cold dungeon. *Maybe I should go talk to her?* My heart raced at the idea. The last time I had seen her was just before passing out after using the *Impotus* spell to remove her magical powers. Anaros mentioned he had attempted to speak with her about the things we had learned from Vander in the village. He asked her about "the Bridge" and what it meant. Her reply had been cold and taunting. She refused to give him any information on the subject, but Anaros was convinced she knew what he was talking about.

I knew the outcome of any conversation I had with her was likely to be the same. I wasn't sure it was worth the time and effort to even try. *But I have to try something.* I stared down at the book of spells resting in front of me, studying the symbols on its cover. In the center there was an open eye outlined with gold. The eye rested on top of a triangle, filled with a green mineral with splashes of white throughout it. Below the triangle, a purple crescent moon curved towards the bottom corners of the book. I recognized both stones as ones often taken from the mines near Theranden. Many of the ornate items of the palace were made with similar material.

A large blue circle encompassed the other symbols. *Lapis.* A rare and valuable stone not native to Selvenor. I remembered Eradoma requesting it from the servants on their visits to Croseline. Lapis had been highly desired by royalty for centuries, and Eradoma was no exception. Whoever had made *The Tahetya* had taken great care to include valuable materials in its cover. *But why? What did the symbols mean? What was the significance of each one and its color?*

Was there a significance?

I rolled my eyes. Everywhere I turned there just seemed to be more questions. I flipped through the pages of *The Tahetya*. Every time I searched within its binding, I hoped to find something new, an answer to just one of my many questions. But there was nothing new to find. I'd read every spell contained in the text at least a hundred times, and none of them gave me any leads to go on.

My eyes rested on the page that contained the incantation for the *Impotus*. The spell had proven useful in defeating Eradoma. I couldn't stop myself from wondering if I could use it on myself. If I could eliminate my own magical abilities, I would be normal. I would be like every other citizen of Selvenor. No one would fear me because the magical powers I possessed would be gone. I would no longer need to hide behind my walls.

I couldn't deny I longed to know what *normal* felt like. But even if I wanted to attempt such a spell on myself, I knew I couldn't. *At least not yet. Not until I figure everything out.* Until the darkness I sensed was gone, I could not allow myself to be selfish. I may be the only one who could protect Selvenor from the threat of evil. If I gave up my magic now, who would defend them? Who would protect the people I loved?

I gently closed *The Tahetya*, staring back into the open eye on its cover. Vander's words reflected on my mind. *Someday you will understand.* I didn't want to wait for someday. I wanted to understand now. How long was I going to have to wait? Surely I needed to understand all of this *before* more darkness descended upon Selvenor? I felt like I was trudging through the dense forest in the middle of the night. There was nothing to light my path and every step had me tripping over branches and boulders. Each question gave way to three more, an unending loop of ignorance.

I sighed, standing up from the desk and moving towards the door. I needed to get out of the room. I needed relief from the solitude of the night. Fortunately, companionship was one thing I *had* obtained on my quest to defeat Eradoma. *Friends. Family. I'm not alone anymore.* It felt good to have family again. Hachseeva had accepted me as her sister without hesitation. I could never thank her enough for making me a part of her family, for being there for me when I needed her. I loved her and Rhemues...and, of course, my spirited niece and nephews. Thinking of them brought a smile to my face.

And then there was Reynard and Delamere. I could never have accomplished my victory without them. They had so much faith and trust in me, even when I didn't think I deserved it. They fought by my side against Eradoma's army of monstrous beasts, paving the way for me to face her myself. Without their efforts I would have never been able to save Selvenor or Anaros.

Anaros. The thought of him made my heart race. We had come so far in such a short amount of time. My feelings for him had only grown stronger since my fight against Eradoma, but I didn't know if he felt the same way. He had been so preoccupied the last few months with rebuilding the kingdom that we didn't have much time to ourselves. I knew it was his duty to put his people's needs first, and I felt selfish for wanting to draw any of his attention to me. *Maybe he doesn't want to spend time with me anyway? Maybe we are just friends?* Now that the intensity of fighting Eradoma's evil reign had subsided, I wondered if his feelings for me had followed suit.

Soon, Anaros would be crowned king. I always knew it would happen should our mission be successful. But the idea terrified me now. Anaros would be burdened with the duties of his kingdom, and with the expectations that accompanied them. The people would expect him to take a wife and to have a family. After all, the future of the kingdom rested on his posterity. The thought made me nauseous. I wasn't sure I could handle the idea.

Even if Anaros still had feelings for me, I knew we couldn't be together. I hated admitting it, but I knew it was true. Anaros would need to make treaties and agreements with other kingdoms, a task that would be difficult to do if they knew he was close to a witch. Magic created so much fear and distrust. Being with me would only jeopardize any progress he made in building a relationship with other kingdoms. I wasn't going to be the reason Selvenor didn't prosper. As much as it made my heart ache, I knew eventually I would have to distance myself from him.

I walked along the corridor, staring at the dark green carpet beneath my feet. I tried to push the thoughts from my mind. As I approached the banquet hall, I could hear laughter echoing from the room. The familiar voices of Hachseeva and Rhemues and the giggling of their three children filled my ears. I stared at them from the entry, watching their happy expressions as they talked. Anaros was sitting at the end of the long table, eating breakfast. He noticed me upon glancing up from his food and sent me a wide smile.

Before I even knew what I was doing, I smiled back at him. I couldn't help but get lost in his gaze. Those dark brown eyes always drew me in and refused to let me go. Guilt filled my thoughts as I stared back , my heart aching at the idea of no longer being close to him. *It will be for the best. It's what is best for Selvenor. It's what is best for him.* I knew it wouldn't be easy to convince myself, but I had to do it. Once I determined Selvenor was no longer in danger, I would have to let him go. I didn't know where that left me. I wasn't sure I could remain here. Distancing myself from him would not be easy for either of us. Even if I chose to walk away, I was certain Anaros would try to stop me. *No. I must leave Selvenor. It's the only way this will work. And when I leave, it must be in secret. He can never know where I've gone.* I wasn't looking forward to the day I would leave Selvenor for good and the pain that would accompany it, but I was grateful that day wasn't today and that I still had time to be with the people I loved.

CHAPTER
Three

I smiled as I watched her enter the banquet hall in a light blue tunic that seemed to make her blues eyes even brighter. Her long, wavy hair brushed against her shoulders I was certain my smile only grew as she approached the table and sat down next to me. Zynnera returned my smile, but I could see she had much on her mind. I'd learned to read her expressions well and could tell when she was fronting a facade.

I had an idea of the culprit. The last few nights I'd awoken to her screams sounding from other side of the wall in the chamber next to my own. It had taken every ounce of my strength not to rush to her side. I wanted to talk to her, to make whatever it was better, but I also knew Zynnera. She wasn't the kind of girl who just accepted help, or sympathy for that matter. I needed to give her space to figure it out on her own, at least until she was ready to confide in me. I tried to keep the suspicion out of my tone. "Good morning."

Zynnera was still smiling as she took the seat next to me, albeit her smile held some suspicion. "Good morning." She could read me as well as I could read her, a fact we knew about each other.

I watched as she began eating breakfast. *She's hiding something. I can tell. Should I say something?* Now probably wasn't the best time. Even if Zynnera was willing to discuss whatever was bothering her, she would not want to do so with Rhemues, Hachseeva, and the children in the room. I made a mental note to ask about it later, planning to find a moment alone with her. I was always up for such an excuse.

Nerene ran to greet Zynnera, wrapping her arms around Zynnera's shoulders as she tried to contain her excitement. "Prince says he is taking us all into the city today!" She jumped up and down, her bouncing nearly pulling Zynnera from her chair. "He says he has a surprise for us!"

Zynnera looked away from her, turning to face me and eyeing me curiously. "Oh, he does, does he?"

I shrugged. "I guess you'll have to come along to find out." I winked at her. I was hoping whatever was on her mind would be pushed aside for today. Perhaps my surprise would provide some temporary relief. I had intentionally told the children, knowing full well their excitement would create enough curiosity to convince Zynnera to come. She hated going into the city, but today I needed her to be there.

Zynnera turned back to Nerene. "What do you think? Should I come?"

Nerene's small body could not contain her enthusiasm. "Yes! Yes! You can walk with me!" Zynnera smiled at her. All three children had become very attached to her the last few months. Zynnera had been exceptionally patient with them. I found myself adding more to her list of admirable qualities and couldn't help but envision us having children of our own. *Our own?* I couldn't deny it was what I wanted, but the idea made my heart race.

"I'd love to walk with you," Zynnera said calmly.

Nerene ran to Hachseeva, still jumping up and down in excitement. "Mama! Auntie Zynnera is going to walk with *me*!"

Both of the boys' expressions reflected their disgust. "Mama, that's no fair!"

Hachseeva sighed. "You can *all* walk with Zynnera for a bit, then you're *all* going to give her some space. Alright?" The children nodded, but I knew they would argue against her later. I laughed a little at their attachment, not that I could blame them for wanting to spend time with her. *I can't blame them at all.*

Rhemues lifted one of the boys onto his shoulder. "Let's go get these three ready." Hachseeva nodded, ushering the other two children through the entry. Rhemues turned to face us before leaving the banquet hall. "We'll meet you by the north entry in a bit."

I nodded. "Sounds good."

Zynnera had eaten very little of her breakfast. I remembered the night we had all found out about her magical powers. Filled with so much guilt and depression, she had refused to eat. The idea worried me. The last thing I wanted was for her to feel that way again. I was torn between my concern and not wanting to push her.

"Zynnera, are you OK?" I hated asking. I was afraid bringing it up would ruin the entire day for her.

Zynnera looked at me with a thoughtful expression. *She knows I can tell something is bothering her.* I waited anxiously for her response. Zynnera sighed, accepting I knew her too well to believe any excuse she might come up with. "I'm OK. I just have a lot on my mind. That's all." She paused for a moment before continuing. Zynnera seemed to realize her answer wasn't enough to abate my concerns. *And she's not wrong.* "Perhaps we could discuss it later tonight?"

I nodded. The fact that she was open to talking to me about it later put my mind at ease. I wanted her to feel safe confiding in me. The last few months had been so busy that our time together had waned. But I needed her to know I was still here for her. And I still wanted her here for me.

I stood up from the table, extending my hand. "Shall we?" Zynnera smiled and accepted the gesture..

We made our way down the long corridor leading out towards the north entry. I found myself stealing glances at her as we walked. Her long brown hair bounced with each step, a few curls swaying against her cheek. I could see her bright blue eyes focusing on the path in front of us as we moved towards the morning light outside. *She's so beautiful. She doesn't even have to try.* My heart pounded harder. I had yet to tell her how I felt. After Eradoma's defeat, I had wanted to desperately, but there never seemed to be a right time to do so. My mind had repeatedly found excuses to avoid the conversation.

Hachseeva, Rhemues, and the children were waiting for us by the north gate. The children jumped excitedly as we approached.

Nerene ran to Zynnera's side, grabbing her hand with a huge smile. The boys seemed satisfied to walk beside her as we passed through the iron portcullis and out into the city. The people were busy in the city center, bustling along with their routines while vendors haggled the prices of their goods. The atmosphere was so different in comparison to six months ago. The city was almost as I had remembered it from my childhood. My kingdom was prospering, and the people were regaining the happiness once lost under Eradoma's reign.

I watched a smile form across Zynnera's face as we entered the square. The sight of the people living without fear was what she always longed for. This was the Selvenor I hoped she would one day see. And while there was still much to do in order to regain everything that was lost, I knew we were progressing in the right direction. I knew one day soon Selvenor would be everything Zynnera had imagined.

I stopped in the middle of the square where tiers of wooden planks towered in front of a large stone statue. I watched Zynnera's face as she approached it, her eyes glazing over as she recognized the face of the stone man in front of her. She turned to face me, obviously fighting back tears.

"It's a memorial," I said, looking into her deep blue eyes. "I wanted to do something so we never forget the people we lost. To keep their memory alive."

The stone man stood, sword in hand, facing out towards the city. His carved eyes seemed to capture the brave expression of the man I once knew, the man who had worked so hard to get us to where we were now. Had it not been for the efforts of Captain Torilus, none of us would be standing here. The kingdom owed their lives to him, and this statue would serve as a reminder of his sacrifice.

Nerene seemed concerned by the tears now flowing from Zynnera's eyes. She tugged at her hand. "Auntie Zynnera? Who is that man?"

Zynnera wiped the tears from her face, crouching down beside her. "That is your grandfather. He helped us defeat the evil witch. We would have never been able to do that without his help."

Nerene smiled. She released Zynnera's hand, running to Hachseeva to tell her all about the stone statue in the city center. Hachseeva's eyes were tearful too. She nodded to me, seeming to thank me for the statue's commission. I moved to stand beside Zynnera, who had inched closer to the statue. Beneath the captain's feet was a large plaque with names inscribed on it. Each one represented someone who had been lost to Eradoma's tyranny.

Tears were still flowing from Zynnera's eyes as she turned to face me again. "Thank you," she whispered. "It's beautiful."

"They deserve to be remembered," I said.

Zynnera nodded, sobbing a little as she stared back at the plaque. I stepped closer to her, gently grabbing her hand and pulling her body towards me until I could wrap my arms around her. She sobbed into my shoulder, her hands resting on my chest as I squeezed her body against my own.

Her words came out shaky. "I miss him so much."

I rested my head on hers, trying to fight back tears of my own. "I know. I miss him too." My hand rubbed the back of her blue tunic in an effort to comfort her. "He would be so proud of you, Zynnera."

Zynnera pulled away from me so she could look into my eyes.

"He'd be proud of us both."

Rhemues approached us, his voice booming to correct our statements. "All of us." He smiled and Zynnera nodded in agreement with his statement. *Yes, the captain would be proud of us all.* We had come a long way in such a short time. It was hard for me to believe only six months ago I was imprisoned in the palace dungeon, my people suffering at the hands of Eradoma's evil magic. Hope had all but disappeared from my mind until the night I met Zynnera in that dark abyss. I hadn't realized then how much things would change because of our encounter. *How much I would change.*

Rhemues was looking at the statue with admiration. "This was a great surprise, Anaros."

"Yes," said Hachseeva. "He did everything he could to protect this city. It is only fitting he should stand guard over it now."

I smiled. "Yes, I agree." I was still watching Zynnera as she studied the face of the stone man. *I wish I could talk to her more. Preferably, alone.*

Rhemues cleared his throat, sensing my thoughts as he watched my expression with a smile. "Hachseeva, we should take the children for a walk in the market." Hachseeva picked up on his plan right away. Rhemues wanted to give me time alone with Zynnera. The two of them had not left their match-making ideas in the forest.

"But what about Auntie Zynnera?" Nerene scrunched her face, obviously not ready to abandon Zynnera's company.

Zynnera looked at Nerene, her focus finally moving away from the statue. Rhemues looked a little panicked as he tried to think of an excuse to leave us behind, but Hachseeva stepped in to save him. "I think Prince Anaros is planning to show Zynnera some of the reconstruction that's been happening in the city." Hachseeva winked at me and I could feel my face flush.

Nerene stomped her foot with a loud thud on the stone beneath her.. "Well, can't I go with them?"

"No." Rhemues and Hachseeva both said it in unison. I laughed a little as Rhemues ushered the children towards the marketplace. I could hear him talking as they moved away from us, promising the children a treat if they behaved.

Zynnera looked at me. I knew she wasn't naive. She was fully aware of what Hachseeva and Rhemues were up to. I wasn't sure if that made things more or less awkward. I shrugged, laughing a little. "Some things never change, do they?"

She smiled, shaking her head. While Rhemues and Hachseeva's attempts to improve our relationship was annoying at times, truthfully I welcomed their help. I wanted Zynnera to know how I felt. I wanted her to know I loved her. *I just need the right moment.* However, I wasn't sure now, amongst the bustling people of Selvenor, was it. Fortunately, there was one thing I *did* want to show Zynnera. Hachseeva's statement hadn't been a complete lie.

We moved along the center street, turning left after a few minutes and walking until we reached a large building. Zynnera's face lit up with excitement as she studied the new windows and clean walls. Her hands covered her mouth in surprise. "I can't believe it! It looks so different!"

I smiled back at her. "Would you like to pay Delamere a visit?"

Without hesitation, Zynnera rushed to the door. Inside, Delamere was talking to a few people while he served them a warm meal. While Eradoma's reign had ended, there were still many struggling to get back on their feet. I had given Delamere a large amount of gold and silver so he could help those in need. Zynnera and Rhemues had told me of his compassion and his efforts to help the people. Knowing I could trust him, I appointed him an overseer of the people. As a man who had been serving the poorest of Selvenor for years, Delamere was equipped to help the people in a way I couldn't, and I was grateful for his willingness to do so.

Upon noticing us, Delamere opened his arms for embrace. Zynnera hugged him tightly, fighting her watery eyes again. "Delamere, this place. It looks amazing!"

Delamere smiled, nodding in my direction. "Well, I have Prince Anaros to thank for that. We're working hard to get the people of Selvenor back on their feet."

Zynnera turned to face me. "Another surprise?"

I shrugged. "Surprises are the only kind of magic I've got." She laughed and I felt my heart stop.. Watching the happiness on her face filled me with a sense of contentment I never thought I could have. I wanted to keep that smile, the pure joy in her expression, there forever.

Zynnera talked to Delamere for a while. Leaning against the wall, I watched the expression on her face turn to pure delight as he told her everything he was doing to help the people. She seemed so happy at the idea they were finally escaping the darkness that ensued during Eradoma's reign. I couldn't help but wonder if she still felt responsible for it.After several minutes, they both approached me. Delamere held out his hand. "I can't thank you enough, Prince Anaros."

I shook my head. "No, Delamere. It is I that owe you a great debt for what you've been able to do."

Zynnera touched the round broach resting on Delamere's chest. "Your family would be so proud of everything you've done, Delamere." I watched the two of them, confused at the gesture and meaning behind her words. Delamere smiled at her. "Not nearly as proud...as I am of you."

Zynnera gave him another hug. My heart was full as we bid Delamere goodbye and left the building. Zynnera's spirits seemed to have lifted from this morning at breakfast, a proud success for me, but I was starting to dread having a conversation with her later, afraid it would only drag her back into depression.

We continued to chat as we walked the streets of Selvenor, taking in all the improvements to the city. Occasionally, Zynnera would glance around nervously, checking to see how many eyes were following us along the stone street. I found distracting her with conversation was the best remedy.

"Have you ever thought about it?" I liked asking her obscure questions, knowing she couldn't resist responding.

"Thought about what?"

I smiled, knowing it worked every time. "Children," I said. "You know, having them. A family...someday."

It felt weird and I immediately regretted it. *Of all the things I could have asked her? Why that? Am I trying to make this awkward?* Zynnera paused, obviously contemplating how to answer the question she hadn't seen coming.

"I...um...well, yes. I have." Her cheeks flushed a light pink as she fixed her gaze anywhere but on me. "Having a family of my own is something I look forward to...someday."

I could feel my pulse quicken. *With me? Have you thought of having one with me?* It was hard to focus over the loud prompts of my out of control thoughts. *No way I'm asking that. Knock it off. Change the subject.* I cleared my throat, but my mouth spilled out words before I could stop them.

"How many?" I felt my face flush now and heard a loud swallow from Zynnera.

"Um..." She was obviously embarrassed. *I'm embarrassed. Why would I ask her that? What's wrong with me?* "Well, I don't know. A few?"

I could hear it in her tone. She was begging me not to ask what *a few* meant, although I couldn't deny I wanted to know. We walked a few yards in silence. I was lost in my own thoughts when my question backfired.

"What about you?"

"What?" I looked at her, trying to determine what she meant by it.

Zynnera laughed. "Children?" She grew silent for a few seconds, moving her gaze back to the street in front of us and fiddling with her fingers like they would provide relief from this strange conversation I had started. "I mean, obviously, you would want them. A royal bloodline and all that."

I bit my lip. *Only with you. Only if they're 'ours'.* I couldn't swallow the lump in my throat no matter how hard I tried. "Obviously." It was the only thing I could pull from my thoughts that didn't sound...more awkward.

Zynnera stopped at a vendor stall, looking at the ornate items and clothing inside. I couldn't help but smile as I watched her. She tried on several hats, choosing to wear the most ridiculous ones first. We both laughed as she even placed a few of them on me. I wanted to stay in this moment with her, keep her carefree and happy expression in place for as long as I could.

Here in the marketplace, away from the palace, she seemed to forget about whatever had been bothering her this morning. For the first time in weeks, I had time with her, and I realized just how much I had missed it. As I stood beside her, looking at the tunics hanging across the side of the stall, two women passed by in deep conversation.

"And can you believe he just lets her stay in the palace with him?" one of them said.

The second gasped. "I know! I mean, the prince is crazy to allow such a *thing* to stay with him. Who knows what she's capable of. The daughter of that evil witch! She could be just like her!"

I felt my stomach curl. I hoped Zynnera hadn't heard them. I stole a glance at her and instantly knew that she had. She seemed frozen, staring directly at them with an expression of intense guilt. The women were still talking, chattering noisily as they walked right in front of us..

"They say the prince fancies her! Can you believe that! The last thing we need is another witch on the throne of Selvenor!" I could feel the anger growing inside me. *How dare they talk about Zynnera that way! She saved them! If it hadn't been for her, Eradoma would STILL be on the throne.*

After a few more seconds, the two women were out of sight. Zynnera rushed out from the stall, walking briskly towards the palace. I ran to follow her, calling her name in hopes she would stop. "Zynnera! Zynnera, wait!" Zynnera didn't slow down. She was determined to leave the city. I grabbed her arm, pulling her to a stop as I stepped in front of her. "Zynnera, listen to me..."

She jerked her arm out of my hand. "No." She was fighting back her tears. Her body was trembling as she looked into my eyes, begging for me to let her leave. "They're right. And you know it."

I stared back at her, shaking my head. "You are *not* Eradoma."

She shook her head and moved past me. I placed myself in front of her again, stopping her progress forward. "Zynnera, please. You mustn't listen to them."

"It's not just *them*! You just can't see it because..." She stopped herself. *I love you.* I finished her sentence in my mind as I stared into her blue eyes. They were so full of pain. I wanted to hold her, to make the pain go away. I wanted to protect her. But I knew the women's comments had only poured salt on an already open wound.

Zynnera let out a shaky sigh. She pushed past me, moving towards the palace without so much as looking back. I felt so angry. How could the people of Selvenor not see everything Zynnera had done for them? How could they hold her in such contempt? I didn't understand it. Eradoma had used her magic to inflict fear within the people. I could understand how easy it would be to fear Zynnera as well, but surely her deeds had shown she was nothing like her mother? Surely they could see how much Zynnera loved the people and wanted to help them?

I wondered how long they would be afraid of her. *It's no wonder she has so much on her mind. This is probably why she rarely goes into the city.* Zynnera didn't deserve to live hidden away in the palace for the rest of her life. She deserved to live in the light and not be feared by the people she had worked so hard to save. I would find a way to help the people understand and accept her. I knew once they saw her for who she truly was, they would love her. I just needed to open their eyes.

CHAPTER
~ *Four* ~

I woke to the morning light resting on my face. It had been the first night in a long time I had actually been able to sleep soundly. It wasn't that my mind had been alleviated from the burden of my memories. They still remained. But I suspected I had been so emotionally and mentally exhausted my mind just couldn't handle another night of spelunking in the dark cave where I was sure the man in the black cloak was still waiting for me. If anything, my mind was even more anxious than before.

Yesterday had been a long day. It started with a sleepless night of haunting memories, both good and bad. I admit they had weighed heavily on my mind as I started my morning. Anaros, of course, could tell immediately something was bothering me. *He can always tell. I think he knows me as well as I know myself.* The fact made me both happy and annoyed. *I can't seem to hide anything from him. At least not anymore.*

Anaros knew all of my secrets, all except one. I had yet to tell him of my vision of the man in the cave. I wasn't sure why I was withholding the information from him. I knew I would eventually have to tell him. My hope was that by the time I needed to explain, I would know more, enough to answer the questions he would likely have. *The same questions I have.*

He would chide me for not confiding in him sooner. And he probably should. Anaros knew my deepest secrets, and my confessions had never caused him to waver. There was no reason to hide anything from him. Anaros had been my support through everything we had faced thus far, and I knew that wouldn't change. *But he has enough to worry about. He's about to become king.* Anaros was about to have more weight on his shoulders than ever before, and the last thing I wanted to do was add to that burden with visions I didn't even understand.

No. Today it's my turn to support him. Today was the coronation. After today, Anaros would be the king of Selvenor. I wanted to be there for him, just like he was for me. Yesterday Anaros had given me something I never expected. He had honored my father and all those who lost their lives to Eradoma's evil reign. I never anticipated his gift, and it had caused me to second guess my decision to leave Selvenor. But overhearing the conversation between the two women in the marketplace had only affirmed what I feared to be true. The people of Selvenor were afraid of me. They were afraid of my magic. Not only was it improper for Anaros to be so close to me, but it was also unwise. I knew what they said was true, even if Anaros refused to believe it himself.

I had left the marketplace angry, but that anger quickly subsided and all that remained was sorrow. The thought of being hated and feared saddened me. It made my heart ache. I didn't want to be the person everyone was afraid of. I didn't want them to think I would ever harm them. But after the things Eradoma had done, I feared they would always see magic as evil. After returning to the palace, I had remained in my room the rest of the day. Anaros had attempted to talk me out of my solitude, knocking on my door every few hours, but I couldn't face him. I needed time to think, time to calm my emotions. As much as I wanted his comfort, I knew I needed to stand strong on my own. Soon I would be alone and needed to rely on my own strength to press forward.

I wanted to push it all behind me. After today, I would leave Selvenor. I would no longer be a burden on Anaros or the people. It was what was best for everyone. I could feel my heart aching at the idea. *This is going to be hard. But I mustn't dwell on it today. Today I will enjoy what little time I have left with him.*

My thoughts wondered to my family. *My family.* The words still felt so foreign to me. The idea of leaving Hachseeva, Rhemues, and the children made my heart hurt even more. Leaving Selvenor meant I would be giving up the family I had just found. It certainly wasn't what I wanted. *Perhaps I'm just destined to be alone? I've done what I needed to. I've saved the people. There is nothing left for me here.* I knew the last thought was a lie. Everything that mattered to me was right here in Selvenor, and I would be leaving it all behind.

I got dressed and made my way towards the banquet hall. My

thoughts seemed to follow me from my room. I felt anxious, but I knew I needed to try my best to hide it from my expression. The last thing I wanted was for Anaros to suspect my plan to leave Selvenor. He would never allow my departure; of that I was certain.

Anaros was sitting in his usual spot at the end of the table, eating a pile of scrambled eggs with a nervous expression. He looked up and smiled as I approached. "Good morning."

He always greeted me the same way. *I'm going to miss that.* "Good morning. Ready for today?"

Anaros looked down at his half empty plate of food. "Honestly, I'm a bit nervous." He looked back at me, forcing a smile. "Well, more than a bit."

"Don't be," I said. "You're going to be a great king, Anaros. You have nothing to be nervous about. You've already done so much for the people. They love you."

Anaros stared at me sympathetically. "The people love you too, Zynnera."

No, they don't. I knew he was just trying to make me feel better after what happened yesterday. But there wasn't anything he could say to change the truth. I knew the people were afraid of me, maybe even despised me. After what Eradoma had used her magic to do, I didn't blame them.

I started to argue with Anaros, but Rhemues's voice boomed from behind me. "Oh boy! There he is! Our new king!" Rhemues's excitement seemed to only make Anaros more anxious. He stood behind him, grasping his shoulder with a tight grip, which made Anaros wince a little.. "It's about time too, I'd say!"

Anaros sighed. "The people are ready, yes. I'm just not certain

I'm ready."

Rhemues laughed. "I figured as much. You were saying the same thing before Eradoma took over. Just remember, Anaros, your father believed you were ready then. And think how much you've grown in the last six months...well, twenty years technically."

Anaros gave him a half smile. "Thank you, Rhemues." His tone didn't change. Anaros was still nervous. I knew there was nothing Rhemues or I could say to make him more confident. He was taking on a huge responsibility; it was only natural for him to feel a bit panicked.

Rhemues turned to face me. "Zynnera, Hachseeva asked me to let you know you are welcome to join her before the ceremony...you know, to get ready." I had guessed it was coming. I thought back on the celebration in the rebel camp. Hachseeva was more than thrilled to help me "get ready." She and Rhemues were still playing match-maker, even now. And even though I knew what they were up to, I wasn't appalled by the offer. Any amount of time I could spend with them before leaving the city would be time well spent as far as I was concerned. It would also be a welcome distraction from the thoughts still racing through my mind.

I smiled at him. "I'd love to."

Rhemues seemed satisfied with my answer. He looked down at Anaros again, who had finished his breakfast. "And *you* are coming with me! We've got to get you looking like a king...and that's going to take some work." Rhemues held his stomach as he laughed.

Anaros laughed too. "Of course. You know best." Rhemues patted his shoulder and walked out of the banquet hall. Anaros stood up from his spot at the table, ready to follow Rhemues through the entry. He stared at me for a moment as though he were debating what he wanted to say. "I hope you'll save a dance for me at the celebration, Princess."

I grimaced. *I hate it when he calls me that. And he KNOWS I hate it.* Technically speaking, princess *was* my title. My mother was queen when I was born, therefore making me royalty. But I despised the idea of it. Anaros, on the other hand, found the title amusing, or at least my reaction to him using it.

He chuckled at my expression. "Still haven't accepted it then?"

"I've no intention of accepting it and you know that. I'd like to forget it altogether, but you seem dead set on reminding me every day." I couldn't help but smile at him. I may have hated his teasing, but part of me also welcomed it.

"Maybe you should just get used to it, Princess. Because I have no intention of letting it go." He gave me a witty smile. I shook my head at his taunting. Anaros glanced down at the floor, his expression more solemn now. "I am serious about that dance, though. I'll be looking forward to it." He gave me a little bow before turning to leave the room.

I watched as he disappeared beyond the entry into the corridor. I felt so torn. *Of course I want to dance with him. But should I?* The closer I allowed myself to get to him, the harder I knew it would be to leave. Still, I needed to keep my facade. I needed Anaros to think everything was fine. I would dance with him, and when the sun rose tomorrow morning, I would be gone. I would leave no trace of where I was going, not that I really knew myself.

I ate a light breakfast and headed towards the East Wing to see Hachseeva. She welcomed me in with a huge smile. "Are you excited for tonight?"

I was pretty sure she was far more excited than I was. "Yes, I suppose." I couldn't deny part of me *was* excited, but I kept reminding myself this would be my last night at the palace. I needed to stay focused.

Hachseeva didn't seem to think my answer was believable. "Zynnera, what's wrong?"

I smiled, continuing my facade. "Nothing. Just nerves, I think."

She considered my smile for a moment, still uncertain she believed me. "Alright, well, have you got a dress to wear?" She looked at me expectantly. I glanced over her elegant red gown, admiring the way it rested on her brown skin. I'd always thought Hachseeva was so naturally beautiful, but this dress seemed to accentuate her beauty even more.

In truth, I hadn't given much thought to my attire. I looked down at what I was already wearing. *She's right. This isn't exactly appropriate for a coronation.* There would be royalty here from many kingdoms. It was bad enough Anaros planned to dance with a witch, but even worse if I went looking like *this*. I was certain the rumors of how Selvenor was freed from Eradoma had spread throughout the land of Virgamor. Everyone would know who I was. Everyone would know *what* I was.

Hachseeva looked horrified by my response to her question. "Surely you weren't planning to go in *that*," she said, pointing to my clothes.

"Well...I...no...but." I sighed. Hachseeva could see right through me.

"You haven't thought about it until just now, have you?" She smiled, shaking her head. "It's a good thing I know you then, isn't it?"

Hachseeva walked towards her wooden wardrobe on the other side of the room. She opened its double doors and pulled out a beautiful dark blue dress. I moved closer to her, admiring the way the fabric flowed from the waist and ruffled at the bottom. The sleeves were trimmed with golden fabric and grew wider towards the cuffs. There was a golden sash around the waist that hung all the way to the bottom of the dress.

"Hachseeva, it's beautiful!" I couldn't help but reach out and touch the soft fabric as she held it up in her hand. I still hated wearing dresses, but I had to admit, I liked this one. *I wonder if Anaros will like it?* I tried to shake the thought from my head. *I can't let myself think like that.*

Hachseeva smiled at me. "I'm glad you approve. Let's get this on you. I can't wait to see you in it!"

I could feel my heart pounding as I removed my clothes and pulled on the dress. It felt so different wearing it in comparison to my normal tunic and trousers. The dress made me feel more like a princess. I rolled my eyes at the thought. *I don't want to feel like a princess. I'm not a princess.*

Hachseeva laced the back of the dress until it fitted tightly around my body. I turned to face her, watching her expression brighten even more as she looked me over. "Oh, Zynnera, you look so beautiful!"

I looked away from her. *Maybe this isn't a good idea? Maybe this will only make things worse...harder.* Hachseeva picked up on my mood right away. "Zynnera, what is it? What's bothering you? You know you can always talk to me."

I tried to hold it all in, but I couldn't. I needed to get the thoughts out of my head; I needed them out in the open. "I shouldn't be trying to impress him." I fought back the tears forming in my eyes.

Hachseeva's face contorted into confusion. "Why not?" She knew exactly who I was talking about. There was no need for me to explain I was referring to Anaros.

I sobbed a little. "Hachseeva, I'm a witch. How do you think the other kings will react if they think...if they see...."

Hachseeva grabbed my shoulders, her voice stern. "You listen to me right now, Zynnera. Whatever those kings think, or anyone else for that matter, isn't important. Their opinions do not matter, and you shouldn't concern yourself with them."

I shook my head. "But they do matter. Can't you see? If we lived in a village, if we were just normal people...but Anaros is to be king, Hachseeva. Who he is with, *that* matters. It could change everything! His relationships with them directly affect Selvenor and the people!"

Hachseeva sighed. "Even so, I think that's a decision for you and Anaros to make. You shouldn't let anyone else make it for you. Besides, there is no reason for a king or anyone else to have an issue with you. You *saved* Selvenor, and you've never done anything but try to help our kingdom."

If only that is how they would respond. I wished it were that simple. I wished I could be judged by my deeds alone. Everything would be so much easier and far less complicated. But it wasn't my reality, and I knew it never would be.

Hachseeva seemed to sense my sorrow. She pulled me into a tight embrace. "Zynnera, please don't do this to yourself. The people, they will come around. And so will everyone else. I'm sure of it."

I wanted so badly to believe her. I wanted to have the same hope she did. Nothing would make me happier than to stay in Selvenor with my family. *With Anaros.* But my visit to the marketplace had only proved it was not possible. I was sure Anaros had told Rhemues about the encounter and, of course, Rhemues was likely to have told Hachseeva.

I dried my tears with my sleeve. "I hope someday you are right." It was all I could manage to say. I needed to move away from the thoughts, from the sadness I felt deep in my soul.

Hachseeva sighed. I knew she was just trying to comfort me. I couldn't have asked for a better sister. She'd been there for me since the moment I met her. My father had told me so much about her, and all of it was true. She was so kind and compassionate. She had such a high capacity for love. I felt connected to her, like I'd known her my entire life.

"Just promise me you won't let anyone come between *us*. No matter what. I don't want to lose my sister."

I felt my stomach curl. *If she knew what I was planning to do, she would be so angry.* "You'll always be my sister, Hachseeva. No matter what."

It seemed to be enough for her as she smiled back at me. "Alright, let's go. The coronation will be starting soon."

I walked beside her, exiting her chamber and walking down the long corridor towards the Great Hall. I felt nervous and excited at the same time. My thoughts were racing with so many things I could barely keep up with them all. One, however, remained very clear.

Today would be my last day in Selvenor, and I intended to make the most of it.

CHAPTER
Five

It felt strange staring at my reflection in the ornate mirror resting against the wall in my room. I moved my body to examine my new attire, wondering if I really liked the way I looked in the ceremonial designs. *This is weird. I look so foolish.* I adjusted the fluffy fur collar around my neck. The outfit may have been traditional, but it didn't mean it was *stylish*, at least not my style anyway.

Rhemues approached me from behind. I could see him holding back a smile and a laugh as his expression reflected in the mirror. "You look...dashing." He snorted. "I'm sorry, this thing is really quite hideous."

I sighed. "Well, I don't disagree, but this *thing* has been handed down for generations, probably since the first king of Selvenor." I tried to adjust the collar again.

Rhemues considered my response for a moment. "Perhaps as king you can, I dunno, order a new tradition?"

We both laughed. Things were certainly different now. Eradoma had changed everything. I now knew the magic in the captain's stories I'd heard as a child was very real. It had been a part of our history, and I suspected it was not just Selvenor that had experienced how powerful those who controlled it could become. As king, it would be my duty to meet with the rulers of other kingdoms. Finding out how aware they were of magic was a high priority to me and something I intended to do immediately.

My thoughts moved to my father. *Why had he not told me? He had to have known. I know he did. So why not tell ME, the one who would take his place?* I couldn't deny the thoughts had bothered me for some time. I couldn't understand why he would keep such a heavy secret from me, and I would never be able to ask him.

Rhemues's reflection was still smiling over my shoulder. "I'm sure Zynnera will still find you attractive." His grin widened as my expression contorted into a grimace. Truthfully, I had already thought about what Zynnera would think of my ugly attire but preferred not to be reminded. *She'll think I look ridiculous. And she'll be right.*

My anxiety swept over me. Thinking about Zynnera made my heart race. It was bad enough I was still terrified of being crowned king, but the thought of the celebration to follow made me even more nervous. It was there that I planned to do it. I planned to ask *the question.*

I turned to face Rhemues, clearing my throat to abate my nerves. "Rhemues, how...how did you ask Hachseeva?"

Rhemues's face reflected his confusion by my question. "Ask her what?"

"You know...to...marry you?"

Rhemues raised his eyebrows. "Marry me?" I could hear the excitement in his voice. Rhemues seemed to guess why I would ask him such a question. "Anaros, are you planning to...are you going to ask Zynnera?"

I could feel my face flush. "Yes, I'm going to ask her tonight at the celebration."

"Tonight?" Rhemues was surprised by my answer. "I mean, don't get me wrong, I'm happy you want to ask her and certainly think you should, but have you even told her how you feel? Kissed her?"

I blinked at him. He knew the answer to those questions already. If I had told Zynnera how I felt and if I had kissed her, Rhemues would have been the first one I would tell. I moved my gaze to the floor, even more embarrassed. "Well, no."

Rhemues was looking at me expectantly. "And you think asking her to marry you before you do either of those things is a good move?"

I rolled my eyes. "Of course not! I mean, I'm going to tell her. And then I'll...I'll..."

Clearly, I was out of my element on the subject. I would be lying to myself if I said I wasn't terrified by the idea of asking Zynnera to marry me. Rhemues was no longer smiling. Instead, he spouted and expression of sympathy.

I sighed. "I know how crazy it sounds. But I know that I...I know how I feel about her."

Rhemues folded his arms. "And how's that?"

I was a little annoyed by his question. *He knows exactly how I feel about her. Why would he even ask that?* I tried to keep my annoyance out of my tone. "Rhemues, you know better than anyone."

"You're right, I do know. Because I know you and I can see it when you are with her...and even when you're not. But what I haven't seen or heard is you ever actually *say* it. Anaros, if you can't say it to me, do you really think you'll be able to tell Zynnera?"

Rhemues had a point. I hadn't ever admitted it out loud. *And why?* What was I so afraid of? The question answered itself. I was afraid. I was afraid of putting my heart in such a vulnerable position. I was afraid of losing Zynnera with my confession should she not feel the same way. I'd never had feelings for anyone in the way I did for her, a truth that both excited and terrified me.

I took a deep breath. "Rhemues, I love her. And I know I need to tell her that. I guess...I'm just afraid. My heart tells me Zynnera feels the same way, but what if I'm wrong? What if it's all just in my head?"

Rhemues chuckled at my statement. "Well, I don't think it's all in your head. In fact, I'm certain it's not. But regardless, you'll never know for sure until you tell her."

"I know...and I will. I'm just not certain how yet." I realized Rhemues had never answered my initial question. "That's why I asked how you did it. How did you tell Hachseeva?"

Rhemues fidgeted a little at the repetition of my question. "You know I had feelings for her for a while...even before Eradoma. And after the captain died, I just...I dunno...was there for her. Eventually we kissed and I told her how I felt. Well, you get the idea, the rest is all history."

For some reason his tone sounded nervous, almost as though he were trying to avoid giving me a detailed answer. I knew Rhemues well enough to know he was hiding something about his engagement to Hachseeva. I raised my eyebrows in suspicion. "And then you asked her to marry you?"

Rhemues cleared his throat. "Not exactly."

For all his mocking of me and my relationship with Zynnera, Rhemues seemed embarrassed to give me advice. *What is he hiding? Whatever it is, he's embarrassed by it.* Hachseeva had always seemed frustrated by Rhemues's sluggish approach to expressing his feelings. I smiled. *That's it! I think I know what he's hiding!*

I couldn't hide the smile on my face. "You never asked her, did you?"

Rhemues looked horrified by my statement and became immediately defensive. "Of course I asked her! I just didn't...I mean...." He released an annoyed sigh, obviously aware I would never let it go until he told me the entire story. "One day we took a walk through the woods. I kissed her, like always. I suppose she was tired of waiting, and well...she asked me if I ever planned to propose to her. So I did, right there in the forest. She obviously said yes, and here we are."

I couldn't help but laugh a little. That certainly sounded like Hachseeva. I remembered when we were in the village and she had helped Zynnera get ready for the celebration. Hachseeva had become annoyed by my slow response to her relationship hints. And even though Zynnera had seemed a little uncomfortable by Hachseeva's match-making shenanigans, I was certain she appreciated them. Admittedly, so did I.

I pulled a small ring from my pocket, holding it in front of me so Rhemues could grasp how serious I was. He nodded his head and smiled. "You really are certain about this, aren't you?"

"I know I love her...and I believe she loves me too. Hopefully after tonight, I'll no longer have any doubts."

Rhemues placed his hand on my shoulder. "I wish you the best of luck, Anaros. Truly, I do. There's not really any advice I can give you other than just be honest with her. If it's meant to work out, it will." He shook his head, laughing at his own statement. "That sounds incredibly cheesy. But it's still true."

I nodded. "Rhemues, I can't thank you enough for always having my back."

Rhemues smiled. "I always will. That's a promise. Now, let's get you down to the Great Hall. It's time to advance your title."

I laughed. *King.* I could feel my nerves taking over again. *Am I really ready for this? Am I ready to become the King of Selvenor?* I felt a little nauseous. It was too late now to decide I wasn't. The coronation was only moments away. By the time the sun set on today, I would no longer be a prince. I would carry the burden of defending my people. I would hold the responsibility of their welfare and prosperity.

Rhemues and I walked along the corridor towards the Great Hall. I tried to focus on my breathing as we moved away from my chamber at the end of the hallway. I stole a glance at the portraits hanging on the wall. They reflected the timeline of all the rulers who had come before, the last frame containing a picture of my father. I stopped in front of his portrait, staring into his painted eyes. *I wish you were here with me today, Father. I wish I could hear your voice, listen to your advice.* Rhemues had stopped to wait for me. He seemed to understand I needed the moment.

After a few minutes we continued towards the Great Hall. I could hear the loud murmur coming from inside as we approached. I allowed myself to peek through the doors. The Great Hall had been filled with chairs to max capacity and every seat was occupied. Royalty and noblemen from throughout the land had journeyed to Selvenor for the ceremony. The idea of being a novice ruler in front of so many only made my anxiety worse.

Rhemues grabbed my shoulders, turning me to face him. "You've got this. You're ready for this." I wasn't sure his words really helped ease my nervousness.

I took a gulp and nodded. Rhemues gave me one last pat on the back before making his way into the room. Standing alone with my thoughts only made my heart race even more. *I'm ready. I can do this.* I took a deep breath, releasing it slowly as I approached the entry. I could see Rhemues sitting with his family. The children were bouncing up and down with excitement as they waited for the ceremony to begin. Zynnera's wavy dark hair moved as she talked to Hachseeva and the children. I smiled, knowing she was here to support me.

The royal Harold was waiting patiently just inside the entry, ready to announce me as I entered the room. I took one final deep breath and nodded to him, moving beyond the dark green carpet of the corridor and into the Great Hall.

The Harold used a wooden mallet to bang against a hollow box, the sound echoing through the room and commanding silence. "His royal Highness, son of King Adikide, Prince Anaros."

I walked forward, keeping my eyes to the front of the room. I didn't dare move my gaze away from the Chamberlain, who waited to perform the ceremony. The man nodded to me, allowing a small smile to escape his impassive expression. His grey hair and wrinkled face provided me with a small amount of comfort as I recalled his role in my father's court. His name was Mefferdus and he had been a close friend of my father for many years before his passing. After defeating Eradoma, it had been difficult to fill the royal court. Many of the people who had served under my father's reign had been killed. Mefferdus was the only member of the royal court who remained. And while I hadn't known him well before our kingdom was besieged by Eradoma, I felt he could help me obtain a sense of normalcy for the sake of the people.

Mefferdus gestured to a small green cloth resting on the floor. I knelt down on it, keeping my focus on him to abate my nerves. I could feel the eyes of the room all on me. Mefferdus took a short ornate rod in his hands, placing it on each of my shoulders. It was riddled with green gemstones embedded in its gold frame, an item that had crowned each of my ancestors to the throne of Selvenor. Mefferdus began reciting the coronation rite, but I found myself unable to focus on his words. I thought of my father and how he had looked forward to this day. I couldn't help but feel a sense of loneliness at his absence. *I want to make him proud. I want to be the king he thought I would be.*

At the conclusion of his words, Mefferdus gestured for me to stand. I followed his instruction, turning to face the full room behind me. I didn't dare steal a glance at Rhemues or Zynnera, fearing I would lose my nerves completely. Instead I focused on the strangers in front of me, the strangers I was likely going to become quite familiar with in the upcoming months.

The Harold's voice echoed from the back of the room. "Presenting his royal majesty, King Anaros, King of Selvenor."

Everyone in the room rose to their feet. I moved slowly towards the back of the hall, suddenly aware of the heavy crown on top of my head. I'd been so lost in my own thoughts, I hadn't even noticed Mefferdus place it on my head. I could feel my body trembling as I moved through the Great Hall, the soft chattering of the people filling the room as I passed beyond the entry. The doors closed behind me with a soft thud. *Finally. It's all over.* I felt like I could finally breathe a small sigh of relief. *Now if I can just get through the celebration.* But I knew my nerves would not be any calmer. I thought of Zynnera. Would I really have the courage to tell her tonight? To follow through with my plan and ask her one of the most important questions of my life?

I made my way back to my chamber. The servants would need time to set up the Great Hall for the celebration and I intended to spend those short hours in my room alone, hoping to ease my anxiety. I sat on my bed for a long time, pondering my plan to steal away time with Zynnera tonight. My thoughts raced with phrases and words, trying to sort them into coherent sentences that might sweep her off her feet. No matter how hard I tried, they all sounded stupid to me.

I could see the sun setting low in the sky when a soft knock sounded from my door. *It's already time?* I sighed. I was no closer to being ready now than I had been hours ago. I opened the door to find Rhemues bolstering a huge smile. Enthusiasm seemed to radiate from his expression as he looked me over. I had taken it upon myself to remove the hideous ceremonial attire and regalia, replacing it with something I was more comfortable in. My usual black trousers, white shirt, and a new green overcoat were accompanied by a black cape, the underside of which also flashed a dark green.

"I see you've changed," said Rhemues. "Not brave enough to go to the celebration in that fashion challenged ensemble?"

I laughed, moving away from the door. "Definitely not." Rhemues followed me, still chuckling as he closed the door behind him. I was glad he had come to see me before the celebration. There was something I needed to discuss with him. "Rhemues, I know I've already thanked you this morning, but I feel as though I should do so again."

Rhemues smiled. "Anaros, you're my best friend. My family. You know I'll always have your back."

"Yes, I know," I said. "And I know you'll always do what you can for Selvenor and the people." Rhemues nodded, watching me expectantly. He seemed to sense I had more to say to him than just a simple *thank you.* "Rhemues, you know I've been filling positions on the court."

Rhemues nodded. "Yes, of course. I imagine it will be good to delegate some of your responsibilities."

"True. But there is one position I have yet to fill. And I was rather hoping you might accept my invitation to it."

Rhemues stared at me, completely baffled by my words. "You want...me? You think I should be your royal advisor?" He remained surprised even as he clarified my offer.

"Rhemues, you've been there for me through everything. Our whole lives. *And* you're next in line for the throne should something happen to me. I trust you with my life, with the kingdom, everything. It only makes sense for you to continue the role you've always played."

He stayed quiet for several moments, fighting tears as his eyes glazed over. "Anaros, I don't know what to say."

I smiled. "I'm hoping *yes* will be your response."

Rhemues laughed. "Yes. Of course, I accept. I'm honored you would want me in such a prestigious position. Truly honored."

He was still fighting back tears. I knew how much this meant to him. "I assure you, the honor is mine."

We both smiled at each other for a few moments. I couldn't be more grateful for everything Rhemues had done for me. He was always there, no matter how tough things got. Rhemues let out a shaky sigh. "Well, we should probably get going. As your royal advisor, it's my advice that we get you to the celebration."

I laughed. "Right. Yes, we should go."

As I walked with Rhemues down the corridor to the Great Hall, I could feel my anxiety returning. I still had no idea what I would say to Zynnera...or how I would start the conversation I knew needed to happen. *Just stay calm. Don't overthink it. Be natural.* If only it were as easy as my mind made it sound.

Once again, the Harold announced my arrival into the Great Hall. I made sure he was aware of Rhemues's new title as well. I watched surprise spread across Hachseeva's face as the Harold announced Rhemues as the royal advisor. Rhemues approached her with a bright smile, whispering to her what I knew were the words from our conversation in my chamber.

Slowly the Great Hall filled with kings and queens, princes and princesses, and other royal court members from across the land. My heart pounded as I waited for the name that really mattered to me. *What's taking so long? Is she coming?* I felt a tap on my shoulder. I turned to find Hachseeva smiling at me. She seemed to know exactly what I was thinking.

"Don't worry," she said. "She'll be here. She wanted to wait until after the Harold finished announcing everyone. I think she was a bit nervous to have him mention her name."

I nodded. What Hachseeva said certainly made sense. Zynnera was struggling with the idea of being accepted by not only our people, but also those of the surrounding kingdoms. I understood why she desired to hide her identity from everyone, but I wanted to protect her from those fears of judgment. I wanted Zynnera to understand I didn't care what anyone else thought about my relationship with her.

The room was loud with chatter now as the minstrels began playing music in the background. Some of the guests even began dancing, bouncing to the sounds of the flute and mandolin. I kept my eyes on the entry to the Great Hall as much as I could, waiting for Zynnera to appear. Other diplomats would occasionally ask for my attention, shifting my focus only long enough to engage with them before it returned to the empty space leading out of the room.

After several minutes I turned to face Hachseeva, hoping her expression would provide me some comfort. Hachseeva sighed. She seemed as worried about Zynnera's absence as I was. But as I watched her face, Hachseeva's expression contorted into a smile as she lifted her hand to point towards the entry.

As I followed the direction of her gaze, Zynnera came into view, walking through the entry and into the Great Hall. Time seemed to stand still as I looked at her through the crowd, watching her dark blue gown graze the floor as she walked. She stared at me for a few moments and I realized my body had begun to move towards her without permission from my mind. Zynnera stared down at the floor as I approached, obviously nervous by the attention that followed me.

I stopped in front of her, my heart pounding as I convinced myself to speak. "You look beautiful," I said.

Zynnera moved her gaze from the floor to my eyes. I could see how nervous she was, although her expression tried to hide it. I watched her take a deep breath and tuck her hair behind her ear. The motion made me smile. *She still does that. I love that she does that.* Zynnera grabbed both sides of her dress, performing a little curtsey as she continued to look at me. "Thank you, Your Highness."

I couldn't help but smile at her. I knew how nervous she was in this moment. She looked around the room, a little frantic at the amount of attention her proximity to me had created. But none of it mattered to me. I was happy she had finally arrived.

I held out my hand in front of her. Zynnera stared at it for a moment before placing her hand in mine. She still seemed uncertain of dancing with me in front of the crowd whose eyes were all watching us both carefully. I pulled her to the center of the room where others were already dancing. We placed our palms together, moving in a circle as we bounced to the quick rhythm of the music.

A smile finally stretched across her face as we danced. Hachseeva had spent several days teaching Zynnera how to dance, and the experience seemed to make her more at ease. For the moment, everything was easy, simple. Zynnera's concerns appeared to melt away, along with my own. It felt nice to just be with her, to enjoy a moment with her.

The music stopped momentarily as the minstrels began a new song. This one was much softer and slower. I placed my hand around Zynnera's waist and pulled her closer to me. I could see her anxiety return as she looked past me at the crowd around us. She seemed almost panicked at their whispers. I knew she wasn't imagining their detest, but I was determined to show her I didn't care what their opinion of us was.

I placed my hand on her face, turning it until she was looking at me. "Look at me. Don't worry about them. Just focus on me." I could feel her body trembling as we started to dance again, her blue eyes reflecting the fear I knew she felt. After a minute or two she seemed to relax a little, allowing me to lead her to the music. I smiled at her. "It's not so bad, is it? Dancing with me?"

Zynnera forced a little smile. "You know it's not that."

My smile faded. "I do. I understand." I placed my mouth right next to her ear, whispering. But I want *you* to understand I don't care what they think."

Zynnera closed her eyes and shook her head. "Anaros..."

"Excuse me, Your Highness." A man with white hair and a beard down to his chest interrupted Zynnera before she could finish. She stared at the floor, avoiding eye contact with him as he spoke. "I'd like a word with you before I leave Selvenor."

I watched him stare at Zynnera with a disapproving expression. I recognized the man as the King of Dunivear, King Lenear. He had been to Selvenor on many occasions during my father's reign. Our kingdoms had once been allies before Eradoma's assent to power and I suspected he was eager to discuss those treaties again now that she was gone. I knew it was my obligation to engage in such discussions, but I didn't want to abandon Zynnera because of Lenear's timing.

King Lenear was looking at me expectantly. "Alone, of course." He flashed Zynnera a fake smile. I was certain she could see through it.

I paused, still not wanting to leave her standing alone. The man at his side spoke up, obviously sensing my hesitation. "I'd be happy to finish this dance if it pleases you, Your Highness." The man turned to Zynnera, smiling as he gave her a shallow bow. I wasn't sure I liked the idea of her dancing with someone else, but I couldn't back out of my duties. I'd only been king for a few hours, and I knew the occupants of the room were watching my every move.

King Lenear pointed to the man standing beside him. "This is Elric, my advisor. I assure you the girl will be in good hands in your absence."

There was something cold about the way he said *the girl*, not to mention disrespectful. He talked about Zynnera as though she weren't standing right in front of him. I was annoyed at his dismissal of her, but what choice did I have with everyone watching? "Very well." I turned to Zynnera, sympathy in my eyes. "I'll be back soon." I wanted her to know I had no intention of letting this interruption conclude our evening.

King Lenear followed me into another room just down the corridor from the Great Hall. It was a fairly small room with a large table in the center. My father had used it to meet with the leaders of his army and plan during times of war. A huge map hung on one wall, featuring the fine details of Selvenor and the kingdoms beyond our borders.

I turned to face him, hoping to make my conversation with him quick so I could return to Zynnera. "What is it I can do for you?"

King Lenear sipped the wine from the chalice he had brought with him from the Great Hall. He seemed to be in no hurry to begin our discussion. "I'm sure you are aware of the arrangements between myself and your father?"

"Yes, as I understand it, you had both trade and peace agreements," I said. He walked a few paces around the large wooden table, still drinking from his chalice. I tried to hide my frustration from my expression. *Just get to it already.*

"That's correct. I would like to renew those agreements, assuming that is something you are interested in?"

"Of course. I see no reason why Dunivear and Selvenor should not remain allies."

King Lenear walked to the side of the table where I was standing. He placed his chalice down, turning to face me. "You may not see it, but I certainly do."

My face contorted into confusion. "See what exactly?"

I could hear the tension in his voice. "Your Highness, you are young, and so I will excuse your lack of experience and insufficient ability to make wise decisions. But I will also be blunt. As long as the threat of the witch remains in Selvenor, there will be no agreements between our kingdoms."

I bit my lip. I was trying hard to keep myself calm, but his words repeated in my mind, making me more angry with each pass. "There is no threat in Selvenor. Zynnera took care of that." I was glaring at him now. If he thought I was going to just stand by while he questioned Zynnera's character, he was sorely mistaken.

King Lenear didn't back down. His tone became even more serious, almost threatening. "Your *witch* may have rid Selvenor of Eradoma's dark magic, but it will fall to hers. I assure you of that."

"Zynnera is nothing like Eradoma. She has only used her magic for good..."

Lenear interrupted me, shouting above my voice. "Don't be naive, boy! You think that witch hasn't thought of using her powers against you and every single one of the people in this kingdom? Mark my words, she will turn on you and your people. And when she does, I will not send my army to your rescue. I will not sacrifice my people so you can have your little fling with the witch. The destruction of Selvenor will be on your head!"

I couldn't hold back my anger. *He has no idea who Zynnera is. She would never turn her back on the people or on me.* "You don't know her, nor do you know me. You're asking me to exile the person who saved this kingdom. If it weren't for her, none of us would be standing here tonight. I have no intention of doing this."

King Lenear's voice calmed. "You should consider this decision wisely, Your Highness. Either you cut ties with the witch, rid your kingdom of her magic, or lose an ally you can't afford to. The decision is yours. But I assure you, the economic repercussions of alienating ties with your neighbors, and not just Dunivear, will devastate Selvenor in ways you never dreamed." He made his way to the entry. "I'll be awaiting a messenger to bring your decision."

My blood boiled as he left the room. Once he was out of sight, I slammed my fists on the table and purposely knocked the half-full chalice to the floor. I breathed hard as I leaned over the wooden table, propping myself up with my hands. I'd been king less than a day and already I could feel the enormous weight on my shoulders. How was I supposed to make this decision? Lenear wasn't wrong. Having no allies or trade agreements with the surrounding kingdoms spelled disaster for Selvenor. I couldn't let my people fall into poverty, not when we had worked so hard to get them back on their feet. But accepting Lenear's conditions would mean asking Zynnera to leave, and that was something I refused to do. *There has to be a way around this. There must be a way to make them understand, to see who Zynnera really is.*

I didn't have an answer. I hadn't even been successful at helping my own people see Zynnera for the kind and compassionate person she was. How was I supposed to convince anyone else? The whole thing made me sick. I had no idea what I was going to do, but one thing was certain. *I can't tell Zynnera. She can't know. I won't let her leave.*

CHAPTER
~ *Six* ~

The minstrels proceeded to play, filling the room with the sound of music. I could feel my heart pounding as Elric placed his hand on my waist. I hesitated to take his other hand as the music continued to play in the background. *I've never danced with anyone except Anaros. I don't know if I feel comfortable doing this.*

Elric smiled, seeming to sense my thoughts. "It's only a dance. I'm sure King Anaros will return promptly."

I accepted his outstretched hand, and we began to move to the soft sounds of the mandolin. I still didn't feel comfortable with the whole situation. I found myself wishing for Anaros to return each passing second. The night had already been hard enough as every person in the room watched me with suspicion and distrust. I could feel their eyes on me even now as I danced with the royal advisor of

Dunivear.

He was a tall, handsome man, a bit older than myself. He wore all black: a cape, trousers, and what looked almost like thin armor over his chest. I couldn't help but wonder why he felt the need for it at a coronation. He presented himself as someone accustomed to his noble rank, but I didn't sense the same disdain emanating from him as I did from the crowd around us. Elric seemed tolerant of my magical lineage, almost accepting. I found his lack of concern both comforting and misgiving. There was just something odd about him that I couldn't put my finger on.

I could feel him staring at me as I glanced around the room at the herd of grimacing faces. He leaned closer to me, whispering in my ear. "You know they are never going to trust you, don't you?"

I turned to face him, looking deep into his light brown eyes. I wasn't sure how to take his comment. He was probably right, of course, but I wasn't sure why he felt it necessary to say it. Part of me felt angry he would even say such a thing to me. *He doesn't know me. What difference does it make to him, anyway?*

Elric smiled at me again. "Every last person in this room knows how powerful you are. They know what you can do with your magic, should you choose to. People always despise what they fear...and what they cannot control."

"So...what? Are you saying I should just bow to their will? Let them believe I exist solely for their use? To execute whatever purpose they see fit?" I knew my face reflected my anger and I didn't care.

Elric laughed. "No, I think you should be appreciated. Of course, my opinion isn't exactly the popular one. You, Zynnera, you could have this entire kingdom if you wanted it. Yet you stand here, placing yourself on display only to be hated and rejected. And why? To impress a king who will dismiss you? Reject you the same way the people of Selvenor have."

I could feel my face flush. "I've no desire to rule Selvenor. And you don't know anything about Anaros. He would never betray me, cast me out. He is a good man..."

Elric interrupted me. "A good man, yes. But a man nonetheless. And one who now bows to the will of his people. Anaros may be king, but he is still subject to rule on behalf of the people. And when they come to him with complaint, when they...demand the witch be removed from their city, what then, Zynnera? Do you honestly believe he will stand by you? Face rebellion just to keep you here?"

I pulled my hand from his and used the other to remove his hand from my waist. I could feel my eyes glazing over. There was nothing I could say to him. Everything he had spoken was the truth and I knew it. But hearing it out loud, and from a stranger, was harder than hearing it within my own thoughts. I turned and walked away from him. *I need to get out of here. I need to leave.*

Heads turned to follow me as I walked out of the Great Hall. As soon as my feet touched the green carpet of the corridor, the tears I'd been working so hard to retain gushed from my eyes. I stood against the wall, sobbing as Elric's words still lingered in my thoughts. I knew everything he said was true. It was why I had already planned to leave on my own. Being in Selvenor only complicated things for Anaros. My presence would only put a strain on his reign and create unnecessary problems as he tried to rebuild the kingdom. I didn't want that. I didn't want to add to the burden I knew he already carried.

Hachseeva appeared in the entry. *She saw me leave. She knows Elric upset me.* I wiped the tears from my face, hoping to hide my emotional state. Hachseeva approached me, her eyes full of sympathy and concern. "Zynnera, what happened?"

I shook my head. I didn't really want to talk about it, but I knew she would never let it go until I did. "I don't think I can do this. I can't live like this."

Hachseeva moved to my side, placing her arm around me. "Like what, Zynnera? What did that man say to you?"

"Nothing that wasn't true," I whispered.

Hachseeva's tone became annoyed. "Well, I'd like to be the judge of that."

I sighed. "Hachseeva, Anaros is trying to rebuild everything Eradoma destroyed. The people of Selvenor don't trust me...and neither does anyone else. And I don't expect them to. How can Anaros bring Selvenor back to prosperity when people are frowning at his relationship with me...when they see me as a threat to their lives?"

"Zynnera, I told you. They just need time to see."

I shook my head again. "Time isn't going to solve this, Hachseeva. It just won't." I moved away from her, stopping after a few steps. "I think I just need some rest. Please tell Anaros I'm sorry when he returns."

I didn't turn around to check her response. I knew if I did, she would only continue to argue with me and try to convince me to stay. But I couldn't. My mind was racing as fast as my heart. I *needed* to get away from it all, away from everyone in that room.

The only visitor who hadn't judged me was Elric, but his blunt statements of my current situation left me hating him nonetheless. King Lenear had also been slow to hide his disgust with me. I could hear it in his tone when he interrupted my dance with Anaros. I hoped their discussion hadn't been about me.

Guilt crept into my thoughts. *Maybe it would have been better if I had left before the celebration? Maybe I should have gone months ago?* No. Anaros would have only come looking for me. *At least if he does so now, he will have already been crowned king. The other leaders have accepted his royal position. Now I can leave. Anaros will have no choice but to let me go, knowing he has a kingdom to maintain.* I hoped the last part was true. I hoped he really would let me go.

As I moved along the corridor of the West Wing, my mind raced with thoughts of tomorrow. *Tomorrow I'll leave. I'll leave without telling anyone.* I still had no idea where I was going to go. I just needed to get out of Selvenor, somewhere beyond its boundaries that was far enough away so that Anaros would stop looking for me. *Because I know he will. The minute he knows I'm gone, he'll have people looking for me.*

I thought of Croseline. I had never been there, never seen the ocean. It seemed a good place to start. Once there, perhaps I could barter passage aboard a ship. I could go anywhere as long as it put more distance between Selvenor and myself. The idea scared me. Only a few short months ago I was leaving the city of Selvenor for the first time in my life. Even then I hadn't voyaged beyond the borders of the kingdom. Everything about this trip would be new and I would be facing it all alone.

I returned to my chamber. Everything inside was shrouded with the darkness of night. I lit a small lantern and placed it on the table beside my bed. I moved to my wardrobe, pulling a large satchel from its hiding place behind some of my clothes. I placed a clean pair of clothing and *The Tahetya* inside the brown sack. It seemed a bit empty, much like how I felt preparing to leave the only home I'd ever known. *I'll go to the kitchen tomorrow morning before I leave. I can fill the satchel then. At least have a bit of food to start my journey.*

I placed the satchel back inside my wardrobe to keep it hidden in case I had any visitors. The last thing I wanted was anyone to become suspicious and realize what I was planning. There was only one thing left to do, and it was the one I was dreading most. *Sleep.* If I could even call it that. I felt certain tonight would be no different than any other, filled with memories and nightmares that prevented any amount of actual rest. Still, I knew I needed to try. Tomorrow would be a long day. *A hard day.*

I plopped down on my bed, leaning against a pillow as I stared at the ceiling. I still had so many questions. I wondered if I would find any answers on my journey away from Selvenor. I could feel myself drifting off to sleep as I imagined the places I might visit. As my eyes closed, those thoughts were replaced with visions of a beautiful city resting on the Sea of Maleze. My father's voice penetrated my thoughts as he described Dunivear. I envisioned the warlocks who left the city to escape persecution from the people they had worked so hard to save.

A darkness filled my thoughts. I could see a large village surrounded by a dense forest of birch and pine. My mind raced through a mountain pass where a small stream forced its way over rocks and into a pool below, forming a small waterfall. I could hear it as though I were right there, as if everything inside my mind were tangible. I could feel the mist from the river as it crashed on the surface below and even smell the water in the air.

I suddenly found myself standing along the riverbank beyond the falls. Everything seemed so quiet and peaceful. The light from the moon reflected onto the surface of the water as the river widened and the flow slowed to a calm trickle between the banks. I couldn't help but think it would be a nice place to go. *If I could find a place like this. Somewhere safe. Somewhere away from everyone.*

But my thoughts were interrupted as a cloaked figure appeared near the falls. I could see it moving towards me, its face hidden beneath a hood. My heart began to pound hard. I had an uneasy feeling about the mysterious figure as it moved closer to me. It stopped a few yards away, hovering over another figure resting on the ground. As it stood towering over the other, I could hear faint whispers from the one on the ground.

I struggled to make out the sounds. "Please. Why are you doing this? Please."

The cloaked figure did not respond to the whispered pleas. It waved its hands over the other, a blue aura surrounding them. I could hear screams. *I have to do something! What can I do!* The blue aura from the cloaked figure seemed to absorb the green aura from the figure on the ground. I watched as the green light left their body and entered that of the figure standing over it. The screams continued until the spell was completed. The cloaked figure waved its hand a second time, using a spell I recognized.

The Morso. The spell of death. The body on the ground was motionless. I knew what had happened. I knew the result of the spell. *Did I just witness a murder? No, this...it can't be real. It's only a dream, nothing more.* I couldn't shake the feeling that I was lying to myself. It all felt so real.

The cloaked figure turned towards me as if it could see me standing by the bank of the river. My heart felt as though it would beat out of my chest as it began to approach me. *This isn't real. This is a nightmare. I'm not really here.* The words didn't seem to convince my mind. I had to do something. I had to wake up! What was going to happen to me? Would the mysterious figure do to me what it had to the other lifeless body on the ground?

It continued to approach me. I could hear the panic in my own voice as I stumbled backwards. "Please...I don't...I just...." I didn't know what to say. I had no idea who this cloaked person was or even *where* I was. The figure stopped in front of me, waving its hand as a blue aura surrounded them. "No! Please!" I could hear myself screaming, but it didn't seem to stop the nightmare in front of me. "No!"

I felt the warm touch of someone's hand on my arm. "Zynnera! Zynnera, wake up!"

I sat up on the bed, gasping as I looked frantically around the room. Anaros was sitting beside me with a terrified look on his face. *It was only a dream. It wasn't real. It wasn't real.* I was still trying to convince myself, but I couldn't seem to find any truth in the words.

Anaros's hand was still resting on my arm. "It's OK. You're safe."

I stared at him. What was I supposed to say to him? He was obviously concerned. Had I screamed in real life and not just in my head? "I'm fine. Just a nightmare."

Anaros didn't seem convinced. "About what?" His question was serious.

I shook my head. "It doesn't matter. I'm fine, really." Looking into his deep brown eyes, I knew my answer wasn't enough for him. But did I dare tell him? What if he figured out I was planning to leave?

"Zynnera, this isn't the first time I've heard you screaming at night." I gulped. *Fantastic. He's not going to let this go.* I suddenly regretted being in the room right next to his. Anaros sighed. "Zynnera, you need to tell me what's going on. Please."

I felt so overwhelmed. I couldn't fight it. I wanted to tell him so badly that the words escaped before I could stop them. "I don't know. There's a darkness, the same darkness I felt in the cave. It haunts me. I feel as though something evil, something powerful is coming." I shook my head, tears flowing down my face and onto the soft blankets on the bed.

"Why haven't you told me before now? Zynnera, look at me." His fingers curled under my chin, forcing my eyes back to his eyes. Anaros tucked my hair behind my ear so he could see my face.

I sobbed a little. "I don't know. I just...you have so much already. You're king...I didn't want to burden you with anything else."

Anaros shook his head. "You're not a burden to me, Zynnera. You never have been and you never will be. Surely you must know that?" I glanced up at him. I knew I should keep my dreams to myself, but I wasn't sure I was strong enough. Anaros grabbed my hand. "Please tell me."

I let out a shaky sigh. "When we were in the cave and I had the flashes, I...there was one I didn't tell you about. There was a man with black hair in a black cloak. He was repeating this phrase over and over again. I couldn't understand him, but I know it has something to do with Virgàm."

I paused to give Anaros a chance to process what I was saying. I was sure he would have questions. He thought on my words for a few moments. "And you think this man is somehow linked to the darkness you sense?"

I nodded. "Yes. I feel it every time my mind takes me back to the cave. I just wish I knew what it meant! I wish I knew who he was!" I felt so frustrated. It felt good to tell Anaros everything, but the fact that I had no explanation only made me angry with myself. What good did it do to tell him any of this if we had no idea what it meant?

Anaros was still looking at me, waiting for me to continue. When I didn't say anything, he pushed me with another question. "And tonight? Was this what you were dreaming about? This man in the black cloak?"

I bit my lip, still uncertain I wanted to tell him everything. Anaros sensed my hesitation immediately. "Zynnera." His tone chided me.

I sighed. "No. This one was different. There was someone else, someone with magical powers. They attacked another person. It was like they were draining the magical energy from them. I thought they were about to do the same to me...in the dream, I mean."

It was a lot to take in. I could see Anaros analyzing the details in his head. I knew I needed to tell him my plan. If I left now, having told him all this, he may never give up searching for me. "Anaros, I...I think I need to leave Selvenor."

He looked up at me, studying my expression to decide if I was serious. "Why?" I looked away from him. I didn't want to answer, but my avoidance only seemed to agitate him. "Zynnera, if it's because of the King of Dunivear, then the answer is no." I smiled. If I wanted to leave, Anaros could do little to stop me. *And he knows that.* The King of Dunivear was only a small reason for my desire to leave.

The name repeated in my mind. *Dunivear.* It was like a soft whisper, calm and instructive, more feminine than the voice of the man in the black cloak. *Go to Dunivear.* I looked at Anaros, who was still waiting for me to answer his question. "I think I need to go to Dunivear." It sounded strange coming out of my mouth. *Am I really listening to a voice inside my head?*

Anaros's face contorted into confusion. "Dunivear? Why would you want to go there?"

I didn't really have an answer, at least not one that made sense. My father's story flashed through my mind again. "There are people like me there."

Anaros seemed surprised by my response. "You mean people who can use magic?"

I nodded. "My father used to tell me stories of a people who lived deep in the forest of Arnfell. A whole village of people with magical powers. As a child I often imagined going there." *With him. I imagined going there with him.* The thought saddened me.

His free hand moved to his mouth as he spoke. "Zynnera, I don't know. Dunivear isn't exactly friendly towards the idea of magic. That was certainly made apparent tonight." Anaros fidgeted a little as if there were more to his statement than I was aware of.

"If there are other witches there, perhaps they could help me understand these nightmares? Maybe they could tell us what Virga'm is, the Bridge, all of it." I realized my hand was still resting inside his. I placed my other hand on top of it, hoping it would help my plea. "Anaros, I have to figure out what these dreams are about. I have to understand them. It feels important."

Anaros nodded. "Alright. But Reynard should go with you. I don't like the idea of you going alone." I started to argue with him, but he stopped me. "Just...to ease my trepidation a bit." Anaros smiled at me, knowing I hated the idea but would agree.

"OK," I said, looking into his light brown eyes. I was surprised by how easy it had been to convince him. It still didn't solve my problem of affecting his ability to connect with other kingdoms, but at least I could leave without worrying he would try to find me. At least I didn't have to lie to him, not yet anyway.

Anaros rose from the bed and walked towards my chamber door, pausing in the entry. "Just promise you won't leave without saying goodbye."

I smiled back at him. "I promise." My stomach curled. *Why would you promise that?*

"I'll see you in the morning then," he said as he exited into the corridor.

I fell back onto my pillow again. I was grateful Anaros had understood. Going to Dunivear hadn't been part of my initial plan, but it was where my journey would begin. The voice in my head had been so certain it was where I should go. *Maybe I'll be able to find some answers there? But was it my own thought or something else? Someone else?* I felt shivers flood across my body. *I hope I can trust that voice, whoever it was.*

CHAPTER
Seven

Sleep would not be possible, of that I was certain. The idea of Zynnera leaving to find some rogue group of witches left me feeling uneasy to say the least. I was worried about her, but not just because she was leaving Selvenor for the first time in her life. I had heard her mumbling, screaming in her sleep, for a while now. Her nightmares seemed to be getting worse. I couldn't blame her for desiring to get some relief from them, but my understanding of the situation didn't alleviate my concerns.

I had forgone returning to my chamber to rest, choosing instead to visit the palace library in hopes of gathering more information. Zynnera said her father had told her of a village of witches and warlocks deep in the forest of Arnfell. There was only one issue with her statement. Arnfell covered a massive area. The village could be hidden anywhere within the deep timberland, and the longer it took her to find it, the longer she would be gone.

In addition, the King of Dunivear had made his opinion of magic and those who used it quite clear. I dreaded what would happen should he discover Zynnera exploring his land unannounced. I was hoping the library might hold some answers as to where the village might be located. The less time Zynnera spent in Dunivear, the better.

I made my way down the dark corridor until I reached the library. The room was quiet as I lit a few lanterns to help me see. There were three walls of long shelving, each stretching from the floor to the ceiling. Every shelf was completely full of books and parchment. *Where should I even begin?* I moved closer to one wall, holding my lantern near the books so I could read their bindings. *Royal Genealogy of Izarden, Resource Survey of Theranden, Selvenor: Traditions and Rites, Kingdoms of Virgamor.* I moved to another shelf, looking for anything about Dunivear. *History of Dunivear. Yes!* I pulled the book from the shelf and placed it on the wooden table in the center of the room. The lantern light exposed the text as I flipped through the pages. The book covered everything from the kingdom's founder, Arnfell Dunivear, to King Lenear. My eyes moved through the pages, searching for any mention of magic.

After several hours I began to lose hope of finding any pertinent information. The book was detailed about each king who had ruled over the land and every war with other kingdoms and invaders, but there was nothing about witches or warlocks. There was no mention of magic, not even a suggestion that it existed. Whatever story the captain had told Zynnera didn't seem to appear in Dunivear's history book. I couldn't help but wonder if the lack of information was intentional.

I slammed the book closed, frustrated with my lack of progress. Instead of easing my concerns, I had only made them worse. I rubbed my forehead with my hand, trying to fight the exhaustion as the hour grew late. It had already been a long day, and both my mind and body desperately wanted to rest.

A man's voice came quietly from the entry. "A bit late to be scouring books in the library, My King." Reynard was standing just inside the door, holding his own lantern in the darkness.

"Zynnera is planning to leave," I said. "I was just trying to find information to help."

Reynard walked towards me, stopping at the end of the table. "Leave? What for?"

"Lately she's been having nightmares. She sees a man in a black cloak. She says she saw him when we were in the cave in the forest." I paused for a moment. There was still so much about our trip to the village that none of us understood. Zynnera felt she needed answers and, admittedly, I felt I did too. I turned to face Reynard. "Captain Torilus told her stories about a village in the forest of Arnfell, where witches and warlocks live. Zynnera thinks they might be able to help her find answers. Maybe explain what it is she sees in her dreams. What they might mean."

Reynard nodded. "I see. If these nightmares have become as bad as you say, it would be wise for her to seek out their meaning. Did the captain say where this village is? Arnfell is not exactly a small area."

I sighed. "No. That's what I was hoping to find, but there's nothing. Not a single mention of magic in this entire book. And after my discussion with King Lenear today, I can't say I'm all that surprised."

Reynard raised his eyebrows. "Discussion?"

"Yes, he insisted on talking to me tonight during the celebration. He threatened to withhold all peace and trade agreements if I refused to cut ties with Zynnera."

"What! That's ridiculous! It is only because of Zynnera that Selvenor is free from Eradoma's evil magic in the first place." Reynard was obviously angered by Lenear's disregard for Zynnera's accomplishments. I understood the feeling all too well.

I smiled, chuckling a little. "Yes, I know. Believe me, I wasn't exactly happy with his expectations either."

Reynard gave himself a moment to calm down. "What are you going to do? You haven't told Zynnera, have you?"

"No, I haven't. It would only upset her. I figured it would be best to keep the information to myself, at least until I do decide what to do. How am I supposed to make a decision, Reynard? I can't just abandon her."

Reynard thought for a moment. "I don't know, My King. It's unfair King Lenear would ask this of you. I'd say he fears Zynnera's magic. I can think of no other reason for his demands. But I trust you know trade agreements with Dunivear are essential to Selvenor's prosperity. Without it, rebuilding our kingdom will be difficult."

I knew he was right. The future of Selvenor depended on our relationships with other kingdoms throughout Virgamor as much as it did on our own drive for success. I would have to find a way around King Lenear's conditions. If I could find a way to make him see Zynnera posed no threat to his kingdom and, if anything, she was an asset to our defense, perhaps I could persuade him. But I knew it was not going to be easy.

I laughed a little. "I hope being king isn't always so difficult."

Reynard chuckled at my statement. "I certainly don't envy your position, My King."

"It's no walk in the woods," I said. I welcomed a distraction from it all. I decided to change the subject. There were other pressing things I needed to discuss with him. "Reynard, how is training going?"

In the six months that Selvenor had begun to rebuild, I had placed Reynard in charge of training recruits for the army. The process was slow at first. The people were so devastated from Eradoma's reign that there were few who were ready to volunteer their services. But Reynard was determined to do his part to bring Selvenor back to the prosperity it once knew, and that included having an army ready to defend against threats. His determination enabled him to grow the army of Selvenor from a few men to a strong two hundred in just a few short months, and that number was increasing on a regular basis.

I knew I could never fully thank him for his efforts; however, I did have an idea that might come close. Reynard had proven himself to be not only an excellent bowman but his skills with a sword had increased dramatically since the time I trained him in the meadow as a new recruit. Once the army had gained enough strength, it was my intention to name him the new General of Selvenor. Of course, I had yet to tell him of my plan, hoping to surprise him when the time was right.

"Training is going well, My King. The new recruits improve every day. I have no doubt your army will one day be as grand as it was when your father reigned."

It sounded so strange, *my* army. I wasn't sure I would ever be used to the idea of the kingdom being under my authority. I always knew it would happen, but I believed my father would be there to guide me, teach me how to be a noble king. Sometimes I felt like I was blundering through everything, generally guessing the best course of action and hoping my choices were adept.

I looked at Reynard. "That's good news. I can't thank you enough for all of your hard work, Reynard. I hope you are right. I can't help but feel Selvenor is going to need a strong army. Whatever this darkness is that Zynnera senses, I fear will affect us all."

"Yes, I agree. A strong army will be crucial in facing the darkness, no matter where it originates from."

Reynard seemed to be thinking. I wondered if he could sense the same thing I could. I didn't have nightmares of a man in a black cloak like Zynnera, but I could feel *something*. There was really no way to explain it. I had hoped after Eradoma was defeated the darkness shrouding Selvenor would vanish, but it hadn't. And whoever this man was that haunted Zynnera's dreams seemed to be linked to it all.

I sighed. "Reynard, I had intended to ask you to go with Zynnera. The last thing I want is for her to travel through Dunivear alone. I don't trust King Lenear nor his men to leave her alone should they find out she is there. But now I'm not so sure. I feel, perhaps, I should go with her as well."

Reynard's expression looked conflicted. "I take no issue in

accompanying her, My King, if that is your wish. I do fear it unwise for you to go without speaking first to King Lenear. It seems your relationship with him has already formed much tension. I do not think he would take kindly to the King of Selvenor exploring his lands unannounced."

I shook my head. "No, you are right. I'm sure he would not. That is why we must first go to Dunivear. I must speak with him."

Reynard considered my words. "It would be risky. If the king denied your request to find the village, he would be sure to force you to leave."

"I know," I said. "But it's worth the risk. I suspect if anyone knows where the village is, it's King Lenear."

Reynard didn't appear to be convinced. "What makes you so sure he'll just give you that information even if he does? You alone, perhaps, but I can't see him allowing Zynnera to become acquainted with more witches and warlocks. It would only increase his distrust of her. This is a very slippery slope, My King. The last thing we want to do is start a war with Dunivear."

I stared down at the book in front of me. *If only I had been able to find the location of the village. Then we wouldn't need King Lenear's help at all. We could have sneaked beyond Dunivear's borders, found the village, and returned to Selvenor with Lenear being none-the-wiser.* But the longer we explored the forest without so much as a hint of where to go, the more likely we were to be caught by his men. And being caught in a kingdom that was not my own would look incredibly suspicious and put Selvenor in jeopardy.

"I know how risky all of this is, Reynard. But I don't see another choice. I fear this darkness far more than I fear Dunivear. It would be unwise for them to go to war against us. With Zynnera on our side, it would be foolish for them to do so."

I never wanted to use Zynnera as a weapon or threaten another kingdom with her magic. She was a person, not an object to be used for war. But if it came to that, I knew she would do all she could to protect our people.

I looked up from the table. "We will go to King Lenear. It's my hope he will help us find the village. But if he doesn't, I want you to go with Zynnera to look for it. I'll return to Selvenor, make him think we have all returned."

Reynard nodded. "Alright, My King. If that is what you wish."

I walked back to the shelves and returned the book to its place. "We should get some rest. Leave in the morning."

I watched as Reynard nodded and then exited the library. I knew I needed to return to my chamber to sleep, but I didn't believe I'd really get any rest. There was so much to take in—the coronation, Zynnera's nightmares, the subtle darkness. I felt overwhelmed with it all. I could only imagine how Zynnera was feeling. I knew our people's distrust was taking its toll on her. *Perhaps leaving Selvenor for a few days will help?* If nothing else, perhaps we would finally have answers to all the questions that had followed us from the forest and start unraveling the mysteries of Virgàm.

CHAPTER
~ *Eight* ~

The shadows flickered behind the light of the small lantern resting on the table beside my bed. I watched them dance along my bedroom wall. My mind refused to stop. I couldn't seem to get the thoughts out of my head; I couldn't convince them to rest. *I need to sleep. Tomorrow is going to be a long day and I need to be well rested.* My body knew it. My mind knew it. And yet here I was staring at the wall in the late hour of night, unable to drift away into unconscious bliss.

I pulled the blankets over my head. Part of me was afraid to close my eyes for fear the nightmares would return again. I had become accustomed to the nightly visits of the man in the black cloak, but this new nightmare made my thoughts race with additional questions. *Who was the cloaked figure by the river? What had it done to the other person?* I wondered if it was the same person as the man in the black cloak from the cave. *No. This person was shorter and just FELT different.* I couldn't even explain it myself, but somehow I *knew* they weren't the same people. While I had sensed a darkness from both of them, the man in the cave was far darker than the one by the river.

I just wish I understood what it all means. Traveling to Dunivear may give me answers. I hoped it would. The longer I dealt with the nightmares, the more important I felt it was to decipher their meaning. The idea of traveling to Dunivear, however, made me anxious in a different way. I knew the king didn't like me. That much was completely clear after tonight. How would he respond if I marched into his kingdom unannounced? The thought made me nauseous. The last thing I wanted was to create tension between our kingdoms.

I threw the blanket back off of my head. *Anaros doesn't need more problems to deal with. Maybe I shouldn't go? Maybe I should stick to my original plan and just leave?* At least then Anaros would be able to establish peace without me being a factor of contention. I closed my eyes, wishing the decision could be easier. *Dunivear. Go to Dunivear.*

I forced my eyes open and sat up. I could feel my heart pounding hard inside my chest. *It's that voice again.* This time I knew I hadn't imagined the soft, gentle whispers. There was a voice inside my head telling me to go to Dunivear, one I didn't recognize, and I was certain it was something more than just my conscience. I couldn't deny it frightened me a little. *Am I going insane?*

I was afraid to answer my own question. *What if I am going insane? What if I'm not?* At this point I wasn't sure which I preferred. I knew I needed to get to the bottom of it, *all* of it. I needed to find answers, and if that meant going to Dunivear, then I would do so. *But where do I even start?* My father had told me about the people living in the forest of Arnfell, but he had failed to give me any details of where they were. I wondered if he had even known.

I sighed. *Just one more thing I don't know.* How was I supposed to ask the people questions if I didn't even know where to find them? I had never left Selvenor, but I knew the forest of Arnfell was huge. I recalled overhearing servants complain about traveling through the dense forest to visit Dunivear and its small villages. The village would be deep in the woodland, away from roads and cities. Finding it without at least having an idea where it was would be nearly impossible.

There is one person who might know where it is. My heart stopped at the thought. The last thing I wanted to do right now was make a visit to the dungeon. I had avoided doing so for six months and preferred to keep it that way. Anaros had also insisted I stay away from Eradoma. He mentioned he had attempted to speak to her while I was still unconscious from our battle. She had yielded no information to him, and I doubted my attempt would be any different. Still, the thought pestered me. *What could it hurt to try?*

I moved out of the bed and grabbed my little lantern. My mind was full of doubt as I walked along the dimly lit corridors of the palace. *Is this really a good idea? Probably not. Anaros would be so angry if he knew I was doing this.* I followed some stairs into the darkness of the dungeon. A lone guard stood watching me as I approached him.

"Who's there?" he asked.

I stopped in front of him. He seemed to recognize me. "I want to speak with Eradoma, please."

He looked at me for several moments. I could tell he was unsure what to do. "Alright, just be quick." His voice was shaky. *He's afraid of me. He's afraid of what I would do if he said no.* I couldn't deny the truth bothered me. I didn't want him to be afraid of me. I didn't want *anyone* to be afraid of me.

For now, his fear worked in my favor. I didn't like it, but being given access to the dungeon prisoners without Anaros's consent was useful right now. I knew how angry he would be if he knew what I was doing. He would insist it was a waste of time and that Eradoma couldn't be trusted, even if she did tell me anything. *And he would be right.*

I flashed the guard a soft smile, hoping to ease his concern. "Thank you, I will."

I moved beyond the dungeon entry and down the narrow path to the last cell. Eradoma was resting inside, unaware she had a visitor. My mind flooded with regret. *This isn't a good idea. I should go back.* I turned to walk away but only made it a few steps before her voice echoed from behind me.

"Well, well. If it isn't my traitorous daughter." I turned to face her, walking back towards the cell so the lantern could illuminate her face. Her expression was harsh and cold. "To what pleasure do I owe a visit from you?"

"I need to ask you some questions," I said, trying to keep my voice even. I didn't want her to know how nervous I was to be talking to her.

She smiled. "Your prince already tried that months ago. I assume he mentioned that?" She was standing with her hands on the bars now, clearly annoyed by my presence.

""King, actually. And yes, he said you wouldn't tell him anything," I said, hoping honesty might somehow win her over.

"Of course, *king.*" She laughed. "And you think I'd be more likely to talk to you?" I stared down at the floor. *I knew she would do this. I knew she wouldn't cooperate. Why did I even bother?* Eradoma seemed to sense my thoughts and chuckled. "Well, go on then. Ask. I'm curious what it is you want to know."

I stared at her for a few moments. She was mocking me. There was little point in asking her anything, but I was already here. *I might as well try.* "I want to know about the warlocks from Dunivear."

She seemed surprised by my request. *She was expecting a different question. She thought I would ask her about the Bridge.* I knew Anaros had asked her about it and she had told him nothing. I thought perhaps she might actually answer a question she deemed insignificant.

"Dunivear? Why?" Her face reflected her intrigue.

I wasn't sure I should explain to her *why.* Telling her about my nightmares would likely only give her more to mock me about. But I had no other reason to ask about Dunivear. "I need to find their village."

Eradoma studied me curiously. "You think they will have answers for you."

It was almost scary how well she could read me. *I suppose I shouldn't be surprised. Technically, she is my mother.* Eradoma had never shown much interest in me, especially as her hope for me joining her destructive path subsided. In truth, she knew very little about me, but I still felt connected to her. Whether it was our blood relationship or through some unknown magical force, I wasn't sure.

I stared down at the stone floor. "I'm hoping they will, yes." Eradoma remained quiet as though she were still analyzing my question. I looked up at her, my patience thinning. "Are you going to help me or not?"

She laughed. "You're in such a hurry to go there, Zynnera. You've no idea what you are getting yourself into. Dunivear isn't exactly friendly to those who wield magic."

I folded my arms. "I guessed that, funny enough. Doesn't change the fact that I need answers. If Dunivear is where I need to go, so be it."

Eradoma raised her eyebrows. "And you're sure Dunivear is where you need to go... *why?*"

I realized I had never answered her question. *I'm not going to get anywhere with her if I don't tell her why.* I swallowed hard, preparing to admit my reasoning. "I've been having visions. I don't know what they mean and I'm hoping to find a Seer. Someone who might be able to understand..."

Eradoma interrupted, even more curious with my confession. "Visions?"

"Yes," I said. I wanted it to be enough for her, but I wasn't naive. But before I gave up any details, there was one thing I wanted her to know. "I've been there...to the cave. *Your* cave."

Eradoma stared at me with a perplexed expression. She seemed uncertain about engaging in questions before fully understanding what I was referring to, almost as though she wanted to keep the details of her past a secret. "What cave?"

She tried to portray ignorance, but I knew better. I had seen her there. I had watched her raise the Vlenargans from the depths of the earth. "You know what I'm talking about," I said. "The cave where you learned dark magic. The cave with the spells on its walls."

Eradoma's expression didn't change, but I could sense her surprise. "I'm not certain I understand the point you're trying to make, Zynnera. What does this cave have anything to do with you having visions?"

I placed my hand on the cell bar. "Because it's where they began. And I've had them ever since." I stared into her dark eyes. The curiosity was still there. *I have to keep playing the game. Intrigue is the only thing that keeps her talking.* "I had visions of you. The Vlenargans." I paused for a moment. Was I sure I really wanted to tell her more? Once I allowed the details to escape, I would never be able to take them back. "And a man with black hair in a black cloak."

Eradoma's face flushed to a pale white. She appeared shocked by my words. "What about this man? What is it you saw?"

I shook my head. "Who is he?"

She became annoyed. I wasn't about to tell her more without first getting information from her. Eradoma seemed desperate for me to answer. Holding the details hostage was the only chance I had at getting more from her.

Eradoma recognized my plan at once. She moved away from the cell door and into the moonlight shining through the small window in the prison wall. *I'm losing her. I have to keep her talking.* "Tell me who he is, and I'll tell you what I saw."

She considered my words for several minutes. "It matters not what you saw. Soon he will return and there is nothing you or your prince, forgive me, *king* can do to stop him."

"He will return?" I heard the words leave my mouth before I even had time to think about what I was doing. I had fallen right where she wanted me. Eradoma knew she was in control of our conversation now and her expression didn't bother to hide it.

"Oh, Zynnera. You are so naive. So ignorant of the magical world that exists around you. A world that has existed for centuries. Did you honestly think defeating me would end the darkness? It can't be stopped. *We* won't be stopped until mankind pays for their misdeeds. Until we are given the respect we deserve. We will bring light to this world by putting those who stand against our power in their place."

Her voice was so cold it sent shivers through my body. I could feel a surge of darkness spread across the room, the same darkness I had felt in the cave. *The same darkness I feel in my nightmares.* I choked a little on my words. "*We?*"

She could hear it, the fear in my voice. There was no point in trying to hide it. Her words had shaken me to my core. Whoever the man in the black cloak was, Eradoma knew him...or at least knew of him. She spoke as though she were somehow part of his plan. *His plan? What is his plan?* Eradoma said they would put those who stood against them in their place, that mankind would pay for their misdeeds. But what did she mean by it?

Somehow I felt more confused than I had before coming to the dungeon. Eradoma laughed at my expression. "You'll find out soon enough, I'd wager. But you won't get any information from me. You're just wasting your time."

That was it. Our conversation was over. I hadn't gathered any helpful information and there was no use in continuing to interrogate her. Eradoma would not give up her secrets, of that I was sure. The only thing I knew was that she did, in fact, know what my nightmares meant. But this information didn't help me if she refused to explain. I still didn't know where to look for the village in Dunivear, and I still didn't know anything about the man in the black cloak.

I turned to leave the dungeon, taking a few steps before Eradoma's cold voice stopped me with another question. "Dunivear. You still haven't said why you feel the need to go there?"

I didn't care anymore. I could tell her everything and it wouldn't matter. The worst she could do was continue to mock me. "A voice. There's a voice in my head telling me to go."

To my surprise, Eradoma said nothing. Instead, she studied me curiously again. She seemed unsure what to make of my comment. I left her alone in her cell, making my way past the guard and back up the stairs. The corridor was still dark as the night continued to press on. *That was a waste. I got nothing from her. Nothing but more...QUESTIONS.* I was agitated with myself. *I never should have allowed myself to go down there. What was I thinking? Did I honestly expect Eradoma to just hand over all of her secrets, to suddenly be the mother I never had?*

I hated to admit it, but part of me wished she would. Despite everything she had done, I still longed for a connection with her. Perhaps it was because she was the only person who could understand what I was going through and how I felt. She had experienced the hatred and the fear from the people, not that it bothered her as it did me. I imagined Eradoma in the darkness of the cave beyond her village. She would have felt so alone, forced away from everything she'd ever known and cared about because of her actions. And while I did not condone the things she had done, I felt sympathy for her. I knew what it felt like to be hated. I knew what it felt like to be alone.

CHAPTER
Nine

My eyes greeted the morning light as a faint knock interrupted my sleep. I struggled to force myself to sit up, exhaustion still compelling my body and mind to rest. It had been a long night, preceded by an even longer day. Much of it still weighed heavily on my mind. There were decisions to make and I wasn't sure I was prepared to make them.

A soft thud sounded from my door again. I moved towards it, opening the door to find Rhemues standing in the corridor. He certainly looked more rested than I did, but his expression reflected one of concern.

"I'm sorry to bother you so early," he said. "But Zynnera is in the banquet hall. She has a satchel. And Reynard is readying the horses as though they are leaving....Anaros, what is going on?" His voice was calm but I could sense his underlying panic.

I nodded. "I know. We are going to Dunivear."

Rhemues raised his eyebrows. "We?" I moved my gaze to the floor. Last night I had promoted Rhemues to the position of royal advisor. I stood by my decision to do so, yet here I was already making heavy decisions without talking to him first. I felt guilty for not seeking his counsel last night. He should have been the first one I discussed my predicament with.

I motioned for him to come into the room, shutting the door behind him. I needed to tell him everything that happened with King Lenear, and I didn't want Zynnera to accidentally overhear. "King Lenear asked to speak with me last night."

Rhemues nodded. "Yes, I know. I saw you leave with him. Elric danced with Zynnera for a few minutes after you left, but then left the Great Hall upset. Does this decision to leave have something to do with that?"

I returned a perplexed expression. I hadn't heard anything about Zynnera leaving the Great Hall upset. She had already disappeared by the time I returned. Hachseeva had given me her apologies but said nothing more. I had assumed she left because of the murmurs and disgruntled faces of the people in attendance, but now I wondered if there was more to it than that.

"What exactly do you mean, upset?" I was hoping Rhemues would fill in the details where Hachseeva had chosen not to.

Rhemues shook his head. "I'm not really sure. Hachseeva spoke with her. But she seemed upset when she left, almost angry. I thought perhaps she mentioned it to you?"

"No, she hasn't. Do you think Elric said something to her? I know she was already anxious when I left, but..." My voice trailed off as I thought about the night and how it unfolded. I wished I hadn't been obliged to leave her alone in the Great Hall while I spoke to King Lenear. What was more, her leaving had also taken away my chance to propose. *I wish the night could have ended the way I planned it in my head.*

Rhemues sighed. "I don't know. Hachseeva said Zynnera didn't give her the details. She didn't want to talk about it. If I had to guess, I'd say Elric did upset her. But regardless of that, you haven't explained why Zynnera is leaving?"

I wrapped my belt around my waist and sheathed my sword. "King Lenear demanded I cut ties with Zynnera."

Shock spread across Rhemues's face. "What? How dare he demand such a thing! Who does he think he is exactly!"

"Well, he is the King of Dunivear. And if I don't comply with his request, he's threatened to end all peace and trade agreements." The reminder of our conversation made me angry all over again.

"How absurd! He can't...I mean, he can but..." Rhemues sighed. "What are you going to do?"

I chuckled. "You're supposed to be the one giving me advice, remember?"

Rhemues moved his gaze to the floor, deep in thought. "Right, yes, I suppose I am. But I'm not certain I should? I mean, you know...I want you and Zynnera to..." Rhemues paused for several moments as a smile spread across my face. He looked up at me. "Anaros, I think I may be too biased to give you advice."

I laughed hard at his remark. "Don't worry. This is exactly why I'm going to Dunivear with her. Maybe I can talk some sense into him."

Concern returned to Rhemues's face. "Anaros, I'm not certain that's a good idea."

I placed my hand on his shoulder. "I know. I realize it's risky. But Zynnera feels she needs to find more people who wield magic. And they live somewhere in Arnfell."

Rhemues followed me as I exited my chamber, making my way down the long corridor. "Wait...wait, are you saying there are more witches living in Dunivear?"

"According to Zynnera, yes. She said the captain told her about them and, well, his stories have proved to be based in truth."

Rhemues nodded as he walked beside me. "I certainly can't deny that."

"I'm leaving you in charge," I said without looking at him. I knew he would panic at the statement and felt it best to keep walking.

"In charge! Wait...no, Anaros, you can't just..."

"I'm king. I certainly can." I didn't even bother to hide my smile.

I could hear Rhemues sigh in objection as we entered the Great Hall. Zynnera was seated at the long table, poking at her breakfast. She didn't seem to have actually eaten any of it. I suspected she was anxious to leave, probably even a little afraid.

She smiled as I approached her, as if my presence now gave her permission to go. She stood up and started to speak, but I cut her off. "I'm going with you...so sit back down."

Surprise spread across Zynnera's face. "You're what? No, Anaros, you can't..."

I interrupted her. "Why does everyone insist I can't do things? I thought I was crowned king yesterday?" I flashed Zynnera a wide grin, but she didn't seem amused.

"Anaros, you have a kingdom to run." She started to argue with me, but my decision had already been made.

"I'm going," I said as clearly and bluntly as I could. I sat down at the table to eat.

Zynnera rolled her eyes and sat back down. *She knows I won't change my mind or let her go on her own.* I tried to hide the amusement from my face as Zynnera started eating her breakfast, realizing she wouldn't be permitted to leave yet. Rhemues was standing in front of us. I could tell he was still uncertain about being left in charge. He didn't seem to like the idea of it, but there was no one I trusted more with the kingdom than him.

Reynard entered the banquet hall. He displayed a bright smile as he gave me a little bow. "Everything is ready when you are, My King."

I nodded towards him. "Thank you, Reynard. Please, have breakfast with us before we leave." Zynnera rolled her eyes again at the word *we.* She was clearly annoyed with me insisting on accompanying them. Reynard smiled, sensing Zynnera's disapproval. *I think he finds her funny too.*

After breakfast we all made our way to the north entry. Reynard had prepared three horses with supplies for our journey. Hachseeva and the children had also come to bid us goodbye. They seemed saddened by the idea of Zynnera leaving.

Hachseeva wrapped her arms around Zynnera in a tight embrace. "Promise me you'll be careful."

Zynnera nodded. "I promise."

Rhemues was standing beside them, his body trembling a little in the cool morning air. I approached him, hoping to ease his nerves before I departed. I held out my hand. "Rhemues, everything will be fine. We'll be back soon."

He stared at my outstretched hand for several moments before pulling me into an embrace. "Are you certain about this?" he whispered, releasing me so he could see my response.

"No, I'm not." I glanced at Zynnera. *But if it means helping her, I'll go. I'll do whatever it takes.*

Rhemues seemed to understand what I was thinking. "Just be careful." I nodded and patted his shoulder.

We all mounted our horses and passed through the north entry and into the square. I could tell Zynnera was uncomfortable as the people watched us make our way down the streets of Selvenor. She tried to hide her discomfort, but I could see relief sweep across her face as we rode through the gate on the south end of the city. Once Selvenor was behind us, she seemed to relax. *This will be good for her. She needs some time away from the city.*

We rode in silence for nearly two hours. I followed close behind Zynnera, who seemed to be taking in everything around her. I reminded myself this was her first time leaving the borders of our kingdom. I couldn't help but wonder what she was thinking as we trotted along the dirt road. She appeared so content to just enjoy the peaceful sounds around us. I wanted to talk to her, but I also wanted to allow her to benefit from our current solitude.

We stopped to rest at the base of the mountains in a small grove of trees. Reynard pulled some food from a supply bag, and we ate a light meal as we sat on the ground. Zynnera was watching the birds as they chirped overhead. She turned to face me as I moved closer to her. "How are you feeling?" I asked.

"Fine." I watched a smile form across her face. She knew I wanted more than that and her smile was intended to taunt me. "Better. It's sort of nice to be away from everything."

I smiled back at her. "Just like old times."

She laughed. "Yes, I suppose it is."

My hand felt the metal ring resting in my pocket. I didn't know why, but I'd felt the need to bring it. I had no intention of proposing to Zynnera in the forest, but I hadn't been able to convince myself to leave it behind. Zynnera turned her attention back to the singing birds. I found myself admiring her beauty once again. Her dark brown hair rested behind her shoulders, a few pieces falling against her cheek when she moved her head. Rhemues's words entered my thoughts, mocking me. *You haven't even kissed her yet.* I would find a moment. Now that we were away from Selvenor, I would find more time alone with her. I would tell her how I felt.

Reynard stood up from his spot abruptly. His expression looked stern as he stared down the dirt road towards Selvenor. I rose to stand beside him. In the distance I could see a horse, running towards us with swift speed. For a moment my heart pounded hard until I recognized the burly figure riding on it. Rhemues stopped when he reached us, dismounting the brown steed.

I moved closer to him. "Rhemues, what are you doing here?"

"I had to come," he said. "Please don't be angry. I'm your royal advisor. I should be going with you to Dunivear."

I sighed. "But Rhemues, I left you in charge."

Rhemues smiled. "Yes, and I left Hachseeva in charge. No one is going to mess with Selvenor, trust me."

We all laughed. I still wasn't sure I liked the idea of leaving the kingdom unattended. Part of the reason I asked Rhemues to stay was because he was next in line for the throne. With both of us gone, there would be no heir to take over should something happen to us. I tried to shake the thoughts from my mind. *Nothing is going to happen to us. Everything will be just fine.*

Rhemues was still beaming. "Anyway, I thought I could use a short vacation. I...um...probably won't be getting much rest in the near future."

I stared at him. *What does he mean by that?* Reynard looked as confused as I was. The only one who seemed to understand was Zynnera. She had covered her mouth as a loud gasp escaped. Rhemues seemed pleased that someone understood the meaning behind his statement.

Zynnera moved forward, hugging him with a smile. "That's wonderful news, Rhemues! Congratulations."

I was still lost. "Can someone explain to me what..."

Zynnera interrupted me, rolling her eyes as she spoke. "Hachseeva is expecting!"

"Oh," I said. "Expecting..."

Zynnera laughed. "A baby!"

I scrunched my face. "Yes, I knew that, thank you." In reality I hadn't been certain it was what Rhemues was referring to. Zynnera didn't seem to believe my response either. I shook Rhemues's hand. "Congratulations!" Reynard shook his hand as well, patting him on the back with a bright smile.

"Thank you. I appreciate that. Technically speaking, I wasn't supposed to tell you until we got back." Rhemues stared at the ground guiltily but with a smile. "But I was a bit excited."

Zynnera chuckled. "Well, I think we can all still pretend to be surprised."

I bit my lip. "Rhemues, are you certain you should come? I mean, perhaps you should be with Hachseeva?"

Rhemues shook his head. "No, I'm sure. Besides, Hachseeva insisted I come. You know how she is." He laughed. "She said I should go with you. Keep you out of trouble."

Reynard mounted his horse. "Well, we should get moving. I think we can make it to Lake Athenasi by nightfall tomorrow if we keep pace. It will be a good spot to make camp."

"A lake?" Zynnera's tone reflected her excitement. I looked at her curiously. She quickly tucked her hair behind her ear at the realization of how enthusiastic she sounded about something so insignificant. "It's just...well, I've never seen a lake."

I laughed. "Well, then it will definitely be a good place for us to camp." Zynnera tried to hide her red face. *She's embarrassed she's never seen one.* Zynnera was often embarrassed by her lack of experience. Things that seemed second nature to me were still new for her. At times it was fun to watch her experience something new, and I couldn't deny I enjoyed witnessing her excitement over small things like seeing a lake for the first time.

We all mounted our horses and continued our journey along the dirt road towards Lake Athenasi. We spent the night amongst the pines, talking beside a warm fire. After a long day of travel, I was eager to get some rest, especially after having been awake nearly the entire night before. Zynnera seemed to sleep well that night. It was the first time in a while I didn't hear her screaming from the terror of her nightmares. I hoped perhaps they wouldn't follow us on our journey to Dunivear. She deserved a break from them.

The next morning, we continued south along the dirt road, stopping only for a short while to have lunch. I thought about Lake Athenasi as the sun made its descent across the sky. I was looking forward to resting by the lake, listening to the sound of the calm water as it lapped against the shore. *Sounds like a good place to talk to Zynnera...alone.* I couldn't deny I was looking forward to being with her. We had so little time together in the last six months, rarely a moment to ourselves. *Perhaps I can finally tell her?*

I wanted a moment with her, free from the concerns of her nightmares and the impending darkness that still seemed to follow us. I wanted to give her a break from that darkness, even if just for a moment. There was little I could do to ease her nightmares. Until we solved the mysteries that haunted her mind, I knew she would never be able to rest. *But I can help her do that. I can persuade King Lenear to help us and to see her for who she really is.* I just wasn't sure how yet.

As we neared the top of a hill, I rode beside Zynnera. We looked out over the land before us as Reynard and Rhemues continued towards the water. I watched a smile form across her face as she peered out over the lake. The light from the setting sun glistened off the surface of the water and into her bright blue eyes.

"It's more beautiful than I could have imagined," she said.

I smiled, still watching her expression. "Yes, beautiful."

Zynnera turned to look at me, returning my smile. She seemed to understand it wasn't the picturesque scene before us I was referring to. As I watched the gentle breeze blow through her wavy hair, I could feel the depth of my emotions. *I love her. And I intend to tell her.*

CHAPTER
~*Ten*~

Light from the setting sun glistened off of the surface of the gentle waves as they lapped onto the sandy shore. I listened to the sound of the water splashing lightly against a few large boulders on the edge of the lake. It was so peaceful here, so beautiful. Watching the sun set over the lake had to be one of the most magical moments I'd ever seen.

I laughed at myself and the use of the word *magical*. A witch who could cast spells calling a sunset magical would probably seem silly to most. But to me, that is exactly what it was. There was something beautiful about the serenity of nature's natural processes, almost mysterious. *I can't believe I've never seen a lake before. I can't believe what I've been missing.* I'd spent so much of my life alone, locked within the chambers of the palace walls. I wondered how much I had missed out on; what beauty had gone unseen. If there was one thing leaving Selvenor would do for me, it would be experiencing something new. Maybe by the time this trip was over I would no longer feel like the girl who'd been imprisoned her entire life, the one who knew little of the world she lived in.

Perhaps it will also give me confidence in my decision to leave. I still planned to depart from Selvenor, although I was unsure of where I would go. My lack of travel experience did concern me, but I was hopeful this visit to Dunivear would help alleviate that. Then there was also the prospect of answering the many questions that ravaged my thoughts. If I could find answers to even a few of those questions, I would feel better about leaving. I still worried about my nightly visions and the darkness that filled them. I feared leaving Selvenor with the darkness hanging over it like an ominous cloud preparing for a spring storm would be a mistake. The last thing I wanted was for something horrible to happen to the people I'd worked so hard to save.

I could see Anaros approaching me out of the corner of my eye. I tried to hide my smile as he stopped at my side. The gentle breeze lifted pieces of his light brown hair as he stared out over the lake. I waited patiently for him to say something. Finally, after several minutes, he turned to face me, his dark brown eyes staring deep into mine as he spoke. "Zynnera, are you OK?"

I smiled. This question had been the start of so many of our conversations. *He's always so worried about me.* I couldn't deny the thought brought me happiness. I knew he cared about me. And although he had never said it, I believed his feelings for me were far more than merely friendship. Even the people of Selvenor could see it. But as much as I wanted it to be true, part of me also hoped it wasn't. I knew I loved him. I couldn't pretend otherwise. But if Anaros returned those feelings, it would only be more difficult for me to leave.

"I'm fine," I said, still smiling. For once it was the truth. At the moment, I wasn't feeling as overwhelmed as I had been back at the palace. While the uncertainty and fear still remained, I did feel a little relief now that I wasn't surrounded by people who constantly judged me because of the power I possessed.

Anaros cleared his throat. He fidgeted as though what he was about to say weighed heavily on him. He seemed uncertain he wanted to tell me at all. "Zynnera, before we go into Arnfell, we need to go see King Lenear."

I stared at him. *Is he crazy! I can't go see him. He already doesn't like me.* I shook my head. "Anaros, that's a really bad idea. You and I both know he isn't fond of me."

Anaros sighed. "Yes, I know. But if he finds out we are venturing around his kingdom without permission, I fear his reaction. I know it's risky either way, but I think being upfront with him is the better choice."

I wasn't sure I shared his conclusion. Visiting King Lenear was not something I had planned or wanted to do. "What if he forces us to leave? We'll have lost our chance of finding answers. Anaros, I need to find answers. I *have* to." I choked a little on my words. My mind was desperate for relief. I feared telling King Lenear of our plan might slaughter my only hope of getting it.

"I know. Believe me, I do. I want answers too. But we do have to approach this cautiously. And besides, if there is anyone who is likely to know where the village is, it's King Lenear."

I considered his logic. I couldn't disagree with him. When my father told me the story of the two warlocks departing into the forest of Arnfell, he said the king had sent spies to follow them. It was very likely the king knew where the warlocks had made their home. I imagined such information would have been passed down through the generations. King Wilhelm feared the warlocks were a threat to his kingdom. His idea that magic was a danger to his people would not have just vanished with succession. King Lenear's despise of me and my magical ability was likely the result of a long line of hatred for magic, one passed down from King Wilhelm.

I sighed. "Yes, you're probably right. I hate the idea of seeing him again, but if it helps us find the village, I'm willing to do so."

"I know you don't trust him. And I'm not asking you to. Just trust me, Zynnera. I'll never let anyone hurt you..." Anaros paused, likely realizing there probably wasn't anyone in Dunivear who could actually hurt me. "I mean, I know you don't need my protection...anyone's protection. You're perfectly capable...I mean, I just..." He laughed at himself and his inability to form his thoughts into a coherent sentence.

I laughed too. "It's OK. I understand what you mean." Anaros smiled, his face still a little red with embarrassment. *What he doesn't understand is that I do feel safe with him. Protected.* I may not have needed physical protection. That was something I could certainly handle on my own with my powers. But it was protection from myself I seemed unable to accomplish. I needed protection from my fears, from my own self-doubt. That is what he protected me from, and I suspected he didn't even realize it.

Anaros turned to face our campsite. Rhemues and Reynard had finished setting up a large tent and proceeded to build a fire, Rhemues's arms in a constant motion in an effort to fight away the bugs swarming around his face.. Reynard had insisted on a single, large tent for our journey to help maintain an obscure presence. "We should probably have something to eat and get some rest," he said, nodding towards the camp. "I'm guessing tomorrow will be a long day."

We both moved to sit by the fire, chatting casually until the sun had completely set and the darkness of night descended upon us. It didn't take long for Rhemues to fall asleep inside the tent, his light snores echoing around us. I stared into the darkness at the cloth tent above me for what seemed like hours. I knew I should sleep, but part of me was afraid of what would happen should I try. *Will the nightmares find me here? Will I scream out in my sleep if they do?* I already had Anaros worried with my nightmare from two nights ago, and I wasn't eager to add to his concerns.

I rolled over to face him. He was already lost in a deep sleep. Resting between us was the brown satchel I had hidden in my wardrobe back at the palace. *The Tahetya* still resided inside the thick cloth. I had brought the book along partly because I needed to keep it close to me, to keep it safe, and partly because I was still hopeful I might find some answers within it. I'd searched through it so many times I doubted I'd ever find any, but having it nearby seemed to make me feel better nonetheless.

I fought my exhaustion for as long as I could, but eventually my eyes yielded to it and my thoughts were swept away to a place I'd never been. Once again my body was standing along the banks of a river. I could hear the sound of the water as it passed over the rocks and flowed past me. The area was beautiful and calm, just as it had been that first night. I could feel my heart pounding as the foreshadow of what came next filled my mind.

A black cloaked figure stood along the bank in front of me, hovering over two trembling bodies on the ground. I could make out the details of their faces this time. A woman with beautiful wavy red hair grabbed the arm of a bulky brown-haired man. They seemed to tremble in the darkness, cowering beneath the powerful presence of the cloaked figure. I desperately wanted to help them, to stop the attack I knew was coming. But my legs were unable to move. It was as if my presence within the dream was unreal enough to make any physical progression.

The cloaked figure unsheathed an item from his belt. I could see the blade of a jagged dagger pointing from his hand. For a moment I thought the figure might stab the two helpless people on the ground, but instead I watched as he twirled the blade around until it was facing him. He exposed the handle, pointing it towards the man and the woman. *What is he doing? What is he going to do to them?*

I felt my breathing quicken. The figure's voice echoed in my ears. I could tell it was a man's voice, deep and cold, as he began reciting the words to a spell I didn't recognize. An aura formed around both the man and the woman, one green and one purple. Slowly it passed away from their bodies as they screamed and moved towards the handle of the jagged dagger. As the man continued the incantation, a small blue gem on the hilt illuminated. It glowed a bright blue until the man had finished his spell and the screams had ceased.

I could hear the man on the ground pleading with the other.

"Please! You've got what you wanted. Just let us go. Please!"

The cloaked man remained quiet for several moments before responding. "I can't have you warning the others. I'm afraid this is the end for you. But I promise your magical energy will be put to good use."

The man and woman begged harder, but their pleas did not stop the blue aura as it hit their bodies. It did not stop the *Morso* from taking their last breath and leaving their bodies motionless on the cold ground. The man returned his dagger beneath his cloak. *WHY! Why would he kill them!*

The cloaked man turned to face me, as though he had become aware of my presence. He moved towards me, my heart pounding harder with each step forward. He stopped in front of me, his face still hidden inside the shadows of his hood. Fear had taken over me. I couldn't move. I couldn't speak. The man held out his hand, a purple flower resting in his palm. I didn't understand. *Why is he offering this to me? What is it?*

His voice whispered from beneath his hood. "Zynnera. Join me, Zynnera." I shook my head. I wanted nothing to do with the man I just watched murder two people. But his voice persisted. "Join me and together we can set *him* free."

Him. Who is he talking about? Was it the same person Eradoma had mentioned? I watched the man in the cloak disintegrate from in front of me. The familiar words sounded through my mind like a trumpet issuing the call to battle. *Pukurae mayart Virgàm.* The phrase repeated as the man with the black hair appeared before me. Everything else around me became shrouded in darkness and I could no longer see the banks of the river. I could see the red streaks in his hair as he moved closer to me. His eyes were black and dark like everything around us.

He reached out and touched my arm. Chills ran throughout my body. *Pukurae Mayart Virgàm.* His voice grew louder with each repetition. I wanted to be free from him, free from the nightmare. I couldn't move, but I could feel the tears rolling down my face. *Zynnera.* The man spoke my name. *Zynnera. Bring it to me.* His voice was cold and demanding. *Bring me the Virgàm. Join me, Zynnera.*

"No!" I forced myself to scream with as much effort as I could. "No, I won't!"

*Zynnera....*His voice became a soft whisper. "Zynnera!"

I sat up, frantically taking in my surroundings. Anaros was sitting beside me, his hand resting on my shoulder. He looked terrified, proving my fear that I had once again been shouting in my sleep. Rhemues and Reynard were also studying me with expressions of concern. *Great. They all heard me. I probably look crazy.*

Anaros wiped a tear from my cheek. I hadn't noticed real ones falling from my face. His eyes looked deep into mine as his expression softened from terror to sympathy. "Another nightmare?" He asked the question, but I was certain he already knew the answer.

I nodded. "Yes. I'm sorry to have woken everyone."

Rhemues shook his head. "You don't need to be sorry, Zynnera. It's not your fault."

His effort to excuse me didn't make me feel any better. I looked down at my blanket and noticed Anaros's other hand tightly holding my own. "Do you want to talk about it?" he asked. There was still concern in his tone. Whether I wanted to or not, I knew telling him what I saw was the only way to appease his concern.

"It was like before. There was a person in a cloak, a man. I heard his voice this time. He attacked two people with magic. I don't know who they were, but I think he stole their powers and somehow put it inside his dagger."

Anaros scrunched his face. "Inside a dagger?"

I realized it must have sounded crazy. But I had seen everything happen so clearly. "Yes, a dagger. It was jagged and had a blue gem on it that lit up as he performed the spell."

"Any idea what the spell was? I know you said it took their powers, but are you certain?"

I shook my head. "Not one I've ever heard. But I'm certain it is what happened. Anaros, after he took their power, he killed them. They couldn't even fight back." I took a deep breath. I needed to get it all out of my head. I needed to tell him everything. "After he killed them, he asked me to join him. He asked me to help set *him* free."

"What do you mean? Him who?"

I fidgeted a little. I hadn't told Anaros I'd been to see Eradoma. I knew he wouldn't be happy. "I don't know, but..." I looked into his dark brown eyes, begging for understanding. "Please don't be angry with me."

Anaros shook his head. "Why would I be angry with you, Zynnera?"

I gulped. "Eradoma said something similar."

"Eradoma?" He kept his expression even, but I could tell from his tone he wasn't happy where our conversation was going. "You went to see Eradoma? ...alone?"

"I'm sorry...I just...I thought maybe she might tell me where the village is."

Anaros sighed. "Zynnera, I told you I tried to talk to her. And besides, we can't trust any information..."

I interrupted him, "I know. I know that. I just..." I stared guiltily at my blankets. "I was just desperate to make them stop. The nightmares." I couldn't fight back the tears any longer. I let out a small sob.

Anaros wiped more tears from my face. "It's OK, Zynnera. I'm not angry with you." I looked up at him. There was so much sympathy in his eyes. I hated feeling so vulnerable.

"You said Eradoma said something similar," said Reynard. "What exactly did she say?"

"I told her about my visions of the man in the black cloak. She seemed to know who I was talking about but wouldn't tell me who he was. All she said is that he would soon return." I shook my head. "I just wish I understood what it all meant."

I stood up from my bed, grabbing the brown satchel from where it rested on the ground. I walked out of the tent before any of them could say more, practically running towards the lake. The sun was low in the sky and its morning light touched the clouds with colors of pink and orange. I plopped down on one of the grey boulders on the water's edge and pulled *The Tahetya* from the bag. I began scouring through its pages earnestly, hoping something new would magically catch my eye.

Anaros had followed me from the tent. He leaned against the boulder I was sitting on for several minutes, watching me flip through the pages. "Zynnera, what are you doing?"

I wiped a few tears from my face. "I'm looking for a spell. Something to make them stop."

Anaros sighed, moving in front of me. He placed his hands on mine to stop me from turning the pages. He closed *The Tahetya*, pulling it off of my lap and placing it back inside the satchel. I stared back at him, fighting against a complete emotional breakdown.

"I'm tired of being afraid." I sobbed. "I'm tired of being afraid to close my eyes. Tired of being weak. I don't want to be afraid anymore."

Anaros wrapped his hand around mine. "Everyone has fears, Zynnera. All of us."

I shook my head. "You don't ever seem to be afraid."

Anaros tilted his head back and laughed. "That's certainly isn't true."

I squeezed his hand. "What are you afraid of then?" I didn't really believe his words.

"I'm afraid I'm not strong enough. Not adequate enough to be king. At least not the king the people deserve. And I'm afraid of losing the people I love, of this darkness that still settles over Selvenor." He paused for a moment, taking the time to tuck a piece of my hair behind my ear. He flashed me a smile. "Snakes. I'm afraid of snakes."

I laughed. "Snakes?"

He nodded. "We're all afraid, Zynnera. Fear makes us human. Having fear doesn't make us weak; however, facing it does make us strong."

I shook my head again. "What if I can't face it? What if I don't know how?"

"We'll do it together. Just like we always have. I promise we will figure it out. Whatever comes our way, we'll face it together."

I nodded and the tears started flowing from my eyes again. Anaros hopped onto the rock and placed his arm around me. I leaned against him, watching the waves crash into the rock in front of us. *How am I ever going to leave him? I NEED him.* I knew it was the truth. A new fear filled my mind, the fear that I would not have the strength to do what needed to be done. All I wanted was to stay with him, to find comfort and security in his arms. It was selfish of me to put my own desires over what was best for the people of Selvenor. Every moment I spent with him made leaving even harder, and I knew it would only make things harder for Anaros as well.

I don't think I can go through with it. I don't think I can leave him. I could still feel the tears flowing down my face. Anaros tightened his hold around my body. I closed my eyes. *Stay.* The word penetrated my deepest thoughts. I could feel my heart pounding hard inside my chest. *Was that my own consciousness trying to convince me, or does someone else think I should stay too?*

CHAPTER
Eleven

The morning air was cool as we sat around the small fire, eating breakfast. It had taken some time to calm Zynnera down. I had hoped her nightmares would not follow us on our journey to find the village, but I was only disappointed. Zynnera had described in detail what she saw and, admittedly, those details worried me. *She witnessed a murder in her visions. I can't imagine what that would have been like.* I stole a quick glance at her. For the moment she seemed fine, but I was sure the vision had her shaken.

There was so much about her visions we didn't understand. *Were they real? Was what she saw actually happening?* Even Zynnera didn't have the answers. She had often taken the time to describe everything she knew about magic to me. Zynnera said her father had explained there were three types of special gifts a witch or warlock could possess. I tried to recall the details of her explanation. The first was easy, a Protesta. It was easy because I knew it was the gift Eradoma possessed. Her power was very strong as far as witches were concerned. But Zynnera had defeated her. *Does that make Zynnera a Protesta? She was stronger than Eradoma?* I mulled over the idea for a few minutes.

But what about these nightmares, these visions? The second gift Zynnera had mentioned had a strange name, one I couldn't recall. I did remember, however, what it meant. *A Seer. Someone who could see the future.* Zynnera's nightmares left me wondering if perhaps she possessed this gift. *Maybe these nightmares are flashes of the future? It would make sense.* The nightmares had been increasingly persistent and seemed to be more detailed each time she had them. I sighed. *But if Zynnera is a Seer, how did she find the strength to beat Eradoma? Had it all been luck?* I didn't believe that was the case.

The third gift Zynnera described suggested the person had control over the elements. I had never seen anything to suggest Zynnera had such control but, to be honest, she rarely used her magic at all after defeating Eradoma. *She's afraid the people will see. She still feels the need to hide her powers.* The thought saddened me. I didn't want Zynnera to feel she had to hide any part of herself. She deserved to live freely, to be herself and be accepted as such.

After finishing breakfast, we packed our things and continued to travel south. Zynnera rode quietly along the dirt road. I suspected she was deep in thought, thinking both about her nightmare and our impending meeting with King Lenear. I forced my horse to catch up to hers, trotting beside her for several minutes while I thought of something to say.

Zynnera seemed to sense my concerns, flashing me a smile after I remained quiet. "I know you're wanting to ask. But I promise, I'm fine. At least no less so than when we left Selvenor."

She knows me too well. I smiled back at her. "I can't help worrying about you. I don't like seeing you upset."

"I know. But I think, at this point, I'm getting used to being plagued by nightmares, by questions. I've just accepted that until I find answers they aren't going anywhere."

I studied her expression. *She's so much stronger than she knows. Handling something like this with as much composure as she has...it's impressive.* I thought for a moment before asking her another question. "Zynnera, have you thought about the gifts of magic you told me about? Thought about how they could be related to your nightmares?"

Zynnera stared out in front of us. "Yes, I have. I know what you're thinking. You think I might be a Seer."

I laughed. "Yes, that's exactly what I was thinking." I paused for a moment, making my tone more serious before speaking. "What do you think?"

Zynnera shook her head. " Honestly, I don't know what to think. But I'm hopeful finding the village will provide some answers. Perhaps the people can help me understand both myself and my visions."

I hope she's right. I think I want answers as much as she does. I need to focus on what I'm going to say to King Lenear. He's our best chance of getting the answers we need. My first encounter with him as king had not gone well. He had been angry by my response to his disapproval of Zynnera. I didn't really care what he thought of her, but I knew it would impact both our journey through Arnfell and the future of Selvenor. I needed to be very cautious with the way I approached him. *I have to keep calm. I have to ACT like a king.*

The sun was making its descent to the horizon as we rode to the top of a hill, stopping to overlook the city of Dunivear. It had been a long time since I'd seen the city, but it was just as I remembered. Dunivear was surrounded by a massive stone wall that stretched past the shoreline and into the sea, creating a closed harbor for a vast array of trade ships. I moved my gaze to Zynnera, realizing this would be her first time seeing the ocean. I could see her smiling as she looked out upon the waves glistening in the sun.

"It's amazing! Look at all the ships! The city is even bigger than I imagined!"

I tried to hide my laugh but was unsuccessful. I couldn't help but smile at her excitement. "Wait until we go inside the city walls. It really is a beautiful place."

Zynnera smiled as we moved forward, leaving the dirt road behind us as we entered the city gate. Dunivear was bustling with people, and the streets were far more crowded than those of Selvenor. Zynnera retained her excitement as we rode along the paved streets. *It must be nice for her to be out in this city where no one knows who she is. She doesn't have to worry about what people think.*

We rode across a large bridge in the center of the city. The river flowing from Lake Athenasi moved right through the middle of Dunivear until it met the sea. The stone bridge only added to the beauty and elegance of the city, something Zynnera seemed to be thoroughly enjoying.

The palace lay just across the bridge at the end of a stone paved street. I could see Zynnera's expression change to one of nervousness as we approached the palace gate. Two guards stopped us before we could enter. "Please state your business here. We are not expecting guests today."

I dismounted my horse, stepping forward to face them. "I have need to see King Lenear. He is expecting a message from Selvenor." I wondered if I should tell them who I was. Announcing myself as king still felt strange to me, and I preferred not to if it wasn't necessary.

The two guards stared at me blankly for a moment. "We'll need to verify with the king's advisor before allowing you to pass. If you'll wait a moment for us to request him."

I nodded, moving my gaze to Zynnera. She looked even more nervous at the mention of the advisor. I had never asked her why she had left the Great Hall so upset the night of my coronation, but I suspected he had something to do with it. One of the guards disappeared inside the palace.

We waited only a few minutes before Elric returned with him, a broad smile spreading across his face as he approached. "Your Highness, we were not expecting to see you again so soon!" The two guards looked at each other nervously, obviously scared for not having known of my royal status.

"I thought it best to come myself," I said. I was certain as the king's advisor, Elric would know all about the conversation I had with King Lenear. For all I knew, he could have been the one to suggest its necessity in the first place.

Elric held out his arms as though welcoming us inside. "Please, I will request an audience with King Lenear at once. I'm sure he will be happy to continue your discussion." I wasn't convinced by his facade. The last thing King Lenear was likely to be was happy. Elric moved his eyes to Zynnera, his expression changing to a scowl. "Forgive me, Your Highness, but I'm afraid Miss Zynnera will not be permitted to enter the palace."

Zynnera stared at the ground in front of her, obviously upset by his comment. I felt my skin grow hot. *Just stay calm. Keep it together.* "And why's that?"

Elric sighed sympathetically. "I'm sorry, King Anaros, but it is by our law. Magic and those who wield it are not permitted in the city, let alone in the palace. I must ask that Zynnera leave. Willingly is preferred, by force if necessary."

It was getting harder to control my anger. I was afraid to respond, knowing full well I wouldn't be able to keep it in if I did. Zynnera rode her horse closer to me. I looked up into her sad blue eyes. She knew how upset I was by Elric's comments and she probably knew my temperament wouldn't handle them well. "It's OK," she said. "I'll wait for you outside the city." I started to argue with her, but she shook her head. "Really, it's fine. You need to go and speak with him. I'll be fine on my own, I promise."

I didn't like it at all, the idea of leaving her on her own in a city she'd never been to. But I knew she would be fine by herself. I stepped closer to her horse, releasing a heavy sigh. "I'm sorry." I wanted her to know how much I hated what was happening. She seemed to understand, flashing me a small smile.

"Take this street," I said, pointing southwest of the gate. "It will take you out of the city. Wait for us there...*please.*" I debated asking Reynard to accompany her, but I knew it would only make her more frustrated with the situation. *Please, just wait.*

Zynnera nodded, her smile growing a little as if she knew what I was thinking. "I promise."

Zynnera nodded and turned the horse to follow my instruction. Elric seemed pleased by her willingness to follow his orders. Reynard and Rhemues dismounted their own horses, frustration growing in their own expressions. Elric gestured for us to enter the gate. "Please, follow me."

We left our horses tied beside the palace entry. I couldn't stop my thoughts as we walked down a long carpeted corridor. *This has to stop. There is no excuse for the way he's treated Zynnera. I won't stand for it.* I reminded myself to stay calm. *I must be diplomatic. I can't lose my cool; otherwise, he'll never help us.*

Elric left us in a large room while he proceeded to tell King Lenear of our arrival. I looked at Rhemues, who was studying the emblem of a snake stitched into a cloth bearing Dunivear's crest. Reynard was watching me, obviously concerned by my frustrated expression. "It's unfair the way they treat her, My King, but you must look past it for the time being."

Rhemues looked back at me upon hearing Reynard's words. "He's right, Anaros. I know how angry you must be. Reynard and I don't like it either, but we have to remember why we are here. We need information. We can deal with this prejudice later."

I nodded, taking a deep breath to calm my emotions. But I wasn't sure I would be able to maintain it. *I need to focus on asking him questions. Try to forget about Zynnera long enough to get information. Rhemues and Reynard are right. There will be time to deal with that later.*

We waited for what felt like an eternity for King Lenear. When he finally entered the room, his face was expressionless. I suspected he was curious about my unannounced arrival into Dunivear. I waited for him to speak the first word, hoping to gage his mood by his tone.

He held out his hand in formal greeting. "King Anaros, I am surprised to see you. I was not expecting you to come in person."

Stay calm. Just stay calm. "I felt it would be best to speak with you in person," I said.

"So, have you considered our discussion? Made a decision?"

I kept my tone even and my stare firm. "I have. But that is not what I wish to speak with you about today."

King Lenear eyed me curiously. "I think it best I hear your decision first."

I could feel my skin growing hot. I was certain he could see it in my eyes. Rhemues moved forward, hoping to stop me before things got worse. "His Highness was hoping you might have information about a certain village in the forest of Arnfell. He is in need to visit it...with your permission, of course."

King Lenear became temporarily distracted by Rhemues's statement. "Village in the forest? What village?"

Rhemues looked frantic. "Uh...well, we don't know what it's called..."

King Lenear looked annoyed. I knew I needed to move the conversation forward while he remained distracted. "A long time ago two warlocks were exiled into the forest. It's rumored they remained there, in their own village. I need to find it."

I kept my request short and to the point, hoping he wouldn't feel the need to ask many questions, but I was only disappointed. "Why? What business do you have with warlocks?" His tone reflected his suspicion. "If it's something to do with that witch standing outside my city wall, then I'll give you no such information. What are you and her up to!"

I clenched my jaw and clenched my fists. Rhemues could sense my anger and proceeded to step in again. "It does involve Zynnera, yes. Please allow me to explain." King Lenear glowered at him. Rhemues cleared his throat nervously. "Zynnera has seen visions. We are only hoping to find someone who might be able to decipher their meaning."

King Lenear laughed. "Visions. You welcome this magic in your midst as though you trust it. You are blind to what's in front of you. But you will see soon enough. You will know the destruction and evil it brings."

My anger was taking over. I couldn't hide it from my tone. "Zynnera's visions could affect all of us, not just Selvenor. There is a darkness hovering over Virgamor, and I'd wager you can sense it as well as I can!"

King Lenear looked taken aback by my statement. His expression only confirmed I was right. Whether he wanted to admit it or not, he could feel it too; I knew he could. King Lenear sneered at me. "I'm already knee deep in issues with magic as it is. I don't need you adding to the problem."

I scrunched my face in confusion. "What do you mean?"

King Lenear stared at me for a moment, unsure whether he

wanted to discuss his kingdom's problems with me. "Perhaps it will make you see," he said, giving in to his better judgment. "Perhaps you will rethink this ideal of magic being something you can trust."

King Lenear gestured towards Elric, who had been standing by the entry this entire time, listening to our conversation. Elric seemed to understand what he meant without words. A few minutes later he returned with several servants carrying a wooden board with a white linen draped over it. They set the board on the floor in front of me, moving away from it as soon as their fingers released its sides. I looked at King Lenear, who nodded towards the board, encouraging me to investigate for myself. I could feel my heart pounding as I pulled the linen away from what I feared was a body, judging by the bulky shape.

Unfortunately, my assumption was correct. A cold, pale-faced man lay completely still on the wooden plank. There were no signs of physical damage on his body, no blood or evidence of foul play. I looked back at King Lenear. "What happened to him?"

He stepped closer to me. "Magic. This man was killed by magic."

"How can you be certain..."

"I am certain!" His voice was loud as if offended by my question. "This man was perfectly healthy. He was found dead on the street outside the palace, not a mark on him. No sign of a struggle. No sign of sickness."

I shook my head. "There are plenty of sicknesses you cannot see. Things that could cause this."

King Lenear's face went red and his eyebrows tightened. "No! This man was killed by magic. And he is not alone. There have been others. Many others. Always the same, dropping dead in the middle of the street with no sign of a struggle. It's been going on for months. There was even a witness to this man's death. Now I am more certain than ever."

"A witness? What did this witness see?" I couldn't deny his predicament had caught my interest.

"A woman entered the street and saw this man lying on the stone pavement. She said she saw a man in a black cloak leaving his side, leaving the city. She said she saw a blue mist around him."

King Lenear seemed pleased by my reaction as I remained crouched by the lifeless body, my expression reflecting my surprise. "A man in a black cloak?" I recalled Zynnera's description of her visions. In both nightmares she had mentioned there was a man in a black cloak. I felt impressed that these occurrences inside of Dunivear were related. "Zynnera's visions contained a man in a black cloak."

King Lenear seemed surprised by my statement. I knew he didn't trust Zynnera but thought I might be able to use his story to convince him to help us. "Help us locate the village," I said. "Zynnera feels there could be someone there who could interpret what she has seen. It might shed light on what is happening in Dunivear. If we can figure out who this man in the black cloak is, then perhaps we can stop him."

He considered my words for several long moments. I still sensed he was uncertain helping us was what he wanted to do. His gaze moved to Elric, silently asking his opinion. Elric thought for a moment, then replied with a steady, diplomatic tone. "I think it wise to allow this, My King. It may give us the opportunity to catch this man."

Lenear nodded. "Elric, bring me a map of Dunivear."

Elric obliged to follow the king's command right away. He returned in minutes with a map, rolled and tied with a piece of string. King Lenear placed it on a small desk, unrolling it to reveal a map of his kingdom. He used a feathered quill to mark a place on the parchment. "Here," he said, pointing to the spot. "This is where you will find Bogumir. Follow the road for a day—there will be a path leading into the forest. It is unmarked and unmaintained. Follow it due east towards the mountains. It will lead you to the village." He paused for a moment to make sure I understood before continuing with a stern voice. "I shall expect your return with information."

I nodded and took the map in my hand. Rhemues, Reynard, and I walked towards the room entry. I stopped before exiting, desiring to ask one last question before our departure. I turned to face King Lenear, who was watching me curiously. "If Zynnera helps put a stop to these deaths, if she helps protect your people, will you reconsider your request?"

King Lenear studied me for a few moments before responding. "Perhaps." I started to turn away, but his voice stopped me. "Whatever spell she has you under, it's certainly a strong one."

I was losing control again. *Calm. Stay calm.* "I'm under no spell."

Lenear scoffed. "Love is always a spell, just not necessarily one produced by magic."

I don't know why his comment surprised me. Certainly my feelings for Zynnera were obvious. Anyone could see it. I still didn't know how to respond to his blunt observation. I bit my lip, turning to move past the entry and leave him alone in the room. *At least he'll consider it. At least there's a chance I can change his mind.*

It was enough for me. Just the idea that he would consider it was more than I'd actually hoped for. This was the chance I needed. *Zynnera needed.* If she could show King Lenear she only wanted to use her magic for good, perhaps he would change his mind. *She can show him she is nothing like Eradoma. Nothing like this man in the black cloak.* And once she had, Selvenor would be able to retain the trade and peace agreements it had with Dunivear.

As I began making my way down the hall to leave the palace, Elric's voice sounded from behind me. "Your Highness!" I turned to face him, still uncertain how I felt about the man after what Rhemues had told me of his dance with Zynnera. "I just wanted to wish you luck, Your Highness. I hope you find this man, for both Dunivear's and Zynnera's sake."

I considered his words, wondering if he really meant them. "Thank you, Elric. I must ask, as the royal advisor, King Lenear will hold your opinion in high esteem. If there is anything you can do to persuade him, I'd greatly appreciate it."

Elric placed his hand over his heart. "Of course, Your Highness. I give you my word, etched in stone."

He smiled at me with his oath. I wasn't sure I found his words genuine, but it didn't hurt to ask for his help. "I will prove to him Zynnera is nothing like Eradoma." Elric nodded and turned to leave me standing alone in the hallway.

In my mind, this proof of Zynnera's character was just as important as finding the answers we needed about her visions. She was desperate for those answers, but I was desperate for her to feel at peace with herself, to feel accepted by our people and those of the surrounding kingdoms. After all, I planned to ask her to marry me. That would make Zynnera the queen of Selvenor and she deserved the respect that came with such a title. *They'll see. They'll all see. I just need time to show them.*

CHAPTER
~ *Twelve* ~

The waves crashed into the shoreline as the sun set over the Sea of Maleze. I watched the colors of the sky change from a soft blue to bright oranges and pinks. The water seemed to sparkle as the light touched it, shining down on the ever-rolling waves from the west. I could smell it. *The sea.* It was nothing like I'd ever smelled before. *I can't believe this is the first time I've seen the ocean.* This journey had already been full of so many new experiences, and I was grateful for them. At least they provided a small distraction from everything going on inside my mind.

I turned to face Dunivear. The city wall lay only yards from where I sat looking out over the ocean waves. I wondered how things were going inside the palace. *I hope Anaros is making progress with King Lenear. If he refuses to help us, I fear we may never get answers.* My mind reflected on our approach of the palace gate only an hour ago. Seeing Elric greet us upon arrival had made me nervous...and angry. I was still upset about the way he had spoken to me the night of the coronation. Even though I knew his words had held truth, I couldn't get past them. It bothered me how accepting he had been of who I was, only to turn around and suggest I had no resolve to fix my problem. Of course, his idea of a solution involved me taking something I simply wasn't interested in. I had no desire to rule Selvenor or the people and certainly didn't want any harm to befall them.

I still felt there was something odd about the man. Perhaps it was because he had been accepting of me, a feeling I wasn't exactly used to having. He had said his opinion wasn't the popular one, another factual statement on his part. There were very few people who didn't look at me with distrust and without fear. I hated that I was starting to get used to the idea of never being accepted for who and what I was.

My mind became more anxious with the passing minutes. *What's taking them so long? Is it good or bad that they've been in there for over an hour? What if he kicked them out of Dunivear? How would I know? What if he comes after me?*

Fear was taking over my thoughts. I inhaled a big breath, releasing it slowly with my eyes closed. *I can't let myself panic. I have to stay strong.* My mind wandered back to Elric and the palace entry. I had not been permitted to pass through the iron gate leading into the palace yard. And what was worse, Elric had stated I wasn't allowed to be in the city at all. I recalled my father's words from his story of Dunivear. King Wilhelm had made it law that no magic was allowed inside the city walls and vowed to destroy all those who could wield it. The memory made me feel as though I had a target on my back, sitting here in the open while I waited for the boys to meet with the king.

I sighed. *I hope Anaros is able to keep a level head while he's in there.* I could tell Elric's words had angered him. Starting out angry before even meeting with King Lenear certainly wasn't going to help the situation. *Rhemues is with him. He will help keep him in check...I hope.* I felt sick to my stomach. The last thing I wanted was for this to end badly, especially as a result of Anaros trying to defend me. I didn't want to be the cause for contention between our kingdoms, not while Selvenor was working so hard to rebuild everything it had lost.

But I knew the odds of King Lenear willingly helping us were probably slim. Not only did he dislike me and my involvement with Selvenor, but Anaros also seemed to be hiding the details of the conversation he had with him. I suspected their discussion had involved me, and I was concerned my relationship with Anaros had already begun to erode his relationships with other rulers.

I closed my eyes again, listening to the sound of the waves hitting the shoreline in front of me. My mind carried me away from the ocean, away from Dunivear, as though it desired to answer my question. I found myself standing inside a building, and it was one I easily recognized. I'd spent my whole life inside the palace walls and there was nothing that could make me forget the stone corridors lined with dark green carpet.

I was standing in a hallway just beyond the Great Hall. A set of voices echoed from a room at the end of the corridor. I walked slowly towards them, trying to make out the words as I approached the room. I recognized the voices right away. One belonged to Anaros and the other to King Lenear. My heart pounded harder. *This can't be...I can't be seeing the past?*

It didn't make sense to me, but curiosity pushed me forward until I was standing in the entry of the room. King Lenear was walking around a wooden table, while Anaros stood at one side, his expression reflecting an obvious amount of frustration.

"Don't be naive, boy!" Lenear said. "You think that witch hasn't thought of using her powers against you and every single one of the people in this kingdom? Mark my words, she will turn on you and your people. And when she does, I will not send my army to your rescue. I will not sacrifice my people so you can have your little fling with the witch. The destruction of Selvenor will be on your head!"

"You don't know her, nor do you know me." Anaros's voice sounded with anger as he argued with Lenear. "You're asking me to exile the person who saved this kingdom. If it weren't for her, none of us would be standing here tonight. I have no intention of doing this."

Exile? Had King Lenear asked Anaros to banish me? "You should consider this decision wisely, Your Highness. Either you cut ties with the witch or lose an ally you can't afford to. The decision is yours. But I assure you, the economic repercussions of alienating ties with your neighbors will devastate Selvenor in ways you never dreamed."

I felt my hand cover my mouth as I gasped. King Lenear moved towards the entry, stopping just in front of me before he spoke. "I'll be awaiting a messenger to bring your decision." He stormed past me and down the corridor out of sight. I moved my gaze back to Anaros, watching him slam his fist on the wooden table and knock a chalice to the floor. *What have I done? What position have I put him in?* I assumed his discussion with Lenear had been about me, but I never imagined the depth of that conversation. King Lenear had given Anaros an ultimatum: cut ties with me or lose any potential agreement with Dunivear.

I knew how important such arrangements would be for Selvenor's prosperity. *He has to let me go. We can't do this! It's his duty to protect our people, not put them in danger because of me.* I feared that was exactly what was happening. Anaros had come with me not just because he wanted to find answers, but because he wanted to persuade Lenear.

I felt myself being pulled away from the palace and back to my spot just above the sandy beach. I was breathing hard, trying to regain a sense of where I was. My vision had taken me on a journey to the past. I had witnessed Anaros's conversation with King Lenear for myself. And while I was upset that Anaros had withheld the details of their discussion from me, there was something more pressing on my mind. *How did I just see a vision of the past?* The three magical gifts had been a topic I frequently pondered during the last few weeks, and I was still unsure which one I possessed. The longer I was haunted by visions, the more certain I became that I was a Seer. But this vision was different. There was no doubt I had seen an event from the past. *That's not how it works, at least not how it's supposed to work. A Seer should see visions of the future, not the past.* I mulled over the thought for a moment, feeling even more frustrated than before. *What is wrong with me! Can nothing about me just be normal?*

The sound of horses walking along the stone path caught my attention. I turned to face the gate into the city. Anaros, Rhemues, and Reynard were riding towards me. I could feel myself holding my breath, anxious to learn the result of their discussion with King Lenear.

Anaros dismounted his horse after stopping just a few feet in front of me. I couldn't wait another moment for him to tell me what happened. "Well? How did it go?"

Anaros stepped in front of me, a wide smile forming across his face as he held up a piece of rolled parchment tied with a string. "Better than expected."

I stared at him, surprised by his reply. "Really?"

"Really," he said. Anaros unrolled the piece of parchment he was holding to reveal a large map of Dunivear. I could see markings where someone had inked in a large "X" over a grove of trees. Anaros pointed to it. "Bogumir. That's the name of the village."

I continued to stare at him, unable to comprehend what he was telling me. *Is this really happening? King Lenear actually agreed to help us?* "I really didn't expect King Lenear to be OK with us being here, let alone help us."

"Well, he wasn't onboard at first, but let's just say he's helping us to help himself."

I raised my eyebrows. "And what does that mean exactly?"

Anaros smiled. "It means we should go make camp, and then I'll tell you all about it."

I had almost forgotten how late it was. The sun had nearly set over the water now, the last bit of light streaking directly across the surface. We rode down the dirt road for several minutes until we found a clearing away from the city wall. King Lenear may have agreed to help us, but I suspected his opinion of me and the magic I wielded had not changed. I was anxious for Anaros to explain how he had managed to convince him to give us any information at all.

"Alright," said Rhemues as he swatted some bugs away from his face. "The tent's all set. Let's start on that fire, Reynard." Anaros walked to his side, ready to help, but Rhemues shook his head. "No, no. You take a walk." Anaros's plain expression changed to confusion. Rhemues tried to give him a discreet wink, but I caught it out of the corner of my eye. "Go. Take. A. Walk."

Anaros glanced up at me, obviously hoping I hadn't noticed Rhemues's poor attempt at being subtle. "Right. A walk." He walked nervously towards me, trying to hide behind a forced smile. "Zynnera...uh...would you like to..."

"Take a walk with you?" I flashed a witty smile in Rhemues's direction. He only returned my smile, passing another wink to me.

Anaros smiled, holding out his hand in front of me. "Please, take a walk with me."

"Well, if I must," I said sarcastically. I placed my hand in his, following his footsteps towards the beach. We walked along the sandy ground for several minutes, his hand still wrapped tightly around mine. The moon was shining brightly over the waves, giving us just enough light to see. I could make out the small fire dancing in the distance behind us, where Rhemues and Reynard sat with our horses.

Anaros stopped walking and turned to face the water. "Zynnera, I'm sorry about today. That you weren't permitted to go into the palace with us."

"It's not your fault," I said. "I knew how King Lenear felt about me before we got here."

"I know. But there's really no excuse for his actions. I'm hoping we can change that, though."

I stared at him for a moment before turning to face the water. Everything I had seen in my vision reflected across my mind, and I felt a twinge of anger towards him. *He should have told me. He shouldn't have hid it from me..* "You mean so I don't interfere with the peace and trade agreements?"

Anaros scrunched his face, clearly surprised by my knowledge of their conversation. "How did you...?"

"I had a vision," I answered before he could finish. "I had a vision of your discussion with him the night of the coronation." I continued to stare out at the water in front of us. I was sure Anaros felt guilty for not telling me, and I couldn't deny it had made me a little angry with him.

"When? How long have you known?"

"While you were in the palace," I said. I wasn't sure how to feel about it, him withholding those details from me. I was trying not to sound annoyed but knew I was failing with my tone.

Anaros sighed. "Zynnera, I'm sorry. I didn't tell you because...well, I knew how it would make you feel and I was afraid..." Anaros pulled on my hand so I would turn to face him. "I was afraid you would leave."

My heart pounded hard. Leaving was *exactly* what I was planning to do. I sighed. "I just wish you would have told me, Anaros. Things are different now. But I really don't want to argue about it. You said you thought King Lenear might change his mind?" I had to admit I was curious as to why. He had seemed pretty set on hating me at the celebration.

"King Lenear has a bit of a problem, Zynnera. There are people dying on the streets of Dunivear."

His statement surprised me. "What? What do you mean dying?"

"Several people have just dropped dead in the street. No signs of physical assault. No blood. Nothing. Lenear believes magic may be behind the murders."

I stared blankly at him. "And you think that would make him trust me... *why?*"

Anaros shook his head. "There was a witness to the last murder. A woman. She said she saw a man in a black cloak standing over the body."

"A man in a black cloak?" I could hardly believe the words as they escaped my own mouth. The idea that the same person from my nightmares could be killing people on the streets of Dunivear made my heart race. I was terrified that not only was he very real, but possibly very close.

Anaros released my hand and grabbed my shoulders. "I told him about your vision, Zynnera. That is why he agreed to help us. Gave us a map to find Bogumir. He may not trust you, but I think he knows that only magic can stop magic. You getting answers helps him get answers."

I knew what he was suggesting. Anaros thought we could find the cloaked man and put an end to his murderous scheme. But he didn't understand. King Lenear was no longer my concern. Right now, it didn't matter what he thought of me. It didn't matter if

Anaros had a plan to change his opinion of me. I could feel my body trembling and so could Anaros. I could feel my eyes glazing over. "I'm scared, Anaros. I'm scared of this man in the cloak. I don't *want* to find him."

Anaros seemed unsure what to say. I could tell he didn't want to push me, knowing how much of a toll my nightmares had already taken on me. "I'm not saying we are going to go looking for him, Zynnera. But if we can at least figure out who he is, maybe we can stop him. This man is killing people and for whatever reason seems to have a connection with your mind. Finding him might be the only way to stop the nightmares."

I nodded, brushing away the tears that had managed to escape my eyes. "I know. I know you're right...it just doesn't make me any less afraid."

Anaros placed his hand on my cheek, swiping away my hair and tucking it behind my ear. "You don't have to do it alone, remember? You have me. And Rhemues, Reynard...we are all three right here with you."

All I could do was nod in response as Anaros pulled me into a tight embrace. His head rested on mine, and I felt his hand rub between my shoulders. As much as I wanted his comfort, I couldn't shake my fear.

We walked back to camp in silence, his hand still tightly holding my own. We enjoyed the warmth of the fire for a short time before entering the large cloth tent. I wanted to rest, but my fear kept me awake. It was taking everything I had not to break down into a full-on sob.

Rhemues and Reynard seemed to have no trouble falling asleep almost immediately. I envied them. *It must be nice to sleep like that. To actually be able to rest.* I sighed. I might never know what that felt like again.

"Zynnera," whispered Anaros. I turned to face him. He was sitting up, watching me fight my body's desire to sleep. "You need to sleep, Zynnera. You need to rest."

I sat up, holding the blankets tight in my hands. *Don't cry. You don't need to cry.* "I'm not really tired."

I completely lied and he knew it right away, chiding me with his tone. "Zynnera."

I let out a shaky sigh that seemed to give my body permission to shed the tears it had been holding back since we entered the tent. "I'm afraid to close my eyes. I don't want the nightmares to come back."

Anaros scooted closer to me and wiped the tears off my face. I watched him place a bag of our supplies behind my pillow and lean against it. "Come here," he said, gesturing for me to lean against him.

I hesitated for a moment, not because I didn't want to, but because I wasn't sure if I should. *I know I shouldn't, but...*I couldn't help myself. I wanted to feel safe, and being with Anaros was the only time I ever did. I leaned against him, resting my head on his chest. His arm wrapped around my shoulder and rested on my arm. He used his free hand to pull my blanket over me. I could feel my eyes growing heavy almost immediately. He didn't speak; he just held me until I drifted to sleep, a guard to protect me from the thoughts within my own mind.

CHAPTER
Thirteen

Light peeked through the wall of the cloth tent just enough to pull me from a deep sleep. I started to move but stopped when I realized Zynnera's body was still resting against mine. I didn't want to disturb her, at least not yet. Not when she was finally getting some much needed rest. I could feel her hand resting on my chest alongside her face. She seemed so peaceful lying against me.

I stroked her arm with my thumb. She had remained snuggled against me the entire night, a night that had been free of the nightmares that typically haunted her. Although she had hesitated to accept my gesture, I knew I had made her feel safe. The thought made me smile. I *wanted* to make her feel safe.

Still smiling, I tilted my head to rest against hers. I wanted to enjoy the moment. I wanted to retain that feeling of being her protector. Her body moved gently as she breathed, unaware morning had come and its light had chased away the darkness of night. I allowed myself to press my lips against her head. *I have to tell her. She needs to know how I feel.* It was moments like this that might push me to actually follow through with my plan. It was moments like this I wanted more of.

I shifted my eyes to see if Rhemues and Reynard were still sleeping. To my surprise and embarrassment, Rhemues was staring at me with probably the widest grin I'd ever seen. I could feel my face flush as I met his eyes and watched his smile miraculously grow even bigger. He raised his eyebrows and nodded to me. "Good night, I presume?" He kept his voice at a low whisper to avoid waking Zynnera.

I rolled my eyes. *Well, there goes that moment.* Rhemues had made everything sufficiently awkward now, and the worst part was I couldn't excuse myself from the situation without waking Zynnera. I was stuck, torn between enjoying my proximity to her and escaping Rhemues's uncomfortable stare.

Rhemues let out a soft chuckle, still whispering as he moved toward the tent opening. "Don't mind me. I'll just join Reynard for breakfast while you..." He gestured towards Zynnera, smiling as he disappeared beyond the cloth walls.

The whole situation annoyed me. I could picture Rhemues standing outside, telling Reynard all the details. The thought only made me more embarrassed. I looked down at Zynnera as she whimpered in her sleep. *I hate waking her. I wish I didn't have to. But we've got another long day ahead of us.* I stroked her face, whispering softly to not startle her. "Zynnera. Zynnera, it's morning."

She took in a deep breath as she sat up, blinking sleepily at me.

When she realized she had still been lying against me, her face turned a bright red and she quickly tucked her hair behind her ear. The movement made me smile. I had called her out on the habit months ago in the forest, but despite her obvious attempt to quit, she still fell to the subconscious movement anytime she became nervous.

"How did you sleep?" I asked. There was really no need for my question. I knew she had slept better with no nightmares haunting her in the darkness. But I wanted to have a conversation with her, and it seemed the perfect way to start.

She moved her gaze to the pile of blankets at her feet, her face still red with embarrassment. "Better than usual."

I suspected she was still uncertain allowing herself to be so close to me was proper. It was a legitimate concern, especially with the people of Selvenor watching us both so closely. But we weren't in Selvenor now, and I didn't care about any of that. Truthfully, I never had.

"That's good," I said. "I'm glad you were able to get some rest."

Zynnera seemed unsure how to respond. "Anaros...I...last night..." She paused for a few moments to gather her thoughts. "Thank you." Her tone was soft and genuine. I could tell the decision still weighed heavily on her mind.

"You're welcome," I whispered. Staring into her eyes, I wanted to say more. I wanted to tell her now. But I couldn't bring myself to do it. The fear of how she would respond remained inside my mind. *Why can't I overcome it? Why can't I just say it?* I had talked to Zynnera only days ago about facing her fears, yet I still couldn't face one of my own. She had bluntly asked what I was afraid of and I had been honest with her. However, I had left out one of my biggest fears and it was the one that haunted me the most right now.

My thoughts were interrupted by the growling of my stomach. "I suppose we should have breakfast. Pack camp and get moving."

Zynnera continued to stare into my eyes as if waiting for me to move first. The problem was my mind had yet to convince my body to actually do so. *Just say it. Tell her.* My body rose from the ground, ignoring the desperate pleas in my head. I held out my hand to help her up and she accepted it. Once again, I found myself angry at my lack of courage. No matter how many times I convinced myself I would find the right moment, I inevitably let them escape me every time.

We ate breakfast and packed camp before continuing our journey south down the dirt road. We rode along the coastline for hours, eventually following the road into the dense timberline. Zynnera seemed much more relaxed. It was amazing what a restful night free of nightmares could do for her. I thought about King Lenear's words. He had said to follow the road south for about a day before turning east towards the mountains. That meant we would be camping another night in the woods before we reached Bogumir. *Will Zynnera want to sleep next to me again? Should I offer?* It was obvious it had helped her sleep more soundly, but would she feel comfortable doing so again? I also wasn't sure I wanted to endure another awkward moment with Rhemues, who had found the whole situation quite amusing.

The day seemed to pass quickly as I contemplated my dilemma. The sun was low in the sky by the time we reached the spot King Lenear had told us about. An unmarked road stretched due east through the forest. It looked more like a dying trail than an actual road and I suspected it was meant to be that way. It was unlikely anyone from Dunivear ever ventured towards Bogumir and just as unlikely the people of the village ever left the forest. I couldn't blame them for wanting to avoid the judgmental wrath of King Lenear and the people of Dunivear.

We followed the path through the dense wood for about an hour before stopping to make camp. My heart pounded hard as I helped Rhemues set up our tent while Reynard collected a stack of firewood. Rhemues would flash me a smile every few minutes, obviously wondering the same thing I was. *Should I ask Zynnera? It's probably not appropriate. But if it helps her sleep...* I was no closer to making a decision and now the sun was beginning to set. The whole thing was making me sick to my stomach.

Rhemues swatted at the bugs as they flew around his face. "One thing I *don't* miss about living in the woods." He started gagging, holding his throat with a dramatic expression. "I think I swallowed one!"

"Bugs should be the least of your worries," said Reynard, unloading another stack of wood onto his pile. "There are plenty of things that are worse."

Rhemues stared at him nervously. "Like what? Giant bears?" He looked past Reynard into the dark shadows of the forest.

Reynard hid his smile, but I knew he was enjoying his tease. "I'm thinking something smaller. I might have seen a few furry critters running around the tent last night."

"What? You mean like...like rats. I don't like rats..." Rhemues's voice grew quiet as he looked anxiously at the tent. It didn't take much to get him wound up when it came to animals lurking in the night. Rhemues was a burly man, but even the smallest creatures made him jumpy.

After dinner we all crawled into the tent. Reynard seemed to fall asleep almost immediately, and Rhemues appeared to be resting quietly on his own pile of blankets. I couldn't help but wonder if he was actually asleep or just pretending so he could listen in on any conversation I might have with Zynnera. She seemed hesitant to lie down in her own bed, and I suspected her mind was racing as much as mine.

I cleared my throat, preparing to address the uncomfortable tension between us. "Zynnera, if...I mean you're welcome to...if it helps..." My heart was pounding so hard I thought it might explode.

"Yes," she said before I could actually make a complete sentence. Her face turned red at the swiftness of her answer. She had obviously been waiting for me to make the offer.

I tried to keep myself from smiling at her response. I didn't want to make this more awkward than it already was, but I felt almost giddy at the idea of holding her again. Within minutes she was snuggled against me in the same position as the night before. I wasn't looking forward to seeing Rhemues's ebullient grin when the morning light penetrated the cloth tent, but it was worth it. *It's worth dealing with his taunting. It's worth it to make her feel safe.*

Zynnera fell asleep much faster than I did. My mind seemed to think it needed to remain awake until I knew she was sleeping peacefully and she wouldn't be pulled into another vision. Time appeared to race by in the darkness, and the light of morning greeted me before I felt ready to begin the day. *At least Zynnera got another night of rest.* I looked down at her resting on my chest. Once again I was faced with the dilemma of not wanting to wake her from a peaceful sleep. Both Rhemues and Reynard had already left the tent, something I felt grateful for, but I knew I couldn't stay here with her all morning. Admittedly, part of me wanted to.

We should reach Bogumir today. We should get going. I sighed. *I HATE having to wake her.* "Zynnera." I stroked the top of her head with my hand. She sat up, nervously moving her gaze away from me. "We should probably pack up camp," I said. "We're not far from Bogumir now."

Zynnera's expression looked even more anxious. I knew she was eager to find more people like her, people who could wield magic and possibly answer the many questions she had, but I was certain the whole thing also made her nervous. There was no telling what we would find in our efforts to decipher her visions. *Or who.* It was that part I assumed had her on edge. She was afraid we would find the man in the black cloak.

I reached forward and touched her hand. "Remember, we'll face it together."

My statement seemed to reassure her as she flashed me a bright smile and nodded. "Thank you, Anaros. I admit I'm really nervous for today. But it still feels right. I still think it's where we need to go."

"Well, then let's go. You're not the only one who is anxious."

We both exited the tent to find Rhemues and Reynard eating breakfast around a small fire in the crisp morning air. Rhemues's expression immediately formed into a giant smile upon seeing us. He drew in an exaggerated breath. "I sure did sleep well last night. What about you Reynard, how did you sleep?"

"I'd wager we all slept well," he answered, flashing me a crooked smile.

Is this what the rest of this trip is going to be like? It was harder to make any kind of move with the two of them taunting me. *Maybe if I'd actually make a move, they'd stop. It's obvious that's what they want.* I stole a glance at Zynnera to see if she had picked up on their teasing. She seemed to be avoiding eye contact with all of us. *She's noticed, no doubt.*

Reynard unrolled the map of Dunivear on the ground in front of us. "We're really close. We should be there around noon."

I suspected we were all anxious to leave. After all, the entire trip had been building up to this moment. We were so close to finding the village, to finding answers. And we weren't the only ones hoping to find them. King Lenear would be waiting for our return as well. He still lacked trust in Zynnera, but this trip to Bogumir could change all of that.

"Let's get going," I said. "I have a good feeling about today."

We packed the camp and began making our way down the overgrown path through the woods. At times it was difficult for the horses to maneuver through the fallen trees and dense brush. We often had to stop and move obstacles that blocked our path. Zynnera's magic was especially helpful for moving the downed trees and thick brush that covered the hidden road. It was rare to see her actually using her magic, and I couldn't deny watching her golden aura clear our path so easily was fascinating.

As the sun moved overhead through the leafy treetops, I could feel my anxiety growing. We stopped to eat a light lunch among the birches and pines, and I could tell Zynnera was becoming more nervous as the day trudged on. Reynard was examining the map again. "We should be very close. *Very* close." I hoped he was right. I wasn't sure how much more anticipation my mind could take.

A large snap resonating from the trees caught our attention. We all turned to face the spot where the noise had sounded, moving to our feet in preparation for what lay hidden in the shadows of the forest. My hand rested on the hilt of my sheathed sword as I stared into the trees. After several minutes of silence, Reynard shouted out into the shadows, "Is someone there!"

There was no reply, but I couldn't shake the feeling that someone was watching us. Zynnera moved closer to me, pointing towards the trees. "There! Someone is behind that tree."

I could hear the panic in her voice as she spoke. I stared at where she was pointing. There didn't seem to be any evidence of a person hiding amongst the trees. But I knew better than to question her. The last time she had insisted she'd seen something in the woods, she had turned out to be correct. I pulled my sword from its scabbard, ready for what I feared could be an ambush.

After several more minutes a figure peeked out from behind the tree. "There!" Zynnera shouted. "I see them!"

The figure heard her and darted deeper into the woods. Before I knew what was happening, Zynnera took off after them. I could feel panic sweeping over me as I sheathed my sword and ran to follow her. "Zynnera! Zynnera, wait!"

I could see her running through the trees ahead of me. The figure wasn't too far in front of her. *This could be a trap. We could be running right into a trap!* I wanted to shout out to her, to beg her to stop, but I knew it would do no good. Zynnera seemed determined to catch the figure, and all I could do was follow her. I could hear the rustling of leaves and snapping of branches from behind me as Rhemues yelled my name. He and Reynard were following us as best they could, but the harsh overgrowth was making the pursuit difficult.

I forced my way through the dense overgrowth of the forest until I came to a clearing. Zynnera had stopped, facing a large crowd of people with scowls on their expressions. I could see her body trembling as she looked into their unwelcoming faces. The figure we'd been chasing was glaring at us from within the crowd. *We have been lured into a trap, it seems.* Reynard and Rhemues arrived seconds after me, breathing hard from their attempt to keep up.

"Anaros, you shouldn't have..." Rhemues started to speak, but I held up my hand to stop him. His expression changed to fear upon noticing my reason for silencing him. My hand automatically moved to my sheathed sword, preparing to defend us from the crowd. I watched Reynard react in the same manner. He seemed to sense their silent threat as the tension between us mounted.

Zynnera stepped backwards until she was standing beside me. One man from the group stole the moment to address us. "Leave here. You're not welcome in our midst." His tone was stern and demanding.

My mind was racing. Behind the group I could see cottages lined along the clearing. *I think we've found Bogumir.* But the thought didn't provide me any comfort. The people here obviously wanted to be left alone, to remain in their isolation. They seemed prepared to defend their village at whatever cost.

Zynnera took a step forward and held up her hand in an effort to calm them; her voice was shaky as she spoke. "I need your help."

The man shook his head. "I said leave. I won't ask you again." A purple aura surrounded his hands as his threat became more real. I wasn't sure what to do. I knew the man would not hesitate to attack us, and, quite frankly, the only one who could stop such an attack was Zynnera.

"Please," she pleaded. I could hear the desperation in her voice, but it did us no good to find the village if they would not give us a chance to explain why we were there.

In seconds, the man shot a bright beam of purple energy past us. My body trembled as I watched it crash into the trees. I glanced at Zynnera, hoping she had a plan to defend us if attacked again. She remained focused on the man, a bit of uncertainty in her eyes as she faced him.

"Please. I don't want anyone to get hurt," she said. Her tone was still begging him to retract his threat.

The man forced a second purple beam of energy towards us. My heart felt like it stopped as the light approached. Zynnera waved her hands, producing a giant golden shield to protect us. The purple beam clashed against it, dissipating only moments later to reveal the expressions of shock from the crowd in front of us. I could hear them murmuring to one another, almost as if they were stunned by Zynnera's ability to wield magic.

The man stepped forward, his eyes partially hidden behind strands of long black hair "Who are you?" His tone had changed. It no longer weighed heavy with demand. He no longer sounded threatening but instead emanated a desperate curiosity.

"My name is Zynnera. I've come seeking a Seer. I need someone who can help me interpret the visions I'm having."

Surprise remained on the man's face. "The same Zynnera who defeated Eradoma to save Selvenor?"

Zynnera seemed taken aback by his question. She hadn't been expecting anyone to know her name or what she had accomplished for our kingdom. I smiled at the idea of these people appreciating what she had done. "Yes," I said, moving to stand beside her. "Zynnera saved our people. We owe her a great debt."

The man looked at me. "And you are?"

Zynnera answered for me, "He's King of Selvenor. And this is Rhemues, the royal advisor, and Reynard. He is training our new army."

The man seemed to take in everything that she said. He was still curious of our presence in their village. "It is an honor to meet you, Zynnera. Please forgive me for earlier. It is not often we have visitors and when we do, they are often not friendly. I'm sure you know of King Lenear's despise of our people?"

Zynnera looked at the ground in front of her. "Yes, I have unfortunately become aware."

The man shook his head. "Don't let it bother you. Now, you said you were having visions? I think we can help with that. Please, come with me."

He gestured for us to follow. I could feel myself calming. *This is it. We are going to get answers.* Through our entire journey I had been hopeful we would find them, but now I was certain. Everything about this encounter made me more optimistic. Not only did they seem to want to help Zynnera, but they also appeared to recognize and respect her. They were aware of what she had done for

Selvenor, and I felt they were ecstatic to have her in their village. *I've only just met them, but I trust them. They are going to help us. I can feel it. They are going to help Zynnera in a way I can't.* I now understood why Zynnera had felt so strongly about coming here. *This is where she is meant to be.*

CHAPTER
~ *Fourteen* ~

Dozens of cottages were aligned in rows through the village. The main path was paved with large flat stones and there were several side streets branching to either side. I could hardly believe what I was seeing. When my father spoke of a village of witches and warlocks hidden in the forest of Arnfell, I never imagined something so large and sophisticated. The village of Bogumir looked more like a small city, and a thriving one at that. Undoubtedly, magic had helped them create such a beautiful place to live, and I was eager to see all of it.

Upon first arriving, I had been concerned the people would refuse to help me. They had become immediately defensive, not that I really blamed them. The man said their visitors were often unfriendly towards those who wielded magic. I wondered if King

Lenear had ever sent his men to spy on them. *I bet he has. He probably keeps very close tabs on them.*

It was amazing how quickly their mood had changed upon seeing me form a shield to defend us. They seemed surprised by my ability to use magic. But they weren't nearly as surprised as I was at their recognition of my name. It was true, I had defeated Eradoma and saved Selvenor. However, the idea that I had somehow become famous amongst an isolated people this far from my home baffled me. The mere mention of my name was enough for them to welcome me into their midst and protect us from their magic.

We followed the man through the village until we reached a large stone cottage at the end of the main paved street. He knocked softly on the door and was greeted by an older woman in a dark blue dress. There was a pendant hanging around her neck. I recognized the shape immediately as the same symbol embedded in the cover of the book resting in my satchel. "I'm sorry to disturb you, Adeara," said the man. "But I think it would be best for our visitors to speak with you."

She looked at us curiously, her eyes stopping when they reached me. I couldn't be sure, but it seemed as though she could sense my magical abilities, like she knew I was different from the others. Adeara sent me a bright smile and gestured for us to enter her home. *I feel so nervous. Why do I feel so nervous?* I stole a glance at Anaros, who was looking back at me. Suspecting my hesitation, he nodded towards the door to encourage me to follow her.

Adeara's home was very modest, filled with the most basic essentials and free from all manner of useless items and decorations. She invited us to join her as she sat down at a large square table by a window. Anaros and I both joined her with Rhemues following suit after a bit of hesitation. Reynard remained standing beside the man who had brought us to the cottage. He seemed uncertain he yet trusted anyone in the village.

My heart and mind were racing. *I hope we can trust them. I hope she can help me.* I could feel my hands shaking as they rested on my lap below the table. I was glad she couldn't see them there and how nervous I was. Anaros was sitting beside me, and my nervous shaking hadn't gone unnoticed to him. He reached over in one subtle motion and grabbed my hand in his own. *It will be OK. I'm not facing any of this alone.*

The man moved forward to the vacant side of the table, looking at me with a serious expression. "Show her. Show her your magic." I looked at him suspiciously. *Why? Is this some kind of test? Do I need to prove to this woman I can use magic?* The man smiled at my confused expression. "It's OK, Zynnera. You'll understand in a moment. Please, show her."

I felt Anaros squeeze my hand. After releasing a shaky sigh, I moved the other hand above the table, giving a small wave until my golden aura surrounded it. Adeara's expression reflected her surprise and fascination as she gasped in awe of my magic. "The prophecy is fulfilled!"

I stared blankly at her. "The prophecy?" I had no idea what she was talking about. I had assumed the murmurs of the crowd were due to their surprise I could use magic, but now I wasn't so sure.

She smiled at me. "There is a prophecy known to us who use magic, passed down since the very beginning. One day a person will come, destined to find the Virgàm and save us from the darkness."

Anaros seemed anxious for more information. "Virgàm? Could you tell us what it means? It's not the first time we've heard the word."

"The Virgàm is an ancient item with mystical powers. It is the source of all magic in humans. It connects us. Protects us. Keeps the world in balance."

Without skipping a beat, Anaros proceeded with another question. "You say this person in the prophecy is destined to find it. Does no one know where it is?"

Adeara seemed intrigued by Anaros's attention to detail, almost pleased by his desire for information. "The Virgàm has always been hidden from the world. It reveals itself only to those worthy of its power. Those occasions are rare, only once in the last few centuries."

"Centuries?" Anaros raised his eyebrows. "Then how is anyone supposed to find it?"

"There is only one person who can," said the man. "The prophecy speaks of a Bridge. The Virgàm will reveal itself to them so they can use its power to stop the darkness."

My mind was still racing. *Bridge. Vander spoke of this. This must be what he was referring to when we met him.* I was sure Anaros was thinking the same thing I was. Vander had said someday we would understand. The mystery behind his words was finally coming to light.

Anaros continued to press for answers. "What do you mean by *Bridge?* A man told me I was destined to help *the Bridge* find Virgàm. Are you saying I'm part of this prophecy?"

I was glad he was so eager to ask the questions rampaging through my mind. Right now I didn't feel like I could soak in the information fast enough to ask anything. My thoughts were pulling me in every direction imaginable, trying to prioritize what question I should seek an answer to first. They all seemed equally important, and the dilemma only left me frustrated. Listening to Anaros query for details provided me time to analyze the information and collect my thoughts.

"It's quite possible," said Adeara. "I can't say I have an answer for you. Much has been lost of the prophecy through the years. But this much I know, the Bridge is destined to fight the darkness. As the name suggests, they will be a bridge between magical abilities. Only someone who can wield all three can protect us."

My heart skipped a beat. "All three? You mean it's possible for someone to possess more than one ability?" I felt as though I knew the answer as the question escaped my mouth. All this time I'd been struggling to understand which ability I had been born with, trying to determine if I had one or the other. I'd never given thought to having more than one. *But what does that mean? If I do have more than one....am I the one she's talking about? Am I the Bridge?* The idea made my head swirl.

Adeara smiled at me, nodding her head. "Yes, the Bridge will possess all three. They are the only one who can do so."

Her confirmation left me panicked. *I can't be this Bridge. I just can't. I'm not strong enough to defeat the darkness she speaks of. I'm just...me.* I knew I needed to ask. I needed to be blunt. But I was afraid of her answer. I was afraid my suspicions would be correct.

"When you saw my aura, you said the prophecy is fulfilled. You think I am this Bridge, don't you?" I swallowed hard as I waited for her response. Part of me was begging for it not to be true. I wasn't interested in carrying such a heavy responsibility.

Adeara looked at me sympathetically. She seemed to sense my fear. "The original prophecy spoke of a sign, a way for us to know when the Bridge presented themselves among us. They would have a golden aura, a far different aura than any witch or warlock has ever had."

I could feel my body shaking again as Anaros tightened his grip around my hand. He could undoubtedly sense how afraid I was. I couldn't deny this was all something I had already suspected. From the moment Vander told us about the Bridge, the Virgàm, and that Anaros was destined to help, part of me knew I *was* the Bridge. It was an idea I had pushed to the back of my mind for fear it was true. The woman had only validated something I had already suspected, and I was certain Anaros had too.

"I've never had the ability to control the elements," I said, grasping at my last effort to invalidate her claim.

"Every gift requires time and nurturing. With proper training, I have no doubt you will wield the power of an Elementalist as well as the other two abilities. Unfortunately, there are no Elementalists among us at present, but I know the people of this village would be happy to assist you in furthering your power as a Protesta and Seer."

Anaros studied the woman curiously. "How does one know what type of ability they have? Is it something you just figure out over time?" His question wasn't really relevant to me, but I was still curious to know the answer.

She waved her hand, emanating a purple aura as she moved it through the air. "Color. Color lets us know to which group we belong."

Anaros turned to face me. "Eradoma's aura was blue."

I nodded. "Yes, and Larena's was purple."

Adeara removed the pendant from around her neck and laid it on the table in front of me. I had been right about the symbol; it was the same as *The Tahetya*. I quickly pulled the book from the satchel hanging across my shoulder and placed it gently beside the pendant to compare them. Adeara smiled, realizing the information was beginning to make sense to me.

She used her finger to outline the triangle. "Green. Elementalist." She proceeded to the crescent moon hanging below it. "Purple, for the Seer."

I moved my own finger around the blue circle surrounding them. "Protesta."

The woman nodded. "And here, the golden eye in the center. The Bridge. *You.* The one who will wield all three."

I couldn't believe it. All this time I had searched *The Tahetya* for answers and thought I'd found nothing. All this time it had been right in front of me. Everything was starting to make sense now. I had beaten Eradoma because I was a Protesta. My thoughts raced back to the night of my battle with her. I recalled her expression when she witnessed my magic for the first time. At the time, I believed the shock on her face was merely a sign of surprise that I had kept my secret from her for so long. *But that wasn't it. She may have been surprised, but that isn't why she looked afraid. She saw my gold aura and she knew what it meant. She knew I had more power than she did.*

And then there were my nightmares. I had suspected they might be visions of the future, but now I was certain at least some of them were. *I am a Seer too. My nightmares are visions.* I looked at the woman for a moment. "I've had visions, nightmares. Could you help me understand what they mean? Is there a way to control them?"

The woman sighed. "It is one of the unfortunate cons of being a Seer. Of all three abilities, it is the one with the least control. Our visions seem to come and go as they please. There is very little we can do to control them. I can help you decipher what it is you've seen, but I think it may be a lesson for another day."

I looked beyond her and out the window. The sun had set and the moonlight filtered through the glass panes. I couldn't believe it was already nighttime. It seemed like we had only just entered the village minutes ago. I'd been so focused on the information she presented that I hadn't noticed the setting sun.

The man walked to the old woman's side. "Adeara, I'll see to it our guests are comfortable in the spare cottage. It sounds like they may be with us awhile."

"Yes, thank you," she answered. "Zynnera, please visit with me again tomorrow afternoon. We can discuss your visions then."

I smiled at her. "Thank you, Adeara. For all your help."

Adeara nodded and I felt a warm sensation come over me. The information she had presented had produced a great deal of fear and anxiety in me, but somehow those feelings seemed to vanish. For the moment, I felt at peace with everything she had told us. There was still much I didn't understand, but having even a few answers gave my mind permission to rest. *If she can help me understand the visions tomorrow, maybe I can finally move past the nightmares. Maybe they will cease to haunt me.*

The man guided us to the edge of the village to a small cottage and welcomed us inside. "We keep this cottage vacant for when we have visitors," he said. "We get an occasional rogue witch or warlock seeking refuge from Dunivear. Give them a place to shelter for a bit. Some of them end up staying, others continue on. But you are all welcome to stay as long as you like or need."

"Thank you," said Anaros. "We appreciate your hospitality. You haven't told us your name." He held out his hand in formal greeting.

"Ah, forgive me. I was so taken by Zynnera I forgot pleasantries. Aldous is my name."

Anaros smiled. "Thank you again, Aldous."

Aldous nodded. "I'll check on you in the morning. You're welcome to have breakfast with my family."

He waved goodnight and left the small cottage. I plopped down on a bed, my mind completely exhausted by the events of the day. Anaros sat down beside me, sensing how overwhelmed I was. "You feeling OK?"

I didn't know how to answer him. Truthfully, in some ways I felt better than usual. But in other ways I felt worse. I felt free from some of the questions that had bothered me for months, for *years*. But the answers to those questions had brought an unprecedented burden that I wasn't sure I was ready to carry.

"I don't know," I answered honestly. "I'm not really sure what to think or how to feel right now."

Rhemues, who had been unusually quiet through this entire encounter, moved closer to us. "So, let me see if I've got this straight. You're basically an all-powerful witch that can beat the boogers out of anyone else who uses magic. Oh, and you're meant to save the world from evil. Does that about sum everything up?" His tone was partially sarcastic but still heavy with concern. I imagined the revelation of my destiny had him worried about both my safety and sanity.

I laughed. "Well, I don't know about all-powerful. I certainly don't feel all-powerful."

"Well, you did beat Eradoma," he said. "She seemed as powerful as they come."

I nodded. I didn't want to worry him, but I also didn't want to lie. "Eradoma was very powerful, yes. But this darkness Adeara speaks of...Rhemues, I don't know. It definitely feels stronger than she was. Stronger than I am."

Anaros placed his hand around my shoulder. "They've offered to help you, Zynnera. You should let them teach you. You told me you felt you needed to come to Dunivear to find answers, and you were right. But maybe it wasn't just answers you need."

I considered his words. Anaros was right. I did come looking for answers, but now that I had them, I felt there was more I needed to do here. "Yes, I should learn what I can. I feel as though I'm going to need it."

Reynard was standing a few feet away with his arms folded. "I'm glad you found what you were looking for, Zynnera. The people seem eager to help you. I think it would be wise for us to stay here a few days and give you time to learn."

"I agree with Reynard," said Anaros. "We've come all this way. We should make the most of it."

I was grateful for their support, but I couldn't help but feel guilty for keeping Anaros away from Selvenor. He needed to return as soon as possible, and his desire to stay with me was keeping him from his duties as king. I knew he would chide me for suggesting we return sooner rather than later. *A few days. We'll just stay a few days and then go back. Once I get some answers, learn a little magic, we can go back.*

I found it difficult to fall asleep. Even within the safety of the warm cottage, I couldn't escape my thoughts. There was so much information for my mind to reflect on, I wasn't sure I'd ever be able to shut it off. *We've come so far in the last few days. We're so close to understanding everything.* I contemplated what having answers would mean for me. Before starting our journey, I had been determined to leave Selvenor. I'd felt sure it was what I needed to do, what was best for both me and Anaros. Now I was uncertain. But I couldn't decide if that feeling was the result of how much I loved him or because there was really no reason for me to leave. I suspected my emotions would never allow me a truthful answer.

Anaros had seemed so sure he could persuade King Lenear to reconsider his demands. *If King Lenear can change his mind, maybe everyone else can as well?* After all, no one seemed to despise me more than he did. I closed my eyes. I could feel it now, the exhaustion taking over my body and mind. I started to drift to sleep just as Elric's words entered my thoughts. *You know they're never going to trust you...*I hoped he was wrong. I *needed* him to be wrong.

CHAPTER
Fifteen

The air was warm inside the small cottage. I rubbed my eyes groggily as I sat on the edge of the bed, looking around the room. The building consisted of a single large room with five beds lined along the length of the north wall and a wooden table in the southeast corner. There was a fire smoldering inside the stone fireplace, providing enough heat to curb the coolness of a typical spring morning.

I moved my gaze to the bed beside me where Zynnera was still resting peacefully. Another night free of nightmares had come and gone. I wondered if our discussion yesterday with Adeara was the reason for their absence. *I'm sure it was. Adeara answered so many of our questions. I can't imagine how overwhelmed Zynnera must be feeling.* I understood what it felt like to have the weight of so many on your shoulders. I was still struggling with the burden of being king, and I couldn't imagine what it would be like to be destined to save everyone. That would be a lot of pressure to place on anyone.

But despite the tremendous burden Adeara's information had placed on her, Zynnera had accepted it without hesitation. I knew the day I met her she was different; she was strong. And while Zynnera had often rejected my insistence of these traits, I knew they were part of who she was. I found her inner strength just as attractive as her outward beauty, and both presented far more in her than anyone I'd ever met. Add those to her genuine love for the people and it was obvious why I had grown to care for her so much.

My fingers played with the metal ring resting inside my pocket. I still hadn't found the *moment*. I hadn't told Zynnera how I felt about her. *I don't know why this is so hard? There is no doubt in my mind how I feel. Why do I hesitate? And I know she feels the same way; otherwise she wouldn't have spent the previous two nights snuggled against me.* Recalling the memories made me smile. Admittedly, I had missed feeling her body against mine last night. I was glad she was able to sleep soundly on her own, but part of me missed the opportunity to comfort and protect her.

A series of snores echoed from beneath the covers of Rhemues's bed. I laughed quietly to myself as I thought of Hachseeva. *I bet she is grateful to have a break from that.* He let out another loud snore, waking himself from his deep slumber. Rhemues sat up in his bed and looked around the room, trying to remember where he was.

He smiled upon spotting me. "Good morning!" I shook my head, pressing my finger against my lips to shush him, but it was too late. Zynnera sat up in her bed, obviously still half asleep as she rubbed her eyes. Rhemues's expression changed to a guilty frown. "Sorry, Zynnera."

She blinked at him. "What...oh, it's fine. I should probably get up anyway."

Reynard entered the cottage, greeting us with a smile. "About time the three of you woke up."

Rhemues folded his arms. "Huh! Says the man who never sleeps past sunrise! Some of us prefer to sleep in on occasion!"

Reynard laughed. "On occasion? Besides, I've told you, no amount of beauty sleep will ever help you."

Rhemues rolled his eyes. "Oh yes. Ha, ha. We are all so very amused."

Zynnera laughed hard at their banter as she pulled on each of her black boots. We had both become accustomed to their friendly raillery, but it never ceased to be a source of entertainment. *Never a dull moment with these two.* Zynnera flashed me a smile and I knew she was thinking the same thing.

"Aldous asked me to let you know breakfast is ready," said Reynard. "He's expecting all of us to join him and his family."

Rhemues chucked the blankets off of him and began pulling on his own boots as quickly as he could. "Oh! I could do with a decent breakfast. Let's go."

Once ready, we all followed Reynard to a cottage on the other side of the village. Aldous welcomed us in with a bright smile. His home was about the same size as the one we were staying in, with four beds along the north wall and a large wooden table. We were joined by his wife and two children, who ate their breakfast quickly before ecstatically leaving the cottage to play with their friends outside.

"I found someone who is willing to train you, Zynnera," said Aldous. "His name is Takias and he is a Protesta. He was quick to volunteer; I think he is impressed by you."

I felt my body grow warm and my stomach churn. *Impressed by her? What's that supposed to mean?* I recalled how Aldous had mentioned the village knew of Zynnera's defeat of Eradoma. *Well, of course he is impressed by her. Who wouldn't be?* I wasn't sure why I had become so annoyed by Aldous's statement.

"Thank you, Aldous. Any help I can get is appreciated." Zynnera placed her utensil on the empty plate in front of her. "Did he say when or where?"

Aldous nodded. "He said he would come by in an hour or so to give you time to eat. I imagine he will be here shortly."

A light knock on the door sounded as if to answer his statement. Aldous welcomed Takias into his home. I looked him over, studying his tall, muscular form and nervous expression. He appeared to be the same age as Zynnera and me, but I reminded myself that meant little as far as witches and warlocks were concerned. For all I knew, he had granted himself immortality and lived in this village for centuries.

Takias moved forward, holding out his hand to greet Zynnera. She grabbed his hand in response, ready to shake in formal greeting, but Takias quickly moved her hand to his lips and smiled. "It's a pleasure to meet you, Zynnera. The stories don't do your beauty justice."

Zynnera's face turned a bright red at his comment. I was sure she hadn't been expecting such flattery from him. My stomach twisted again, and my skin felt hot. I'd just met the man and already I was annoyed by him. I swallowed hard, trying to keep my emotions in check.

"Um...thank you," she said, pulling her hand away from him. "Um...Aldous says you can teach me more about magic. Train me?"

"Yes, of course. I'm more than happy to." There was no hiding his exuberance. Takias was clearly smitten by her. The thought hit me hard. I understood why I felt so easily annoyed by him. *Jealous. I'm jealous. Just stay calm. It doesn't matter.* The pep talk didn't seem to curb the growling monster inside me.

"OK...thank you." Zynnera was obviously uncomfortable with his boldness. It was about the only thing that was keeping me sane and from saying something I might regret. I shot a glance at Rhemues, who was biting his lip at the awkwardness Takias had created.

"Great," Takias said. "Let's you and I get going then."

I was even more annoyed now. Takias had made it clear no one else was invited to go with them. I hated the idea of Zynnera being alone with him. *Should I say something? Should I ask to go? No. I don't want to be overbearing. Zynnera needs this. I need to stop being selfish.* I wasn't sure I could, especially when Takias was so clearly interested in her. The idea that Zynnera might return his sentiments was already driving me crazy and they hadn't even left.

Zynnera looked at me anxiously. I could tell she was uncertain about the situation. There was sympathy in her eyes as she spoke. "I guess I'll see you later."

She wasn't naive. I was sure she could sense how much I disliked the idea of not going with her. It took everything I had to front a fake smile and nod in response. *I've got to get a grip. It's only for a* *few hours. She couldn't possibly fall for him...*I stopped the thought before it could finish. I realized how hypocritical I sounded. It hadn't taken *me* much longer than a few hours to fall for Zynnera. I didn't have claim over her; I hadn't even told her how I felt.

"Adeara would like to meet with her this afternoon, Takias. She asked that you be back by then if you don't mind." Aldous smiled as Zynnera stood up from the table. "Good luck."

I could feel my heart pounding as I watched her leave the cottage with him. I released a long sigh the moment the door closed. Rhemues moved to sit beside me. "It's fine. I'm sure it's fine." His words didn't really make me feel any better. *What am I supposed to do all day? Just sit here and wait for her to get back?*

Reynard was sitting across the table from me. I was sure he could sense my thoughts by the expression on my face. "My King, perhaps we should take some time to speak with Adeara while Zynnera is away."

I looked up at him. "Speak with Adeara? About what?"

Reynard folded his arms. "Well, I was thinking it may be wise to ask her about the things we discussed with King Lenear."

The murders. After everything we learned yesterday, I had almost forgotten about them. We still needed to get to the bottom of those deaths and figure out who the man in the black cloak was. It was an essential part of my plan to earn Lenear's trust for Zynnera. Talking to Adeara was definitely a good plan.

"Reynard, that is a *fantastic* idea," said Rhemues as he turned to face me. "As your royal advisor, I suggest we do that." While Reynard's suggestion was a good idea, I knew it wasn't why Rhemues was pushing me to agree. He was hoping the distraction would help me forget about Zynnera being alone with Takias. I couldn't deny I hoped he was right.

"It's settled then," I said. "Let's go speak with her."

We thanked Aldous and his wife for breakfast and made our way to Adeara's cottage. I hoped speaking with her would provide us more insight, but I also welcomed the idea of a distraction. Upon opening the door, she greeted us with a smile and gestured for us to come in.

"I've been expecting you," she said, inviting us to sit down at her table. "I suspected you had more questions."

I laughed. "More than you know, I think." I liked Adeara. She was very warm and kind. I felt at ease in her presence and sensed she was more than willing to answer any questions she could. Rhemues, Reynard, and I joined her at the wooden table.

"What is it I can help you with?" she asked.

"Before we came here, we stopped in Dunivear to speak with King Lenear. He told us of several murders that have taken place inside his city. He felt certain they were committed by someone who wields magic."

Adeara looked at me curiously for several moments before speaking. "I trust you know King Lenear isn't particularly fond of us. May I ask what made him certain these murders were the result of magic?"

"Yes, I am aware. In fact, I'm hoping to change his mind. But to answer your question, he stated that there was a witness to the last murder. A woman insisted she saw a man in a black cloak standing over the body and a blue mist surrounding him." I paused for a moment. I didn't want to sound accusatory. "I didn't believe his assumption at first either, but I can't deny it does sound as though magic is involved."

Adeara let out a long sigh and nodded. "Yes, it does sound that way. I must admit I fear you are right. There have been similar things happening here in Bogumir."

I was surprised by her response. "What do you mean, similar things?"

"We have lost a few of our people as of late. Their bodies were found by the river not far from here. There was no sign of physical harm. As you probably know, we are able to heal most physical ailments, so it is unlikely they would fall victim to disease. The most likely cause is murder, but we've had no success in gathering any information to verify this."

I felt at a loss for words. The things happening in Dunivear were also happening in Bogumir. I was more certain than ever Zynnera had felt the need to come here for a reason. Her visions could be the key to stopping the murders. I tried to recall the details she had shared with me.

"Zynnera has been having visions. I know you intend to speak with her later, but she said she witnessed murders. She said she thought a man was stealing the magical energy from those he killed. Is something like that possible?"

Adeara's expression twisted into concern, a hint of terror apparent in her wrinkled forehead. "Zynnera said this? She said this is what she saw?"

We could all feel how anxious she was. The idea that someone was stealing the power of others clearly frightened her. I nodded. "Yes, Zynnera seemed certain that was the case. But she wasn't aware of any spell that could do this, so we were uncertain."

"That is because a spell such as that would only be known or used by someone connected with the darkness. Such dark spells exist, yes. Through the ages most of us have strived to live in light, to use our magic to help others. But there are those who choose to use their magic for dark purposes. I fear this man in the black cloak could be one of them. If this is true, it is essential we get to the bottom of it, and as quickly as possible."

I knew there was far more I could tell her about Zynnera's visions and even the things Eradoma had mentioned. But I felt it best to let Zynnera have those discussions with her. She would be able to convey the details I couldn't, and those details could make all the difference. Adeara's reaction to the information made me feel uneasy. *How is it possible for this to happen in the presence of so many witches and warlocks? How did this man get away with it? And why had those who were murdered not fought back?*

"Adeara, you're a Seer. How is it that no one else has had these visions? Seen any of this before or after it happened?"

Adeara considered my words for a moment. "As I told Zynnera yesterday, a Seer has very little control over when they have a vision or the subject of those visions for that matter. I cannot answer as to why only Zynnera has seen these things. I am certain it has much to do with her destiny, a destiny we do not have a clear understanding of. As for seeing these events after they happen, well, it is not in a Seer's ability to do so."

I scrunched my face in confusion. "You mean you can't see the past? You don't have visions of things that have already happened?"

"No," she said. "We are only permitted to see the future."

My mind was racing with a thousand questions again. My thoughts returned to the cave in the forest where Zynnera had been so dramatically affected from a simple touch of the cave wall. I remembered her telling me of the flashes of Eradoma and the Vlenargans. *Those were things that had happened in the past. Perhaps being in the cave had a unique effect on her abilities? No, that can't be it.* Zynnera said she had a vision of my discussion with King Lenear. *That was a vision of the past also?*

My thoughts left me feeling even more confused. "Adeara, Zynnera has had visions of the past. She saw visions of her mother, from before she was born. And she's even had visions about me. Seen discussions she wasn't present for."

Rhemues and Reynard were staring at me with surprise. I hadn't told them Zynnera knew the subject of my discussion with King Lenear. I had been shocked to learn she'd seen the entire conversation. She knew of King Lenear's threats to end all agreements with Selvenor. I still felt guilty for both not telling her and the weight such information placed on her shoulders.

Adeara also appeared shocked by my statement. She stared down at the wooden table for several minutes, obviously deep in thoughts and questions of her own. "This ability to see events of the past, it is a very unique gift. I've never heard of anyone being able to do so before. But as the Bridge, there may be more to Zynnera's powers than any of us are aware. I wish there was more I could tell you but, unfortunately, there are some things Zynnera will have to discover on her own."

I sighed. It seemed there were always more questions than answers. I knew Zynnera felt the same way. For every one answer, two new questions seemed to emerge. I hoped one day we would be able to sort them all out. I hoped one day we would be able to put an end to all of the uncertainty. But for now, there was still much to uncover about Zynnera and her connection to the darkness that shadowed the land.

"Adeara, thank you for answering my questions...well, trying to anyway."

Adeara smiled. "You're very welcome. I only wish I could be of more help."

We all made our way to the cottage entry, ready to leave Adeara to her own thoughts. I couldn't deny my mind felt even more heavy now than it had when we first arrived. There was much to think about, and it only complicated an already complex situation.

"King Anaros." Adeara's voice stopped me before leaving her home. "May I have a moment with you?"

Rhemues nodded to me. "We'll wait for you outside."

I closed the door behind them, a little nervous at her request. Adeara continued to smile at me, her eyes soft as she proceeded. "Zynnera...you care for her."

I could feel my body shaking at her blunt observation. *It really must be obvious if even Adeara has noticed.* I sighed. "I...um...yes. I do care about her."

Adeara shook her head, smiling even more. "No, I mean you *really* care for her. You love her."

I bit my lip. I knew there was no point in trying to evade her question. "Yes, I love her."

Adeara walked towards me. "You shouldn't worry yourself over her spending time with Takias." I scrunched my eyebrows. *How*

does she know that? How does she know I was worried about it?
Adeara laughed at my confusion. "I could sense it the moment you walked in. But don't worry, I also sense Zynnera is very loyal to you. Those feelings are mutual."

As awkward as it was for Adeara, an almost complete stranger, to tell me Zynnera loved me, I still felt giddy over the revelation. I desperately wanted her statement to be true. "I intend to ask her," I blurted without thinking. "To marry me, I mean."

Adeara nodded. "I suspected as much. You play with your pocket more than you realize."

My eyes moved immediately to the metal ring resting inside my clothing. I laughed. She was probably right. I imagined I did play with the contents of my pocket subconsciously on a regular basis. After all, proposing to Zynnera seemed to be a regular subject of my thoughts.

Adeara placed her hand on my shoulder. I stared into the blue eyes partially hidden behind strands of long silvery hair. "You are good for her and your destinies are intertwined. That much I can see. But you should tell her yourself."

"You say our destinies are intertwined. Have...have you seen something? A vision of our future?" I could feel my hands shaking nervously as I asked the question. I wanted her to answer now more than ever before.

Adeara stared back at me with a cunning smile. "It's not always best to share visions of the future, King Anaros. But let's just say I have a good feeling about the two of you."

It definitely wasn't the answer I was hoping for. I wanted a clear confirmation that there was more to our destiny than finding the

Virgàm and saving everyone from the darkness, but I had no such luck. One thing, however, was becoming very clear to me. My love for Zynnera was obvious and apparently so were her feelings for me. This clarity alone should be enough to push me into being honest with her, into being open. But I still hesitated, and I was beginning to understand why. Part of me was afraid, yes, but another part of me wondered if the disclosure was best for Zynnera. She had found people like her, a place to be who she was without fear of rejection and despise. Zynnera could be happy in Bogumir, living among people who understood and could help her. The thought left my heart aching, but I knew it was true. The only problem was if Zynnera remained here in the forest, we could never be together. I was king of Selvenor; I *had* to go back. But I wasn't sure it was right for Zynnera to return, and the idea was already beginning to haunt me.

CHAPTER
~ *Sixteen* ~

Everything was peaceful as we made our way through the dense woods. The familiar sounds of the forest seemed to put my mind at ease, something I desperately needed. This journey had been long and exhausting, and there was still a long way to go to find all of the answers I needed. Being surrounded by other witches and warlocks had made me feel both accepted and inadequate. Most of them had decades, if not centuries, of experience practicing magic, and I was only just beginning to understand how to use my powers.

Takias was walking just a few steps ahead of me. I had promised myself I would keep a little distance between him and myself, especially after the awkward moment at Aldous's cottage. Takias had shown interest in me, and not in a soft friendship kind of way. I could sense immediately how jealous Anaros had become of him.

Part of me liked that he had responded with annoyance at Takias's obvious attempt to flatter me. It felt wrong that his jealousy had made me happy, but knowing Anaros cared about me enough to have those feelings only confirmed I meant more to him than a friend.

It would be so much easier if he would just tell me. Why doesn't he just tell me? Maybe I make him too nervous? At times it seemed I did. I could recall several occasions where talking to me had him stuttering and stumbling over his own words. The memories made me chuckle to myself. Then there were the moments he pulled me close without hesitation. It was in those moments that I felt the depth of his affection for me. *But he hasn't said it. He hasn't ever told me how he feels.* I sighed. If only he had. Then I could honestly explain to Takias why I felt the need to withdraw from him and his compliments.

Perhaps it won't be as bad as I think? If I can keep him focused on teaching me, there'll be no room for his attempt at courtship. I doubted the thoughts as soon as they swept through my mind. Takias had been anything but subtle, even in front of everyone in the cottage. There was no reason to think he would be here in the forest, where we were completely alone.

After several minutes we arrived in a large, grassy clearing at the base of a mountain pass. Looking out into the meadow, the land was exceptionally beautiful. The tall mountain peaks towered over the lush, green plain below, both resting beneath an open blue sky. *This place is so beautiful. Like something from a story.* Part of me envied the people of the village for having such a picturesque place to live, not to mention secluded from those who feared their magical powers.

Takias turned to face me, a wide smile forming across his face. "Well, this is my favorite place to practice or think...or do anything really." He laughed. "I thought you could use a bit of peace and quiet. Somewhere away from everything and everyone else."

I wasn't sure how to respond to his comment. I did enjoy being in the quiet of the forest and meadow, but I hadn't felt the need to escape *anyone* in particular from the village. *He's referring to Anaros.* I realized he was trying to assess my response to his assumption. "It's a beautiful place, but I don't mind the village or anyone there in the slightest."

Takias studied my expression carefully. He was trying to decide how to take my answer. *Maybe it's a good idea to keep him guessing. Keep him distracted.* "So, should we get started?"

Takias nodded. "Yes, of course. Well, let's start with you showing me what you know. Then if there's anything I can teach you, we can go from there."

I didn't really need to show him every spell I could perform. I reached into the satchel and pulled *The Tahetya* from within its cloth walls. He seemed surprised by my possession of the book. "Here," I said, handing it to him. "Everything in here is what I know."

Takias held the book in his hand and blinked at me with a shocked expression. "Where did you get this? And you know all of the spells in it?"

The Tahetya was no small book. It likely contained the incantations to over a hundred spells. Most of them were small and simple, but it also contained more difficult spells such as the *Impotus.* I'd been through the book, studied each page, so many times in search of answers, I had since memorized its contents.

"It belonged to my...family." It was the only response I could think of that didn't involve the explanation of my entire life.

"And you know them all?" he repeated as he flipped through the pages with excitement.

"Well...yes...I mean I'm sure you know just as many, don't you?" I knew the answer from his lingering shocked expression.

Takias laughed. "No, Zynnera. Most of the magic I know I've learned from those who taught me and only by them showing me how to do it. Books like this are incredibly rare. And even with it, memorizing the entire thing...well, I'm just impressed."

I gulped. The last thing I had wanted to do was impress him more. I'd never felt I excelled in memorizing spells, but apparently it was yet another abnormal thing about me. I wondered if it was because I was this *Bridge* from the prophecy Adeara told me about yesterday. I hadn't felt adequate enough to be considered someone destined to save everyone from the darkness, but she seemed certain my golden aura positively identified me as such.

Takias was flipping through the pages as though trying to decide whether there was, in fact, anything he could teach me. "And you've successfully performed all of these?"

"Uh...well, no. I mean, some of them I haven't fully projected. And, of course, there are some I've had no need to attempt."

He rubbed his mouth. "Alright, well, let's start there then. Tell me one you haven't been able to project."

I moved to stand beside him and my heart did a flip as I felt his breath against my skin. "OK, there's this one." I turned the page to a spell I'd practiced a handful of times.

"The *Illustris*. Well, at least you picked one I know so I don't have to look like a complete fool." Takias smiled at me.

I laughed. I suddenly felt more at ease around him, connected to him. I found myself staring into his big brown eyes and returning his smile. Takias was certainly handsome with his golden brown hair and light brown skin. My gaze lingered long enough to make me nervous. I turned back to *The Tahetya*. "I...um...from my understanding, the spell creates an orb of light. One that the caster can control. I imagine it would be useful at night or in caves...and such."

Takias chuckled. "Yes, it is quite useful. Let me see you try, and then we can figure out why it hasn't worked for you."

Closing my eyes, I repeated the incantation in a soft whisper. My golden aura surrounded my hands and slowly formed into a small yellow orb of light. As soon as I opened my eyes, however, the orb dissipated into the air. "See. I can form it, but I've never been able to maintain it more than a few seconds."

Takias nodded. "I see. What are you thinking about when you say the incantation?"

"What am I...thinking about?" His question left me perplexed. *Is there something I'm supposed to be thinking about? I thought just focusing on the words was the proper procedure.*

Takias laughed. "Yes. Hmmm...let me see if I can explain. Our magic is directly connected to our emotions, Zynnera. The more in touch our spells are with those emotions, the more powerful they will be. Does that make sense?"

I thought about what Takias was telling me. It made a great deal of sense. When I had faced Eradoma, I was fearful my magic would never be enough to stop her. I held my own against her power for a while, but it took everything I had to defend myself from her assaults. But when she unleashed a direct attack on Anaros, something changed. Something felt different. It was in that moment I felt more magical power surging through my body than I had ever felt before. My response to her attack on someone I loved had sparked deep emotion inside me, the desire to protect at all cost. I now understood why I was able to defeat her. In essence, her attempt to harm someone I cared about resulted in her own downfall.

"It does make sense," I said. "But how do I connect with a spell? I mean, I understand if I'm defending someone. But something as simple as this?"

"Our minds are quite magical in and of themselves. We can recall memories and those memories often retain the feelings we experience during them. Something like this, a light, needs a warm memory. It needs something that evokes the feeling of happiness inside you."

I nodded. "Alright, I'll try again." I closed my eyes and began reciting the incantation. I allowed my mind to fill with a memory, one I knew would provide the feelings Takias described. I thought of Hachseeva and Rhemues; how they had welcomed me into their family. I thought of my niece and nephews. I loved them all more than I could ever describe. I *loved* having a family.

As the warmth of those memories flowed through me, I opened my eyes. A bright yellow orb was hovering in the air in front of me. *I can't believe it! I did it!* I waved my hand, moving the orb through the air with ease. I couldn't stop myself from smiling.

"Well done! You see, emotion makes all the difference! For example, if you were to attempt the *Morso...*"

I interrupted him with a stern seriousness in my tone. "I've no intention of *ever* using that spell. Ever."

Takias seemed to understand the sincerity of my words. "Right, of course not. I only meant it as an example." I nodded, but the mention of the spell admittedly had me on edge. The last thing I wanted was memories of my vision flooding my mind.

We spent the rest of the morning practicing various spells from *The Tahetya.* Takias seemed to be learning as much as I was. I couldn't deny he had helped me in a way no one else had, and it felt nice to have some guidance from someone who both understood and related to me. Once the sun had reached its highest point in the sky, we returned to Bogumir. Takias walked with me to Adeara's home.

"You improved so much today," he said. "I know I already said I was impressed, but I'm even more so now. You're a fast learner, Zynnera."

I could feel my face flushing bright red. I had never felt so torn. His flattery was appreciated, I couldn't deny that. It was nice to connect with someone who could use magic. But part of me felt guilty for enjoying his company so much. I didn't want to betray Anaros or the feelings I had for him.

"Thank you, Takias. I truly appreciate all of your help."

Takias beamed a bright smile. "Of course." He stared nervously at the ground just outside Adeara's home. "Would...would you like to get together tomorrow...to practice, I mean?"

My mind wanted to answer immediately, but my heart hesitated.

Why do I feel like this is such a dangerous road to travel? There's no reason for me to feel guilty. It's just training. Nothing more. Despite my attempts to convince myself, I feared it wasn't the truth.

I nodded gently. "OK. Tomorrow morning?"

Takias nodded and the sunlight caused a light shimmer on the hairs in his beard. "Tomorrow then."

I smiled, then turned to knock on Adeara's door. I could hear Takias's footsteps as he walked away from me. *What am I doing? Was that really a good idea?* My stomach felt nauseous thinking about it. I already had enough on my mind, and adding this did nothing but make it worse.

Adeara smiled upon opening the door. "Come in, Zynnera."

I was grateful to be alone with her in the cottage. I needed to escape from everyone else right now. I sat down across from her at the wooden table, my eyes staring out the small window behind her.

"Is everything OK?" she asked.

I smiled, shaking my head. "Yes, fine. Admittedly, a bit overwhelming."

Adeara nodded. "I can only imagine how you must be feeling. But perhaps we can shed some light on these visions you've been having. King Anaros mentioned they were quite dark. That you've seen murders."

My heart pounded hard inside my chest. "Anaros...told you that?"

"Yes, he came to see me this morning. I think, perhaps, he was seeking a distraction. But he did tell me about the murders in Dunivear and those in your nightmares."

I nodded. I didn't even know where to begin. *I suppose from the beginning is best.* "It all started about six months ago. We were in

the forest, searching for a way to defeat Eradoma. We found this
cave with strange markings on the walls. When I touched one of the
symbols, I had these flashes...visions, I suppose. I saw a man. He
repeated this phrase over and over again. He asked me to bring him
the Virgàm."

Adeara studied me curiously with a great deal of concern on her
face. She nodded for me to continue. "Then I started having this
second vision. It was slightly different each time, but there was
always a man in a black cloak. It looked like he stole the powers of
other witches and warlocks, and then he..." My voice had become
shaky. It was hard to describe the details without the memories
flooding my mind. Everything about those visions felt very real and
they terrified me. Recounting them only forced me to relive the
nightmares.

"Murdered them," whispered Adeara. She looked at me with
heavy sympathy in her eyes. I nodded, trying to fight back the tears.
Adeara reached across the table and grabbed my hand. "It's OK,
Zynnera. It's OK to cry. You don't have to hold it inside."

I let my tears flow from my eyes freely. I wasn't sure I could hold
them back even if I wanted to. Something about talking with Adeara
made me feel comfortable enough to let them fall, to feel safe in my
vulnerability. "I'm terrified," I whispered. "I want them to stop."

Adeara sighed. "I can imagine, Zynnera. But I fear until the
darkness is conquered, they will continue to haunt you."

I nodded. I'd known all along there was little chance of being rid
of my nightmares. Intuition told me they could not be cast away with
a simple spell. But I held hope of finding some sort of relief,
anything to help me get through them. I wiped the tears from my

face, regaining my composure.

"Are there any more details you can tell me from this vision where people are murdered? Anything? Even small details could help us identify the culprit."

I took a deep breath. "Um...well, I'm always standing along the banks of a river, somewhere in a forest. I can hear loud water in the distance...a waterfall, I think."

"A waterfall?" Adeara seemed lost in her own thoughts. "Zynnera, when I spoke with Anaros earlier, I told him something similar to what is happening in Dunivear is also happening here in Bogumir. Several villagers have come up missing. We found each of their bodies on the bank of the river. There is also a waterfall nearby. I believe your visions were of these people. A witness to their deaths."

"Here?" My voice was shaky again. I had hoped coming here would help me escape my nightmares, not lead me right to them. The idea of being anywhere near the man in the black cloak terrified me beyond comprehension.

"I'm afraid so. If what you say is true, about this man stripping them of their powers, then things are far worse than I feared. I've sensed the presence of dark magic and now I am certain it is among us."

"Wait, you think the man is here...in Bogumir? As in, he lives here?" I couldn't comprehend what she was saying...or perhaps I didn't want to. The idea that the killer could be in the village or that I had even met him shook me to my core.

"It's very likely, yes. But I have no suspects that come to mind. Most of these people have lived here for decades, many their entire lives. I hope I am wrong, Zynnera, I do." Adeara released a heavy sigh. "But I fear I am not."

"What do we do? How can we figure out who is doing this? Better yet, *why* is he doing this? I don't understand how anyone could do such a thing." I stared down at the table. No matter where I turned there seemed to be more death, and magic always appeared to be involved. I had always believed magic could be used for good, but what use was it if there were those out there using it for evil? Perhaps it would be better if no one had magic at all?

"All we can do is be vigilant. Keep watch, look out for one another. And if your visions present any more details, let me know straight away. I fear the motive behind these attacks. Whoever is doing this seeks power and, at the moment, they are getting it. I don't think they will stop, and that puts us all in danger."

There was one more detail I needed to tell her, and it was important. "Adeara, when the man steals their power, he uses a dagger. It's almost as if he is storing their magical energy inside it. When he drains them, their aura sort of disappears inside a gem on the hilt. It's a blue gem and the man's aura is..."

Adeara interrupted me. "Blue." I nodded in response. She seemed to understand what I was getting at. "The man in the cloak is a Protesta. Well, it certainly narrows down the list of possible suspects, but there are hundreds of Protesta here. And that's assuming it is, in fact, someone who lives here in the village."

"Yes, but at least it gives us a place to start," I said. "Something to go on."

Adeara nodded. "I agree. You should go now, Zynnera. Take a break from all of this. You've earned that much. But we should keep the details of your vision quiet for now. At least until we have more to go on."

"I understand," I said. "I'll let you know if I see anything else."

I started towards the door, but Adeara's voice stopped me. "Zynnera, one last thing before you go. I know how afraid you are of your visions, and I don't blame you after the things you've seen. But you must face them. You must find a way to fight against the darkness, even within your own mind."

I flashed her a final smile. "I'll do my best. "

My mind raced as I left the cottage and proceeded down the main paved street to our cottage. Everything Adeara and I had discussed weighed heavily on my thoughts. The burden on my shoulders only seemed to grow with the additional information. I wondered how much more I could carry before I completely broke down. I never imagined my life would become so complicated. Six months ago, my only thought was how I would manage to defeat Eradoma and free Selvenor from her evil reign. Now I faced another darkness, one I couldn't even see. I didn't know how I could overcome such a force when I couldn't even keep it from breeching my own mind. *I have to push forward. I have to do everything I can to fight it. I have to try.* It was all I could do, and I hoped it would be enough.

CHAPTER
Seventeen

Time seemed to move by at a painfully sluggish pace as I sat at the wooden table inside our cottage. I caught myself looking out one of the small windows every few minutes, hoping to see Zynnera walking towards our temporary home. Every second that passed tore my thoughts away from reality and pushed me towards my worst fears. *What is Zynnera doing? Is she still with Takias? Maybe she would rather spend time learning magic with him than come back here? How long have they been gone anyway?*

I could feel my leg shaking with nerves. *I've got to get a grip on myself. This is absolutely ridiculous.* However, it didn't matter how much I wanted to push the thoughts from my mind, I knew I couldn't, at least not for any substantial amount of time. I was jealous of Takias, and it was clear the idea of Zynnera being with him was driving me into insanity. The sun had already reached its highest point in the sky hours ago. *She was supposed to meet with Adeara this afternoon. She should be back by now. Perhaps she is with Adeara now? Maybe I should go check? NO!*

I stood up from the table and moved to stare out the little window at the streets outside. Rhemues approached me from behind, his tone filled with sympathy and concern. "I'm sure she'll be back soon, Anaros. You really need to stop worrying."

I knew he was only trying to make me feel better, but it wasn't working. The truth was I was feeling exceedingly torn right now. From the moment we entered the village and the people witnessed Zynnera's magic, they had accepted her. This was something she had never experienced in Selvenor from our own people. I had been happy to see her at ease, to be able to be herself without fear. Zynnera seemed content here, or at least more so than she did at home.

It wasn't that I didn't want such happiness for her. I wanted it more than anything, but I feared what finding such happiness would mean. Living in Bogumir could provide Zynnera a life she deserved. As much as I hated to admit it, living in Bogumir was a far better option for her than living in Selvenor.

But my mind knew what such thoughts meant. If Zynnera were to remain in Bogumir, there was little chance we could ever be together. Staying here would mean an end to whatever relationship we had developed over the last six months. The selfish part of me didn't want her to stay. I wanted her to return to Selvenor. I wanted to ask her to marry me. But should I? I felt like I knew the answer and it wasn't the one I wanted.

Rhemues placed his hand on my shoulder. He knew me better than anyone and I was sure he could sense my despair. "Anaros, you're letting this get to you. Really. Zynnera isn't going to just run off with Takias."

I shook my head. "Perhaps she should. Perhaps it would be better if she did...easier."

The expression on Rhemues's face reflected his confusion. "What do you mean, it would be better? How would that be better?"

I sighed. "Rhemues, maybe Zynnera should stay here. She would be with people who understand her. Who can help her."

Rhemues shook his head in frustration. "No. No way. I know what you are thinking, Anaros, and I wholeheartedly disagree. Zynnera may be with people who are like her right now, but in Selvenor she is with people who love her! She's with her family!"

Accepting this would not be easy for me. It would not be easy for Rhemues. My mind wandered to Hachseeva. I hated the idea of having to tell her that Zynnera had remained in Dunivear. I couldn't fathom any conversation that would convince her it was best for Zynnera to stay. *How can I make them understand? I know it's the right thing to do, but...*

It would be hard to convince everyone else when I wasn't sure I could even convince myself. I turned to face Rhemues, tears starting to form in my eyes. "Rhemues. I think she needs to stay. I think it's what's best for her."

Rhemues shook his head again. "No, what's best is her being with people who care about her."

"The people here will take care of her. They will care about her. I think some of them already do."

Rhemues raised his voice, spouting his frustration. "I can't believe this. I can't believe you would willingly just leave her here!"

"You think this is easy for me? You think I want to do this? Of course I don't! It's the last thing I want to do!" I felt my skin grow hot. I knew Rhemues would not agree with the idea of leaving Zynnera, but he had to see the logic behind my decision.

Reynard was watching us both carefully. I sensed he was uncertain how he felt about the conflict. "My King, we've only been here a day. Perhaps we should hold off on making any drastic decisions until we know more."

I moved back to the table to sit down, hoping it would calm my emotions. "The longer I stay here, the longer I stay with her, the harder this is going to be. I can't let my selfish desires be the reason Zynnera remains unhappy."

"Unhappy? Really?" Rhemues folded his arms. "Do you honestly believe Zynnera is unhappy? For the first time in *years,* she has a family. People who actually care about her. You think she'll want to just give all of that up for a bunch of people she doesn't even know?"

I drummed my fingers on the table while I listened to his rebuke. "I don't think she'll want to, no."

Rhemues looked shocked by my response. "So, what? Are you planning to just up and leave? Planning to banish her so she'll stay here? Do tell, Anaros. What exactly are you planning? Because I think I have the right to know."

He leaned forward onto the table across from me, propping his body up with his hands. Looking into his eyes, I could feel his anger. I could feel his frustration. But I didn't blame him for reacting this way. I hated the way I felt and wished I could push it from my mind completely. "I don't know," I answered honestly. "I don't know what I'm going to do."

"But you're considering it? You're actually considering this?" Rhemues tightened his hands into fists, clearly trying to control his rage. "As your advisor, I highly recommend against this, Anaros."

"Well, you're not exactly unbiased, are you?" My tone came across a little more aggressive than I intended. I could tell the comment bothered him. I hated upsetting him, making him angry with me, but it might be the only way to end his arguing. "You said it yourself, remember? You're too biased to give me advice when it comes to Zynnera."

Rhemues nodded in irritation. "Right, well, I guess I am. But I can't help but wonder if you've given *any* thought to asking Zynnera how she feels about this? Or maybe you just prefer to make the decision for her? Taking away her choice makes you no better than the people of Selvenor!"

That was too far. I stood up from the table, taking a few steps to stand in front of him. "That's not true. You know I would never do that to her!"

Rhemues laughed. "Funny, because it's *exactly* what you're doing. But by all means, Anaros, be king. Demand she stay here. Exercise your authority."

I slammed my fist onto the table. "This has nothing to do with me wanting to exercise authority and you know that!"

Reynard stood up, staying a few feet away from us but ready to step in. Our heated debate was headed to a more physical confrontation. I didn't want to fight with him but would if it came to that.

"Tell me then, Anaros. What is it then? Why do you want to leave her here?"

"Because I love her!" I shouted.

Just as the words escaped my mouth, the door to the cottage flung open. Zynnera stood in the entry, staring at the three of us with a doleful expression. I stared at the floor, wondering how much of the argument she had actually heard. The silence seemed to drag on for hours as each of us waited for someone to speak.

Rhemues was still fuming. "Well, if you love her, then maybe you should ask Zynnera what she thinks, instead of presuming you know what's best for her." I winced at his words. He turned and stormed past Zynnera and out of the cottage.

I folded my arms, still staring at the floor to avoid eye contact with her. I could hear Reynard release a heavy sigh. "I think perhaps it would be best to give the two of you the room." Reynard proceeded to leave the cottage. He flashed Zynnera a sympathetic smile as he closed the door behind him.

I could feel Zynnera's eyes on me as we stood there in the silence. I wanted to say something, but I didn't know where to begin. I was still fuming about Rhemues's comments. *How could he think any of that? Exercise my authority?* And it wasn't just those words that had me frustrated. Rhemues had clearly stated that I loved Zynnera, intentionally forcing the words out of his mouth so she could hear. *This isn't how I wanted to tell her. This isn't how I wanted her to hear those words.* But it was too late. Zynnera had heard them, and I wasn't sure what to say to her.

She moved closer, stopping just in front of me as she attempted to gain my attention. I continued staring at the floor, still hoping to find the right thing to say to her. Even though she'd already heard Rhemues state the words I'd been holding back for so long, part of me still wanted to say them directly to her. But I knew I could no longer allow myself to do so. Saying them now would only make things harder for both of us. I didn't want to add to the heartache. I didn't want to add to the pain.

After a few more minutes of silence, Zynnera touched my arm. I allowed myself to look up at her, fighting against the tears forming in my eyes. She looked back at me with sympathy and concern, her blue eyes seeming to stare directly into my soul. "Anaros, what's wrong? Please tell me what's going on."

I released a shaky sigh. *I have to tell her. I have to tell her I'm leaving.* "Zynnera, I need to go back to Selvenor."

"Yes, I know we have to go back..."

I shook my head at the word *we.* "Not we, Zynnera." I hated myself for thinking it, for saying it. But I knew it was the right thing to do.

She stared at me for a moment. I could see her eyes glazing over. "You think I should stay." She bit her lip. "You want me to stay."

I shook my head again. "Not want." I paused. *I need to explain. I need her to know this isn't what I want at all.* "I just...Zynnera, you could be so much happier here. With people who are like you. Who understand. Who won't judge you."

She looked away from me. I could tell her mind was racing. I wasn't sure if continuing to talk would make things better or worse. She let out a long sigh, turning to face me again. "I don't know. I don't know if I want to stay here. I understand what you are saying, and I know it's coming from...because you care. But I just don't know."

I nodded. "Just promise me you'll think about it. Please." I didn't want to force her to stay. I wanted her to make that decision on her own. But I feared she wouldn't because of how she felt about me. The last thing I wanted was for Zynnera to give up a life of potential happiness because of me.

"OK," she whispered. "I'll think about it."

"I think I need some fresh air." I moved past her and left the cottage. It felt cold, the way I left her standing there alone in the room. I hated it. I hated everything about the situation. But if forcing a cold tone was how I could convince her to stay, I would put on the facade.

Rhemues and Reynard were standing only a few feet away from the cottage. "We're leaving in the morning," I announced, not giving them so much as a quick glance as I walked past them. I imagined my tone had made Rhemues even more angry with me, but it didn't matter. I knew what needed to be done. As much as I wanted to fight the idea that this was best for Zynnera, I just couldn't. I loved her too much to not want the best for her.

I continued down the paved street until I met the edge of the forest. I stopped just in front of the tree line to catch my breath. I'd been fighting back tears since my conversation with Rhemues began, and I was still struggling to keep them at bay. *I've got to be strong. I've got to let her go.* Convincing myself was proving to be difficult.

The sound of rustling leaves interrupted my thoughts. I could see a figure leaving the woods. I recognized them as soon as they left the shadows of the forest and entered the clearing of the village. The man stopped abruptly upon seeing me standing alone. His expression shifted to concern as he studied my face.

"Is everything alright, King Anaros?" asked Takias.

Takias was probably the last person I wanted to speak to right now. Just seeing him only made me feel worse as the monster of jealousy growled inside me. *With me gone, he'll be free to make whatever move he wants. He'll have Zynnera all to himself.* I could feel my skin growing hot again. *It doesn't matter. This is where Zynnera needs to be. Maybe knowing there is someone here who cares for her is a good thing.* I didn't particularly like the thought, but I accepted it. Maybe Takias could help? Maybe it would help me feel better about leaving her here.

I sighed. "I'm going back to Selvenor tomorrow."

"Oh," he said, still holding a bit of confusion in his tone. "So soon?"

I could tell his question wasn't concern for me leaving, but rather Zynnera. He wanted to know if she was leaving too. "Yes, well, I do have a kingdom to run."

Takias nodded. "Of course. I shouldn't have expected such a long visit from all of you."

He was pushing for the information he wanted, trying to be subtle. It annoyed me, but I knew I needed to be blunt with him. "Takias, I think Zynnera should remain here in the village. I've asked her to consider it. I don't know what her decision will be, but if she does decide to stay..." I stopped, staring down at the ground in front of me. It was difficult to force myself to say the words, to ask for his help. "Would you keep an eye on her? Look out for her?"

"Absolutely, Your Highness. It would be my honor. You needn't worry; Zynnera will be in good hands here."

I wasn't sure his reply made me feel any better, but I nodded. "Thank you."

We stared at each other for several long moments. I wondered what he was thinking. I imagined his mind was jumping for joy at the idea of me leaving and Zynnera staying here in the village. My stomach felt like it was tied in a knot. I still didn't know if all of this was really the right thing to do. There were still people being murdered, a mystery we had never solved. Leaving Zynnera in the middle of it left me feeling uneasy, but I knew she could take care of herself. Being surrounded by other witches and warlocks wasn't a bad thing either.

"Just keep her safe," I said finally. "I don't want anything to happen to her."

Takias smiled as though he understood all too well the depth behind my words. "I give you my word, etched in stone."

He moved past me and proceeded down the stone paved street and into the village. I remained by the forest edge, lost in my own thoughts. There were still so many unanswered questions. My mind wandered back to Dunivear and King Lenear. *What am I going to tell him? I promised to bring him information when we returned?* There wasn't much I could give him. The only thing we had learned was that there seemed to be attacks happening in Bogumir as well. I wasn't sure this information would be of any use or concern to Lenear.

I knew Zynnera would continue to work towards finding an answer even after my departure. I knew she would figure it all out. She could still find a way to stop the man in the black cloak from killing more people. *Perhaps she can rekindle a relationship between those who use magic and the people of Dunivear by putting an end to the murders?* It appeared to be another good reason for her to stay. If Zynnera could put an end to the hostility between them, everyone would be safer. Even Selvenor would benefit from her remaining here. Although I despised thinking of it that way, things would certainly be less complicated.

It's for the best, I know it is. And she'll be happy. I want her to be happy. But would I be? I wasn't sure I'd ever be able to move on, to let her go. I loved her more than I ever thought possible. My heart was already aching at the idea of never seeing her again. Tomorrow was going to be the most difficult day of my life, and I wasn't sure I was ready to face it.

CHAPTER
~*Eighteen*~

The ceiling of the small cottage was void of anything interesting, but I couldn't seem to remove my gaze. There was so much going through my mind I barely noticed when Reynard and Rhemues both entered the room an hour after Anaros had stormed out. They stayed quiet, leaving me to my thoughts as I lay in my bed, mulling over the argument I had walked in on.

Anaros said it. He said it out loud. I heard him. He said that he loved me. I had opened the door just in time to catch the words leaving his mouth. His feud with Rhemues had been a heated one, and now that I knew the topic of their contempt, I understood why. Anaros felt it would be best for me to remain in Bogumir, and Rhemues had obviously found the idea unacceptable. I wondered what Reynard thought of the whole ordeal. Had he taken a stance at all on the matter or stood quietly by while Anaros and Rhemues battled one another's opinions?

I sighed. *I guess it doesn't really matter, does it? Anaros asked me to consider staying and I promised I would do so.* My eyes remained fixated on the wooden beams that crossed overhead. *The only problem is I'm torn. I don't know what I want to do.* Staying here wasn't a bad idea, if I was to be perfectly honest with myself. To live among other witches and warlocks would be like a dream. I'd be with people who understood me, understood how I felt. They knew what it was like to be hated by those who couldn't wield magic. The people of Bogumir had created their own safe haven in the forest of Arnfell, one that didn't rely on much of anything from the outside world. In Bogumir I would be safe from the harsh judgments of Selvenor. I would be free to use my magic without fear of repercussion.

But that wasn't the only positive for remaining in the village. I knew that if I was no longer in the picture, Anaros would have a far easier time forming relationships with other kingdoms. He would be able to focus on the people instead of focusing on how to convince them to accept me. King Lenear had already made it clear he was not interested in being allies with a kingdom that welcomed magic. I imagined many other leaders would feel the same way. But if I stepped aside, there would be no reason for them to not make such agreements, and Selvenor would finally begin to prosper as it once had.

It was all logical, the benefits to staying in Bogumir. My mind seemed to agree with every thought. But it was my heart that held me back. No matter how sensible it was for me to stay here, my emotions fought against the idea. There was no way I could deny how I felt about Anaros. My heart had become too invested to just push those feelings from my mind. I knew it was selfishness that urged me to return to Selvenor, and I wasn't sure how to eliminate the deepest desires of my heart.

I knew Anaros was struggling with it as much as I was. He resented even asking me to consider staying. I could see it in his eyes, all the pain and regret. There was no way for him to hide it at this point. And after listening to him say the words I'd been longing to hear for so long, I wasn't sure I was strong enough to turn my back on them.

It's not just Anaros I would be losing. The thought sent a sharp pain through my heart. Staying here meant I may never see Rhemues and Hachseeva again. I may never see my niece and nephews. *And the baby. I would never get the chance to meet it.* I bit my lip in an effort to fight back my tears. After years of being alone, I had finally found family, people who cared about me. And I cared about them more than anything in the world. *How can I leave all of that behind? Give it up so willingly. I know I was planning to leave Selvenor on my own, but....*

This felt different. Perhaps it was the idea of not being able to say goodbye to people I loved? Or perhaps I just wasn't strong enough to go through with my plan, despite my efforts to convince myself otherwise. *It doesn't matter now; I have to make a decision. They are leaving in the morning and I have to decide what I'm going to do.* I closed my eyes, allowing a few tears to stream down my face and land on the blankets below. *Stay.* The voice came clear and stern. I was certain it was not my own subconscious. The word only made me cry more. I knew it was right. The voice in my head was right and I needed to listen. But it didn't make things any easier.

I rolled over so my face was hidden from Rhemues's and Reynard's view. I didn't want them to see me quietly sobbing into the folds of the blankets.

When my eyes opened again to the light of morning, I realized I had cried myself to sleep, passing out from the sheer mental exhaustion the previous day had brought. I sat up quickly, feeling frantic as my eyes darted around the room.

Rhemues was sitting at the wooden table, his expression filled with sorrow. Both Reynard and Anaros were nowhere to be seen. I wondered if Anaros had even returned at all last night. I got up and walked to the table, sitting down beside Rhemues. He didn't look at me, almost as though doing so might cause a complete meltdown to ensue.

"Rhemues," I whispered. "Rhemues, please look at me."

He turned to face me with an apologetic expression. "I'm sorry, Zynnera. I'm just...not feeling like myself today."

I sighed. "I know you and Anaros don't agree about whether or not I should stay here."

"Of course I don't agree!" He raised his voice for a moment, then paused to calm down before continuing. "I don't want you to stay here. I want you to come home. Come home to your family. I don't understand why he feels the need to abandon you."

I shook my head. "That's not what he's doing. You know that, Rhemues." Rhemues sighed in frustration. He knew I was right. Anaros would never just abandon me. His reasons for asking me to consider staying made sense. I knew Rhemues understood that; it just didn't make the idea any easier to swallow.

Rhemues muttered under his breath, still agitated by my words. "If he really loves you the way he says he does, he would never ask you to stay."

I bit my lip in an effort to fight back the tears. "I know he loves me. *You* know he loves me. And it makes this incredibly hard for me...and for him. Rhemues, Anaros is only trying to do what he thinks is best *because* he loves me."

Rhemues looked at me, raising his eyebrows. "Why does he get to decide what's best?"

I gently shook my head. "He left the decision up to me, Rhemues. It's my decision and...I think he's right. I need to stay."

Rhemues shook his head in disbelief, moving his gaze towards the small window. He couldn't accept my decision and I knew he was holding Anaros responsible for it. I placed my hand over his. "I need you to put your anger aside, Rhemues. If not for Anaros, then do it for me. He *needs* you. He needs someone who can help him navigate through all of this."

"I can't, Zynnera. I can't do this...not when I disagree with it."

"I'm not asking you to agree," I said. "Or even understand." I paused for a moment to think. I needed Rhemues to accept that this decision was mine. The last thing I wanted was for them to leave in contempt of one another. I didn't want Anaros to be alone. "The day before we left, I heard a voice in my head. At first I thought it was my own subconscious, but it's not. It's something else. That voice told me to go to Dunivear. There was a reason I needed to come here, Rhemues. Almost as though someone is guiding me."

Rhemues stared at me, a little concerned by my confession.

"Does Anaros know? About this voice in your head?"

I shook my head. "No. I never told him. I didn't want him to worry. But that same voice is telling me to stay." A few tears trickled from my eyes and down my cheeks. "I don't know why, Rhemues, but there is a reason I need to stay. And maybe it's for a short time, maybe it's not. I don't know. But it's clear to me that staying in Bogumir is what I *need* to do."

I watched a few tears escape his eyes. "What am I supposed to tell Hachseeva?"

I smiled through my tears. "The truth. And tell her I love her. And I miss her."

He nodded, fighting to retain what little composure he had left. I felt horrible for putting him in such a position. I knew how upset Hachseeva and the children would be, but I couldn't deny the voice in my head. It had been clear about coming to Dunivear, and it had now clearly told me to stay. *There must be a reason. There must be.*

"Rhemues, I need you to promise me something," I said, staring into his grey, teary eyes. "I need you to promise me you'll help him. Help him forget about me. Move on. He needs to focus on Selvenor, and to do that he has to let me go." Rhemues started to shake his head, but I couldn't allow him to argue. "Please...please do this for me."

Rhemues let out a long, shaky sigh. "I'll try, Zynnera, but I can't promise you more than that."

It would have to suffice. It wasn't fair of me to ask any of this of him. But I couldn't stand the idea of Anaros wallowing in depression and alone. Knowing Rhemues would do what he could to console him only numbed the ache inside my heart, but it was better than nothing at all.

The door of the cottage swung open and Reynard's eyes met the two of us. "Everything's packed, Rhemues." He lingered in the entry, waiting for a response. I knew he was expecting me to say something. Rhemues was the only one who knew my decision, and the time had come for me to tell Anaros. I dreaded the idea so much that it took everything I had to convince my body to stand.

Rhemues followed me to the door and out onto the street. Anaros was standing by his horse, strapping down the last bit of their supplies for the return trip. Several of the villagers had gathered near them to say goodbye.

"It was nice to meet you, King Anaros," said Aldous as he held out his hand towards him. "I wish you safe travels back to Selvenor."

Anaros took his hand with a smile. "Thank you, Aldous. I appreciate your family's hospitality."

I could feel my heart pounding. I was terrified to tell Anaros my decision. *What if I'm making a mistake? What if I should go back?* I swallowed hard and took a deep breath, trying to calm my nerves. *Stay.* The voice sounded loud through my thoughts. There was no denying the clarity of its instruction.

Reynard nodded in my direction, signaling to Anaros that I had come outside. He glanced at Rhemues and then walked towards me with a solemn expression. I could feel despair emanating from him as he approached, forcing himself to ask the question I knew was coming. "Did you make your decision?"

I nodded, unsure I could form the words to answer him. I knew what I needed to do, but it wasn't what I wanted. The idea of this being the last time I spoke to him sent chills through my body and made my stomach knot. I could feel my eyes glazing over as the words left my mouth in a hushed whisper. "I have to stay."

Anaros stared at the ground, nodding after a few moments. "I know." He looked back into my eyes and I quickly regretted my decision. I wanted to change the words. I wanted to say I was going home. But I couldn't bring myself to do it.

Rhemues moved past Anaros and pulled me into a tight embrace. I could hear the sadness in his shaky voice. "Stay safe, Zynnera. Know that you can come home anytime. You will *always* be family."

I couldn't stop the tears from flowing. Reynard also wrapped me in a warm embrace as he told me goodbye. None of it seemed real. My mind had not allowed the reality of what was happening to settle in. I looked again at Anaros as Rhemues and Reynard mounted their horses. He was still standing in front of me, obviously conflicted with how he should say goodbye. I wanted to hug him, to feel his arms wrapped around me one last time. But I feared doing so might push my mind over the edge and alter my decision to stay.

Anaros sighed. "Goodbye, Zynnera."

It was all he said. He mounted his horse, and in minutes the three of them had vanished into the shadows of the forest. I remained standing in the center of the street, staring out into the dense brush and thick timberline. *They're really gone. They've actually left. I might never see them again.* I could still feel the eyes of several villagers watching me. When I could no longer hold in my emotion, I turned and ran to the opposite end of the village. I continued past the last cottage and into the woods, pushing my body through the overgrowth until I reached the meadow. I collapsed to my knees, running my fingers through the lush grass as I sobbed uncontrollably. *What am I doing! I can't do this. I just can't...*I knew if I ran, I could still catch up with them. I could still go home. I couldn't deny it was what my body wanted to do. *Stay...*

"Why!" I shouted out loud at the voice in my head, my tears flowing so heavily I thought they may form a puddle on the ground. "Why?"

A man's voice echoed from behind me. "Zynnera?"

I turned to see who it was. Takias was staring at me from just in front of the tree line. I felt embarrassed by my lack of composure, but there was little I could do to regain control of my emotions. The pain was too heavy to silence.

He seemed to understand my lack of response, moving to sit beside me on the ground. "Everything will be OK, Zynnera. I think you will be happy here, I really do."

Right now I felt anything but happy. The only thing keeping me from running after Anaros was the voice inside my head. I didn't understand where it came from and part of me wanted to convince myself not to trust it at all. But it was the voice that had led me here in the first place, led me to the answers I knew I needed to find. As much as I hated it, I knew it was guiding me with purpose and that I should listen.

"I've never felt so torn in my entire life," I whispered. "I miss them already. I miss my home, my people."

"The people of Selvenor, do they like you? Welcome you?"

He asked it as a question, but something about his tone told me he already knew the answer. I wasn't sure I really wanted to answer him either way. "No. Not exactly."

"Then why would you want to go back?" Takias was smiling, but I knew there was seriousness in his tone. He seemed to realize his question had left me a little offended. "I guess I just don't understand why you would miss them if they don't treat you well, that's all."

He made a valid point. I didn't really understand why I worked so hard to gain their trust. *Why should it matter if I fit in there or if they like me? It shouldn't matter.* But I knew the reason. Gaining acceptance of the people was the only way I could ever be with Anaros. Now that he was gone, there was no reason for me to worry about what they thought of me, to feel the need to earn their trust.

"They are still my people. Some of them are my family." I sighed. I didn't expect him to understand, and I knew he was right anyway. "I've spent my whole life hiding, keeping my powers a secret for one reason or another. I suppose it's time I embraced who I really am. I'm just not sure I actually know how or where to start."

Takias smiled again. "Well, I'm happy to help in any way that I can. If there's anything I can do, just say the word."

I returned his smile, wiping the tears from my face. "A distraction would be nice."

Takias laughed. "I think I can do that. Anything in particular you had in mind?"

"I know it sounds silly, but I wouldn't mind training with you more. Perhaps not today...but tomorrow?" I fidgeted a little. *What am I doing? This was so uncomfortable last time. Why am I putting myself in this situation again?*

I realized I was so desperate for something to distract my thoughts, I was willing to accept it from anywhere. Training with Takias had been a bit awkward yesterday, but only because Anaros had displayed so much jealousy at the idea of me being alone with him. *But Anaros is gone. There's no reason for me to worry about it.* I knew the next few days were going to be difficult. I knew how hard it would be to move on and let go of the past. If Takias could make the transition even a little easier, then I should let him.

"Sounds like a plan," he said.

We spent the entire day in the meadow, just talking and enjoying one another's company. Every once in a while my mind would remind me Anaros was gone and I would dive back into an emotional state. I tried to maintain my facade, but I was sure Takias could sense each instance of mood change. He handled it all with patience and compassion, something I was grateful for. It was good to have at least one person I could lean on for support.

When the sun began to set, we returned to the village. Takias walked with me to the door and bid me goodnight. I dreaded entering the cottage, knowing I would be staying there alone. I felt so empty as I lay on my bed in silence. There was no one to stop the memories and thoughts from forcing their way into my mind. No one to distract me. I found myself sobbing again into the soft blankets, crying until my eyes were too exhausted to stay open. *I hope this was the right decision. I hope this wasn't goodbye forever.*

CHAPTER
Nineteen

Crickets chirped as the last of the sun's light peeked through the trees. Reynard was busy building a fire while Rhemues quietly helped me set up the tent. We had spent the entire day riding in silence, and I had no intention breaking it now. Rhemues and I had not spoken to each other since he stormed out of the cottage, angry with my decision to leave Zynnera in Bogumir. I was certain he was still unhappy with the idea of leaving her, even as he helped me prop up the cloth with wooden poles. The worst part was I didn't blame him for being upset and I'd spent the last several hours fighting my regret.

Once the tent was completed, I threw our supplies inside. Rhemues sat down on a fallen log beside Reynard, swatting away the bugs swirling around his face. I joined them around the fire, sitting by myself on my own log. The silence seemed to stretch on forever as we ate some of the food Aldous had been kind enough to send with us. I forced it down, not feeling hungry in the slightest.

Reynard cleared his throat. "We will be in Dunivear tomorrow. Have you given any thought as to what you are going to say to King Lenear?"

I hadn't given any thought to Lenear. My mind was so weighted by the idea of leaving Zynnera that I hadn't been able to focus on anything else. I knew it was something I needed to figure out before tomorrow. King Lenear would be expecting us to return with information, but there wasn't much I could really give him. We had learned very little of the man in the black cloak, only that his murders were happening in Bogumir as well as Dunivear. But I doubted such information would be of concern to King Lenear, who despised the villagers for their magic.

I sighed. "I don't know what I'm going to say to him."

Reynard stole a glance at Rhemues, who was fidgeting with his fingers. "My King, we *will* have to speak with him. He's expecting..."

I interrupted him with an agitated tone. "I know he's expecting us. Doesn't change the fact that I have nothing to tell him."

Reynard and Rhemues looked at each other. I could tell they felt uneasy about my lack of having a plan. *What do they expect? They know everything I do...and it's not much more than we knew the first time we talked to Lenear.*

Rhemues moved restlessly on the log. "Anaros, I know we haven't found the man responsible, but we can't just avoid speaking with him. You know that, right?"

I could hear the fear in his tone. He was afraid I would avoid returning to the palace at all. I knew the repercussions of such action would not end well. Lenear would take his frustration out on Selvenor; he would view my avoidance as a threat. Such suspicion could even cause problems for the people of Bogumir. *For Zynnera.*

I had no intention of backing out on my word to return to the palace, but my anger towards Rhemues stopped me from clarifying my intentions and easing his concerns. "Why not? Can't I just exercise my authority and ride right past Dunivear?"

Rhemues didn't know how to react to my aggressive response. I stood up from the log and stormed past them into the woods. *I need to be alone. I need time to think.* Part of me felt guilty for being so angry with him, especially when I didn't blame him for it. There was nothing about this situation that I liked. The idea of speaking with Lenear admittedly had me stressed, and the reminder of my lack of preparedness only made me feel worse. As I sat down and leaned against a small pine, my mind raced with anxiety. *What am I supposed to do? What am I going to say? Sorry? We didn't find anything? Good luck keeping your people safe?*

I shook my head. Being diplomatic when I felt like such a mess wasn't going to be easy. I realized my hand had subconsciously moved to the metal ring inside my pocket. I pulled the ring from its hiding place to examine it. A circle of gold met a bright green gem, held in place by four slender prongs. The band itself was marked with etchings of flowers and vines. The ring was a family heirloom, one worn by my mother when she sat on the throne of Selvenor with my father. It had always been his intention that I pass it to the woman I married.

A sharp pain struck my heart at the thought. I had every intention of telling Zynnera that I loved her. I had every intention of presenting the ring to her and asking her to marry me. But now there was little substance to those intentions. Now I needed to find a way to let her go. I couldn't help but wonder if I would ever be able to give the ring to anyone.

The sound of someone walking through the forest towards me forced the ring back into my pocket. Rhemues emerged from the shadows with a sullen expression. I stared at him for a few moments, unsure of his intention. "If you've come to chide me, I'm not really in the mood. You can take your comments back to camp."

Rhemues moved his gaze to the ground in front of him. He seemed unsure what to say to me. After a few moments he moved closer and plopped down on the ground beside me. We sat there in the silence for several long minutes, listening to the sounds of the forest as night settled over us. Rhemues turned to face me. "I promised her, you know." I looked at him with confusion, waiting for him to clarify. He stared out into the shadows. "I promised Zynnera I would be there for you. Help you move on."

I bit my lip. *Of course she made him promise. She knew I would be a complete wreck. She didn't want this to come between us.* I looked out into the forest. "Zynnera has a habit of asking for promises."

Rhemues shook his head. "How am I supposed to help you move on, when I don't know how to do it myself? Every ounce of me is screaming to go back. To go get her. Anaros, what am I supposed to tell Hachseeva? The children?"

I closed my eyes. "I know this was my idea, but it was her decision. I didn't force her to stay. I wanted it to be her choice."

Rhemues turned to face me again. "I know. I know you never wanted to just abandon her there. I didn't mean what I said at the cottage. I just..." He paused for a few moments, fighting back his own emotions. "Anaros, I'm sorry I blamed you. You only want what's best for her, I know that, it just..."

"Doesn't make it easier," I finished.

He nodded in agreement. "As hard as it is for me, I know it's a thousand times harder for you. I wish I knew what advice to give you; how to help you. But I don't."

I couldn't fight back my tears anymore. "I don't know if I can leave her. I don't know if I *can* move on. Every second I have to convince myself not to go back. I have to convince myself I did the right thing. But the truth is, I don't know if I did." I wiped the tears off of my face with my arm. "How am I supposed to forget everything we've been through? Forget all the moments. The feelings. I can't just make them vanish."

"Perhaps we should go back and see if Zynnera has a spell for that?" Rhemues chuckled.

I laughed. "I'm afraid if I went back, I wouldn't be able to leave without her anyway."

"Anaros, you don't think King Lenear will be angry if he finds out she is still there, do you? I'm worried he might be suspicious. Worried what he might do."

I could hear the fear in his voice. His statement was something I had considered. "Even if he is, what could he do to them? He would be a fool to attack them. I'm more concerned with what he will do to Selvenor if he thinks we are conspiring against him. Hopefully it does not come to that."

"I hope you're right," he said, moving to his feet. "Come on, we should get some rest. Tomorrow will be a long day." I nodded, pushing myself off the ground to follow him back to camp.

I stared at the cloth roof for what felt like hours before finally falling asleep. Even then my thoughts were filled with memories of Zynnera. I couldn't seem to push her from my mind even in my sleep. My thoughts took me back to when I first met her. I recalled every detail of that night in the dungeon: the way she had studied the cell, her surprise when I told her it was pointless, and how she had chided me for being hopeless. I remembered hearing her sarcastic replies in response to my pessimism. I remembered standing in front of her, the moonlight illuminating her face and her blue eyes pulling me so deep I thought I might drown. It hadn't taken much time for me to *feel* something for her, and not a whole lot more to admit it to myself.

All of those moments leading up to dancing with her in the rebel camp seemed like they had been weeks instead of days. I felt as though I had known her my entire life, like someone I'd known even before Eradoma. Holding her that night had only solidified what I knew was happening. I had been falling for her. *Perhaps, I'd already fallen completely.*

The more time I spent with her, the more I knew it was the truth. Nineteen years I'd had before evil swept through my kingdom, and not once did I recall the feelings I was experiencing. I never stumbled over my words, never worried about impressing a *girl*. In a matter of days, Zynnera had changed all of that. *She'd changed me...and for the better.*

Fate had put her in that lonely cell with me and, though I didn't know it at the time, it was the start of a long journey together to save our people. Zynnera and I had come a long way since that dark night in the dungeon, facing Vlenargans and fighting against Eradoma's magic. But things had not gotten any easier since defeating her; in fact, they had seemingly gotten worse.

The nightmares had started almost right way, occasionally visiting her while she slept. As the months progressed, they became worse and more frequent. I had often heard her screaming in the night, calling out in fear and begging for them to stop. It was impossible to listen to the pleas in the room next to me and not be filled with concern. I was scared for her, and that fear only grew as I began to realize there was little I could do to help.

I had hoped traveling to Dunivear would provide the answers Zynnera needed to end the nightmares. I wanted her to obtain relief from them. But the answers she received from Adeara had not explained the meaning behind the dreams or who was responsible for the murders within them. Instead, the murders had only become more real when we learned that they were taking place in both Dunivear and Bogumir. The crimes were certainly connected, but the information left us no closer to solving them. At first I had been happy to find a way for Zynnera to gain King Lenear's favor. By solving the mystery that plagued his people, I hoped she would gain his trust. But I hadn't succeeded, and it seemed my trip to Dunivear had accomplished nothing.

The only positive to come from our trip was that we finally had answers to our questions about the things Vander told us. We now understood what he meant by the Bridge and that the Virgàm was an item from which all magic originated. Zynnera was destined to save mankind from darkness, a revelation passed down from prophecy. I couldn't help but wonder if there was more to the vision than what Adeara had told us. She said much of it had been lost through decades of recitation. *Does that mean there is more information out there? More details that might help Zynnera know how to defeat the darkness?*

I sat up, staring out into the night. The sun had barely begun to press its light through the overgrowth of the forest. I was certain I hadn't slept at all as my mind mulled over the thousands of questions still rampaging through my thoughts. There was so much I didn't know or understand, and all of it sprouted fear inside me. The thought of Zynnera facing the darkness on her own made my heart race. *But she's not facing it alone. She's surrounded by hundreds of witches and warlocks. They are going to help her. They are going to teach her.*

I knew I would never be able to convince myself it was enough. What I wanted was an excuse to go back, to stand by her side while she followed her destiny. Memories of Vander flashed through my mind. *It is your destiny to help the Bridge find the path to save us all.* The phrase repeated in my thoughts for several minutes. I wondered what exactly he had meant by it. I had helped Zynnera on her path to defeat Eradoma. I'd always believed that was what Vander had meant. But part of me hoped there was more to his words than that. I wanted my destiny to still be intertwined with hers. Even Adeara seemed to think it was. *It doesn't make sense. If I'm supposed to help her, then why do I feel so strongly that she should stay in Bogumir? Why do I feel like I'm being pulled away from her?*

The more I thought about it, the more frustrated I became. I'd spent the last six months guessing what I needed to do. It seemed moving my title to king had not changed that. I often felt like I had no idea what I was doing or how I should fulfill my duties as a leader. *I suppose this afternoon will be no different. I have no idea what I'm going to say to Lenear.*

Reynard sat up in his bed, rubbing his eyes as he took in a deep breath of morning air. His expression changed to concern when he realized I was already awake. "You haven't been awake all night, My King?"

"Would've gotten just as much rest if I had, I'm afraid."

He flashed me a sympathetic smile. "I'll go make us a fire."

Our conversation had pulled Rhemues from a deep sleep. He rolled over to face me. "Any mid-night inspiration on what you are going to tell Lenear?" There was still concern lingering in his voice. I wished I could put his mind at ease, but that would require me to actually have a plan.

I shook my head. "No. But I suppose our best option would be to just tell him the truth. There is still a chance Zynnera will figure out who is responsible."

"That's true." He nodded. "Maybe she can figure it out."

I could tell he was agreeing with me in hopes that it would ease my trepidation. I wasn't sure anything could at this point, but I appreciated his effort. "Come on. Let's have breakfast and get going."

I was anxious to begin our journey. The sooner we got to Dunivear, the sooner we could leave. I hoped putting more distance between myself and Bogumir would help keep me from retreating back into the forest of Arnfell. *I have to keep moving. I have to take this one moment at a time.*

We ate a quick breakfast and started packing camp. I found myself moving slowly, almost as though my body were fighting against the idea of leaving. I tried to push Bogumir and Zynnera from my thoughts, a nearly impossible task.

Rhemues folded the cloth tent cover and placed it with our other supplies. "If things go well with King Lenear, do you think he'd let us spend the night at the palace? Not going to lie, having a bug-free place to sleep is a nice thought."

I shook my head. "I think it would be best to speak with him and keep moving."

He seemed to understand my logic. Staying in Dunivear would only give me more time to contemplate turning back. Then again, Rhemues wouldn't be saddened by the idea of doing so. I think he missed her almost as much as I did.

The sound of horses echoed from the road beyond us. I could hear them trotting closer as I turned to Reynard, slightly concerned that anyone would be headed towards Bogumir. At least a dozen men approached us, mounted on horses and bearing the crest of Dunivear on their armor. They appeared as though they were ready for battle, and my heart raced at the thought of where they were headed.

They eyed us with suspicious expressions as they stopped in front of the camp. All of them dismounted, stepping into our camp with aggressive haste. "Who are you?" demanded one man. "What business do you have here?" He seemed to be the one leading the group on their escapade through the forest.

Reynard stepped forward before I could answer. "We could ask you the same question. We have permission to be here and are under no obligation to answer your question."

The man's tone was cold and stern. "We are here under direct orders from Dunivear. You *will* answer our question."

We all stared at him in silence. None of us were sure we should tell him anything without knowing the reason they were this deep in the forest. The only village along this road was Bogumir, and there was no way I was telling them anything if they planned to attack it. *I won't put Zynnera in danger. I won't tell them anything until I know what they are up to.* I glanced at Reynard, who seemed to be thinking the same thing I was.

The man stared at us for a moment as if giving us one final chance to answer. "Very well then. Take them back to camp. General Jehaz will have questions for them." He gestured towards us and the men immediately surrounded us on all sides. I reached for my sword only to realize I had not yet put my belt around my waist. It was still sitting by the small smoldering campfire.

Rhemues started to pull his own sword but stopped upon noticing Reynard shaking his head. He allowed them to bind his wrists. "It's best we sort this out with the general," he said as they pulled him away. "Don't fight them."

The idea of allowing myself to be taken captive was not one I relished. The last time I was bound, I had subsequently been beaten and tortured. It wasn't a memory I was fond of, nor did it give me any interest in handing myself over without a fight. One man grabbed me by the arm. I jerked away from him, punching him in the nose just before two others grabbed me from behind. I struggled against them, refusing to let them wrap their ropes around my hands.

Rhemues had already been bound, following Reynard's advice. "Anaros, you must stop. We'll speak with the general. Stop fighting them!" he had proceeded to shout as they pulled him away.

I pulled myself free of their grips, but more of them surrounded me now. They seemed to understand I wasn't planning to go willingly. Several of them grabbed me at once. I continued to fight against them until the man in charge grew tired of my refusal to bend to their will. He walked towards me, pulling his hand into a tight fist before swinging at me. The moment his hand met my face, everything around me disappeared and my mind became quiet.

CHAPTER
~*Twenty*~

Water rushed over the ledge and fell into the pool below. Sunlight had just begun to penetrate through the dark clouds as it met the brisk morning air. I found myself standing along the familiar banks of the river, searching frantically for the shape I knew would appear from the mist. I moved closer to the waterfall, pausing with each cautious step. The morning fog was so thick I could barely see two feet in front of me, and my heart pounded with the anticipation of what might be lurking in the haze.

I continued forward until I could hear voices. The sound of a woman pleading for help filled my ears. Part of me wanted to stop, to refrain from going any closer. *But I have to see. I have to know...* I took a few more steps until two figures became visible through the fog. The man in the black cloak was hovering over a terrified woman.

"Please! Please don't!" she begged as she attempted to drag her body away from him.

The man pulled the dagger from beneath his cloak, tilting the blue gem on its hilt towards the woman as he recited the incantation. Within moments a purple aura flowed from the body of the woman and the air was filled with her screams. Her magical energy drained into the gem and then the man proceeded to use the *Morso.* I knew the moment his spell ended that she was dead. Her body remained motionless on the ground as he returned the dagger beneath his cloak.

"No!" I shouted at him. "Why! Why are you doing this?"

He moved towards me, causing my body to shake with fear. "Join me, Zynnera. Help him return."

"Who! Help who return?" I desperately wanted an answer. I needed to understand how my nightmares were connected to the darkness I still sensed. For the first time, I felt the courage to face the man in the black cloak. I wasn't afraid to ask questions. I wasn't afraid to stand against him.

The man only smiled at me. There was no response to my question. Everything started to disappear into a black swirl. The man in the black cloak seemed to disintegrate, bringing my mind to face another man, the one with the red streaks in his hair. I felt all of the courage I had managed to accumulate leave my body. The darkness emanating from him was like nothing I'd experienced. He held out his hand towards me. *Bring it to me, Zynnera. Bring me the Virgàm.*

"No." I shook my head, stepping away from him. "No!"

I felt myself gasp as I sat up in the bed. I was breathing hard as I looked around the cottage, alone in the morning light. *It happened again. There was another murder.* There was no time to waste; I needed to go see Adeara right away. I pulled on my boots and left the cottage, nearly running along the stone paved street to her home.

I tried to keep myself calm as I pounded on her door. *Please be home. PLEASE be home.* After a minute Adeara opened the door with the usual smile resting on her face. Her expression quickly changed to concern upon seeing my distress.

"I need to talk to you," I said with a shaky voice. "I've...I've had another nightmare."

She gestured for me to come inside. "Come in, Zynnera."

She started to walk towards the table, offering for me to follow. I shook my head at her hospitality. "I think it's happened again. Someone else has been murdered."

Adeara placed her hand on my shoulder. "Are you sure? Zynnera, tell me everything you saw."

"We were by the river again, same as before. There was a woman. He drained her power and then he...then he..." I couldn't stop the sobs. The reality of what the nightmare meant had finally caught up with me.

"It's OK, Zynnera. It's alright."

I took a deep breath. "He killed her. And then I was facing another man. A man with red streaks in his hair. He asked me to bring it to him. To bring him the Virgàm."

Adeara pondered my words. She looked deep into my eyes and I could sense her fear. Something about my nightmare truly terrified her. "What is it?" I asked. "What does it mean?"

She shook her head. "I wish I knew, Zynnera. But I fear that this man is responsible for the darkness. I fear he is trying to get to you through these nightmares. It is essential you keep fighting against him. You must not give in, no matter what. It could mean disaster for us all."

I felt as though the weight of the world rested on my shoulders. The burden was so heavy. *How am I supposed to do this? How do I carry this alone?* I'd spent my entire youth feeling inadequate, feeling like a disappointment to Eradoma. And while I never longed to gain her approval, I still hated the feeling of failure. I didn't believe I was capable of defeating this darkness Adeara spoke of. I didn't believe I had the strength to overcome it.

"I know how afraid you are, Zynnera. But I need you to stay calm. Keep this quiet. I will send a few people to the river. Until then, we don't want anyone to panic."

I nodded. "It was near the waterfall. Just at the base."

Adeara placed both hands on my shoulders. "We will get to the bottom of this. Stay strong."

I nodded again, unable to form any more words. I still felt like I was in a state of shock as I left the cottage. *Stay calm? How am I supposed to stay calm?* I didn't know what to do. Sitting alone in my cottage all day certainly wasn't the answer. That would only allow my mind to wander back to the river. *I can't. I need a distraction.* I remembered my conversation with Takias yesterday in the meadow. *A distraction.*

I rushed to Takias's cottage, hoping he wouldn't mind how early it was. Taking a deep breath to regain my composure, I knocked softly on the wooden entry. Takias opened the door, rubbing his eyes groggily. *I woke him. I should have waited. The sun has only just come up.*

Realizing who it was knocking on his door, Takias flashed me a bright smile and attempted to flatten his disheveled hair. "Zynnera! Good morning! I'm sorry, I wasn't expecting you so early."

I sighed. "Yes, I'm sorry. I didn't mean to wake you. I forgot how early it was. I just...I, um..." It was taking everything I had to fight back my tears. I suddenly felt overwhelmed. I stared at the ground in front of me, allowing a small sob to escape my mouth.

Takias immediately moved to my side. "Zynnera, what's going on? It's OK. You can tell me."

I nodded, looking at him through my tears. "Not here. Not in the village."

"Alright. Give me a minute to grab my things. We'll go to the meadow." He gestured to a small wooden bench sitting against the wall of the cottage. "Wait here?"

"OK," I whispered.

I knew I had to tell someone. I needed to get the thoughts out of my head. Telling Adeara what I had seen hadn't seemed to help at all. If anything, I felt even more scared. As soon as Takias had gathered his things, we walked to the meadow. I was still fighting against a complete emotional breakdown as we moved through the dense forest. *Adeara asked me not to tell anyone. But I need to talk to someone. I can trust him?*

The last thought came as more of a question; however, I wasn't sure why. *Surely I can trust him?* He'd been nothing but kind and understanding, completely patient while I faced the emotions of losing everyone I cared about. Yet my instincts still remained unconvinced. *I barely know him. Perhaps that's all it is?* But I knew it wasn't true. The moment I met Anaros I had given him my complete trust. Something about Takias was different.

We sat down in the grassy meadow, staying quiet for several minutes. Takias turned to face me. "Tell me what's going on, Zynnera."

I drew in another deep breath. I wasn't sure I should tell him everything. As much as I wanted to, I knew I shouldn't. "I just...I've been having visions. It's a bit overwhelming. I was hoping you could..."

Takias smiled as he finished my sentence. "Distract you?"

I laughed shyly. "Yes. Distract me."

"Alright. Well, tell me what I can do to *distract* you."

"Could we just...practice some spells? It doesn't matter what. Just anything." I knew focusing on magic would draw my attention away from everything I had seen in my vision this morning, and I was eager to push them from my mind.

Takias only smiled. We practiced dozens of spells as the day continued on. He was able to pull me away from all the worry and fear trapped within my mind. I found myself smiling, and even laughing at times. Performing magic seemed to be the remedy I needed to get through everything that overwhelmed me. All this time I had fought so hard against it, against being myself. I never imagined the one thing I tried so hard to hide was the only thing that seemed to help me through the pain.

As the sun began its descent, I sat with Takias on the grass, watching the clouds move across the sky. I couldn't deny how much better I felt after spending the day with him. "Thank you, for this," I said. "For today. I can't tell you how much it helped."

Takias laughed. "Well, I don't think I've actually taught you anything you didn't already know."

"No, probably not." I laughed with him. "But that doesn't mean it hasn't made a difference. I needed to get out of my own head."

"Glad I could help."

He was staring at me with his bright brown eyes. It was strange that I felt connected to him. *Maybe I have a thing for falling fast.* The thought scared me. *Is that what this is? Am I... falling?* I could feel my heart racing. So many things went through my mind as I stared back at him. Something about him drew me in. He'd been the support I needed the last two days, saving me from my own thoughts. He'd been my *Anaros.*

I realized now what it was. I wasn't falling for him. I was grasping for anything or anyone who reminded me of him. Anaros was who I wanted sitting beside me. Anaros was the one I wanted pulling me into a tight embrace when the world became too overwhelming. Takias wasn't Anaros, and I felt guilty for allowing myself to replace him.

Takias stared at me for several moments before his lips plunged towards mine, leaning in to kiss me. It all happened so fast, my hands moving to push against his chest and my head moving away from him. I could tell from his expression that my withdrawal had hurt him.

I cleared my throat. "I'm sorry. I just...I can't. I'm not ready to..."

Takias bit his lip and looked out into the meadow. "Because of him, right? King Anaros?"

There was disgust in the mention of his name. I wasn't sure how to respond. Of course Anaros and my feelings for him still remained a part of me. It hadn't been *that* long since he left. *Does he expect me to just forget? I'm sure he knows I had feelings for him.* And it wasn't just Anaros that stopped me. I felt connected to Takias, but not in the same way. I couldn't put my finger on it, but I knew something was different. Regardless, my resistance to his advances seemed to have offended him.

I decided to be honest with him. "Anaros is part of it, yes. I just don't think my mind can take on anything else right now. There is so much I don't know or understand. Not to mention I've left the only home I've ever known and my family."

"I'm sure it's all overwhelming, Zynnera. But you have to let it go. Let *them* go. Surely you must know they were only holding you back. *Here*, in Bogumir, that's where you're supposed to be."

I swallowed hard. I wasn't sure what Takias meant by his statement, but it left me feeling a little agitated. "No...no, they weren't holding me back."

Takias laughed. "You may not realize it now, but you'll see. Once you get over all the pain, you'll see the truth."

I hated that he laughed. I hated that he implied they had a negative effect on my life. I tried to keep my voice calm. "What truth is that, exactly?"

He turned to face me. "That those who can't wield magic hate us. They hate us, Zynnera. Some out of fear. Some out of jealousy. But it's true of them all. Believe me, no matter how much you help them, they will always turn on you. They will always find a reason to make you their enemy."

I felt baffled by his statement. "Anaros has never done anything to intentionally hurt me. He would never turn on me. I'm sorry if this happened to you, but not everyone is like that."

Takias shook his head, sneering at my comment. "I don't get it. I don't understand what you see in him, that *human*. Poor excuse for a leader, not to mention he has no respect for your true power."

"Anaros has more respect for me than anyone. And he's going to be a great king." I could feel my skin growing hot. I couldn't believe what he was saying. All this time I thought he was compassionate and kind. *But only if you wield magic. Only if he deems you worthy.* "We are all human, Takias. Magic or non-magic. We are *still* human."

He shrugged. "Perhaps. But some of us are better humans. Some of us deserve to be in control. We were chosen to have magic, Zynnera. Not them. It's our destiny to rule over those unfit and unworthy of this power."

"We should use our power to help people, not control them." I could feel my body shaking. I couldn't deny his words made me upset, but they also scared me.

He nodded sarcastically. "Let me tell you what happens when you use your power to help them. My mother, she was just like you. Always striving to help the poor, pathetic humans. Then one day she saw a man drowning in the river. She brought him home, took care of him...healed him. And after she had done all of that, after she had opened our home to him and used her magic to save his life, he murdered her while she slept. Slit her throat with a knife and made off with anything of value he could carry. That is what happens when you use your power to help those who don't deserve it."

I could feel my heart racing. "Takias, I am sorry for what

happened to your mother. I truly am. But that doesn't mean everyone is bad or evil. That man committed a horrible crime, but it doesn't excuse us to exercise our power to harm anyone." I stared deep into his eyes. I could feel the hatred, the anger. It had been there for a very long time, consuming his soul.

I stood up from the grass. My instincts told me to leave. Takias was showing me a side of him I never expected. There was something dark about the way he spoke. There was so much rage in his tone. I feared his anger and what he might be capable of. "We obviously don't see eye to eye on this. I think it best I go back to the village."

I started to walk away, heading towards the forest with the sun behind me. Takias's voice echoed with a stern, dark tone. "We will bring light to this world by putting those who stand against our power in their place, Zynnera. We will make this world what it was meant to be."

I could feel my body trembling. *Those words. I've heard them before.* I didn't respond to him, moving into the forest as quickly as I could without making him suspicious. My mind was racing. *Eradoma said those exact words to me in the dungeon. But what does it mean? Could Takias really be linked to the darkness like she is?* The thought scared me more than I wanted to admit. I was glad I hadn't given him the details of my visions. If nothing else, I certainly didn't trust him with the information.

After several minutes, I entered the village clearing. I kept moving down the street, terrified to check if Takias was following behind me. In the center of the village a large crowd of people were gathered around in a circle. I pressed through them to see the cause of their commotion. The cold body of a woman lay on the ground in front of them. I recognized her immediately as the woman from my vision.

I felt my hands cover my mouth as I gasped. The reality of my visions had now come full circle. There was no doubt everything I had seen actually happened. Adeara was standing beside the body. She marched towards me, pulling me away from the crowd where we could speak without being overheard.

"Zynnera, is this the woman you saw in your vision?" I nodded, unsure if I could speak. Adeara pulled me in closer to her. "They found her by the river. Same as the others. If there is anything else you can tell me, anything at all?"

I wasn't sure what to say. Everything in my gut told me Takias was somehow involved, but I had no evidence to prove his guilt. Other than my sense that there was a darkness in his soul, I had nothing to go on. The last thing I wanted to do was push my suspicions only to find out I was wrong. Condemning someone who was innocent, regardless of what they believed, was something I had no intention of doing.

"I don't know anything more for certain," I answered. "But when I do, I'll let you know right away."

My answer seemed to be enough for her as she stared back at the lifeless body on the street. The entire crowd resonated with murmurs. They were obviously frightened by the woman's murder. *I can only imagine what their terror would be if they knew what I did.* The man in the black cloak had once again stolen the magical power of another, storing it inside his jagged dagger. *And why? What is he going to do with all of that energy?*

My mind was once again full of questions. I wondered if there would ever be an end to them. *I have to figure this out. I have to put a stop to this.* I was more determined than ever, but I still had little to go on. My vision had failed to give me any new details that might lead me to finding the culprit. But I did have a place to start. Regardless of having no evidence, there was one person I had to speak with. *I must speak to Takias. If he's innocent, then I can move on. Keep searching.* But my instincts felt certain he was somehow involved. I wasn't ready to name him the killer, but I was determined to find out.

CHAPTER
Twenty One

The tent was filled with all manner of weapons and supplies. My face winced at the pain of my throbbing head as I looked around. Flashes of what happened entered my mind. I remembered the group of soldiers entering our camp. I recalled struggling against them as Rhemues and Reynard were bound and taken away. *That man punched me. Apparently hard enough to knock me out.* I glanced around the tent, one eye squinting through swollen skin, hoping to get an idea of where I was. In the corner there was a mountain of bows and swords. It appeared as though these men were preparing for battle.

The thought left my stomach in knots. The only reason they would have for traveling the overgrown path to Bogumir was not one I was fond of. I knew how King Lenear felt about the warlocks and witches who lived there. He saw them as a threat to his kingdom. *But it would be foolish of him to attack the village. He stands no chance against hundreds of people who can use magic.* I tried to think of another logical reason for the army's presence in the forest, but came up with nothing.

I attempted to move. My hands were bound behind my back, wrapped around a wooden beam in the center of the tent. The soldiers obviously didn't trust me, and there was no sign of Rhemues or Reynard. I wondered if they had told them who we were. *Surely they would let us go at the mention of my title? Assuming they believed them.* I twisted my hands in an attempt to free them, but it was no use. The rope around them was too tight and wiggling my hands only caused it to cut into my skin.

I could hear the voices of at least a dozen men outside the tent. I wondered how long I had been out. *I've got to get out of here. I have to warn them.* The thought of returning to Bogumir made my heart race. Would Zynnera change her mind about staying if she saw me again? Would I change mine? Part of me hoped that was the case, but I felt selfish for it.

The tent opening parted and two men walked in, stopping just in front of me. Rhemues and Reynard followed a few seconds later. One of the men pointed towards me. "Untie him. Now!" He sounded angry, although I wasn't certain the source of that anger.

The second man crouched behind me and cut the rope from my hands. Rhemues rushed towards me, offering his hand to help pull me from the dirt floor. "You alright?" he asked, placing his hand on my shoulder and the other pointing to the eye that felt swollen.

I stared at the man who had untied me and realized it was the same one who punched me in the face back at camp. I touched my eye and winced a little. *I bet that's black.* "I'm fine. Just a severe headache."The man moved his gaze to the floor in an expression of guilt. The other man stepped closer to me, his tone remaining stern. "My apologies, Your Highness. My men weren't aware of who you are. Not that it's an excuse." He glowered at the man, obviously angered by the way he had treated us. "General Jehaz." He held out his hand in formality.

I accepted it, still uncertain I trusted him. "What are you doing here? Why are you headed to Bogumir?"

I realized my tone came across as accusatory and nothing short of suspicious. General Jehaz seemed irritated by my demand for answers but obliged nonetheless. "We are headed to Bogumir, yes. It is where he has most likely gone."

I released a frustrated sigh. "He? He who?" I didn't really have time for this, nor the patience. I wanted answers. My head was still throbbing from where the man had hit me in the face and the pain wasn't helping to calm my frustration.

Reynard appeared to sense the irritation growing inside me and spoke up to progress the conversation. "King Lenear has been taken, My King. They are looking for him."

I could feel my expression move into one of shock. "Taken? What do you mean taken? By whom?"

General Jehaz sighed. "We aren't certain who or at least not who he *really* is. Several guards witnessed the abduction. They said the royal advisor betrayed the king and that he could wield magic."

"Elric? Elric is a warlock?" I could hardly believe the words as they left my mouth. All this time I knew there was something strange about him, but I never expected this. I never expected him to possess magic. *All this time Lenear has banned magic from within his own city, his own palace, and it was right under his nose.*

The general shook his head. "Not quite. I can't explain it really. I've known Elric since he was born. Known his family for decades. About a year ago he started acting strangely. *Different.*"

I folded my arms. "Different how?"

Jehaz shook his head again. "Like I said, I'm not sure how to explain it. When you know someone, you just know them. They say certain things. Act certain ways. But then his whole demeanor just changed. Like he was an entirely different person overnight. Only those of us who knew him well ever noticed."

I believed the general's words, mulling over everything he said as I contemplated what it really meant. "And King Lenear? Did he think something was off about him?"

"I did bring it to his attention once. But he assured me everything was fine. I've tried to keep a close watch on Elric since then, but I have other duties I must attend to. Now I fear I've failed my king by not listening to my instincts."

I could see the regret in his eyes. General Jehaz had taken the blame of the king's capture upon himself. But there was still so much that didn't make sense. *Why would Elric suddenly be different? Act different?* The memory hit me hard, pulling me back to the night we had sat around the fire and listened to Rhemues tell the story of Eradoma's control over Captain Torilus. The man I knew would have never helped project her evil power on to the people without being forced to do so. *Captain Torilus was under the influence of magic. She controlled him.* The answer certainly seemed to make sense.

"General, when Eradoma reigned over Selvenor, she used her magic to control one of our captains. Do you think there is a chance the same thing happened to Elric?" I could see the surprise on Rhemues's face. The reminder that magic could control someone he cared about brought back the same anger he had expressed that night around the fire.

General Jehaz nodded. "Yes, that does seem to make sense. However, it doesn't explain why. What purpose would anyone have to control Elric? Why not just control King Lenear himself?"

I pondered his words. He made a valid point. If someone wanted to get to Lenear or use him, why had they not enchanted him directly? Based on what the general said, Elric seemed to have been under their control for some time. Why had they not acted before now? My theory also didn't explain the fact that Elric had performed magic. *Perhaps he had been hiding his powers all this time? But if he really could use magic, why had he not protected himself from being enchanted?* What I thought was a sure answer only melted away as more questions filled my mind.

I sighed. "The only way we are going to know for sure is if we find them, Elric and King Lenear." I understood now why the men were traveling to Bogumir and why they had felt the need to bring the vast array of weapons that were sitting in the tent. If Elric was a warlock or being controlled by someone who was, Bogumir was the first place to search for answers. "I believe the villagers of Bogumir will help us. I'm going with you."

The general seemed pleased by my statement. I felt certain the idea of marching into a village of witches and warlocks had his courage dwindling, not that I blamed him. *We'll go to Adeara. Maybe she can help us? Maybe she has seen something? If Adeara hasn't, then maybe Zynnera has?* The thought of Zynnera sent my heart pounding again. What would happen when I saw her? Would she even want to see me?

I tried to force the thought from my mind. "General, have there been any more murders in Dunivear? King Lenear told me of them when we passed through."

General Jehaz nodded. "Yes, there have been several more since then. I think they are somehow connected to Elric, or whoever is controlling him."

"Yes," I said. "I think so too. And there have been murders in Bogumir as well. There is a good chance that whoever is behind this is responsible for them as well. They likely live in the village."

The general seemed surprised by the revelation. "Murders in Bogumir?" He paused as he thought about the statement. "Yes, we should go there immediately. There is a chance King Lenear is still alive, and we must move with haste."

I recalled everything Zynnera had told me about the murders in her visions. If King Lenear was taken by the person responsible, then there was a good chance the man in the black cloak intended to kill him. *He may already be dead.*

I looked at Rhemues. He nodded his head, seeming to agree with the idea of going back. "We have to stop this. This man needs to be stopped."

Going back was necessary, but I knew how much it would complicate things. It had been hard enough leaving Zynnera there the first time, and I wasn't sure I could do it again. *I can't think about that right now. I'll worry about that later. Right now, I need to focus on finding Lenear.* I didn't particularly like the man, mostly because of his despise of Zynnera, but I knew I needed to do anything I could to find him. This wasn't something I could just walk away from.

"Alright, let's go," I said, moving towards the tent opening. A few feet from the outside air, my body collapsed. Everything swirled around me as I hit the ground. I could faintly make out the panicked screams of Rhemues from behind me. My heart pounded hard as a loud voice filled my thoughts. *Go back. Save her.* I didn't know what to do. My whole body felt numb and unresponsive. *Go back to Bogumir. Save her, Anaros.*

My mind flashed with memories of a few days ago. I saw myself standing in the corridor of the palace in Dunivear. I could see Elric bidding me good luck. I watched him place his hand on his heart as his promise sounded in my ears. *I give you my word, etched in stone.* In another swift moment the memory was gone and a new one took its place. I saw myself standing on the outskirts of the village, watching as Takias departed the forest. I remembered how it felt forcing myself to ask him to take care of Zynnera, but it was his response that now sent chills through my body. *I give you my word, etched in stone.* The same phrase, in complete exactness, had been used by Takias as he promised to look after her.

I felt Rhemues's hands on my shoulders as my mind drifted back to the tent. I was gasping for breath. Rhemues's expression reflected his terror. "Anaros! Are you alright? What happened?"

Reynard was crouched beside him, also displaying a high amount of concern. I shook my head. "I...I don't..." I couldn't find the words.

I had no idea what had just happened. I could feel sweat dripping down my forehead and forming in my palms.

Rhemues shook his head at Reynard. "He needs to rest. We can't go back to Bogumir just yet. Not like this."

I held up my hand in defiance, still gasping to catch my breath. "No...no, we have to go back. I have to go back right now!"

I attempted to move to my feet, but I felt dizzy and my body collapsed back to the floor. I sat up again, propping myself up with my arms. My rapid breathing had Rhemues in a state of panic. "You are absolutely not going anywhere!"

I shook my head. "She's in trouble, Rhemues. Zynnera...she's in trouble." I felt as though I might completely pass out, but I was fighting it with everything I had. "I have to go back. I have to save her."

"You're in no condition to go anywhere, Anaros." He tried to argue but I could hear the fear in his tone. He could sense the urgency in what I said.

I needed to make him understand. This wasn't just a sudden urge or desperate excuse to see her again. "Takias. He's involved."

Rhemues was shocked by my statement. "What? Takias! But he's the one that was training..."

I could see understanding begin to sink in by his expression. We had left Zynnera in the village. We had possibly left her with the murderer. I forced myself to my feet again, staggering to remain standing. My body moved without thought. The only thing I could focus on was getting to Bogumir. *I have to leave now. I have to get to her now!* Before I knew what I was doing, I found myself climbing onto one of the horses outside the tent. Several men tried to stop me as I forced the horse forward, galloping onto the path into the forest. Rhemues and Reynard were both yelling at me from the camp, but I couldn't stop. I didn't have time to wait for them. *I have to get back there as fast as possible. Zynnera could already be in danger.*

I hated myself. I hated that I had left her there. Not only had I abandoned her in a village of strangers but one where a murderous monster lived. And to top it off, I believed I had asked that very monster to look out for her, to take care of her. *If he lays one finger on her, I'll kill him.* I knew the thought held little weight. There wasn't anything I could do against magic and I knew it, but I wasn't going to let that stop me from trying. I wasn't going to let that stop me from saving her, even if it meant risking my own life in the process.

CHAPTER
~Twenty Two~

The air had already begun to grow cool as I made my way down the street. In another hour the sun would set and darkness would reign over the forest. I knew what I needed to do, but it terrified me. I knew I had to get to the bottom of the murders that plagued Bogumir and my nightmares. For so long I had feared the man in the black cloak and with good reason. He was stealing the magical energy of witches and warlocks, storing it inside the jagged dagger he kept beneath his cloak. Takias was suspect of being the man from my nightmares, and I was determined to verify my suspicions before another murder took place.

I had spent an hour in my cottage alone, scouring through *The Tahetya* in an attempt to find a spell that might ease my anxiety. It had accomplished nothing. I knew every spell contained in that book and that knowledge would have to suffice. Takias had acted impressed by my memorization of spells, but if he was involved, there was a good chance he knew spells I'd never even heard of before.

I made my way to his cottage as my heart pounded with anticipation. *What should I say? Should I just be blunt? If he is the murderer, is this even a good idea?* I realized I probably shouldn't be doing this alone, but I still didn't want anyone else to hear my accusations before I proved them to be true. Additionally, if it turned out I was correct, then involving others would only be putting more people in harm's way. The man in the black cloak was dangerous, that much was certain, and he was willing to do anything to get his hands on the magical power of others.

My heart raced even more at the thought. *What am I going to do if he is the murderer and he tries to take my power?* The idea of having to defend myself from yet another person with decades of magical experience terrified me. I still wasn't convinced my defeat of Eradoma had been anything more than luck. What was I going to do if my luck had run out?

Am I really sure about this? Am I sure Takias can really be the one responsible for the deaths of so many people? I didn't want to believe it. He had helped me in so many ways that it was hard to imagine him as a monster. But after my conversation with him today in the meadow, I knew my suspicions were justified. Takias had revealed his true nature, and his feelings towards those who were unable to wield magic could not be filled with more hatred and despise. After what happened to his mother, part of me understood his need to hate those without magical ability, but it was no excuse for the type of destruction and control he desired.

We will bring light to this world by putting those who stand against us in their place. The same words had been uttered by my mother in her dungeon prison. I had felt the darkness emanate from them as she spoke, and I could feel that same darkness as Takias recanted them. I knew it was no coincidence they had used the exact same phrase. *It's coming from somewhere...or someone. This idea that those who use magic should reign over those who don't...it has something to do with the prophecy. I know it does.* Whoever was in control of the darkness, or rather wanted to spread it, was pushing this idea of complete dominance.

It's my destiny to stop it. I won't let anyone force the people I care about into subjugation. It would all start now. Takias was going to give me answers. I knew he was involved, although to what extent I wasn't certain. But he was the only lead I had, and I would not allow it to pass unresolved.

I inhaled a deep breath as I knocked lightly on his door. For several minutes there was no response. *Perhaps he is still in the meadow?* Footsteps sounded from inside. The door creaked open to a face I wasn't expecting to see. A tall man with golden brown eyes and royal apparel stood looking back at me with a bright smile.

"Hello, Zynnera," he said. "It's good to see you."

I remained silent for a moment with my mouth gaped open. "Elric?"

There was no denying that was who was standing before me, but I couldn't seem to find any logical reason for his presence. Elric continued to smile at my shocked expression. He gave a short chuckle, one that felt a bit forced, almost nervous. "I'm assuming you are here to see Takias, yes? He's not here at the moment but will be back shortly. I'm sure he wouldn't mind if you waited here for him."

I wasn't sure what to do. Elric's presence complicated things. It would be much harder to confront Takias with him here. *But why IS he here?* I still couldn't wrap my head around it. What business did the royal advisor to King Lenear have for being in the home of a warlock, especially one I felt was, at minimum, suspect to criminal activity?

Elric laughed at my hesitation and gestured for me to come inside. "Come on, I don't bite, you know."

I knew the only way I was going to get answers was by speaking to Takias. Elric's presence would make things awkward, not to mention dangerous, for him. If Takias turned out to be a murderous monster, confronting him in front of Elric would only put his life in danger. *I'll have to find a way to get him to leave. Maybe he won't stay long anyway.*

I accepted his invitation inside. Takias's home was warm with a small fire burning in the fireplace on the east wall. I sat down on a chair at a small table in the corner. Elric smiled at me from across the room, only making me more nervous about the situation.

"So," he said. "What brings you to see Takias tonight?"

I thought for a moment. What was I supposed to say to him? The last thing I wanted to do was to tell him my suspicions. "There is something I need to discuss with him. Something important."

I left it at that. I had no intention of discussing this any further with him. Elric stared at me, as though he were unsure whether to continue pushing for information. "Well, it's good to see you again.

How are you? Had any luck finding information about the murders in Dunivear?"

Once again, I wasn't sure how to respond. Elric seemed to be fishing for answers and I didn't want to drag him into the situation any further than he already was. "Nothing concrete. However, I did learn there have been murders here as well."

"Really? Well, that's interesting. Do you think they are related?"

I stared blankly at him. "Possibly."

Something about all of this didn't feel right. I didn't know what, but I knew something about the whole thing seemed *off.* I watched Elric pull two cups from a cupboard and fill them with water from a small black pitcher. He moved towards the table, holding the cup in front of me.

"Thank you," I said. I placed the cup in front of me, still trying to unravel everything in my head. "So, why is it you're here?"

Elric smiled. "Ah, Takias is a friend of mine. King Lenear has been particularly distraught with the murders. I thought perhaps Takias could help. Possibly know who could be behind them."

I considered his words as I took a drink from my cup. "Takias is your friend?"

"Yes," he answered, laughing. "This surprises you? Zynnera, I feel as though I should be offended. I told you the night of the coronation I thought those who wielded magic should be appreciated."

"I remember. I'm just surprised King Lenear is OK with his royal advisor being close to a warlock. As you know, he's not exactly fond of my relationship with Anaros." Thinking of Anaros was painful on every level imaginable. I longed to have him here with me, to help me solve the mystery behind the murders. *It's better he's not here. Safer. I don't want him anywhere near this.*

Elric nodded at my comments. "Yes, well, what is it they say? Desperate times call for desperate measures. King Lenear is very adamant about getting to the bottom of it all."

We stared at each other for what felt like hours. It was starting to get awkward now and I still didn't know how to get Elric to leave the cottage. "Do you know how soon Takias will be back? I can have him come find you after I speak with him. I assume you're staying in the village tonight?"

Elric smiled again. "That's very kind of you, Zynnera. But I think I'll wait."

I was running out of ideas. If Takias returned and Elric was still here, I wasn't sure what I would do. I didn't want him to be an innocent victim of the magical battle that could ensue from my accusations. I took another sip of water. *I've got to get him out of here.*

"Listen, Elric," I said. "I don't want to be rude, but what I need to speak with Takias about is...uh...personal." I was hoping he would get the hint. I needed to speak to Takias alone.

"Oh, don't worry, Zynnera. I'm very good at keeping a secret."

I rubbed my forehead with my hand in annoyance. *This guy has got to be the most dense person I've ever met.* Clearly, I was going to have no luck getting him out of here with my subtle hints. Elric was staring out one of the small windows, a wide smile resting on his face. I wondered if I should just tell him the truth. *Even the truth probably wouldn't make him leave.*

"Oh!" he shouted with excitement. "Takias was telling me he's started his own collection. Said he kept it in the cellar."

I raised my eyebrows. "Collection of what?"

Elric laughed. "He didn't say. But told me I would find it fascinating. We should go have a look." He moved to a spot on the west wall, near an unmade bed. He pulled a small rug away from him, revealing what appeared to be a trap door in the floor. "Ah! Here, this must be it. He told me it was under the rug near the bed."

Elric pulled the metal latch and lifted the door. I watched him peer down into the hole with an excited grin. He took a few steps down the stairs into the darkness before glancing back at me. "Are you coming?"

I stared back at him. "I...uh...no, I really think I should just wait here for Takias."

Elric shrugged. "Alright. Suit yourself."

He disappeared beyond the trap door. I waited for several minutes, listening for any sound from him. Curiosity began to get the best of me. I stood up and walked to the hole leading into the darkness below. "Elric?" I listened for a response, but there was nothing. *Where did he go?* I rolled my eyes. *GREAT. I suppose I should go find him before Takias comes back.* Not only was Elric's presence inconvenient, but it was quickly becoming annoying. His inability to read my hints for him to leave had me wondering just how much advice he could possibly offer King Lenear.

I descended down the stairs and into a dark corridor. The stone walls were wet and covered in a moss. Torches lined the wall, forging a lighted pathway through the darkness. It only took a minute to reach the end of the corridor, where the narrow passage emptied into a small open room. It was cold and eerie, dimly lit with three or four lanterns flickering as they rested on two wooden tables.

"Elric?" I called out for him.

"I'm here, Zynnera." He was standing in front of a third table against the wall. A huge smile formed across his face. "Decided to join me, I see. I knew you would."

I sighed. "Elric, we have to get out of here now. It's a lot to explain, but I need you to come with me."

Elric laughed as he leaned against the table. "A lot to explain...oh, Zynnera, please do try. I would love to hear it."

I scrunched my face in frustration. "This isn't a joke, Elric."

"No, of course it isn't," he said, turning to face the wall. "After all, you're afraid Takias is a murderer. Isn't that right?"

I felt my heart begin to race. "How did you know that?"

Elric laughed again, his body moving as though he were playing with something on the table. He picked up a small stone bowl and held it out in front of himself to show me. "Do you know what this is, Zynnera?"

"A mortar and pestle," I answered. "But I'd really prefer you answered my question before asking about irrelevant items." I was watching him carefully. Everything inside me said I had made a mistake following Elric into the cellar. He knew I suspected Takias, but how I wasn't sure. The only logical explanation was that Takias was also aware of my suspicions and had told Elric. *And if that's true, it's likely Elric is also involved. Elric has a part in all of this.*

I could feel my body trembling as Elric reached for another item resting on the table, still laughing at my response. "Irrelevant. Hardly the word I would use." He held up a beautiful purple flower by the stem. It was like nothing I'd ever seen. The flower seemed to almost glow in the darkness, like it emanated its own magical aura. Elric smiled as he watched me study it with nervous fascination. "And this? Have you ever seen this before?"

I didn't want to answer. My instincts were screaming for me to get out of the room. When I didn't answer, Elric only cackled. "Puniceas," he said. "A very rare flower. It grows only in darkness, requiring no sunlight. But that isn't its most impressive feature." He plucked the petals from the flower and placed them in the mortar. Elric began grinding them with the pestle until all that remained was a purple powder. "When ground into a fine powder and mixed with water, it becomes completely invisible. It has no effect on most, but to those with magical energies...well, let's just say it numbs the ability to do magic."

"Numbs their power?" My breathing quickened as I recalled the nightmares that had plagued my dreams for the last few weeks. Every single person the man in the black cloak attacked had not attempted to protect themselves. *Because they couldn't. They couldn't defend themselves.* It all made sense. *The man in the black cloak used this flower to overpower them.*

A muffled scream sounded from a second room, pulling my attention for a moment. I glared back at Elric, who began laughing at my expression of mistrust. "Ah, yes. That will be the king."

I felt a sharp jolt in my heart. *The king? Anaros...*I ran to enter the second room. The area was completely empty except a single chair in the center where King Lenear sat, bound and gagged. I felt a small sense of relief sweep over me at the realization it had not been Anaros that Elric was referring to. But that relief was short lived. My mind was racing with questions...and fear.

Elric stood in the entry, still laughing at my terrified expression. King Lenear continued to scream through his gag, pleading for help. I could feel my body trembling as my mind caught up with everything Elric had said. "You're working with him, aren't you? You and Takias are responsible for all the murders, both here and in Dunivear."

Elric stepped closer to me. "No, Zynnera. Not quite. How frustrating it must be to come so close to the answer only to miss it."

He was mocking me. Suddenly there was a darkness surrounding him. I could feel it, the same sensation I had felt in the cave so many months ago. I stared at Elric, fighting to maintain my composure. "Then why don't you explain it to me. I'm tired of playing games." My voice was shaky. I had tried hard to maintain a calm tone, but I knew Elric saw through the facade.

Elric smiled and nodded. "As you wish." He waved his hands until a blue aura formed around them. His entire body became surrounded by it. I watched in shock as his body changed in front of my eyes. His face shifted to someone completely different as the image of Elric faded away. Once the blue mist had dissipated, it was no longer Elric staring back at me but someone else altogether.

"Takias?" My mind was racing in a thousand directions. I had suspected Takias was involved, but this was beyond anything I imagined. My voice changed to a more demanding tone. "How?"

He returned a smug smile. "Simple, really. Time consuming, of course, but fooling these petty humans required very little effort. Most of them never even noticed when I replaced the real Elric. Naturally, I had to dispose of him to take on his role of royal advisor. A simple spell was all it took to convince them I was him."

"You killed Elric to become the royal advisor of Dunivear. Why?"

Takias laughed. "At first my only intention was to gain control of Dunivear. I needed to learn about Lenear, all his little traits and quarks." He tilted his head to see around me where Lenear was groaning through his gag.

I gulped, understanding his plan. "You were going to *be* him." King Lenear whimpered at my comment.

Takias smiled. "Very good. Yes, I planned to take over Dunivear. And with my newfound power, I would begin to put those who could not wield magic in their place. As king I would lead the army of Dunivear to battle against the people of Bogumir. Of course, they would completely decimate Dunivear's soldiers. The people of Bogumir would wish to retaliate, and I would lead them in a war against the kingdom. I would make them see that we deserved to rule, not be exiled to the forest like animals. Make them see magic deserved to reign. But then the announcement came. Eradoma, Queen of Selvenor, a witch, defeated by another. I knew then I had to meet you. I had to find out more about you."

I felt disgusting as I recalled my dance with the man I thought was Elric at the celebration. Takias had been lying to me for weeks, before I even knew his real name. How had I let so much slip past me? How had I believed his deception so easily? Takias had fooled everyone, and there was no remorse in his actions. My mouth felt dry and I could feel sweat forming on my forehead.

I moved away from him as he took another step towards me. "A trip to Selvenor. Now that was interesting. Meeting you changed everything, my entire plan. I could sense it from the moment I met you. You were different. You held a power far greater than anything I'd ever sensed in the village. And I wasn't wrong. When you showed up and I saw your golden aura, I knew you were the one from the prophecy. I found a new purpose, a new plan, if you will."

"Then why take him?" I nodded towards Lenear, who was still pleading through his gag. "Why bring him here? Why risk blowing this charade completely?" My eyes felt heavy. Something felt off. I felt different and it was growing harder to focus on his words.

"Because I *despise* them. *All* of them." I could see the hatred in his expression. The entire room felt cold. "I will rid this world of his prejudice and then I will take over his pathetic kingdom. Magic will reign supreme. His city will bow to my power...and to yours. To everyone here."

The room was starting to spin. I didn't know what was happening. My body felt weak, but I fought against it. "Everyone? And what about the witches and warlocks you killed? Were they not worthy of this so-called move to reign?" I could see each of their faces flash across my mind. I could see the dagger and the blue gem on its hilt. There was more to his plan than he was telling me.

Takias smiled. "I'd be happy to explain it all to you, Zynnera. But first, I have a loose end to take care of."

Lenear began to scream even louder as Takias aimed his palm at him. He seemed to understand his intention. A blue aura formed around his hand, and I knew I had to move quickly. I placed myself between Takias and Lenear, forming a golden shield as the *Morso* hit it with great force. Takias kept his spell short, realizing I was willing to protect Lenear with my magic.

I felt strange, almost as though I might pass out. I could hear myself gasping. *Something's wrong. I don't know what it is...but something doesn't feel right.* I shook my head, fighting the dizziness. "I won't let you kill him."

Takias sighed. "Ah, Zynnera, so noble. So willing to protect those who are least deserving. I still don't understand, but it matters not. Your shield will not hold a second time."

His comment made me angry. *He thinks I'm weak. He thinks he is stronger than I am.* I waved my hands, producing another golden shield in front of us partially out of spite. But it didn't last long. In seconds the shield of energy vanished into the air. I felt panicked, waving my hands in an attempt to reform it for protection. Nothing. I could barely produce a small spark of golden energy. I stared down at my hands, my heart pounding even harder. I was sure my expression reflected the confusion and fear I felt.

Takias sneered. "I told you, Zynnera. You certainly are stubborn, aren't you? I suppose that's part of why I admire you. You fight so hard for the things you believe in. But fighting for these *humans* is just folly. Protecting him, a man who despises you? You waste your efforts, your power. But it doesn't have to be that way, Zynnera. You don't have to live in the shadows."

My entire body was shaking as the room continued to spin and my voice came out shaky. "What...what did you do to me?"

"The same thing I've done to others. I suspect you've seen it, haven't you? That's why you've felt so overwhelmed with your visions. Did you see me? Did you see what I did to them?" Takias seemed to relish the idea that I knew what would become of me at his hands. "This will be fun. You knowing my intentions. The others were completely blind. Didn't see any of it coming. Like a fox caught in a trap, realizing too late the danger of the shadows."

I broadened my stance in an attempt to keep myself from falling over. My mind flashed with memories from only minutes before. Elric had offered me a glass of water and I had unsuspectingly drank the entire contents of the cup. "The...Puniceas?" I was fighting harder with each passing second. My body wanted to collapse.

Takias walked forward until he was standing right in front of me. "Yes, Zynnera. So you were listening? Very good. It numbs the consumer's ability to do magic, an effect that has already set in for you."

I felt my knees hit the floor as Takias continued to talk. I tried to prop myself up on my hands as my vision blurred. He crouched down beside me, swiping my hair away from my face and behind my ear. He placed his fingers under my chin, tilting my head up to look into my eyes. "Unconsciousness. A short side effect as the Puniceas takes hold. Convenient for me, really. It gives me just enough time to get you out of the village. I think you'll like it, Zynnera. The waterfall is beautiful at night with the light of the moon shining over it."

I started sobbing, fighting with the last bit of energy I had. Never had I felt the amount of fear mounting inside me. I once thought facing Eradoma would be the scariest thing I'd ever experienced. But I was wrong. At least I faced her with magic. Without it, I was vulnerable. I was weak.

My arms could no longer hold up my body, and I collapsed to my side. My cheeks were flooded with tears. I couldn't find the strength to speak as I stared into Takias's eyes. He was still smiling as he wiped a few tears from my face. "Shhh, Zynnera. You can't fight it. Just let your mind slip away."

No. I have to...fight it. It didn't matter how badly I wanted to—my body could no longer resist the urge to close my eyes. I felt a tear trickle down my face as my mind started to go dark. The room, King Lenear, and Takias all faded from view as I was pulled into a deep sleep.

CHAPTER
Twenty Three

Everything seemed to flash past me as I forced the horse forward through the darkness. I had never felt my heart pound as hard as it was now. Every moment felt painfully long. I could hear the sound of hooves hitting the dirt road, racing to the village as the last bit of light faded from the horizon. *I must be close. I have to be close.*

I still felt a little woozy from the incident back at the army camp. Nearly passing out while memories flashed through my mind admittedly had me shaken. *And that voice. Where had it come from?* I knew with certainty it was not my own. It had been very clear and direct, almost as though someone were reaching out to me from somewhere far away. The experience was one of the strangest things I'd ever experienced. There had been so much power behind the voice's instructions that I had collapsed and nearly passed out. I could still hear its faint whispers even now. *Go back. Save her. She's in danger.*

Regardless of where it came from, I had not hesitated to follow its commands. Zynnera was in trouble. I could sense the truth behind every word. *I have to get to her. I won't let anything happen to her. I can't...*

My entire body flooded with guilt. I couldn't help but feel this was my fault. I had been the one who encouraged Zynnera to stay. I had asked her to consider it, to make the decision. *If I hadn't brought it up, maybe she would have never considered staying? She wouldn't be in danger right now.* Once again I felt responsible for placing her in a situation where she could get hurt, or worse. I tried to shake the thought from my mind. If anything happened to her, I knew I would never be able to forgive myself.

She might be fine. She could be resting inside her cottage. Maybe this is all just in my head? I knew it was wishful thinking. It was true I had no way of knowing for sure Zynnera was in any danger at all. But I couldn't deny what I had experienced. Those memories flashed across my mind as though someone were helping me piece together the information I needed. *Someone is guiding me to the answer.* It wasn't one I was happy about.

I didn't think I could feel any more guilt weighing down on me. *This is my fault. I never should have left her. I never should have left her with HIM.* I'd been so focused on my jealousy, I hadn't seen Takias for who he really was. He was connected to the murders in Dunivear and Bogumir, although I still didn't have the complete details of his involvement. It appeared he and Elric were working together, enacting some sort of evil scheme. I didn't know how or even why, only that the two of them were responsible.

What am I going to do? I have no evidence to back up any of this. I have no proof that Takias is involved, only my gut...and this voice inside my head. I wasn't sure telling anyone about the voice was a good idea. I knew how it would sound. *They'll think I'm crazy. I would think I'm crazy.* My first thought was to go to Adeara and tell her everything, hoping she would know how to interpret what happened and what to do. But there was no time for that. My first priority was finding Zynnera. Once I knew she was safe, I would deal with Takias. I would expose him. I would find the proof I needed.

And if Zynnera is in danger? If Takias has already grabbed her, killed her? I could feel my blood boiling. If any harm befell her, I would make him regret it. However, if I was to be honest with myself, I had no idea what I would do. It wasn't like I stood a chance against magic. This wouldn't be my first time facing it, and the encounter hadn't gone well the last time. Eradoma had tortured me for hours. I was helpless to do anything to stop her attacks. The pain caused by her spells was like nothing I'd ever felt before...or ever wished to feel again. The suffering she had inflicted upon me had been easy for her, a simple wave of her hand. No matter how much I fought against her, the only thing I succeeded in doing was prolonging my own anguish. There had been nothing I could do to protect myself, and there would be nothing I could do if Takias followed the same means of attack.

It doesn't matter. I have to try. I have to do everything I can to save her. The idea of losing Zynnera only fueled my anger more. While being tortured at the hands of Eradoma had been excruciating, I knew it would pale in comparison to the pain of losing the person I loved most. Leaving her in the forest was the hardest thing I ever had to do, and losing her completely was not something I thought I could bear.

The horse jumped over a fallen log and entered the clearing of the village minutes later. I quickly dismounted, practically running to the cottage at the end of the street. I didn't bother to knock, pushing open the door with great force as I scoured the room. There was no sign of Zynnera in the empty cottage, and *The Tahetya* lay alone on the wooden table. My heart sank to my feet at the sight of it. *She wouldn't just leave this here. Something is wrong. Something isn't right.*

I ran through the open door and back onto the street. My frantic pace caught the attention of several villagers. They murmured as I ran past them, whispering to one another in the darkness with confused expressions. I pounded hard on the entry of another cottage, trying to keep my body calm as I waited for a response. Aldous opened the door, his expression reflecting his surprise by my presence. "King Anaros? What? What are you doing back?"

I didn't have time to give him all the details. "Takias? Where does he live?"

Aldous stared back at me with confusion. "Takias?"

"Aldous, please. I need to know now!" My voice was desperate, and Aldous seemed to hear the panic in my tone.

"OK, I'll take you there now, " he said, closing the door and leaving his home behind him. I walked briskly down the street, Aldous practically sprinting to keep up. "King Anaros, wait! What is going on?"

I stayed focused on the path ahead. "Just take me to his house." I wanted to explain but feared his questions would only slow me down. After a minute or two we reached another cottage. I could see a light flickering inside through a small window. I pounded hard on the door.

Nothing. The seconds seemed to drag on. I knew I needed to maintain my composure, but it was becoming harder by the second. I pounded again. Aldous was watching me carefully now, obviously a bit concerned by my demeanor. *Forget it. I can't wait. I have to get to the bottom of this now!* I turned the handle and pushed open the door, entering the small cottage without invitation.

Aldous gasped from behind me. "King Anaros! You can't just...we can't just..." He followed me inside, still trying to argue as I looked around the room. I started rummaging through some things sitting on a wooden table. There wasn't much, just a few pieces of parchment with spell markings and an empty cup. I started to investigate the contents of a desk, but Aldous placed his hand on my chest to stop me. "With all due respect, Your Highness, I can't let you do this until you tell me what's going on."

The last thing I wanted was for Aldous to feel threatened. I didn't want him to feel the need to use magic against me. It would be hard to help Zynnera if I found myself in a losing battle with him. I sighed. "I think Takias is involved in the murders."

Aldous raised his eyebrows. "Takias? What are you talking about? What makes you think that?"

I stared at the floor, unsure what to say. The truth was I had no proof. "I don't...I just know he is. I don't have any evidence, but I'm certain of it."

"That's an awfully big accusation for having no proof," he said, shaking his head.

"I know. I know it sounds crazy, but I need you to trust me on this. *Please.*" I looked up at him. "Please, Aldous. I think he's got Zynnera. I have to find him."

"Zynnera? You think he's taken her?" Aldous studied my expression. After several moments, he let out a heavy sigh. "Well, then we should find him. We can't get to the bottom of it unless we do."

I nodded, taking a few steps towards the unmade bed beside the desk. "I wish I knew where to..." My comment was interrupted by a board squeaking beneath the rug at my feet. I shifted my weight, listening to the sounds my movement created. Aldous and I both looked at each other and then curiously to the floor. I crouched down and pulled the rug away from the area with one swift motion. I could see the outline of a trap door, secured by a small metal latch.

I looked at Aldous again, who seemed conflicted by our discovery. Finding a hidden trap door only mounted my suspicions, and I wasn't about to stop my investigation now. I flipped the latch and pulled on the door until I could see the opening below. A set of narrow stairs stretched down into the darkness. Aldous fidgeted uncomfortably on his feet. "I never knew that was here. Takias has never mentioned having a cellar."

"I'm betting there's a lot Takias hasn't mentioned," I said with agitation. "But I'm going to find out what secrets he's hiding down there."

I started to descend into the darkness. Aldous looked nervously at the door, ultimately deciding to follow me down the stone steps and into the short corridor below. A few torches glowed on the wall, giving us just enough light to see our feet as we took each step. The corridor met a small room, dimly lit by the light of a few lanterns. Other than several wooden tables, the room was practically empty, but a small luminescent object caught my eye. As I approached it, I realized the object was a purple flower. It seemed to be glowing in the darkness. I had never seen anything like it before. Picking it up, I held the flower in the light of one of the lanterns to examine it.

"Puniceas," said Aldous with surprise as he moved to stand beside me. I flashed him a confused look and waited for more information. "It's very rare. A flower that grows in darkness. I've only heard of them, never actually seen one." I started to hand it to him, but he shook his head. "I dare not touch it. I've heard it can have a terrible effect on those who wield magic."

"Effect? What kind of effect?"

Aldous shook his head again. "I'm not certain the details of how it works, but my understanding is that it weakens our powers or makes us unable to use them."

My heart pounded. "Zynnera said the people in her visions were unable to defend themselves."

Aldous scrunched his face in confusion. "What do you mean? What exactly did Zynnera see in her visions?"

It was clear Adeara had kept the content of Zynnera's visions hidden from the rest of the village, and I understood why. Until she knew who was behind the murders, I imagined she felt it unwise to distribute such information. *What if Takias found out? What if he found out Zynnera knew?* Her knowledge would have put her in danger, a loose end to be dealt with. I felt sick at the thought.

I looked back at Aldous. "The murders. She saw the murders. Whoever is responsible was draining the magical energy from the people he killed." I watched as shock spread across his expression. He started to respond, but a soft whimper from another room interrupted him. Aldous and I both stared at each other as though neither of us was entirely sure what to do. A few more whimpers echoed into the air, pulling us in with curiosity. I slowly peeked my head past the entry while Aldous followed behind me.

This second room was also practically empty, except for a man bound to a chair in the center. I recognized him at once and rushed towards him. "Lenear!" I pulled the gag from his mouth as Aldous began untying his hands from behind the chair. Lenear gasped for air and rubbed his bloodied wrist where the rope had cut into his skin.

"Lenear, what happened? How did you get here?" I felt bad for pushing him for information when he had clearly been through an ordeal, but I had no time to wait for his recovery.

"*He* brought me here," he answered. "My royal advisor, Elric. But it wasn't really Elric."

I was sure my face reflected my confusion. "What do you mean, he wasn't really Elric?"

Lenear shook his head. "He's a warlock. Used his magic to conceal himself."

I still didn't understand what he meant. "Where is Elric now?"

Lenear shook his head even harder. "You don't understand. He wasn't Elric. He waved his hands around and a bunch of blue lights came out. The next thing I know, he's a completely different person."

Shock had settled on to Aldous's expression again. "What did this man look like?"

"Tall, brown hair and eyes. Beard. Evil guy, that's for certain! Did a number on your witch, he did."

I felt my stomach curl. "Zynnera was here? She was with the man you speak of?"

Lenear nodded. "Yes, he brought her down here. I could hear them talking in the other room, so I tried to call out for help. When she saw me, she looked terrified. Then that man pulled his little reveal stunt and tried to kill me."

I was struggling to take it all in. I had so many questions, I didn't know where to start. "Tried to kill you?" Obviously Takias hadn't succeeded because Lenear was still alive and well.

"Your witch, she saved me. Stepped in before he could finish me off. Made some kind of big round gold thing and stopped him. But he did something to her. She tried to make it again and couldn't. She couldn't use magic. Then she collapsed to the floor and eventually passed out."

Fear swept over me and chills ran along every inch of my skin. Zynnera was in danger. Takias had taken away her ability to do magic, and she had nothing to defend herself. He had led her down here like a rat to a trap. I could feel my body trembling as I tried to push a hundred different scenarios from my mind. "What happened then? What did he do?" I feared Lenear's answer. If one thing was certain, Takias had proven he was not afraid to kill his own people. If Zynnera knew his secret, he was unlikely to let her live for long.

Lenear shook his head. "He picked her up. Told me he had some business to attend to. Said he'd be back for me. Then he left with her. Haven't seen him for at least an hour. I thought you were him when I heard you talking. Figured he'd come back to finish the job."

I stared straight into Lenear's eyes. My only chance of finding Zynnera before Takias killed her rested with him. "Did he say where he was taking her? *Anything* at all?"

Lenear stared blankly into the air in front of him as if trying to recall anything that could help me. "A waterfall. He said something about a waterfall and that he thought she would like it."

I looked up at Aldous. "Does that mean anything to you? Are there any waterfalls nearby?" My heart felt like it might beat out of my chest. This was my only chance. If Aldous didn't know where Takias might have gone, the odds of finding Zynnera alive were slim.

Aldous nodded dramatically. "Yes, I think I might know where he has taken her." He helped Lenear to his feet and we all started walking to the narrow staircase. "Every time there has been a murder, the bodies were found along the banks of the river. There is a waterfall there. He's taking her to the same place."

While I was grateful Aldous had an idea of where Takias would take Zynnera, my stomach churned knowing it was the same location as the other murders. Takias was clearly planning to take Zynnera's power and then kill her. "We have to go now. We have to get there before he kills her."

Aldous nodded as we climbed the stairs back into the cottage. He sat Lenear down on a chair at the table. "My King, please wait here. I'll send someone to look after you. I must help King Anaros find Zynnera."

King Lenear nodded, flashing me a glance full of sympathy. "I hope you find her, Anaros. Really, I do. Go."

Aldous and I left the cottage. He pointed towards the forest, where I had seen Takias appear only two nights ago. "Just past the meadow and into the mountain pass. Then we'll follow the river to the falls. Just give me a few minutes to gather some help. It will take more than one of us to take him down."

I nodded, unable to form any words. I watched Aldous as he ran down the street. *I can't wait. Every second counts.* The horse I'd stolen from the army camp was only a few yards away. I knew it was illogical for me to leave without Aldous and the others, but my mind ordered my body to move. I mounted the horse and trotted off towards the forest. Aldous had made the mistake of giving me clear instructions, assuming I would wait for his guidance. But I didn't have time for that. I needed to get to Zynnera before...

I couldn't bring myself to finish the thought. Lenear said Takias had taken her over an hour ago, and I had no idea how long he would allow her to live before ending her life. There was a chance he had already completed the task. *I can't think like that. I can't let myself believe she's gone.* As I raced through the meadow and into the mountain pass, I was determined to save her. I would face Takias myself and protect Zynnera with everything I had.

CHAPTER
~*Twenty Four*~

A land of rolling hills and lush meadows swirled in front of me. It was like something out of a beautiful story. I could see mountains in the distance, where a large peak stretched towards the sky and hid behind thick, white clouds. I could feel the sun warming my skin. I closed my eyes. All the sounds of nature filled my ears. I was alone on the picturesque landscape, but I was at peace. There was no sense of darkness here, only the calm sounds of a warm summer day. I had never seen such a place, and had certainly never felt such peace.

I desperately wanted everything in front of me to be real. I wanted to accept it was where I was and that the darkness I sensed was far behind me. But I knew it wasn't. The place was likely real in the sense that it existed, but I wasn't there. Only my mind could take me to such a place while my body lingered in the cellar of an evil man, one who was determined to use his dark power to threaten the world and everyone in it.

Despite knowing it was all an illusion, I couldn't bring myself to pull my mind back to reality. It was so much easier to stay here, away from the troubles and the dangers of my current predicament. *There's no reason to go back there. There's nothing I can do to stop him.* I had been deceived, and admitting I had failed was an idea I was not fond of. Takias had earned my trust, brought me comfort when I felt I'd lost everyone I cared about. He had pretended to care about me in an effort to gain my trust. *But was it pretend?* I wasn't sure I really believed it was. Takias embraced the darkness, of that I was certain. And he seemed to want to use me and my gifts to further his efforts to subjugate mankind. But I still sensed the feelings he had for me were very real. The idea didn't exactly give me comfort, however. Takias was interested in me because he believed I possessed great magic and he desperately wanted me to join him.

I'd yet to hear him say it to me, to ask me to join his cause. But I knew it was what he wanted. He had already asked me on multiple occasions during my visions, but I wasn't sure if he had truly seen me and said the words. After all, he seemed surprised by how much detail I knew about his crimes.

I looked beyond the meadow where I stood towards a large lake that extended until it met the horizon. The water glistened in the sunlight as a light breeze created shallow waves that crashed against the shore. *I wish I could stay here forever. I wish I could always feel this peace. Perhaps I should stay? Takias is going to just kill me anyway. Why should I go back?*

I bit my lip, realizing I couldn't remember much about what happened. Takias had used his purple flower to affect my magic, to make me unable to use it. It had also caused me to pass out. After that there was nothing. For all I knew, I was already dead. *Perhaps he has already killed me? Is this where the mind goes after...?*

"Not quite, Zynnera," a woman's voice sounded from behind me.

I turned to face her. She was standing in the grassy meadow, staring at me with a bright smile. I wasn't sure what to do. I had no idea who the woman was or where she came from. At the moment, I wasn't too inclined to trust people I didn't know. Allowing Takias to get close to me had been an obvious mistake and I wasn't ready to do so again. Even if this was only happening in my mind, I still didn't know if I could trust her.

She laughed. "Don't worry. I don't blame you for not trusting me."

"Good, because I don't," I said. I waited for her to say something more, but she was quiet, staring out at the lake just as I had been. I felt annoyed. She was interrupting my tranquil bubble and I didn't really feel like interrogating her, but it was clear she had no intention of explaining herself without being prodded. "Who are you?"

"We all ask ourselves that question, don't we?" She turned to face me. "You more than most."

I could feel myself growing more agitated with her deflection. *Who is this woman? And why does she presume to know so much about me? I mean, I know this is all in my head, but...* She laughed again, causing me to scrunch my face in frustration. I looked her over, trying to decide if she was reading my thoughts or if this was all just an illusion created by my mind. She was an older woman, with soft blue eyes and straight silvery hair. I had never met her before, yet somehow she felt familiar to me, like an old friend I hadn't seen in a very long time.

"Your desperate desire to know the truth is what pushes you forward, Zynnera. And your natural desire to protect your people is what will save them from the darkness."

"It seems to me my desire to know the truth is what has me in my current predicament," I said. "Maybe if I wasn't so desperate for answers, I would still be safe in Selvenor."

She nodded, considering my words. "Perhaps. But safe is a relative term. Do you really think Takias would not have found a way to get to you even there? I'd say he was determined to gain your trust, and that is why he went out of his way to speak to you at the celebration."

It was strange, this woman I'd never met knowing so much about my life. How did she know about the celebration? Had she been there? I was so distracted it was possible I hadn't noticed her. However, she spoke as though she knew me on a more personal level. Surely I would remember someone who seemed to know me so well?

"I know how difficult this has been for you," she said. "I know how afraid you are of the nightmares. Of the idea that you're destined to save the world."

I shook my head. "You have no idea how I feel. You don't know me."

My frustration was returning. I didn't want to continue this conversation with a woman who assumed she knew me and how I felt. *She knows nothing of how I feel. Except...* I couldn't get past how familiar she was. There was just something about her that drew me in, encouraged me to trust her. I hated feeling that way. Blind trust only seemed to get me into trouble.

The woman only smiled. "Oh, but I do know you, Zynnera. I know how much the prophecy terrifies you. I know how much you love Rhemues and Hachseeva. How excited you are for them to have another baby. I know how much you love Anaros. How you long to hear him say it out loud, even now, after he gave up his chance to be with you and returned to Selvenor. I know you, Zynnera. Perhaps better than you know yourself."

I couldn't deny her words scared me. There were only a handful of people who knew Hachseeva was expecting. *How can this woman possibly know? How does she know any of this?* I found myself trusting her less and less. She spoke as though she were an outside observer to my life, watching my every move and eavesdropping on my own thoughts.

The woman chuckled. "I know, I'm scaring you. Let me see. Do you remember why you came to Dunivear in the first place?"

I nodded, completely confused by her question. "Yes. I wanted to find a Seer. Someone who could help me interpret my nightmares."

"Yes, yes. But *why* Dunivear? What, or who, prompted you to come here?"

I stared blankly at her. The last thing I wanted to do was tell a complete stranger I was hearing voices in my head. I would definitely sound crazy. *But she already knows. I can feel it. She knows what's been going on in my head.* I sighed. "A voice in my head told me to come here, but you already know that, don't you?"

The wrinkles on her face moved as she smiled again. "Yes, I did know that."

"But how?" I asked before she could continue. "How can you know that? The only person I've ever told is Rhemues."

"You don't have to tell me anything, Zynnera. You and I are connected. I can see everything you see. Feel everything you feel. At least for short moments. I can't maintain the connection for long, but it's certainly there. It's how I've been guiding you."

I swallowed hard. "You've...you've been guiding me?"

It was all starting to make sense to me. I understood why she had seemed so familiar despite never having met her before. I stared into her deep blue eyes and felt a sense of peace wash over me. I knew I could trust her. *I already have trusted her.*

Realizing I finally understood what she meant, she placed her hand on my shoulder and nodded. "That's right, Zynnera. It's my voice you've been hearing."

I shook my head. "I don't understand how?"

"It's quite simple. You are connected to the Virgàm. I am connected to the Virgàm. And so, we are connected to each other. I vowed long ago I would help the Bridge defeat the darkness. I know you have the strength to overcome it, Zynnera. You've come so far already."

"Adeara said I was destined to find the Virgàm. She said it was an item. Where all magic came from. What am I supposed to do with it?" I stared down at the grass in front of me. "I don't think I'm strong enough to fight this darkness. I don't even know where to begin."

"I may be connected to the Virgàm, Zynnera, but I don't have all the answers. I wish I did. You must continue to forge your own path. Just know I will be there to guide you when I can. There is still much uncertainty and much that is unknown. But I believe you will find the answers you need. You are strong enough, Zynnera."

"I wish I were as confident in me as you are," I said. "I wish I wasn't so afraid."

The woman chuckled again. "How did Anaros put it? Facing your fears makes you strong? There is great wisdom in what he told you that day by the lake."

I couldn't help but smile at the memory. I longed for those moments, the ones I had alone with him. I could feel how much he cared about me and I could feel safe. He always knew how to comfort me even when we didn't have all the answers. When I was with him, I felt strong enough to face my fears. A cold sorrow washed over me as I recalled watching him enter the forest and disappear into the shadows. Even in my memories I felt the urge to run after him, to return home with him.

A tear trickled down my face. "I don't think I can do this without him. But you told me to stay in Bogumir."

The woman placed her hand on my shoulder again. "Don't worry, Zynnera. Your destinies are far more intertwined than you know. Your journey with Anaros will be a long one, and you will need each other to get through it. There was a reason you and he met that night in the dungeon. He keeps you strong. Helps you face your fears. And whether you realize it or not, you do the same for him."

Her words made me happy. I knew I was better when I was with him. I had more courage, more hope. When he was by my side, I felt like I could face anything because I knew I wouldn't have to do it alone. But right now, I was alone. I had no way to face Takias. I had lost my ability to use magic and he was about to take it away permanently.

I looked at the woman, wiping the tears from my face with my hand. "You said you can only maintain a connection with me for a short time. How is it we have been able to talk for so long?"

She smiled back at me. "You're unconscious, Zynnera. A blank mind is far easier to reach than an active one. And believe me, yours is usually about as active as humanly possible."

I played with my fingers. I still felt so confused. "I know I have to go back...or wake up, I guess. I have to face Takias, even if I don't know how. I don't suppose you have any guidance to help me now?"

Her blue eyes stared back out over the lake and she stayed quiet for several minutes before answering my question. "Don't lose hope, Zynnera. Not now. I know it seems hard, what you are being asked to face. But the Virgàm chose you to be the Bridge for a reason. You can overcome the darkness. Takias may be strong and he may have the upper hand, but he is alone. You, Zynnera, are not."

I shook my head. "But I am alone."

The woman smiled. "You won't be for long. As I said, Anaros is destined to help you and, because of that, I can occasionally connect with him as well."

I wasn't sure what she meant by her comment. She began to walk away as I mulled over everything she said. "Wait!" I shouted after her. "You never told me who you are!"

"Another time, Zynnera. I know we will meet again. Until then, stay strong. I will be here in your thoughts, in the quiet whispers of your mind."

The woman appeared to disintegrate into thin air. I watched her body dissolve, flowing away on the wind across the meadow. Once again I found myself alone, staring out towards the glistening water of the lake. *I know I have to wake up. I have to face Takias. But I'm still afraid.* I felt a rush of chills flow through my body. I knew I couldn't hide in my mind forever, but it didn't make things any easier.

The woman said I wouldn't be alone for long? What did she mean by that? Was someone coming to save me? I didn't understand, but her words still seemed to be guiding me. She had made it clear I would not be facing this on my own. I took in the picturesque scene in front of me for a few more moments before I closed my eyes and let out a final shaky breath. The world around me began to vanish until there was nothing but darkness.

CHAPTER
Twenty Five

The land was growing dark as I made my way through the mountain pass. The moon was shining brightly overhead, keeping the path in front of me illuminated. I felt lost in my own thoughts. They raced so quickly I could barely focus on one before another took over. It was taking everything I had to not plunge into a fear-induced panic. I knew I had to find Zynnera. The longer Takias held her captive, the less likely I was to ever see her alive again.

The idea of losing her made me sick. I couldn't fathom a world without her in it. I didn't think I could live with losing her, and it wasn't just me that needed her. Adeara had revealed an ancient prophecy to us when we first arrived in Bogumir, and Zynnera was at the center of it. According to that prophecy, Zynnera was destined to save mankind from the darkness. But what would happen if

Zynnera wasn't here to do so? Would this darkness conquer Virgamor with no resistance? It was a terrifying idea. I knew firsthand what those who wielded dark magic were capable of. Eradoma had no remorse for the things she had done. Had it not been for Zynnera, her evil reign would have continued indefinitely. But as evil as Eradoma was, I knew she was not the worst. The darkness that both Zynnera and I sensed was different. The depths of its shadows ran deeper than anything Eradoma had portrayed, and I feared what would happen should it be unleashed. The only chance we had of defending against it was Zynnera.

The air grew cold as I continued to ride through the pass. The moonlight reflected off the snow-capped peaks to either side of me, and the chilling wind stung my face as I fought against it. *I have to be getting close. PLEASE let me be getting close.* Every passing minute put Zynnera in more danger. Even if I managed to find the waterfall on my own, there was a good chance I would be too late. *I can't think like that. I have to keep hope.*

My mind wandered back to the village. By now, Aldous would have known I had taken off on my own and hopefully started the journey to the waterfall with an army of magic. I hoped there would be enough of them to force Takias into surrendering. I wasn't naive enough to believe I could take him on myself. I knew full well I stood no chance against him. But if I could distract him long enough for Aldous and the others to arrive, perhaps I could save her. Even if it meant forcing Takias to move his attention to me instead of Zynnera. Even if it meant letting him kill me. *Zynnera has to live. She's destined to save us. She's the only one who can.*

The idea of running to my death wasn't exactly pleasant, but

Zynnera's life was more important than my own, more valuable. There was nothing I could do to stop the darkness from the prophecy. Zynnera was the key to keeping my people and everyone I loved safe. I would do everything I could to protect her.

I wondered if Rhemues and Reynard had made it back to Bogumir. General Jehaz and his army would find King Lenear safe in the hands of the villagers. He would tell them of Elric, the royal advisor who was only a facade for Takias to gain access to him. He would tell them that Zynnera used her magic to save him and was then taken away into a remote area in the mountains. Rhemues would be upset that I chased after them on my own. He would be angry that I once again ran into danger. But there was no choice. I had to save her or die trying.

After several long minutes, I could hear the sound of the river ahead of me. My heart was racing. *Hold on Zynnera. Stay strong. I'm almost there.* Once I reached the river, I began following it downstream. The water between the banks moved quietly for what seemed like forever. As I continued to follow its path, I realized the water began to gain speed. *This is good. I'm getting closer.*

After nearly an hour of following the river, I finally came to a steep drop where the water rushed over the edge and into a large pool below. The entire area was shrouded in a heavy mist as the water thundered onto the surface below. *This is it. She has to be here.* I tried to remember the details of Zynnera's visions. *She said she was standing on the banks of the river. The waterfall was in front of her, somewhere in the distance. I bet she was on the banks below the falls.*

I forced the horse to proceed down the steep slope on the north side of the river. It was difficult to convince the animal to forge a path down the inclined terrain, but we managed to reach the bottom after several minutes of difficulty. I rode along the bank of the river, searching for any sign of Zynnera or Takias. There was nothing. There were no figures standing in the mist, no screams, and no lifeless bodies. I wasn't sure if this made me feel better or worse. I dismounted the horse and began walking back up the river on foot.

Maybe I missed something? Maybe I didn't? I felt my stomach roll as my fear began to take over. *What if this isn't where he has taken her? He could be anywhere! I might never find her.* My mind suddenly felt overwhelmed. I couldn't hold back the tears forming in my frantic state. I had been so sure Takias would take her here, the same place he had taken his other victims from Bogumir. *What if I was wrong?* I collapsed to my knees, my body trembling in the grass. *I don't know what to do.*

Before I knew what was happening, everything around me swirled away. My body seemed to fly back to the falls, hovering several yards in the air as I passed through the heavy mist. I crossed to the opposite bank, moving closer to the waterfall as the sound of the water deafened everything else. A man in a black cloak flashed into view. I could see him so clearly, the face of Takias hiding just beneath the hood of his cloak. He carried a lifeless body in his arms, one I recognized immediately. I wanted to shout out to him, to stop him in his tracks and demand he let her go, but I couldn't force the words from my mouth. I watched Takias disappear into the shadows near the waterfall. My body desperately wanted to follow him, but I was pulled back to my spot on the banks of the river. The reality of the present swirled back into my view as I found myself face down in the grass by the river, gasping for air just as I had in the army camp.

Did I just pass out? I pushed my body off of the ground, taking in everything around me. The whole thing felt eerie, and I sensed I was not alone. *What just happened? Was that...real?* A voice sounded from behind me. "Yes, Anaros. *That* was real."

I turned around to find a woman with long silvery hair and deep blue eyes. I stared at her with suspicion. "Who are you?"

She laughed. "You and Zynnera are so much alike."

I didn't find any of this funny. Zynnera's life was in danger and this woman was laughing. "Zynnera is in danger. If you know where she is, tell me now."

She blinked at me. "But I just did, Anaros. You were paying attention, weren't you? I'm not sure your mind is strong enough to do this a third time in a row."

I swallowed hard. I hadn't told anyone about the first time my mind went crazy. Sure, Rhemues and Reynard had watched me collapse, gasping to catch my breath, but I hadn't given them the full details of what happened. *How can this woman, who wasn't even there, know about that?* "Who are you?" I demanded again.

"I am the same person who told you Zynnera was in danger. The same person who guided Zynnera to Bogumir in the first place. Let's allow that to suffice for now."

"So you led Zynnera to danger?" My distrust of the woman was growing by the second. I wasn't sure if I really believed she was responsible for everything I had just seen and what happened at the army camp.

She shook her head. "No, I led her to answers. Important information she needs to follow the path of her destiny. Takias has taken her, yes. But that is why I've reached out to you. You, Anaros, are destined to help her. To *save* her."

I could feel my body shaking. "Are you...are you saying she's still alive then?" I didn't trust the woman, but I couldn't help but hope her words were true. If Zynnera was still alive, I had time to save her.

The woman nodded. "Yes, she is alive. But she has lost all ability to do magic. She won't be able to ward off any attack. You must go to her, Anaros. You must save her. I fear the consequences should you fail."

"The darkness, you mean?"

She nodded again. "Yes, the darkness. It fills the hearts of many. They fight for his return. Zynnera must find a way to stop them, or his power will shadow the land and all light will be lost."

I remembered the details of Zynnera's visit with her mother. Eradoma had said *he* would soon return. "Who is he? This man they want to return?"

"A user of dark magic who lived long ago. There is not much I can tell you of him. His time was long before my own. But all of us, even those who cannot wield magic, can sense the darkness. I suspect you will soon find answers to your questions."

"Before your time?" The phrase felt strange. I wondered what she meant by it.

The woman smiled. "My time has come and gone. That is what you were wondering, no?"

I didn't want to answer her. It almost felt like she could read my thoughts, and it wasn't an idea I was particularly fond of. "You're saying...you're dead?" I wanted her clarification. *First my mind flies me around like it was shot out of a cannon and now I am talking to dead people. I think I might be going insane.*

She chuckled, making me even more certain she could sense my thoughts. "Yes. I am. Although, I'm guessing this only makes you more anxious."

I bit my lip. "Talking to someone who is dead is sort of new for me."

Her face formed another big smile. "You're just how I imagined you would be. Interesting how small glimpses can tell you so much about people. I feel like I know you and Zynnera so well. Better than most, I'd wager."

I cleared my throat. Talking to what I assumed was a ghost was awkward enough, but she spoke as though she knew me...and knew me very well. The whole thing made me feel uneasy. "You...you talk to Zynnera too then?"

"I wish I had time to explain more, but I'm sure Zynnera will tell you all about my visit with her. It is time for me to go...and for you, Anaros. Zynnera is counting on you. She needs you. Go save her."

I started to protest her deflection, but her body seemed to melt away in front of me. I felt dizzy as everything around me started to spin until it all went dark. I forced open my eyes and realized I was still lying in the grass by the bank of the river. *What the blazes was that!* I pushed myself off the ground again, feeling a great deal of deja vu as I did so. *Did all of that just happen in my head? Did it even happen at all?* I looked around, frantically searching for the woman I'd spent the last several minutes talking to, but I was alone on the riverbank.

I think I'm going insane...no, I'm definitely going insane. I didn't know what to make of what happened. I thought perhaps my mind was so overwhelmed it created strange illusions to fight my fear. I gazed beyond the river to the falls, where the water rushed over the edge and threw a cloud of mist into the air. The voice of the woman echoed in my mind loud and clear. *Go save her, Anaros.*

I knew where I needed to go. I slid down the riverbank and into the shallows. I pushed my legs into the river, the water rising to my chest as I entered its center. The depth became shallow as I exited on the other side, and my entire body shivered as I walked into the cool night air. But I didn't give much thought to being cold. I was focused on moving towards the falls, towards finding Zynnera.

The mist was heavy as I walked closer. I could only see a few inches past my nose. The moonlight was doing very little to help me see through the haze. I stretched my hand out in front of me to avoid colliding with anything as I pushed towards the rocky bank. I entered a cleared area with steep banks shooting up on both sides. The sound of the falls roared just around the corner of the protruding wall. As I moved farther into the clearing, I could see a large, black opening. *A cave. This is it. This is where he has taken her.* I looked back towards the river, feeling uneasy about leaving the outside air to enter the dark shadows of the cave with no light to guide me.

I released a deep breath. *I have to. I have to go in there, light or no light.* I stepped closer to the cave entrance, examining the sharp edges of the rock wall. One spot, however, appeared to be smooth. Curiosity drew me closer and, when I was only a few feet away, I understood why this section of wall was different. It had been chiseled away until the surface was completely flat. A small symbol was etched in the center. It was difficult to see it clearly through the haze, but I could make out a few shapes if I focused hard enough.

There was a large open triangle with three symbols inside it: another open triangle, the center of which contained a circle that spiraled in on itself, and a crescent moon that hovered over them like a tent sheltering travelers from the elements. The shapes reminded me of the symbol on the cover of *The Tahetya. But these are different. I can feel something about it is different...darker.* I knew for certain this was it. This was where Takias was holding Zynnera captive. I gave one last look to the river. *I hope the others can find it. Otherwise, this may not end well.*

I walked into the darkness of the cave. I couldn't see anything. If Takias was hiding here, even he would need something to light his path. I kept one hand in front of me and the other against the wall of the cave, using it as a guide through the darkness. My steps were small, and I often stumbled on rocks at my feet, but I pressed on as quickly as I could, given the circumstances.

After a few minutes, a strange purple light glowed against the cave wall. I rounded a small corner, only to be left in amazement by what I saw. Hundreds of glowing purple flowers lined the cave floor, illuminating it enough for me to see. *These are the same flowers Takias had in his house. This must be where he gets them.* I could see the flowers only grew in this small portion of the cave. A few yards away the darkness continued with nothing to light the way. I began gathering flowers by the handful, placing them all together in a tight bunch. I held them out in front of me. *Well, it's no lantern, but it's better than nothing.*

I continued into the darkness beyond the patch of glowing purple flowers. *I must look ridiculous carrying this bouquet in a cave...towards a murderer. Zynnera will think I'm crazy.* I rolled my eyes. *Yes, because I'm sure she'll be SO concerned with what I look like right now.* I kept moving, but my thoughts remained on Zynnera. *What will she think when she sees me? Will she be happy I came back?*

I knew the answer, and I couldn't help but feel giddy about it. I was certain Zynnera would be glad to see me. *Assuming we make it out of this alive.* The thought brought me back to reality. *What am I going to do? I have no plan. That's the story of my life, I guess. I never know what I'm doing.* All I knew was I had to do what I could to protect Zynnera until the others arrived. *They have the power to stop Takias. I just hope they get here in time.*

CHAPTER
~Twenty Six~

Even with my eyes closed, I could see light flickering near me. I was afraid of what I would see when I opened my eyes. My mind had returned from a beautiful world, a peaceful place where I felt safe from the situation I had left behind. I knew my magic was still gone. I could feel it, the vulnerability of being defenseless in the presence of a murderer. I couldn't shake my fear. Convincing myself to face Takias was far from easy, even after the mysterious stranger told me I would not have to do so alone.

My fingers moved gently against the soft blanket beneath my body. Takias had laid me down on what felt like a bed, although where I wasn't sure. *Has he taken me back upstairs? Are we still in his cottage?* I hoped that was the case. Perhaps I could call out for help if I was still in the village? But part of me knew it was unlikely.

Takias had taken every one of his victims far from the village to the banks of the river. No one could hear their screams as they became muffled by the sound of the rushing water over the falls.

I tried to keep my breathing calm, still terrified to open my eyes. I heard footsteps approach my side and the creaking of the bed as a body sat down beside mine. I was certain my entire body was trembling. A hand rubbed across my waist and a warm face brushed against my cheek. I could feel the hair from their beard as they pressed their lips against my neck. I forced open my eyes and pushed the body away from me as hard as I could. Takias grabbed both of my wrists and pinned me to the bed as he hovered over me.

"Let me go!" I shouted, fighting to break free of his grasp.

Takias smiled at my struggle. "Always a fighter, aren't you?"

I couldn't hold back the tears. I was too afraid. "Let me go!" I tried to use my feet to kick him, but he leaned his body over my waist and stopped me. I couldn't overpower his strength, unable to move with the weight of his body on mine.

"Relax," he said, holding my wrists even tighter as I attempted to move. "Relax, Zynnera. I only want to talk to you."

"Since when does talking involve you trying to kiss me...or hold me down?"

Takias raised his eyebrows, tilting his head to one side with a sneer. "I suppose I have a weakness for you. Beautiful. Powerful. Smart. I can't help it. It's no wonder King Anaros is always fawning over you."

My breathing was shaky. It was clear Takias desired more than just my power, and the thought terrified me. I hated hearing his flattery. I wanted nothing to do with him. I tried to focus on a spell inside my mind, hoping by some miracle I would be able to produce just one beam of energy to get him off of me. But there was nothing. My magic was still useless as the effects of the Puniceas remained in my body.

I turned away from him, not wanting to look into his eyes as he continued to speak. His grip on my wrists was so tight they were beginning to ache with pain. Takias attempted to gain my gaze. "We could be great, you know. You and me. We could rule over everything. Your power will be unmatched by any other. You could have anything and everything you ever wanted."

I tried to jerk my hand away from him. For a moment I thought I might be successful, but he quickly tightened his grip and placed my hand back against the bed. He laughed at my attempt, which only made me angry. I hated him and I wanted him to know it. "I'm not interested in being with a murderer."

I tried to push him off of me again with no success. Takias ignored me, continuing his attempt to convince me to join him. "Think about it, Zynnera. There would be no need to hide your power. No need to live in fear. You could have anything your heart desired. The people would respect you, worship you. No one would ever disrespect you. You would be free to live your life without hiding. I know it bothers you, the way they see you, *think* of you. I could see it in your eyes when I came to Selvenor and I can see it now. You long to be free of their judgment. You long to be free of the pain their hatred causes you. All you have to do is join me. Together we can change everything. We can make this world what we want it to be. You and I can rule it together."

I shook my head, the tears flowing from my eyes as I sobbed. "I will never join you. I could never be with someone like you."

Takias frowned at my response. "Someone like me? I only want what's best for *our* people, Zynnera. I'm tired of hiding. I'm tired of feeling like we have to distance ourselves from the rest of the world to please those who are only jealous of our power." He leaned in closer to me, his face hovering just inches above mine, causing me to sob in discomfort. "But I suppose you prefer them, don't you? You prefer *them* over your own people. You prefer *him* to me, someone who understands you, who can relate to you. And yet you would still pick that pathetic excuse for a king. Perhaps if I were to remove him from the picture you would change your mind?"

"Stay away from him," I demanded through my tears.

"Or what? You think you can stop me?" Takias smiled, knowing full well there was nothing I could do to him without my magic. "It would be easy, you know. I could break his bones with a quick wave of my hand."

Anger pulsed inside me. Takias's threats only encouraged me to fight harder. I refused to allow him to cause harm to any of the people I loved. *That's exactly what he intends to do. He knows how I feel about Anaros. He won't hesitate to kill him.* Even though Anaros was now far away from me, I was still putting him in danger. I resented being so connected to him. If anything happened to him, I knew it would be my fault. It was because of me Anaros had come to Dunivear and it was because of the way I felt about him that he was in danger. Takias would allow his jealousy to lead him to commit another murder and there was nothing I could do to stop him.

I gathered as much spit in my mouth as I could and then forced it towards his face. The blob landed on his cheek just below his eye. He glared back at me for several moments, the anger growing in his eyes. He released my wrists, standing up from the bed in one swift motion. I sat up, preparing myself for any chance I had to escape.

I looked around the room. We were no longer inside Takias's cottage. In fact, I had no idea where we were. The walls appeared to be made of stone, a natural stone like those found inside a... I stopped at the thought. The walls were moist and the air was stuffy. I could see the etchings of symbols written across the wall in the lantern light. My stomach curled and I thought I might be sick. I'd been in a place like this once before, and the experience still haunted my nightmares. I was suddenly aware of the dark presence that filled the room.

Dark magic. That's what these symbols represent. It's just like before. My heart was pounding hard. I tried to read the markings to no avail. My inability to do so only confirmed what I already suspected. Takias had learned dark spells inside this cave. He had learned how to steal the power of other witches and warlocks, and I feared what he intended to do with that power.

Takias wiped the spit from his face. "You are so high spirited. I hate that it only draws me to you more. I hate that you can't see what we could be."

I kept my voice stern. "I see clearly what we would be and it's exactly why I won't join you. The darkness has consumed you and I want no part in it."

"Perhaps I should do to you as I planned to do to King Lenear? I could control you. Force you to join me. To be with me." His tone was sinister. I could feel fear taking over again. Normally, I could protect myself from such an enchantment, but without my powers I was just as vulnerable to his spell as King Lenear was. Takias stepped towards me. "Of course, I would have to keep you subdued. Forever keep your power from returning. Such a waste."

The idea of being under Takias's control was terrifying, but imagining what he would do to me was worse. I wasn't naive. There was little to guess about the ideas running through his sick mind. I had to keep the thoughts out of my head. I needed to push past his ideas. Distract him.

"How long do the effects of the Puniceas last?" I asked, hoping the question would shift his focus, even if only temporarily.

Takias smiled, obviously aware of what I was trying to do. He played along nonetheless. "A few days."

Days? It wasn't the answer I was hoping for. I thought perhaps I could distract him long enough for my powers to return, but there was no way I could keep him at bay for days. *What am I going to do? I have to find a way out of this.* There didn't seem to be a solution. Takias was in complete control of the situation. My only hope was that the woman from my mind was correct and someone would come to save me.

Takias was still smiling as he studied my nervous expression. "You should accept the fact that there is nothing you can do, Zynnera. There's only one way out of this. Joining me is the only way I'm going to let you live."

As much as I hated to admit it, I knew he was right. The situation looked completely hopeless. *Maybe I can trick him? Make him think I want to join him. Then when my magic returns...* It was a poor plan and I knew it. Takias had proven to be both smart and cunning. He would see right through my plan and he would likely take his anger out on those I cared about. I didn't want to die, but it was better than putting the people I loved in harm's way.

Takias laughed maliciously. "Well, while you decide, you might as well ask the other questions I know you have. Surely you must want to know more of my plan?"

Takias had told me his plan to take over Dunivear by impersonating King Lenear. He planned to start a war with those who used magic in an attempt to force them to see his vision. He wanted to give them a reason to fight. He wanted a reason to justify his plan to rule over those who could not wield magic. But he said his plan had changed upon meeting me. I suspected he had hoped I would join him, eliminating the need to impersonate Lenear at all. If I, the person from the prophecy, was to side with Takias, then many of the villagers would follow me without hesitation.

That can't be it. There has to be more to it than that? My visions flashed through my mind. Takias had stolen the magical energy of other witches and warlocks. He had attacked his own people. I still didn't understand the reason behind those attacks. "If you want *our* people to rule, then why are you murdering them?"

His tone became more aggressive. "I do want our people to rule. But under the supreme power of the sorcerer."

I scrunched my face. "Sorcerer?"

Takias took another step forward with glaring eyes so he was standing right in front of me. I fidgeted on the bed, uncomfortable with his close proximity. "Yes, Zynnera. The Great Sorcerer. His power knows no equal. And once he returns, there will be no one who can stop him. He will usher in a new age where warlocks and witches rule supreme." His words sent chills through my body. It was dark, far darker than anything I'd felt from him.

"Returns from where?" I asked in a whisper.

Takias looked enthralled by my interest in his plan. "A long time ago, he began his plan to subjugate those unworthy of magic. He used his power to destroy any kingdom that stood in his way. But he was defeated by those who disagreed with the idea that humans were our equals. People like you, Zynnera, who believe those without magic hold as much value as us. The sorcerer was unable to complete his mission and make the world a place where we could live freely."

I sneered. "So, what? You intend to bring him back from wherever he is and finish what he started? How exactly do you intend to do that?"

Takias seemed angered by my reluctance to give his plan merit. "His magic was stolen from him, but I've found a way to give it back. He will regain his power, Zynnera. Mark my words."

A way to give it back. I swallowed hard. "Using the dagger..."

"You know of the dagger?" He smiled, bellowing a menacing chuckle at my knowledge of the details. "Of course you do. You've seen it in your visions, haven't you? Yes, Zynnera, the dagger will be the instrument to usher in a new era where magic and those who wield it hold the power in this world." He placed his hand inside his cloak and pulled the dagger into the light. "Beautiful, isn't it? An item forged on Verascene so long ago. Deadly and powerful."

"You're storing their magic in the gem. You're going to give it to the sorcerer."

Takias nodded. "Precisely. And once I have acquired enough

magical energy to resurrect his magic, I will find the final key. I will bring him back to power."

"Final key?" I asked, confused by the phrase. "Are you saying there is more you need to complete your plan?"

Takias snickered. "I think I've given you enough answers, Zynnera. After all, unless you join me, none of this will matter. You will have become nothing more than a loose end. One I will, sadly, have to dispose of."

"I'll never join you," I said. "No matter what you threaten to do to me. But there is one more thing I want to know. That I don't understand." I was stalling now. Takias understood I had no intention of joining his crusade of destruction. It wouldn't be much longer before he decided his attempt at persuasion was in vain and killed me as he had the others. I kept hoping if I distracted him long enough, someone might find us, but my hope was beginning to wane as I ran out of ways to keep him talking.

Takias laughed. "Alright. I'll entertain one more. But I'm afraid your time is up after that. I will require your final decision."

I took a deep breath. There wasn't much more I could do. Once he answered this final question, I would be out of options. My body trembled as I choked on my words. "Why not just take over yourself? Why bring back this sorcerer at all? I don't understand. If you bring him back, you will be under his authority. Why not just claim it for yourself?"

Takias shook his head. "Because I'm not a fool, Zynnera. I know I am not the strongest warlock, the strongest Protesta. There will always be others willing to stand up to the darkness, to our ideas. But with the Great Sorcerer, all will bow to his command. No one will fight against our power."

"He was defeated before. You said so yourself. What makes you think he can't be defeated this time?"

"Because those who defeated him before, the ones who could match his power, are gone." Takias placed the dagger beneath his cloak. "There is so much you don't know, Zynnera. I was so hopeful to have you by my side, but I can see you will never understand."

"There will always be people who stand up to you. It won't stop with me." My voice shook. I knew Takias had grown tired of answering my questions and would soon use his dagger on me the way he had in my visions. I knew he was about to steal my magical energy, and it would be used to bring back the darkness I was destined to stop.

Maybe it was wrong? Maybe the prophecy was wrong? Or perhaps I'm not the one it speaks of. Maybe Adeara got it wrong and it isn't me who is meant to stop this? Could so many people have been wrong about who I was? There was so much that none of us understood, I supposed there was a chance it was true. Either way, it seemed my destiny was to die here in this cave at the hands of a murderous monster. It was my destiny to fuel the rebirth of the darkness. There was nothing I could do to fight off Takias. I had exhausted all hope of surviving. He was going to kill me, and I wasn't even sure if anyone would ever find my body.

Would he leave me by the river as he had the others? Would the villagers find me? I shuddered to think how many more murders would happen before Takias was caught. *He may never be caught.* I had decided not to share my suspicions with Adeara, and without the details of my visions, she may never find the culprit. I felt so full of regret. *If I had just told her. If I had just been honest. Then maybe I wouldn't be here. Maybe I wouldn't be about to die.*

I thought of Anaros. What would he think when he found out? I knew guilt would take over him. He would blame himself for my death. By leaving me alone in the village, I had become an easy target for Takias, who used my grief as a way to get close to me. *He'll never forgive himself. He'll never move on.* A tear rolled down my face, landing on the bed.

I glared up at Takias with both hatred and fear. "If this sorcerer is so hungry for power, I bet he won't keep you around. He'll betray you. You're too ambitious." I wasn't sure why I bothered to continue to talk to him. I knew my time was up.

Takias smiled. "No, he won't betray me. You see, Zynnera, I'm destined to help him return. Me, the last of his descendants, the last of his bloodline."

His bloodline? Takias was related to the sorcerer. It made sense why he was so connected to the darkness. Takias had moved beside me while I was lost in my own thoughts. He swiped my hair off of my face, pulling my mind back to reality. My body flinched away from his touch. He sneered at my disgusted expression. "Such a shame. Someone so beautiful, so powerful. Such a waste."

I could feel my body trembling as he touched my face again. I grabbed his hand to stop him, glaring into his brown eyes with pure hatred. "Don't touch me!"

My empty threats obviously amused him, his loud cackle filling the entire cave. He grabbed me by the arm, dragging me off the bed and into the center of the room. I fought against him, pulling and screaming as hard as I could, but he was far too strong for me to break free. He wrapped one arm around my waist and the other across my chest, holding me tight against his as I faced the cave wall. His hand pressed against my neck to keep me from squirming.

"Let me go," I screamed through gasps and sobs. "Let me go!"

I tried to pull his arm off of me, but it was no use. Takias was not just strong with magic but had enough muscle power to easily hold my tiny body down. I felt his beard rub against my neck again. "I can do what I want with you, Zynnera," he whispered into my ear with a manic chuckle. "There's nothing you can do to stop me."

He enjoyed his dominance over me. It fueled him. I was terrified by the fact that he was right. There wasn't anything I could do. I was at his mercy and I knew it. *Please just let it be over. Please just kill me.* I didn't want to endure it anymore. I wanted him to finish me off. I was crying so hard I could barely breathe. I gave one final jerk, a last effort to resist his advances. "Please, let me go."

"You're mine, Zynnera," he whispered, his face still pressed against my neck. "And once I'm through with you, I'll make it quick. I promise."

I closed my eyes and waited for the new nightmare to begin.

CHAPTER
Twenty Seven

Purple light filtered down in front of me, providing just enough illumination for me to see before taking each step. The path in front of me was still dark, everything black until I was only a few feet away. My grip around the flower stems remained tight, partly because I feared dropping them might leave me completely without light and partly because I was so on edge. At any moment I could stumble upon Takias and Zynnera. I feared what I might find.

The woman said she was still alive. She said I had to save her. The thoughts pushed me through my fears. They kept me going even though I was terrified. I couldn't deny facing Takias, a warlock with magical powers, scared me. I knew an encounter with him would likely result in my own death. *I just have to keep him away from Zynnera for as long as I can. Until someone who can use magic arrives to help.*

The tunnel seemed to go on forever. I felt like I had been walking in the darkness for hours, but I knew each careful step brought me closer to her. As I turned another small corner, I could faintly make out the sound of voices echoing in the distance. My heart pounded harder. *I'm close. I have to keep quiet.* My mind raced with ideas as I slowly moved towards the voices. *I have to keep hidden. My only chance is to surprise him, catch him off guard. If I can do that, there's a chance, a small one, but still...*

After several yards I could see light flickering in the distance. There appeared to be a large opening, completely illuminated by what I assumed was a collection of lanterns. *Zynnera is in there, I know it.* I drew in a deep breath, dropping the bouquet of flowers onto the cave floor. I had to be stealthy. I couldn't allow anything to draw attention to me as I approached them. I would finish the rest of my advance in the darkness without the purple light to guide me.

The voices grew louder as I approached. I recognized them as both Takias's and Zynnera's. I moved slowly over the cave floor, attempting to keep my presence a secret as long as possible. The cave wall protruded out near the open area, giving me the perfect place to hide as I observed Takias from a short distance. I noticed several tables with lanterns, lighting the entire room with enough visibility that I could see the terrified expression on Zynnera's face as she sat on a small bed against the wall. Takias was standing a few feet away from her, his tone cold and sinister as he told her his plan.

Takias placed something into his cloak. I studied Zynnera's face. The sheer terror in her eyes made my blood boil. She seemed deep in thought as Takias moved closer to her, stroking his hand across her face. His touch made her flinch, and I felt my insides curl. My fingers gripped the moist rock wall. It took everything I had not to storm into the room and attack him. The idea of him touching her, caressing her face, made me sick. *Stay calm. You have to wait. If you rush in there now, he'll see you coming and you won't be able to help her.* I clenched my jaw. This was going to take every ounce of self-control I had.

Takias reached out to touch her face again. I had to hold my body back. Zynnera grabbed his hand to stop him. "Don't touch me," she said. I could feel my hands tighten into fists. The anger was almost more than I could control. *If he hurts her, I'll kill him. If he lays one hand on her, he'll regret it.* I allowed myself another deep breath. I still didn't have any sort of plan. It would take very little for Takias to stop any attack I made against him. My hand moved to my waist where my sword was supposed to be. It was only now that I realized it was still missing. I hadn't had it at the army camp, nor had I thought to borrow one from the stockpile in the tent. I had come all this way completely defenseless.

I rolled my eyes. *What was I thinking? How stupid can I be?* I had been in such a rush to get to Zynnera, I had all but forgotten the absence of my belt and sword. They still rested back at our campsite in the forest and were of no use to me now. Facing magic was one thing, but facing it without so much as a weapon was suicide.

Everything happened quickly. Takias grabbed Zynnera by the arm and yanked her from the bed towards the center of the room. She screamed for him to let her go as he wrapped his arms around her in a tight hold. Her desperate sobs sent my heart into a frenzied state of panic. I could hear him whispering to her.

"I can do what I want with you, Zynnera," he said as he pressed his face against her neck. "There's nothing you can do to stop me." My whole body was shaking as I watched her attempt to jerk away from him between her sobs. A sharp pain shot through my heart as I listened to her beg for him to release her.

"You're mine, Zynnera. And once I'm through with you, I'll make it quick. I promise." Takias's chilling deep cackle echoed between her desperate sobs. "We're just going to have a little fun first."

My body moved before my mind could process what was happening. I stormed towards him. They were facing the opposite direction, allowing me to approach them from behind without Takias becoming aware of my presence. I drew my fist, speaking with a stern confidence when I was only feet away from them. "I don't think so!"

Takias turned just in time to catch my fist against his face. My hand hit him hard in the nose, causing his hands to move to his face in response. Takias staggered backwards, tripping over his own feet and falling to the floor. His reaction had released Zynnera from his grasp. She moved away from him, staring at me with watery blue eyes in disbelief that I was really there. I desperately wanted to go to her, but I knew I couldn't. Not yet. Takias was still a threat and I couldn't stop until he was completely subdued.

I moved towards him and pulled his black cloak until he was on his feet, only to punch him in the face again. He staggered backwards for a second time, almost in a daze as he tried to figure out what was happening. I reached out to grab him for a third time, hoping another punch would knock him out entirely, but Takias regained his senses before I could continue my assault. He held out his hand just before I reached him, forcing a bright blue beam towards my chest. As his spell hit me, I could hear Zynnera gasp. My body was sent flying across the room, landing against the cave wall beside the bed.

The room was spinning as I gasped on the cave floor. The spell had knocked all of the air from my lungs, and I struggled to breathe. I started to pull myself to my feet, watching Takias approach me out of the corner of my eye. "You!" he shouted, wiping the blood from his nose as he walked towards me. I could hear the anger is his tone. Takias wasn't pleased to see me, and I knew he would not hesitate to get rid of me, especially after attacking him.

I braced myself for the magical assault I believed was coming, but all I heard was Takias shouting again. Zynnera had run after him, wrapping her arms around his neck in an attempt to stop him. She fought against him for several moments, but Takias overpowered her, clutching his hands around her throat. I could hear her gasping. Her distress pushed me forward. I had to stop him. I had to save her!

Takias saw me move. He released one hand from her throat, aiming it towards me as a blue aura encompassed it. I felt my body stop, frozen despite my persistent demands for it to continue. Takias had restrained me with an invisible force, and the more I fought against his spell, the more pain it seemed to cause. I was still breathing hard, trying to catch my breath through the sharp jolts his magic incurred. Zynnera was squirming, trying to pry his hands from her throat. He threw her to the floor, and I watched her tremble at his feet.

Takias turned to face me again. "You," he said, breathing hard

from our brawl. "I should have known you would come back." I tried
to speak but his spell only hit me harder. I let out a low groan as I
fought against the pain. Takias smiled at my agony. "No matter. I'll
just get rid of you both now."

"No!" Zynnera shouted from the floor. "It's me you want. My
power! Just let him go!"

Takias's shrill cackle flooded the room at her plea. "You still
defend him. Even with no hope of saving either him or yourself.
You know your pleas will do nothing. You know I planned to deal
with him anyway. I told you, Zynnera, every kingdom will fall to our
power." The blue aura around his hand increased in luminance. The
glow was so bright it hurt my eyes to look at it. I felt my body
tremble and my knees being pulled towards the cave floor. I fought
to stay standing, pushing past the pain the struggle created. But after
a few moments it became unbearable. I felt my knees touch the
floor, the rest of my body still frozen in Takias's spell. He smiled at
my obedience to his will. "Every knee will bow to our magic, willingly
or by force."

Zynnera continued to sob as Takias moved closer to me, glaring
into my eyes with a fiery rage. "I'm going to kill you," he said. "But
first you will watch me drain Zynnera of her power. You will listen to
her anguish as I rip it from her soul. And then you will watch me kill
her."

Anger boiled inside of me, compelling me to resist his magic.
The attempt only brought me more pain as my face reflected the
surge in excruciating jolts through my body. Takias seemed to enjoy
my groaning response to his torture. I was certain his torment came
from a place of deep hatred and jealousy. He continued his sneer,

relishing in my anguish as he spoke. "Once I finish with her, I'll dispose of you. I'll kill you off in the most slow, painful way I can come up with."

"You're a monster," Zynnera whispered with a shaky voice.

"Perhaps I am," he said, keeping his gaze on me. "But to be fair, I did attempt to keep my word." Zynnera seemed confused by his comment, waiting for Takias to explain what he meant. I, on the other hand, suspected what he was referring to. I stared back into his cold eyes, the guilt of that night swelling inside me. Takias eyed me with sinister delight as though he could sense my thoughts. "Isn't that right, King Anaros? I gave you my word I would take care of her. I would look out for her."

Takias was lucky his magic worked so well. Without his restraint I probably would have stormed towards him in an angry rage. I hated him so much I knew I would kill him if given the chance. After everything he had done to Zynnera, I would not be able to restrain the fury I felt. *You've done nothing of the sort! If I could get my hands on you...*

I wanted to say it out loud, but his spell constrained me from doing so. Takias continued to mock me. "I gave her a chance, Your Highness. I offered for her to join me. But no, she couldn't move past her loyalty to you, to the people of Selvenor who care nothing for her. Instead she would rather die, give up her life in some noble attempt to combat the darkness. But her power will not be wasted. I've got just the place for it."

Takias backed away from me. I didn't understand what he meant by his speech. I knew he was gathering magical energy, something Zynnera had clearly seen in her visions, but what he was going to do with that energy was uncertain. *He's going to do it now. He's going to take away her magic.* I fought harder against his spell, my groans earning his menacing laugh as he stepped in front of her. I could hear Zynnera's terrified sobs as she waited for what we both knew was coming.

He removed a jagged dagger from beneath his cloak with his free hand, a blue aura forming around it as he began the incantation. "*Manuari lafuk pukurae myart.*" He repeated the phrase, pointing his aura towards Zynnera's body. Within moments her body tensed, and she fell flat on the floor. She screamed in excruciating pain as her golden aura flowed from her body and into to the dagger. Listening to the intense distress in her scream was unbearable. I desperately wanted to be free from my frozen position. I wanted to run to her, to protect her from Takias's magic. But there was nothing I could do to stop him. I was being forced to listen as he tortured the one I loved in the most cruel way. I closed my eyes, trying to push myself past my own pain and overcome his spell with no success.

My face flooded with tears as the sound of her anguish filled my ears. I'd never felt such heartache or so worthless. It ate away at my soul, knowing I had failed her in every way possible. I forced myself to open my eyes, the tears splashing onto the floor below. Her golden aura drained into the gem on Takias's dagger. *This is it. This is MY fault. I left her with him. I left her in danger.*

Several beams of energy stretched from the dark tunnel, hitting Takias in the back with great force. His body flung forward, landing on the ground and rolling across the cave floor. I watched the jagged dagger fly through the air and hit the cave wall, falling between the rocks on the cave floor. I felt my body release from his spell, finally free to move again. Zynnera's screams had ceased and she lay motionless on the cold floor a few yards away from me. Despite being freed from Takias's magic, I found myself unable to move. I was still trying to make sense of what was happening. I watched several figures race from the shadows of the tunnel and into the light of the lanterns. I recognized Aldous and Adeara among the figures rushing towards Takias.

He stood up, preparing to launch a counterattack. Takias pushed his aura towards them, but they were able to extinguish its power by combining their own. Streams of purple and blue energy flowed past me, forcing Takias to go on the defense. He could not overcome the strength of their combined magic. Aldous hit Takias with a spell from the side while he was distracted. He seemed unable to move or defend himself. I wondered if it was the same spell he had used on me. Once they had him disarmed, Adeara began reciting her own incantation.

"*Exhauriat rafik expelle' impotus.*" Her words echoed through the room with beautiful flow, almost as though she were singing a melody in some lost ancient language. I watched as she waved her hands and forced a stream of purple light directly at Takias. He wailed in pain when the spell hit him, his body wrenching in response to its overwhelming power. After a minute, the spell ended and Takias sat gasping on the cave floor.

He stared at his hands in disbelief. I recognized his expression. It was one I had seen before on Eradoma after Zynnera had removed her ability to do magic. Takias shook his head, screaming in rage. "No! No. No. No!" He waved his hands in an effort to produce his aura, but there was nothing to show for his efforts. "No! You will pay for this!"

Adeara shook her head. "No, Takias. I think it's time you paid for your crimes. Those here and in Dunivear." She gestured to two of the men who had assisted in Takias's defeat. "Take him back to Bogumir. I'm sure King Lenear will have some ideas as to what to do with him."

The men each grabbed one of his arms, using another spell to help restrain him as he fought against them. "You'll regret this," he shouted. "*All* of you will regret this! Mark my words!"

I was still trying to catch my breath...and my thoughts. Everything had happened so quickly that I was struggling to comprehend it all. My eyes moved to Zynnera's lifeless body. The image of her lying motionless on the cave floor brought me back to reality. I crawled across the wet floor to sit beside her.

"Zynnera!" I placed my hand on her chest, hoping to still feel her heart beating beneath her skin. *It's there. I can feel it.* The confirmation didn't give me as much comfort as I hoped. I gently shook her body. "Zynnera? Zynnera, please wake up." She was unresponsive to my pleas. My hand brushed her hair from her face. "Please wake up." I felt tears flowing from my eyes. I couldn't stop them. Pure terror filled my mind as I stroked her face. *No. I can't lose her. Please, no. Please wake up.*

Adeara crouched down on the other side of her body. I looked at her, my eyes pleading for her to do something. Adeara placed her hand over Zynnera's body in a waving motion. I watched her expression for any sign she believed Zynnera would be OK. Once she finished, she looked back at me with sympathy. "She will be OK,

King Anaros. But she is very weak. We must get her back to Bogumir."

I felt myself nodding dramatically, the tears still streaming down my face. I thought I might be sick. The idea of losing her had overwhelmed me to the point I thought my heart might fail. The pain of the possibility still lingered, making my heart pound as I stared at her face, the lines of faded tears the only scars of her battle against Takias.

Adeara motioned for Aldous. He stood behind me, placing his hand on my shoulder in an effort to offer me some kind of comfort. "Aldous, take her back to the village, please," said Adeara. "We need to watch her carefully until she wakes."

Aldous nodded, starting to place his hands under Zynnera's body, but I stopped him. "No, I'll take her." The last thing I wanted to do was let her out of my sight. I still felt panicked that I could lose her.

Adeara softly touched my hand, her voice calm and reassuring. "It's OK, King Anaros. We will do everything we can for her. I promise. I think it best you let us take her from here." She nodded to my arms. They were shaking uncontrollably. The entire event had my whole body trembling. *She's right. I'm in no state to carry her.* I sighed, nodding that I understood her reasoning.

Aldous proceeded to lift Zynnera's body and make his way out of the cave. I watched him disappear with her into the darkness. I was struggling to move from the cave floor. I felt almost too overwhelmed to stand. Adeara was studying me with concern. "King Anaros, are you going to be alright?"

I wasn't sure how to respond. At the moment I didn't know. I released a shaky breath. "As long as she's OK...I'll be fine."

Adeara smiled at my response. "You were very brave to come after her alone."

"A little brave. And a lot stupid, I think."

She laughed. "Well, I suspect it is what saved her. I don't think we would have made it in time if you hadn't."

I knew she was right, but it didn't ease the frantic pounding of my heart. I couldn't seem to shake the thought of how close I'd come to losing her. Whether I was brave or not, it wasn't me who had stopped Takias. I hadn't disarmed him or stopped his spell to steal Zynnera's power.

"Anaros!" a familiar voice called from the shadows of the tunnel. Within seconds Rhemues was crouching beside me, the look of pure terror resting in his expression. "Anaros, are you OK? Honestly, what were you thinking? I thought for sure I was going to find you dead. I can't believe you just took off like that. Do you have any idea how worried we were?"

I smiled. "It's good to see you too, Rhemues. Do me a favor and help me up."

Rhemues rolled his eyes but held out his hand at my request. He pulled me from the floor, holding my shoulder until I stabilized myself on my feet. Rhemues stared at his feet, nervous to ask the question I was sure plagued his thoughts. "Is Zynnera going to be OK? I saw Aldous taking her back to the village."

I glanced at Adeara, hoping to get another confirmation. She smiled, obliging at the attempt to ease my concerns. "I think with some rest she will be fine."

Her words did bring me comfort. Listening to Zynnera scream in pain was the worst experience of my life. I knew Takias's spell had only lasted seconds, but it had felt like an eternity with the sound of her pain echoing in my ears. I swallowed hard at the reminder of what he had attempted to do. "Adeara, Takias started to take her magic. Do you think...do you think he succeeded?"

Adeara considered my question for a moment. "It's hard to say how much damage was done by his spell. Only time will tell us for sure."

"If he's taken it, could there be a way to restore it? He drained the magic and put it inside his dagger. Could it be reversed?" I suddenly realized the dagger had been flung against the cave wall. "The dagger!"

I ran to the other side of the cave where I knew it had landed, staggering to keep myself from falling over in exhaustion. I reached the rocks where I saw the dagger land and started to frantically search between them. My fingers found nothing among them.

"It landed right here! I know it did!" I continued to force my hand between the rocks.

A purple aura surrounded the boulders. I backed away from them, turning to see Adeara waving her hands. The rocks lifted into the air as she motioned them into a different spot on the cave floor. Once she lifted them away, it was clear the dagger was nowhere to be found. *This can't be. I KNOW I saw it land here. I mean, I was in a state of shock, but I wasn't delusional.*

Rhemues walked to my side, looking at me with more concern. I stared back at him, feeling the need to defend myself as I sensed his thoughts. "I know I saw it land there. I'm *not* crazy."

Rhemues shook his head. "Anaros, I don't know what happened

here, but clearly you are overwhelmed. Maybe you only thought..."

"No," I interrupted him. I tried to keep my tone calm. I didn't want to be angry with him, but I couldn't help but feel agitated by his reluctance to believe me. "I know what I saw."

Adeara stopped just before entering the shadowed tunnel. "I'll send some people to search for it, King Anaros. I think right now there are more important things that require your attention."

Zynnera. I knew I needed to get back to her. Just being away from her without knowing if she was really OK had my mind headed into panic mode. I needed to return to Bogumir. I stared blankly at the cave floor, void of the item I had been certain was there. *It's gone. It's just vanished into thin air.*

Rhemues placed his hand on my shoulder. "They'll find it, Anaros. We should go check on Zynnera."

I nodded and followed him towards the tunnel, my mind racing as I left room behind us. So much had happened in the last few hours. *Maybe my mind is just overwhelmed? Maybe I'm just confused?* No matter how hard I tried to convince myself, I knew it wasn't true. I knew where the dagger landed. I played the memory repeatedly in my mind, each pass making me more certain than the last. *They won't find it. It's gone. I don't know how...but it's gone.* If there was one thing I had learned about magic, it was that there were *always* more questions than answers.

CHAPTER

~*Twenty Eight*~

The waves lapped gently against the shoreline of the lake. The sky was painted with shades of pink and orange, void of any clouds as the sun neared the horizon. Once again, I found myself standing in the meadow, the peaceful landscape extending in front of me as far as I could see. The sun warmed my skin as I stared at the snow-capped mountains in the distance. *I wish I knew where this place was. I wonder if it really exists?*

It was hard to know if the scene before me was real or just a creation within my own mind. There was a peace about the land, one I had never felt in reality. My mind seemed to desire a place to escape. I knew the events happening now were not any I wanted to be present for. I preferred retreating to this unknown world, where I could be safe from Takias's grasp.

Reminding myself of Takias only filled me with fear. He was so full of anger that darkness had consumed him. He had complete control and I had become subject to his will. His plan would see the return of a dark sorcerer, one I feared would destroy everything I cared about. *And I'm part of his plan. He'll use my power to bring the sorcerer back and there's nothing I can do to stop him.* In fact, Takias's spell to steal my power was the last thing I remembered. The pain was like nothing I had ever experienced. I knew I had left the cave screaming, likely passing out from the anguish of his spell ripping my power from my body.

I wondered if he had completed his spell at this point. For all I knew he had. If that was the case, I wouldn't be around for much longer. It was no secret he planned to kill me once he got what he needed, just like he had with his other victims. My heart raced. *And once he's killed me, he'll go for Anaros.* The thought made me sick. The last thing I wanted was to put him in harm's way. I was glad he returned to Selvenor. I was glad he was nowhere near Takias or the village. I rolled my eyes. *But I was wrong. He didn't go home. That stubborn man came back and now he's in trouble.* I wanted to be angry with him, but I couldn't. After all, the only reason he returned was because he cared about me. How was I supposed to stay angry with him, knowing his intentions?

But those intentions had put him in danger. Anaros was trapped, just as I was. Takias had enchanted him, leaving him unable to move. Guilt swelled in my soul as I thought about what Takias would do to him. He wouldn't just end his life with a swift spell. No, Takias hated Anaros. He resented that I would choose Anaros over him, and that was enough to warrant a long, torturous death. I swallowed hard, remembering how Eradoma had used her magic to torment Anaros to get to me. Watching him suffer at her hands was unbearable. I didn't want to think what Takias would do, knowing the severity of his jealousy.

"Anaros is OK," said a voice from behind me. I recognized it immediately. The woman with the long silvery hair and blue eyes was smiling at me.

"He's OK?" I asked, hoping to receive confirmation.

The woman chuckled. "Yes, he is just fine. And so are you, although I know you are more concerned about Anaros than you are for yourself."

I stared down at the dark green grass at my feet. "Are you sure?" As much as I wanted her words to be true, I couldn't fathom any way for either of us to escape the situation unscathed. Anaros had nothing to defend himself with, and without my magic, I was no good to anyone. Takias had complete control and I didn't see any way for us to get out of the predicament alive.

The woman chuckled again. "Yes, Zynnera, I'm sure."

I stared back at her, trying to sort through the thousands of questions roaming my thoughts. "I'm unconscious again, right? That's why I can see you?"

"That's right," she said. "Takias's spell did a bit of a number on you. But you'll recover."

"You're implying we'll find a way to stop him. But I just don't see how? There's nothing I or Anaros can do to defend against his magic." I looked out over the lake. The idea of failing to protect myself or Anaros weighed heavily on me. I felt guilty for putting him in danger. Although the woman said we would both be fine, I couldn't wrap my head around the idea, not without details describing how we would manage to overcome Takias's power.

The woman smiled at my disbelief. "Takias has already lost his power, Zynnera. You and Anaros are safe, at least for now. But there is still much to do. Much for you to discover, both about the future and the past."

"Lost his power?" I needed to know what she meant by her statement. How could Takias possibly lose his power? *Unless...*Unless someone else who wielded magic found us. Maybe more than one "someone."

"That's right, Zynnera. The people of Bogumir were able to stop Takias. They used the *Impotus* on him, just as you did to Eradoma. Takias can no longer steal the powers of other witches and warlocks. He can no longer accumulate their energy to help the sorcerer return."

"Does that mean I've stopped the darkness? Have I fulfilled my destiny?" I knew the answer before the woman could respond. This didn't feel like fulfillment. There was more I needed to do, and I hated thinking about it.

The smile disappeared from the woman's face and was replaced with a solemn expression. "I wish I could tell you this was all over, Zynnera. But this darkness...it is a strong force. Changing the hearts of men for centuries. I wish it were as simple as defeating Takias, but I think you know that is not the case."

I nodded. "I do, but I wish..." I let out a heavy sigh, feeling guilty for my own thoughts. "I wish I was just normal. I wish I wasn't this person in the prophecy. All I want, all I've ever wanted, was to live in peace and without fear. I want to just..." I was fighting back tears. I didn't want to sound selfish. *Is it too much to ask to have a happy, normal life? To just live and not carry so much expectation?*

"Be with Anaros?" She finished my sentence with a sympathetic smile. I stared down at the grass again, not wanting to confirm, but I knew she could hear my thoughts. There was no hiding anything from her. The woman touched my shoulder. "It's OK to want it, Zynnera. To desire a happy life. If anything, you deserve it. You don't need to feel guilty about that. I hope someday you can live without fear. Perhaps one day the darkness *will* be gone."

"But you don't know? You don't know what the future holds?" I sobbed a little. As a Seer, I had visions of the future. I desperately wanted to have one now. I wanted to know if I would succeed and if there would ever be a day where I could rest. Where I could live and just *be.*

"I don't know. And I'm sorry I don't. There are so many things I wish I could answer for you." She seemed genuine in her desire to help me. I felt I could trust her. But none of that helped me now or provided a path to follow.

"I don't suppose you're going to tell me your name either?" I asked, smiling.

I watched the smile return to her face. "Not yet. I will when the time is right. Until then just know I am a friend and I'll do what I can to help you."

"Well, as my friend, do you have any advice on what I should do now?"

The gentle breeze blew a few silver strands of hair in front of her face. "You need to learn more about this sorcerer. He is the key to understanding your destiny, Zynnera. If you can figure out who he is, perhaps you can find a way to defeat him."

I sighed. "But how? I don't even know where to look." A picture of Eradoma flashed across my mind. *She knows who he is. I know she does. But would she tell me?*

The woman shook her head. "I find that very unlikely. Your mother will not give up so great a secret." The woman's expression changed, reflecting a deep sorrow. "In another time she would have done whatever she could to preserve the light, but the darkness has consumed her heart."

I shifted my weight nervously. "Do you think it's possible for her to change? Do you think there is still good inside her?" I had pondered over the question for a long time. I knew the darkness inside my mother was very powerful. She was filled with anger, promoted by her desire for revenge on those who betrayed her. But I also knew she was once good, someone who helped the people of her village without hesitation. Part of me hoped that side of her still existed and, if it did, there was a way to reclaim it from the dark side of her soul.

The woman stared out over the lake for several minutes. She seemed to be contemplating my questions. I could see her eyes tearing up when she finally looked back at me. "I don't know, Zynnera. I'd like to think so...but I just don't know."

There was something in the way she reacted to my questions. It was as though she longed for my mother's redemption as much as I did, but why I didn't know. I wondered if there were more details she hadn't shared with me, a connection to her like she had with me. *Perhaps the Virgàm connects all of us? Everyone who can use magic?* I wanted to ask but decided against my curiosity.

"What now?" I asked. "What am I supposed to do? You say Takias has already been defeated, but where do I go from here? Do I stay in Bogumir?" *Or do I go home?* I couldn't deny that was what I wanted more than anything right now.

"What do you think you should do?" she asked, flashing me a sly smile.

I wondered if her question was meant as some sort of test. The thought made me anxious to answer, but I decided it was best to be honest. After all, she knew what I was thinking anyway. "I want to go home. I want to go back to Selvenor."

The woman nodded. "Then for now, that is what you should do, Zynnera. I know you think I'm going to tell you where to go, what to do. But this is still your life. It's all your decision. I will guide you, yes, but the choices are still your own."

I sighed, a little agitated by her cryptic suggestions. "But how do I know if I'm making the right choices?"

The woman laughed, her bright blue eyes lighting up with amusement. "Not even us witches can answer that, Zynnera. Magic affords us many things, but a precise map to our lives is not one of them."

I turned to face her, sensing her time with me would soon be over. I felt saddened by the idea of her leaving. There was very little I knew about the woman with the silver hair, but her presence comforted me, and I wasn't sure I was ready for her to say goodbye again. "Will I be able to talk to you again? Visit you?" The words sounded weird. If this was happening in my mind, then visiting her made me sound insane.

"Not to worry, we will meet again. Just keep your chin up and stay strong, Zynnera. Your path is not an easy one, but you are the only one who can follow it. The same is true for us all, really. We are each meant to walk our own path, and only we can do so the way it's meant to be walked."

I pondered her words, staring out at the glistening lake. There was so much more I wanted to ask, but when I turned to face her again, she had completely vanished. I closed my eyes, preparing myself to leave the landscape of my mind. *It's time to go back.*

I felt my eyes flutter open. I was lying on a bed in a small cottage. I could hear crackling in the nearby fireplace. The air was warm and quiet. I turned to my side so I could look around the room. I recognized where I was immediately. Adeara was sitting at her wooden table, studying the markings on a roll of parchment in the silence.

I pushed myself up slowly. My muscles ached and my entire body felt exhausted. Adeara looked up from her studies, noticing I was awake. "Oh, Zynnera," she said, rushing to the bedside. She sat down beside me, her expression full of concern. "How are you feeling?"

I didn't know how to answer her. So much had happened in the last few hours and there was bound to be details I missed while unconscious. I didn't know where to begin with my questions. I felt the need to prioritize. "Is Anaros OK?"

Adeara smiled, seemingly unsurprised by my first question. "Yes, he's just fine. He's outside pacing back and forth with worry, mind you, but fine." I couldn't help but chuckle at the idea of him pacing the streets, worrying over me like he always did. Adeara patted my hand. "He loves you a great deal, you know?"

I nodded. "Yes, I know." I thought for a moment, trying to decide what I should ask her next. "Adeara, can you tell me what happened? I know I blacked out, but how was Takias stopped?" I paused again. "You *did* stop him, didn't you?"

Adeara nodded. "Yes, we did. King Anaros returned to Bogumir. He found King Lenear in a cellar in Takias's basement. Lenear told him Takias had taken you. Of course, King Anaros ran after you before we could even get a group together. Probably good he did. Stalled Takias long enough for us to find the cave. Then we hit him with everything we had. Aldous was able to immobilize him and then I used the *Impotus* to take his powers for good. He won't be using his magic to hurt anyone ever again."

"King Lenear?" I asked. "Is he OK?"

"He's doing just fine, Zynnera." Adeara laughed a little at my questions. "You really are worried about everyone but yourself, aren't you?"

I shrugged sheepishly. "I guess I can't help it."

Adeara studied my solemn expression. I could tell she was still worried about me. "There is still much that bothers you," she said. I knew she meant it as a question.

"There's still so much I don't know...or understand." I sighed. "I don't know what I'm supposed to do from here."

Adeara nodded. "I can't imagine, but I hope you know you are more than welcome to stay here in Bogumir. You are always welcome here, Zynnera. However, I suspect your heart lies elsewhere?"

"I want to go home," I said, fighting my tears as the words left my mouth.

She placed her hand on my shoulder. "Then that is what you should do. Just promise me you'll take things easy until your magic returns? Get some rest?"

My magic? I had almost forgotten that I couldn't use it. The effects of the Puniceas remained in my body, and until they wore off, I wouldn't be able to conjure any type of spell. Flashes of Takias and his attempt to steal my power moved across my mind. He had started the incantation to remove my magical energy and I had passed out from the pain. *Will my magic even return? What if Takias has taken it?*

I turned to face Adeara. "What if it doesn't?" My tears streamed down my face. "How do I know it will come back? Takias was trying to steal my power; what if he succeeded?"

Adeara considered my words for a moment. "Well, I can still sense your power, for one. And secondly, Takias wasn't able to complete his spell. I suppose there's a chance he did take some of your magic, Zynnera. But certainly not all of it. I guess you won't know for sure until the effects of the Puniceas wear off."

Her words provided me with only a little comfort. I hated the idea of not having magic. I had never felt so vulnerable in my entire life. Even when living under Eradoma and keeping my magic hidden, I had felt a small sense of safety. I always knew if I had no other choice my magic would be there to protect me. When Takias had taken that safety away, I felt fear like I'd never experienced before. Feeling helpless against someone with great power was not something I ever wanted to undergo again.

"Thank you, Adeara. For all your help." I stared at the door to the outside streets of Bogumir. "You've helped me in so many ways. I can't say it enough."

Adeara smiled. "Of course, Zynnera. I wish there was more I could do. Just know when the day comes that you should need someone to fight against the darkness, I will gladly join your side. All you need do is say the word."

I stood up slowly from the bed, being careful to check my balance before attempting to walk. My body seemed fine while my mind fought against being overwhelmed. I knew it would take time to understand and move past everything that had occurred the last few days, and it would not be easy. But there was one person I could always count on to get me through, and he was waiting just beyond the wooden door. My hand rested on the metal knob and my heart pounded at the idea of seeing him again. *I'm ready to go home. I want to feel safe again.*

CHAPTER
Twenty Nine

Murmurs whispered from the streets of Bogumir. Every person who dwelled in the village had been awakened by the commotion of bringing Takias to face his crimes. Rhemues and I walked along the stone pavers to Adeara's cottage, where Aldous had taken Zynnera to rest. I could feel my heart pounding hard as I thought about her. My mind was still sick with worry at the thought of what Takias had done and how much worse it could have been. Zynnera was alive, and for that I was grateful, but I feared he had been successful in stealing her powers. Without them there would be no way for Zynnera to fight against the darkness as the prophecy foretold. I worried how she would react to such information if it turned out to be true. I knew the disappointment she would feel in herself and worried her mind would not be able to cope with such failure.

I have to have hope. Maybe he didn't succeed? Maybe she will be just fine? Even if Zynnera retained her magic, I wasn't sure *fine* was the word to use. She had so much weight on her shoulders from the knowledge of her destiny that I wouldn't blame her for breaking down. I understood what it felt like, the enormous pressure of having so many people counting on you, looking to you for protection and leadership. It certainly wasn't an easy idea to cope with.

There was a large crowd surrounding Adeara's cottage. They all whispered as Rhemues and I appeared in front of them. Realizing we had returned, Reynard walked towards us. "My King, I'm glad to see you are safe and well."

"I'm just fine," I said, reassuring him. "Have they said anything about her?"

Reynard knew what I wanted to know. It was obvious I was far more concerned about Zynnera than myself. Rhemues had asked him to return to Bogumir with Aldous, knowing I would want an update on her condition the moment we returned.

He shook his head. "It's just her and Adeara in there now. She wanted Zynnera to have a quiet place to rest. She seemed confident Zynnera would be OK."

I knew Adeara believed Zynnera would make a full recovery with some much needed rest, but it did little to comfort me. Until I saw her eyes open for myself, I would continue to worry over her. I needed more confirmation. My heart needed to see her awake. *And what then? What will I do once I know she is OK?* Today had been the most difficult day of my life. The sound of her tortured screams still resonated in my ears. I couldn't seem to push them from my mind, and each reminder only sparked my anger and fear all over again. I had almost lost her, and the lingering idea terrified me.

I could tell Rhemues was concerned by the expression on his face. He was not just worried about Zynnera but about me as well. If I looked as frantic as I felt, then he had good reason to be. There was so much going through my head I thought my mind might explode.

"She's going to be fine," Rhemues whispered. "You need to calm yourself. Maybe you should try to rest too?"

I shook my head. "There's no way I can sleep right now, Rhemues. I can't...not until I know she's OK."

Several horses trotted down the street, the sound of their clopping hooves distracting him from arguing against my reluctance. Several of the soldiers from Dunivear and General Jehaz moved towards us. King Lenear was riding just behind them, a look of sympathy in his expression as he and the general dismounted their horses. Lenear walked forward until he was standing in front of me, then proceeded to hold out his hand.

"King Anaros, I can't thank you enough," he said, waiting for me to accept his token of gratitude.

I shook my head. "There's no need for that." I took his hand. "Besides, I didn't really do anything. It is the people of Bogumir who deserve your applause."

Lenear nodded, smiling brightly at my words. "Yes, and more specifically...Zynnera, I think. I would have been dead long before you arrived had she not stepped in to defend me." Lenear glanced down at the stone street for a moment as if pondering his words. "I owe her a great debt...and an even greater apology. Aldous tells me she should make a full recovery?"

I wanted to sound confident in my response, but my voice came out shaky. "We hope so."

Lenear pulled his ornate yellow cloak around him as a cool breeze blew against us. The moon still hung over the village in the late hour and the cold spring air nipped at my skin. I was so distracted with my concern for Zynnera I had been oblivious to my body's shaking in response to the frigid air.

"General Jehaz is going to stay here until Aldous and the others have finished interrogating Takias," Lenear said, nodding to the tall man behind him. "Then he will be brought to Dunivear to stand trial for his actions. You have my word he will be dealt with accordingly."

I nodded. "Thank you. I hope his capture will bring your people some peace of mind. Were you successful in obtaining any information from him?" I knew it was a long shot, but maybe Takias had given them some details, something to help us unravel the mysteries of Zynnera's destiny.

King Lenear smiled. "Yes, I'm certain it will. As for Takias, we didn't get much, I'm afraid. He mostly just sneered at us. Stayed quiet. Whatever his plan *was*, he doesn't seem too keen on sharing any details. But rest assured he won't be carrying it out any longer." I sighed. King Lenear didn't understand. Takias may no longer be a threat, but that didn't mean his plan wasn't still in motion. I feared it was only just getting started.

King Lenear turned and mounted his horse again, preparing to leave Bogumir and return home. "Oh, one last thing, Anaros." I looked up at him, wondering what his final remark would be. His eyes were soft and his words genuine. "I still expect a visit from you when you pass back through...you and Zynnera."

He smiled at the mention of her name and I couldn't help but return it. Despite all my planning to help her gain his favor, it had been Zynnera's compassion and protective nature that succeeded. She had gained his trust on her own and I smiled at the realization that Lenear finally understood what made Zynnera the person I knew her to be.

"You have my word," I said.

Lenear nodded. "I'll see you soon then. Take your time and wish her well for me."

I watched him ride towards the forest with a small army of men following behind. It felt good knowing Zynnera would finally be accepted as the good person she was and not some evil threat. I knew the idea of Lenear trusting her would make her happy and offer relief from the constant stress of judgment. It was just one more reason I was looking forward to seeing her awake.

After a few minutes, a man from the village approached us. His expression looked troubled as he started to speak to me. "K-k-king Anaros?" he started, sounding nervous to address me. I guessed he'd never spoken to royalty before and the idea had him stammering.

"Yes?" I replied, trying not to sound impatient.

"Um...we've just finished searching the cave, Y-your Highness. I just thought I should let you know we didn't find it. The dagger you mentioned, I mean."

I blinked at him, trying to make sense of his words. Rhemues moved to my side, obviously disturbed by the information. "You didn't find it anywhere? It can't have just vanished?" He sounded annoyed, practically accusing the poor man of not doing a good enough job.

I placed my hand on his shoulder to calm him down. "It's gone, Rhemues. I don't know how or why...but I know it is. We were never going to find that dagger. I fear someone else may have taken it."

Rhemues shook his head. "No, that's not possible. No one else came out of that cave, Anaros. It has to still be in there."

As much as I wanted him to be right, I knew he wasn't. I knew the dagger was gone. There was no explanation as to how it had vanished. Then again, magic often didn't require an explanation. With magic, anything could happen and it usually left the rest of us confounded. The disappearance of the dagger was no different, although the thought of who might be behind it did have me a little concerned. But there was nothing I could do about that now. Right now my only concern was Zynnera.

I began pacing back and forth in front of Adeara's cottage. It felt like we had been waiting forever for any news of her condition. I was fighting to keep myself from rushing inside to check on her. *Adeara asked for space. She asked for us to let her rest.* I knew it was what Zynnera needed, but it didn't help me fight the urge to go to her side. Rhemues was watching me carefully, becoming more concerned each time I passed him.

"Anaros..." he whispered.

"I know," I said, holding up my hand before he could chide me. "I know I need to calm down. I need to rest. I need to stop worrying." I continued to pace the length of the cottage.

Rhemues sighed. "Yes, you do. This isn't helping anything. You're only stressing yourself more."

I knew he was right. Pacing was only causing me to panic again. I walked away from the cottage, pulling in a deep breath as I tried to calm my mind. My entire body felt hot and everything around me was starting to spin. I bent over, placing my hands on my knees and closing my eyes. I could feel myself gasping in an attempt to calm down.

Both Rhemues and Reynard moved to my side. Reynard placed his hand on my shoulder. "Deep breaths. It's going to be fine, My King. Just breathe."

I tried to follow his instructions, focusing on pulling the air into my lungs and releasing it slowly. When the dizziness subsided, I stood up straight, tilting my head to the sky and focusing on my breathing. I wasn't sure any of this was helping me stay calm.

"What if she doesn't wake up?" I asked, not really expecting an answer. The words had come out without my permission, despite trying to keep them in. I said my greatest fear out loud, and the sound of those words left me empty and afraid.

Rhemues grabbed my shoulders, turning me to face him. "Stop that. You stop that right now!" He held his finger in front of my face, his voice stern. "I mean it, Anaros. You're freaking yourself out. You're freaking me and everyone else out!" He gestured to the crowd of people who were watching us closely. "Aaagh! You're right! What *are* we going to do if she doesn't wake up? Now I'm panicking too!"

Rhemues starting pacing the length of the cottage along the same path I had been. Reynard grabbed him, trying to speak calmly and hide the irritation in his tone. "*This* is not helping."

Rhemues nodded dramatically, his voice frantic. "Right. It's fine.

Everything is fine. We all just need to stay calm." He pushed a fake smile on to his face as he looked over Reynard's shoulder at me. "Nothing to panic over."

I took another deep breath, still gasping a little. The sound of the cottage door creaking open caught all of our attention. My eyes felt glued to the wooden door as it swung open, and I was certain my heart stopped. Zynnera entered the moonlight, her body trembling as she stared out at the crowd in front of her. I could hear a small sob as her eyes met mine. In seconds she was running towards me. My body reacted before I could think, meeting her halfway as she wrapped her arms around my neck. My arms held her tightly against me as I ran my fingers through her wavy brown hair and she sobbed into my shoulder.

There was no fighting my own tears. I let them flow; I didn't try to stop them. Zynnera was safe. She was alive and nothing else mattered. I could feel her holding on to my overcoat with a tight grip. I wondered if perhaps she was afraid to let go, afraid this was all a dream and I would vanish if she released me. I understood the feeling. I didn't want to let her go; I didn't want to let her out of my sight.

"I was so afraid," I whispered in her ear. "I was so afraid I lost you."

She sobbed harder, unable to do more than cry in response to my words. I realized then how much I had taken for granted. Every moment I spent with her was precious. Every moment we spent with the ones we loved had value. There had been so many times I'd planned to tell her how I felt, but I had always allowed them to slip by. *I can't do it anymore. I won't go another day without telling her.*

My body seemed to understand what my heart wanted. I gently pulled her away from me, placing my hands on either side of her face. In a moment I felt my lips meet hers and everything around us seemed to fade away.

I wasn't sure how long it lasted. Time felt differently as I shared the moment with her. I'd waited so long, imagined it so many times in my mind, that I opened my eyes to see if it was real. Her blue eyes were staring into mine as I pulled away. She seemed surprised by the unexpected kiss, although not upset by it. Rhemues was celebrating in the background.

"Haha! Yes! Did you see that?" He hit Reynard on the chest with his hand. "'Bout time it happened!"

Reynard only smiled, keeping his enthusiasm to himself. "I think you've forgotten something in your jubilation."

Rhemues scrunched his face in confusion. "Forgotten something?" After allowing Rhemues to ponder for a few moments, Reynard cleared his throat and held out his hand expectantly.

"What?" asked Rhemues, still confused. "What are you...oooh...right." Rhemues reluctantly pulled a few gold coins from his pocket and slapped them into Reynard's hand, proceeding to move his arms into a folded display of displeasure and annoyance. "You owe me five gold pieces," Rhemues said, pointing at me. "Thought for sure you'd have kissed her *before* we arrived in Bogumir."

I watched a small smile form on Zynnera's face as she let out a quiet giggle. She seemed more amused by their bet than I was. I shook my head. *I'll deal with them later.* Zynnera and I continued to stare at each other. Neither of us knew what to do or say. I moved the hair away from her face as a hum of whispers echoed around us. I felt lost in her blue eyes. I wanted to kiss her again, but the moment was interrupted by an angry voice shouting.

"Get your hands off me!" Takias was being pulled down the street by several men. Aldous walked beside them. He pointed towards General Jehaz, who was still standing near us. The men moved Takias to stand in front of him. Takias sneered at the sight of him. "Ah, General, I suppose you'll be taking me back to Dunivear now?"

I could see the anger in the general's expression. He felt the same way I did. Takias was pure evil and I would have liked nothing more than to see him dead. Zynnera's body trembled upon seeing him. I wanted to take her away, to get her as far from Takias as possible. I watched her take a deep breath, then proceed to storm towards him.

"No, Zynnera, wait!" I started after her, but she was determined to get to him.

Takias sneered as she approached. "Zynnera! Well, it looks like you made it after all. Very good. I suppose now you can be with your..."

He never got the chance to finish his sentence. Zynnera swung her fist, hitting him as hard as she could in the face. Takias's body went completely limp while Zynnera grabbed her hand, flinching at the pain her assault had caused herself. My expression formed into a mixture of shock and delight. *I can't believe she knocked him out cold!* I chuckled under my breath. I couldn't help but feel proud of her.

Rhemues was also happy with how she dealt with the situation, snorting as he pointed to the men hauling Takias's body towards a wagon. "Ha! She knocked ol' Taky out with one swing! I'd pay a lot of gold to watch that again!" His amusement was interrupted by his obvious realization of his lost wager. He stole a glare at Reynard. "At least I would if I had any left."

I walked towards Zynnera. She was bent over, clutching her wrist with her pain-free hand. "Let me see," I said, softly chuckling as I pulled her hand up to examine it.

She winced at my touch. "I know it was stupid, but I couldn't help it."

She sounded as though she thought she needed to defend her actions. I only laughed at her attempt to do so. "Zynnera, you did what I think everyone here wanted to do. No need to feel guilty about it. He certainly deserved it."

"Deserves far more than that," said Rhemues as he walked towards us. "But I gotta admit, watching you punch him was the best thing I've seen in a long time."

Aldous moved to stand beside us. "Zynnera, would you me like to...I mean, I can? I know you don't have your magic back yet."

I watched her face. She didn't like the reminder of not being able to use magic. Zynnera seemed to sense my question before I had the chance to ask. "Takias said the effects would last a few days." I could hear the distress in her voice and I knew she was wondering the same thing I was. There was no guarantee her powers would return at all. None of us knew how much damage Takias's spell had truly caused.

She turned to Aldous, her hand trembling as she held it towards him. "Please," she whispered, trying to fight back tears.

Aldous nodded, waving his hands until his purple aura surrounded her. I could see the relief sweep across her face as the pain vanished. She squeezed her hand to make sure it was fully healed. "Thank you."

"You're welcome, Zynnera. If there's anything else I can do, please don't hesitate to ask." Aldous looked at me. "I can...your face, Your Highness?"

I shook my head. At this point, I'd grown completely used to my swollen eye. It didn't bother me. Zynnera was the only thing I was concerned about and, honestly, I wasn't in a hurry to have spells used on me right now. "Thank you, Aldous, but I'm just fine."

I was grateful for Aldous. It had only been with his help that I had found Zynnera in time. Not only did he give me the directions I needed, but he had come to our aid, fighting against Takias and ultimately helping to defeat him. I owed him a great deal, and I vowed one day to repay that debt.

I grabbed Zynnera's hand. There was so much I wanted to say, but before I did there was something I needed to ask her. *What will she want to do? Will she want to stay?* Zynnera stared back at me. She seemed to understand the distress on my face. The tears flowed freely from her eyes again as she moved back into my arms, resting her hands and head against my chest. I couldn't help but hold her tight against me in an effort to give her comfort.

"I want to go home," she whispered between her sobs. "Please, can we go home?"

My own voice was shaky in response to the desperation in her question. "Yes, let's go home." I rubbed her back with my hand and rested my cheek against her hair. I wanted her to feel safe in my arms. I wanted her to know I would never abandon her again. I loved her more than anything and I didn't care what path she was destined to walk. Whether it was my destiny or not, I would follow her, stay by her side no matter what. We would find a way to stop the darkness together.

CHAPTER
~*Thirty*~

The fire danced in the cold night air. We had returned to the abandoned campsite within a few hours of leaving Bogumir. In a few more the sun would peak over the horizon and light would penetrate through the forest. I had been eager to leave the village, wanting to put as much distance between myself and the events of the past day as possible. But distance would do nothing to block the memories. I worried what effect the trauma might have on my mind. As I sat beside the fire, I couldn't help but wonder what Anaros was thinking.

Rhemues and Reynard were sitting across from us. Our trip through the dark forest had been a quiet one. We had quickly built a fire to warm ourselves from the journey, and now exhaustion was starting to set in. Rhemues stood up from the stump on which he was resting, stretching his arms into the air. "Well, I think I'm going to go get a bit of rest. Won't be much, but I could sure use it."

Reynard nodded. "Yes, I'm sure we could all do with some rest." He looked at me expectantly as though trying to decipher my decision based on my expression. After a moment he smiled, standing up from the log to follow Rhemues. "Well, let us know should you need anything, My King," he said, nodding to Anaros.

I was sure Reynard knew Anaros would not leave my side, and I wasn't certain I was ready to attempt sleeping. Undoubtedly, those memories of Takias and the cave would find me in my dreams. It was likely they would haunt my sleep for a long time, and I didn't want to relive them. Once Reynard had entered the tent, Anaros moved his hand next to mine, slowly covering it with his. I continued to stare at the flickering fire, lost in my own thoughts.

Anaros brushed my cheek with his hand, moving the hair behind my ear. His touch was unexpected, causing me to flinch in response to being brought out of my own head. "I'm sorry," he said. "I didn't mean to startle you."

I shook my head. "It's not your fault. I'm just a little...jumpy."

Anaros nodded. "I don't blame you for that, Zynnera." He paused for a moment as though trying to decide what to say next. I wondered what was going through his mind. I was sure he was worried about me. *He's always worried about me.*

"Zynnera, do you...do you want to try to rest?" he asked finally.

I gulped, shaking my head nervously. "I don't...I can't. I'm afraid..." Tears started to form in my eyes as I attempted to explain. Anaros seemed to immediately regret asking.

"Don't cry, Zynnera. It's OK. I understand."

I wiped the tears from my face. "You should rest, though. You don't need to sit here with me. I'll be fine." Even as I said it, I knew he would not leave me alone in the dark. *He might never leave me alone again.* I felt selfish for keeping him by my side and guilty he was so willing to do so.

"I'm not going anywhere, Zynnera." He laughed a little. "I'm not letting you out of my sight." He tried to sound as though the idea amused him, but I knew how serious he was. After everything we had been through, Anaros was terrified of losing me. I understood the feeling all too well. Takias's threats against his life had left me petrified. Those same feelings had overwhelmed me when Eradoma held Anaros captive, and I felt like I had experienced them all over again.

We sat quietly for several more minutes, his hand still resting over mine. I wanted to talk to him, but I didn't know where to start. I felt like there was so much that needed to be said. "Anaros...I...thank you for coming back for me."

He chuckled. "You say it like you are surprised."

I smiled. "Well, a little. I mean, I really thought you were gone. I guess I had started to accept it." I stopped myself. I wanted to ask him. I wanted to know why he had turned around, but I wasn't sure if I should. I didn't want to make things awkward for him. I knew he loved me; after all, he had kissed me. *In front of everyone, no less.* My heart raced at the memory. His kiss was the last thing I had expected after leaving Adeara's cottage. And while he had caught me off guard, I had enjoyed the brief moment with him.

Anaros chuckled again, studying my expression with amusement. "You want to know *why*, right? Why I decided to come back?"

I sighed. He knew me too well. "Yes."

"Well, we were camped here and when we started to pack up the next morning, we were attacked by soldiers from Dunivear. They took us to their camp." He pointed to his swollen eye, which was now black and blue. "After giving me this. I wasn't *exactly* cooperative." I chuckled as he continued. "They sorted out who we were. Then we found out King Lenear was missing and they were headed to Bogumir. Naturally, I felt like I should go with them."

"Oh," I said, a little disappointed by his answer. I tried to hide it from my face, but Anaros recognized my dismay.

He wrapped his hand around mine, looking deep into my eyes. "Zynnera, I wanted to come back for you the moment we left the village. It took *every* bit of my willpower to not turn around. I never wanted to leave you there, but I thought it was the right thing to do. I thought..."

He sighed. I could sense his guilt. I hated that he felt responsible for what happened. My hand tightened in his. "Anaros, please don't blame yourself for all this. I wanted to stay. I *needed* to stay." I took a deep breath. It was time to be honest. Time to tell him the truth. "Anaros, the reason I decided to stay...was because there's this voice...inside my head. It told me to stay."

I watched his expression for his reaction. I was surprised by his lack of shock and chiding. I had felt certain he would be upset because I hadn't told him before now and that I had based such a heavy decision off something that sounded so crazy.

He stared back at me for a moment with hesitation. "You mean a woman with silver hair and blue eyes?"

His question left me completely perplexed. "How did you know that?"

"I've seen her too. Talked to her. She's the one who told me you were in danger. Showed me Takias was involved. And then when I went searching for you, she led me to the cave." He paused for a moment to give me time to think. "Do you know who she is?"

I shook my head. "No. I haven't a clue. But I think we can trust her? I mean, it sounds like I owe her my life if she led you to me."

Anaros nodded. "I think so too. I tried to ask her more about this man they want to return, but she didn't seem to know much about him. Only that he would bring back the darkness."

"The sorcerer," I said. "The man they wish to return. He lived a long time ago. He wants to rule over all those who cannot wield magic. Subjugate them by force." I stared back into the fire. Takias had told me his plan to use the dagger to bring back the sorcerer. The idea of such darkness returning terrified me, and if he was as strong as Takias made him sound, it would take more than just my power to defeat him.

Anaros appeared as though he had a thousand questions for me. "But Takias didn't say who this sorcerer is? How did he plan to bring him back?"

I turned to face him. "The dagger. It's why he was stealing the power of others. He was going to use it to give the sorcerer back his power. Takias said those who fought against him ages ago had taken his power away from him."

"You think they used the same spell you did. The one you used on Eradoma?"

I nodded. "The *Impotus*. But I didn't know it could be reversed. There's nothing in *The Tahetya* about it." A new thought interrupted my mind. "Takias mentioned something about needing to find the final key. Maybe that's what he meant? Maybe he needs the incantation to do it?"

Anaros sighed. "That would make sense. But where would he find it? Wouldn't a spell like that be in your book? Maybe it's not written down at all?"

"I wish I knew, Anaros. But Takias didn't offer to fill me in on the exact details. It all just adds a bunch of new questions to our ever growing pile." I felt so defeated. I had thought I would at least be leaving Bogumir with answers, but it seemed I was leaving with far more questions. It frustrated me to always feel so ignorant about my own destiny.

Anaros smiled as he perceived my thoughts. "We'll figure it out, Zynnera. Right now, I'm just happy you're safe."

I wanted to tell him how I felt. I wanted him to know how much he meant to me, but I didn't know how to begin. Kissing him was something I'd waited a long time to do. I was ready to do it again. I couldn't deny a small part of me still feared allowing myself to be with him, worried what the people of Selvenor would think. I moved my gaze back to the campfire. *I still shouldn't. I'm still keeping him from his duties and messing up his relationships with other kingdoms.*

A rush of cool air blew through the trees. I felt my body shiver in response to its driving chill. I rubbed my arms in an effort to warm my skin. My cloak didn't seem to be doing much to keep me warm. Anaros pulled his cape from his shoulders and wrapped it around me. Another round of chills ran through my body, but not as a result of the cold.

I couldn't seem to find a way out of his gaze. His dark brown eyes pulled me in and I couldn't escape. He stared back at me, making my heart race again. "Zynnera, there's something I have to tell you," he whispered. "Something I should have told you a long time ago."

I swallowed hard as I waited for him to continue. I thought my heart might beat out of my chest. I knew what he wanted to say. I'd always known. But waiting for him to finally say it made me anxious. Anaros fidgeted and moved his stare to the log below us, obviously nervous about the situation he had just put himself in.

After a few moments he looked back up at me. "Zynnera, I love you."

I had to remind myself to breathe. "I know." I tucked my hair behind my ear, causing him to chuckle. When my eyes met his again, I knew I had to say it. I knew I needed him to know. "I love you too, Anaros."

He flashed me a bright, sarcastic smile. "I know."

We both laughed. All this time we both knew how we felt about each other. It wasn't really a secret. The whole kingdom could see it. But that hadn't made it any easier to confess. It felt good to finally say it, to have the words out in the open. I couldn't help but wonder how it would change things.

Anaros sighed, still smiling in amusement. "I don't know why I waited so long." I stared back at him, unsure what to say. Knowing how he felt somehow only made me more nervous, made me more self-conscious. I felt him squeeze my hand again. "I'm sorry I took so long."

He continued to stare at me. *Is he going to kiss me again? I want him to kiss me again. What should I do? Should I move towards him so he knows? Or should I wait?* My stomach was all in knots and I felt like such a novice. I had absolutely no experience with this sort of thing. I didn't even know how to kiss him properly. It was no wonder my nerves were on edge. I was suddenly aware of just how inexperienced I was.

"Zynnera, I...I'd really like to kiss you again?" He said it as though he wanted my permission. I appreciated his desire to know what I wanted, his care in making sure I was comfortable with his advances. After my encounter with Takias and his forceful attempts to kiss me, it was reassuring to know Anaros would never pressure me into something I wasn't ready for. All I could do was nod nervously. I wanted to kiss him again, but I was still afraid my inexperience would be far from satisfactory.

Anaros leaned in close and pressed his lips against mine. I felt his hand move to the back of my head, gently weaving his fingers in my hair. The rush was like nothing I'd ever felt before. My emotions were all over the place. Somehow I managed to feel nervous, giddy, happy, guilty, embarrassed...all at the same time. The list was unending. It was so strange I couldn't help but wonder if it was normal. Even after the moment had ended, my heart continued to pound. Anaros's forehead rested against mine as his fingers continued to play with my hair. I realized my hands had moved to his chest and I could feel his heart pounding as hard as mine. Somehow I knew he had experienced the same mixture of emotions as I had, and the thought made me feel better.

Anaros placed his arm around my shoulder and pulled me close to him. I laid my head on his shoulder. I felt so safe in his arms I never wanted to leave his side. Being with him gave me courage,

gave me hope. Whatever the future held, I knew I would not have
to face it alone. Anaros rested his chin on my head. "I love you,
Zynnera. I promise that's never going to change."

I believed every word. I knew he meant them. He loved me, and
I loved him. We finally found the moment to tell each other and I
felt relieved. I didn't know how the people of Selvenor would
respond to an open display of affection between us. It still worried
me. I never wanted to put him in a position where he had to choose
between me and our people. But for now, I would follow what my
heart told me was right. I needed him and I felt certain he needed
me.

We stayed by the fire for another hour until the sun began to rise
over the horizon. I felt exhausted, both mentally and physically.
Anaros was tending to the fire when Rhemues and Reynard both
exited the tent. Reynard appeared groggy but flashed me a smile
despite his obvious lack of sleep. Rhemues, on the other hand, was
more chipper than I think I'd ever seen him. He joined me by the
fire with a giddy grin and a display of excitement. He tried to be
stealthy about his gleeful interrogation, but being subtle had never
been something Rhemues was good at.

"Good morning, Zynnera!" He stretched his arms to the sky.
"Beautiful day, isn't it?"

I tried not to laugh at his attempt to probe. "I'm sure it will be."

Anaros was smiling as he continued to place small pieces of wood
on the fire. He knew where this was going as well as I did. Rhemues
sat down beside me, his expression bright with enthusiasm. "So...did
you get any rest last night?"

"Can't say I attempted to," I answered. "Anaros and I were a bit preoccupied."

I knew my answer would send him through a battlefield of questions. I could see the intrigue in his eyes. I stole a glance at Anaros, who was shaking his head with a smile. He knew I was intentionally giving Rhemues just enough to drive him crazy and he found it amusing. Rhemues raised his eyebrows. "Preoccupied?"

I felt my expression form into a smile. Anaros walked towards us, still shaking his head at me. "I kissed her again, Rhemues. Now will you leave her alone so we can have breakfast?"

"Well, that's...that's wonderful to hear. But really, what you do in your personal time is none of my business." I laughed. It may not be his business, but he desperately wanted to know. Rhemues had been rooting for us since the moment he saw us together in the meadow.

Anaros nodded sarcastically. "Right."

After breakfast we packed up camp and continued through the forest. It was good to leave Bogumir and everything that happened there behind me, but I still felt nervous about passing through Dunivear again. My last visit hadn't been welcomed by King Lenear and now that he had been personally attacked by a warlock, I knew he would hate magic even more.

After a few hours we turned north on the road along the coast. *We should be in Dunivear before sunset.* The thought only made me sick to my stomach. *It's fine. I'll just wait outside like before. Assuming Anaros will need to go to the palace anyway? Maybe we'll just pass through?* I glanced at him, debating whether to ask what his plan was. Having an answer seemed better than stressing over the unknown.

I trotted beside his horse. He smiled at my approach and seemed to know what was causing my trepidation. "There's no need to worry, Zynnera."

I gulped. *Does that mean he isn't planning to stop at the palace?* I hated that I wasn't sure what he meant. "I don't suppose there's a way to go around Dunivear, is there?" I held my breath in hopes his answer would provide both clarity and comfort.

Anaros chuckled. "There is, of course, but we won't be taking that road. King Lenear has asked us to visit on our way back through."

I felt my stomach churn. Dealing with Lenear's prejudice was the last thing I wanted to do today. The last few days had been overwhelming enough; I didn't want more to worry about. Anaros seemed to find my concerns amusing, however, which only annoyed me. "Easy for you to laugh," I said. "King Lenear doesn't hate you as he does me."

Anaros smiled. "He doesn't hate you, Zynnera. Or at least...not anymore." I scrunched my face. *What does he mean by that? Not anymore?* Anaros laughed again. "Well, you did save his life."

I hadn't thought about it. Technically, I had saved Lenear from Takias's attack. I had placed myself in his spell's path and created a shield to defend us both. Takias could have easily killed Lenear after I passed out, so I never gave much thought for being the reason he was alive. "Takias still could have killed him. He just chose to deal with me first, that's all."

Anaros continued to smile. "Not how Lenear sees it. He's invited both of us to the palace, Zynnera. Not just me. He also asked me to wish you well."

I was dumbfounded by his comments. I never imagined King Lenear giving me a chance or trusting me. He had been so against magic and everyone who wielded it. I couldn't believe my simple impulse to protect him from Takias had changed all that. *Maybe Anaros just thinks he has changed his mind? He sees what he wants to see because he loves me. He wants Lenear to change his mind. But I don't know. I don't believe he has...I can't.* Whether I believed it or not, we would soon arrive in Dunivear and I would know for certain.

The sun was resting just above the crashing waves when we neared the city. I felt my stomach curl at the anticipation of entering the city walls. Time seemed to speed by as I found myself staring at the palace, waiting for the guards to permit us inside. Neither of them asked me to remain outside the palace walls, but instead welcomed me into the courtyard with hospitality. My heart raced as they led us down the corridor and into the Great Hall, where Lenear was waiting for us.

"Ah, Anaros, it's good to see you again." He held out his hand and Anaros greeted him with a smile. King Lenear immediately turned to me, retaining his bright smile and soft eyes. "And Zynnera, I'm so glad to see you're OK."

I took a deep breath. The whole thing felt weird. Suddenly Lenear acted as though I was his friend. I didn't know what to make of the whole situation. Lenear seemed to understand what I was thinking and chuckled. "I know, you must think poorly of me, Zynnera. I know I haven't treated you well or fairly, and for that I offer my sincerest apologies. I hated magic, thought it was nothing but evil. But you showed me there is light in it; you proved me wrong." He paused for a moment, moving his gaze to the floor as he fought tears with a shaky voice. "And I owe you a great debt,

Zynnera. Please, what can I do to repay your compassion and your bravery?"

I didn't know what to say. I shook my head. "I didn't stop that spell with the expectation of being rewarded. I'm glad you're safe, Your Highness. Nothing more is necessary."

I could see Anaros smiling out of the corner of my eye. He knew I would never accept a reward for saving Lenear's life. King Lenear nodded, studying me curiously for several moments. "Well then, please, stay in Dunivear tonight. The least I could do is offer all of you a warm place to rest. I'm sure you could all do with a good night's sleep."

Rhemues stepped forward with a joyful tone. "Oh! That would be marvelous, Your Highness. We do appreciate the hospitality!" I couldn't help but laugh. Rhemues despised sleeping in the tent...or mostly despised the bugs that came with it.

"Wonderful! I'll have my servants see you to a room." Lenear turned to face Anaros. "I know you must be exhausted from everything, King Anaros, but I wondered if I might steal some of your time? After all, there are a few agreements we need to arrange, if you feel up to it?"

"Yes, I think it would be a good idea." Anaros looked at me. "I'll come find you after?"

I smiled, nodding in response. I knew how important it was for Anaros to form lasting relationships with Dunivear. It appeared King Lenear desired to do so. Somehow I had managed to change his entire perspective on magic, and because of that change I would no longer be standing in the way of Selvenor's prosperity. *If Lenear can change, maybe so can everyone else?* There was hope. Maybe...just maybe the world could accept magic without fear?

As I sat in my room alone, waiting for Anaros, I felt overwhelmed. There was still so much I didn't know or understand. But speaking with Lenear had provided me with a hope I never expected. Takias had been so sure the world would never accept us, but his plan had unintentionally resulted in changing Lenear's mind. I knew magic could be used for good and I wanted to believe the majority of witches and warlocks felt the same way.

We have to stop the darkness. It threatens everyone and everything I care about. If the sorcerer returns, we may never convince the world magic can be used for good. The reminder of the sorcerer sent chills through my body. Takias was willing to do anything to help him return. I wondered if he was the only one; if there were others who would work to achieve Takias's vision? Sadly, I also knew the answer. Takias had never been the only one welcoming the darkness. My own mother had done so. She had ruled Selvenor with absolute power, subjugating all those she deemed below her. *And she knows of the sorcerer. She wants him to return.* The thought brought me sadness and I hated that I felt that way. I wished I didn't care. I wished I could just see her as the evil monster everyone else did.

A quiet knock sounded at my door. Anaros smiled when I opened it and welcomed him inside. "Well? How did it go?"

Anaros's smile grew even bigger. "It went well. Selvenor and Dunivear have officially entered an alliance. Peace, trade, it's all because of you, Zynnera."

I shook my head. "No, it's not because of me."

Anaros laughed, knowing I would never accept credit. "He's

reversing the law against magic, Zynnera. He plans to work with the people of Bogumir. He wants his people to accept magic." Anaros shook his head, chuckling. "I mean, I hoped to change his mind, but I never expected all of this."

I laughed. "Neither did I." My mind wandered back to the sorcerer. Part of me wondered if urging people to trust magic was really a good thing. After all, there were still those who wanted to usher in the darkness.

Anaros stepped in front of me and started playing with my hair between his fingers."What is it? What are you thinking?"

I shook my head. "I'm just worried about the darkness, Anaros. We don't have any idea who this sorcerer is, nor do we know who follows him. It could be anyone. I guess I'm just nervous asking people to trust magic right now."

He considered my words for a moment before responding. "Zynnera, we are all human. Just because there are a few bad witches and warlocks doesn't mean we should lose trust in them all. It's no different than people who can't use magic. There are still criminals in Selvenor." He took my hands in his own. "You know your father once told me we should judge people by their deeds, not by who we presume them to be."

"He told you that?" I asked, fighting back my tears.

"Yes," he whispered, brushing his hand against my cheek to wipe a stray tear away. "And he was right, Zynnera." Anaros sighed, moving towards me to kiss my forehead. "You need to try to rest. Promise me you'll try?"

I nodded. "I promise."

"Then I'll bid you goodnight," he said, smiling as he lifted my hand and kissed it with a sly grin. "Till tomorrow, princess."

I shook my head, grabbing a pillow from my bed and practically chasing him to my door. He pulled it closed behind him, laughing as he continued down the hall. I disliked his teasing, but it still made me smile. *He always makes me smile. Makes me happy, even when I feel like the whole world rests on me.* I realized just how profound the idea was. *Love. Love is what gets us through the most difficult times.* As long as I had him, my family, everyone I cared about, I would find a way to overcome the darkness. I'd find a way to defeat it.

CHAPTER
Thirty One

The mirror reflected my nervous expression. I released a shaky sigh, studying myself carefully. *I just need to be brave. I can do this. What I look like doesn't matter. Why am I staring at this mirror like it does?* Rhemues approached me from behind, sporting a wide, amused grin.

"You look fine, Anaros. Don't overthink it."

I rolled my eyes. "Well, that's easy for you to say. You didn't plan to ask Hachseeva. She told you to ask her." I'd been thinking about it since we returned from Dunivear. It had only been a week, but I felt like a year had passed since I kissed Zynnera that night around the campfire.

"True," he agreed. "But that just proves my point, doesn't it? The more you think about it, the more nervous you're going to be, and what good does that do you? Besides, it's not like you don't know what she'll say."

"I'm not going to assume anything," I said with an irritated tone.

Rhemues laughed. "Alright, alright. At least if we get this over with you can stop worrying over the whole thing. You've been a nervous wreck since we came back, you know?"

I was sure he was right, but I couldn't help it. Ever since kissing her, all I wanted to do was ask the question. The metal ring had traveled all the way to Dunivear and back. Now I was ready to give it to her. It was time for it to leave my pocket for good. I knew Zynnera loved me. She had told me so in the forest, but it didn't make me any less nervous to ask her to marry me. I was worried she still had doubts being with me was a good idea...good for Selvenor. I'd done everything I could to convince her, but I didn't know how effective my reasoning had been.

"You told Hachseeva the plan?" I asked, wanting to confirm everything was ready.

Rhemues rolled his eyes. "When have I ever let you down? Of course I told her. It's not like this is that elaborate, Anaros."

"Should it be?" I swallowed hard. "Am I supposed to make it elaborate?" My own self-doubt was creeping in. I was terrified I wasn't doing this properly.

Rhemues laughed again. "It can be whatever you want it to be, Anaros. I proposed in a forest, remember? Besides, I'm quite certain Zynnera would prefer less elaborate anyway." *That's true. Zynnera likes things simple.* Rhemues continued to talk. "I mean, you're going to do it in front of the whole city. I think that's enough, right there. She'll probably be overwhelmed as it is."

I swallowed hard again. "Overwhelmed?" Rhemues was right; asking Zynnera to marry me in the square would overwhelm her. *I didn't think of that. Why didn't I think of that? Maybe this is a terrible idea?*

Rhemues frantically waved his hands, realizing he had only caused me more anxiety. "No, no! It will be just fine! I'm sure she'll forget all about the crowds of people watching."

"You know, you're really not helping," I said, slightly annoyed at his truthful statements.

Rhemues shrugged. "You were the one who appointed me to royal advisor."

I sighed. "Alright, I need to just...*go.* The longer I stand here the worse I get."

Rhemues nodded, trying to hide his chuckle under his breath. We walked along the corridor and past the Great Hall. The palace was quiet; however, my thoughts were not. I'd never been so nervous in my entire life and I felt like I was over-analyzing everything. I had planned it all in my head, mapped out the entire conversation. I knew what I wanted to say and where. *Just stick to the plan. You've got this. What could go wrong?* I didn't linger on the last thought for fear I might find an answer.

Hachseeva and Zynnera were waiting by the north entry. Hachseeva winked at me as we approached, having been told the purpose of our outing into the city. Zynnera looked slightly uncomfortable standing by the door in her dark blue dress, the same one she had worn to my coronation. I guessed she was nervous about going out into the city, and wearing a fancy dress never helped calm her nerves.

I smiled as I offered her my hand. She seemed hesitant to accept it. I knew she still worried what the people would think of our relationship and I didn't blame her. The people of Selvenor still feared magic and it would take time for them to see Zynnera as different from her mother. But I knew what I wanted, and I wasn't afraid for the people to know it too.

Zynnera placed her hand in mine. She walked beside me into the courtyard as Rhemues and Hachseeva whispered quietly in front of us. I wanted to whack Rhemues with something. I knew he was talking about my plan, and the last thing I wanted was Zynnera to overhear their conversation. I tried to distract myself. "You look beautiful, as always."

Zynnera tucked her hair behind her ear. "Hachseeva insisted on the dress. I've no idea why. I suppose she thinks it might impress the people."

I bit my lip. That wasn't exactly why Hachseeva insisted, but it made for a good excuse. "I'm sure she's just trying to help. And she wouldn't be wrong...about the impressing part, I mean."

She smiled sheepishly back at me. Flattery always made her uncomfortable. We passed through the palace wall and entered the square. It was bustling with people as they went about their daily motions. I could feel Zynnera's hand twitch in mine as more people stopped to watch us. Their stares made her nervous.

I tightened my grip around her hand, letting her know I had no intention of letting go despite their gaping eyes. I glanced at her, watching her release a shaky breath. "It's OK, Zynnera," I said. "Don't worry about them."

She flashed me an annoyed expression as if to say she couldn't. I knew how much their judgments bothered her, but I needed her to get past it. Allowing Zynnera to hide or forcing myself to hide my feelings for her would not push the people to understand or change their minds about magic. It wouldn't be easy, but I was determined to make them see.

We walked towards the statue of Captain Torilus. I stopped, hoping the visitation might ease her mind. She stared at the stone man, a small smile forming across her face. I guessed she was recalling memories of her father, ones full of happiness and love. It was why I chose this spot. This was where I wanted to ask her.

Rhemues and Hachseeva had kept their distance, standing several yards away with anxious eyes. Zynnera pulled her hand from mine, moving to stand closer to the statue. She continued to stare at him, lost in a trance of memory while I fought against my clothes to pull the small metal ring from my pocket. My heart was racing. I prepared myself to kneel, but Zynnera moved. She began walking to the other side of the statue as if admiring every inch of its design.

I didn't know what to do. I had seen the whole thing in my mind. Where I would stand, what I would say. But now I had nothing to go on. I wasn't prepared for an impromptu proposal. I stole a frantic look at Rhemues, who was trying to guide me with nods and facial expressions. He encouraged me to follow her. I moved to the other side of the statue, the ring resting in the palm of my hand. *Alright, I'll do it here then. I'll just kneel down...*I started to make my move, but Zynnera continued around the statue. I thought I might lose my mind. She wasn't cooperating in the slightest and my nerves were becoming more on edge with each passing second.

I followed her again, almost bumping into her in my eagerness.

Zynnera turned to face me, her smile contorting into concern. "Are you OK?" she asked.

I could feel sweat rolling down my face. "Fine."

She raised her eyebrows, studying me for a moment before moving her gaze to the crowd gathering around us. She released a heavy sigh. "I want to go back inside the palace. I don't think I'm ready for this." My heart hit my stomach. I couldn't let her go back inside; it would ruin what little was left of my plan. *If I can get her back to the front of the statue, I can still make this work. I can do this.*

"Just a little longer. Please?" I was practically begging her.

She sighed again, staring at me with sympathy. "I can't."

She started to move back towards the palace gate, but I grabbed her shoulder. "Just...wait." I tried to keep my voice calm, but I was sure I sounded nervous. I rubbed my face with my empty hand. *Impromptu it is.* I cleared my throat and took a deep breath. "Zynnera, I love you. And I think I've practically loved you since the day we met."

Zynnera stared back at me with her blue eyes. She seemed unsure what to do. I had just pronounced my love to her in the open square, and I was sure she was terrified that the people could hear. But I wanted them to hear. I wanted them to see.

"I don't want to spend another day without you by my side. I know you have a destiny to follow, and I promised you I would never let you face that destiny alone. You're a part of me, Zynnera, and I need you more than you could ever know." I watched her eyes start to glisten over as I moved to my knee and she realized what was happening. She gasped a little at the sight of the ring resting between my fingers as I presented it to her. "Zynnera, will you marry me?"

I watched a single tear run down her face. I had left her speechless and the seconds seemed unending. After what felt like forever, she nodded through sobs. "Yes."

There was nothing I could do to stop the smile from forming across my face. I placed the ring on her finger and swiftly moved to my feet and pulled her in. I kissed her right there in front of the statue, in front of everyone. And I didn't care. We both smiled at each other as she continued to cry. I knew these were tears of happiness, and my heart leapt at the idea of her answer.

An ensemble of shouts and whistles echoed from the crowd around us. The people were clapping, celebrating the moment with us. Zynnera looked around, bewildered by their response. All I could do was smile. She had been so concerned about what the people would think of her relationship with me, worried they would judge her based on the things her mother had done. But that didn't seem to be the case, at least for the majority of our people. Most of them appeared happy at the sight of my proposal, applauding Zynnera's acceptance of the ring and shouting with joy at her answer.

Zynnera looked back into my eyes, tears still streaming down her face. All my nervousness had ended as I realized where I was. This was the moment I'd been hoping for, planning for, and now that it was here, I worried it wasn't reality. Zynnera was the most beautiful person I'd ever met, and I knew without doubt that I loved her. As I looked deep into her blue eyes, I could sense that our path forward would not be easy, but it was *our* path nonetheless and we would face whatever obstacles the darkness had in store for us together. I understood why Zynnera had been chosen. She was the most compassionate person I knew, and she would defend everything the darkness threatened to destroy. Zynnera was so much more than the Bridge or someone from a prophecy. She was the light the world needed to face the darkness and I was ready to follow her path through the shadows.

***
The End
***

For more titles in this series, visit:
https://bit.ly/chroniclesofvirgam

Sign up for my newsletter and get free bonus content and *The Prisoner of Magic*, a novella from this series, for FREE:
https://bit.ly/BrookeJLosee

ABOUT THE AUTHOR

Brooke Losee is the author of the series, *Chronicles of Virgàm.* She lives in Utah with her husband and three children. She enjoys writing, gardening, rock hounding, and just being a *mom.* Brooke appreciates the small town lifestyle and adventurous landscapes of where she lives, often using her background in Geology to aid in her writing. She has always had a passion for science, history, and of course, all things books.

Made in the USA
Middletown, DE
28 March 2021